IN THE HEAT OF PASSION

"I will not be addressed in such a manner." She poked at his chest, forcing him to back step. " 'Twas rude and disrespectful and do not think to *handle* me! Do we have an understanding on this?"

Rein only nodded, the blaze in her eyes, the flush to her skin so intense and primitive it ignited a heat in his belly that spread rapidly. God of Fire, she was magnificent in her anger!

"I have been ignored for three years, and now that I do not have to hide, I will not tolerate being sequestered like a mistress."

He leaned down in her face. "You want to make love with me." His gaze slicked over her. "Now. Right now. You are so aroused you cannot stand it."

She blinked, taken aback for only a moment. "Do not think to ply me with passion, Rein Montegomery." She shoved at his chest with both hands. "I am in no mood for it."

He grabbed her to him, his mouth crashing down on hers. He kissed her and kissed her, his strong hands grinding her to his body, letting her feel every tight aching inch. "Tell me now you are in no mood."

She gasped for air, her gaze searching his; then a wicked smile curved her lips and she grabbed handfuls of his hair, dragging him to her mouth, savagely taking his with a force that rendered him helpless.

"Make love to me, now," she whispered.

"I would have you at my leisure."

"I would have you now. Pleasure me, Rein," she whispered. "Pleasure me now."

He covered her mouth with his, backing her toward the bed. . . .

Books by Amy J. Fetzer

MY TIMESWEPT HEART
THUNDER IN THE HEART
LION HEART
TIMESWEPT ROGUE
DANGEROUS WATERS
REBEL HEART

Published by Zebra Books

REBEL
HEART

Amy J. Fetzer

Zebra Books
Kensington Publishing Corp.
http://www.zebrabooks.com

To my 'kid' sisters,
Mimi Wilson,
Mia Castellana

For being the 'Princess' and the 'Duchess' when I was just 'Sissy.'
For never *really* knowing what it was like to be the colonel's daughter,
and the fairy-princess awe when I attended my first birthday ball.
For car rides with my dates, squealing over stolen kisses,
and knowing before I did which man I'd marry.
For coming to me when your hearts were broken
with the absolute faith that I could ease the pain.
And to a future of letting me spoil your babies,
adoring the men you love,
and making me even more proud
than I am at this moment
of the extraordinary women that you've become.

I love you.

ZEBRA BOOKS are published by

Kensington Publishing Corp.
850 Third Avenue
New York, NY 10022

First Printing: November, 1998
10 9 8 7 6 5 4 3 2 1

Printed in the United States of America

One

England, 1778

The silence erupted.

Hooves thundered, trembling the ground.

Michaela's head jerked up, ducklings crowding about her ankles as she searched the countryside for the source.

A flock of quail burst through the treetops, thrashing the gray sky in wild escape.

An instant later, a rider bolted from the forest, demonic, darker than dark, his hair, his tricorn, in the cape snapping against the wind like falcon wings, in the magnificent beast he commanded at a breakneck speed.

And he was bearing down on her, saddlebags slapping, hooves churning the pasture black.

Michaela immediately bent and shooed the ducklings into her apron, gathering them close before darting off the road. She ran.

Yet he kept coming, an unholy dragon swooping down for the kill.

Her lungs burned for air. Her legs quivered with the strain. *I will never outdistance him.* Suddenly, she halted, turning to face him down. One hand clutching the bundle of hatchlings, she reached inside her cloak, her hand curling around the worn wood pistol stock, her finger slipping around the trigger.

Rein chanced a look behind for the highwaymen, their pursuit driving wildlife from the forest and into open country. Great thunder, he'd hoped they'd given up by now. He dug his heels deeper, urging Naraka to prove his ancestor's blood.

Then he saw her, a lone cloaked figure, and he knew she would either be run down by the brigands or their next target. The last thing he needed was another rider, but leaving her defenseless did not bear questioning, not when he brought the plague of thieves with him.

He bore down on her, primed to snatch her from the ground.

She raised her arm, and a split second too late Rein recognized the gun in her hand and the determination in her eyes. She fired, her hood falling back with the recoil, the ball ripping through his shoulder, nearly jerking him from the saddle. A splendid cap to a bloody rotten day, he thought as pain spiked through his back and down his arm. He clutched the pommel, the pump of blood flowing with his heartbeat. Yet he'd no choice but to take her along; he leaned to the side, his uninjured arm out. Her eyes rounded as he neared and she scrambled to reload. The opportunity fled as Rein clapped her waist, yanking her off the ground and tucking her to his side.

She fought. The contents of her apron spilled.

"The babies!"

Baby?

He jerked back on the leads and Naraka reared, pawing the air.

"Oh, nay, they'll be trampled!" she cried, struggling against him.

Rein brought the animal to heel as his gaze scanned for a child. "We tarry for bloody *ducks?*" The last he said with a quick squeeze, chasing the breath from her lungs, yet with his blood draining down his chest, his anger stronger than his hold, she escaped his grip, dropping to the ground.

She hastened around the dangerous jumble of hooves to gather the ducks.

"Leave them, woman, we have company!"

Michaela straightened, pushing deep red hair from her view and scanning the surrounding area. Four riders raced toward them. She spun about, looking imploringly up at her victim.

Her expression nailed him in the chest. Damn those eyes, he thought. So wide and pleading. He ignored their effect. "Quickly, manslayer." He offered his gloved hand. "I assure you, their aim is far better than yours."

"I can't." The carved line of his mouth tightened with irritation. It was his only feature not obscured by the shadows of his tricorn. "I can't leave them to die." Michaela gestured helplessly to the hatchlings, stooping to catch one.

Exasperating female. He'd no time to argue over her ridiculous heroics and twisted in the saddle, judging the distance and their chances, then slid from the mount, wincing at the blaze searing through his shoulder. *Today, I am a mush-hearted fool,* he thought, pressing his lips together. He chased a duckling, dumping it into her apron, then scooping up another.

"They are scared."

"Enough! Make haste." Blood slithered down his arm, filling his glove, and he cursed his fortune to cross paths with this little killer and caught the last bird, shoving it at her before remounting the stead. He leaned out for her.

Michaela looked at the approaching thieves, then him.

The lesser of two evils, he thought, a bit amused.

"They will not catch me . . ." His deep voice rumbled like a storm beneath the ocean floor. "But you . . . ?" He let the sentence hang, wiggling his fingers.

Feeling much the cornered rat, Michaela jammed her foot into the stirrup and slapped her hand in his. He yanked, depositing her on the saddle before him. His mount surged, slamming her back against his broad chest, his groan of pain driven under the sound of hooves.

Ducks quacked wildly, tossing in her apron folds as they rode, their pursuers rapidly approaching.

Michaela tried stealing a look, but he shoved her forward.

"You will unbalance us, and I am not in a state to control this horse."

Though his voice was soft, Michaela felt the bite and closed her eyes, unable to look at him nor the tear in the cloak. The scent of his blood filled her nostrils and her stomach pitched. *Oh, what have I done?* she thought, and was truly surprised he'd not left her to her own devices.

He charged the hillside, the overtaxed mount slowing. Michaela heard his curse as he withdrew a pistol and twisted.

He fired.

The motion revealed his blood-soaked shirt, the jumble of knives and flintlocks at his waist.

"Why did you not shoot afore? My lord, you are weaponed like an arsenal."

He jammed the spent pistol into his waist belt, then drew another, sparing her a tight glance. "Of the thirty-two ways to fight, the best is to flee with your life." He turned and fired. A rider tumbled from his saddle, trampled by his cohorts. They kept coming. "Peaky little devils," he muttered, digging his heels into horse flesh. Shots rang around them as they crested the hill, an estate looming ahead, and Rein knew once the thieves saw they were near help, he and his slayer would have the chance of escape.

He headed toward the main house.

She stiffened in front of him. "We cannot go there!" Fear colored her words. " 'Tis the earl's home."

"Is it? Well, then, 'tis the safest haven available. And we need it."

"But the earl—" Michaela clamped her lips shut. If she crossed the earl's path, she would be recognized and in an hour, word of her doings would reach her uncle. That could never happen, wounded scoundrel or nay.

"His lordship will never know," he assured close to her ear, his arm limp around her waist, his chest pressing to her back. She felt his struggle to remain in the saddle. Guilt pounded on her soul and she covered his hand with hers.

He scarcely felt the soft touch, his lungs working for air, stars bursting behind his eyes. His shoulder throbbed with the mercy of an English beating. *The bullet is still inside,* he thought, cursing this chit and her hand with a weapon. They crested the rise and Rein spoke to Naraka in Hindi, promising grain and a long rest if he brought them to the rear of the massive house. The horse bolted and he directed the mount in a wide berth toward the left side, slipping behind the stables and a cropping of trees. Rein maneuvered the horse close to a wall, aching to brace himself against it and succumb to the pain, but instead, he slid from the mount, pushing Naraka back from sight, then peering around the edge of wood. He clutched his shoulder beneath the cloak, wincing. *Damn me, but this one hurts.*

Three men appeared on the hilltop, horses prancing, and even at this distance Rein could feel their indecision. *Come, approach, show yourselves the larger fool,* he thought. *Then I will shred you where you stand.* Yet, it was not their thievery nor the fight he'd endured to get away, but their continued pursuit that stirred his suspicions. Relieving him of his coin was secondary to their quest for spilling his blood, and though he had his share of enemies, though none recent, nor cowardly enough to send five men to take him down. He withdrew a handkerchief and pressed it to his wound, his need to groan no more than a hiss through clenched teeth. He could not maintain a foothold on his faculties for overlong, he thought. He was bleeding too rapidly. *Gain control or we will both die,* he thought and concentrated, forcing the pain to a place that could not touch him. For several seconds, he was perfectly still, his mind challenging the wound, smothering the flow of blood. The gush eased, yet Rein knew that without his thoughts centered and sharp, it was temporary.

He glanced briefly at the woman, struck again by her vivid beauty the pounds of wildly curling hair and threadbare cloak could not hide. The ducklings shifted in her apron and she slipped her hand inside, bringing a velvety yellow baby to her cheek. The creature trembled and she cooed, soothing it, the tender sight and sound peeling away a layer Rein did not want gone. A mothering spirit, he thought fleetingly, and a sadness swept him so quick and profound, he flinched, tearing his gaze from her. He returned his attention to the landscape, cursing the delay in his plans and laying the blame at her dainty feet.

Michaela stared at his broad back, his straight shoulders offering more muscle than bone, the expensive cut of his clothing bespeaking affluence. His Spanish saddle and the quality of horseflesh beneath her added to her assumption. A gentleman, mayhap titled, she thought dispiritedly, envisioning her remaining days spent in the gaol. But my word, he was a tall one, a towering dark creation of masculinity, she thought, stretching her neck for a better look. And so different than the Englishmen she'd known, in more than appearance. Even now, she felt his steadfast vigilance, a keen awareness of their surroundings unsuppressed by the wound. And his next words confirmed it.

"The birds, they are yours?"

She lowered the hatchling to her lap, frowning. "Nay."

"Then what was your intention? To mother them, mayhap learn them to swim?"

The wealthy, she thought, imagined themselves rather witty today. "Do not be facetious. 'Tis most unbecoming." Irritation sharpened her voice. He'd not bothered to meet her gaze and she'd yet to have a thorough look at his face. "And if you insist on prying in my affairs, sir—"

"You *are* my affair, lass."

Her breath caught at the possession in his tone, as if he did not speak the like often, and Michaela felt a sudden unexplained pleasure trip through her. "I was taking them home," she blurted over the unwanted feeling. "The poor dears have lost their mother."

He twisted. His dark head tipped back a fraction and something flared in his eyes just then, sharp and hard, like a spark or a slap. Michaela caught her breath, captured in his gaze. He possessed the palest blue eyes, and within the startlingly dark features, it was terribly arresting. Terribly. For she wanted to remain there, probing for the secrets seething behind those eyes, beneath the undeniable power surrounding this man.

He stared.

Saddle leather creaked.

And Michaela's world suddenly narrowed, to him, to the lure of darkness and a knowledge of things of which she could never begin to dream.

Distantly, the jingle of a carriage harness, the incessant grind of wheels to stone, pricked the silence. Wind floated down the hillside, rustling tall grasses like a hand across green velvet, spinning the fragrance of wild heather around them.

His mount shifted beneath her.

He tilted his head ever so slightly, into the breeze, and within the feathery streams of black hair, Michaela glimpsed a silver ring piercing his lobe. For reasons she could not lay a name, the sight of it left her utterly breathless.

And a single word rose in her mind like a phantom's whisper. *Exotic.*

Her skin, her every pore, suddenly careened to life and she swallowed to stem the tide, feeling unseasonably warm, unrealistically stripped beneath his intense gaze. It touched her features with the heat of a freshly lit tinder, yet with the delicacy of spun sugar.

Wind kicked at his cloak.

His eyes roamed.

For the breadth of a heartbeat, she did not move, expecting the stomach-churning revulsion she often felt under such close regard. That it did not come scared her as much as what did, and she immediately tried to dismount.

But he was there in an instant, forcing her back into the saddle, then climbing unsteadily up behind her. "What are you doing?" she asked.

He closed his eyes, briefly, demanding control from his body, his floating thoughts, then reined around. "Taking you with me."

"Nay, I cannot!" Her uncle would beat her if he discovered her absence.

He caught her jaw, forcing her to meet his glacial gaze and be prisoner. "I have lead that needs removing, and since you so efficiently put it there, 'tis only fitting you tend it." Fierce, unbendable. And he stole the choice and maneuvered the horse to a quick pace toward the trees beyond a pond.

"Wait!"

"Woman! I cannot delay!" The highwaymen were still in the hills.

Regardless, she slid off the prancing horse, stumbling, righting herself, then running to the small pond and untying her apron. She knelt, the babies tumbling from their cradle and waddling toward the mature ducks in the pond. Just as quickly, she stood and turned back to him. Rein gazed down at her, the wind whipping at her long coppery dark hair, her cloak. An exquisite creature, he thought, and not for the first occasion wondered why she was wandering the countryside without escort.

Of course, he thought ruefully, the girl was adept enough at arms to protect herself.

He motioned impatiently for her to mount, and when she hesitated, he impaled her with a challenging stare.

The sudden hard look held more power than a loaded weapon and, without a word, Michaela obeyed, her body crashing into his, his groan of agony and her regret hanging in the air between them. Removing her apron, she rolled it into a ball and twisted to press the cloth to his wound. His expression did not alter a fraction, though she knew he was in tremendous pain. Without visible motion, the horse broke into a brisk canter and Michaela struggled to stem the flow of blood and maintain her seat in the Spanish saddle.

Except for the pallor of his bronze skin, her dark rescuer appeared unaffected by this whole sordid mess.

They rode into the forest, skirting the villages. "Have you a name, manslayer?" he said after awhile.

She ducked to avoid a branch, holding it away for him. "Aye." Quickly, Michaela debated the reasons not to reveal her name, then realized he would know little of her circles.

His lips quirked at her hesitation. "And 'tis?"

"Michaela."

He repeated her name, the sound rolling off his tongue with a deliciously strange accent. There was little English in his tone, his accent a strange mix she couldn't name, and she wanted to hear more. Of course, it was not proper without introductions.

"I am Rein," he said to the unasked question.

"Where do you take me?" The magistrate, was her first panicked thought.

"My ship."

"Oh, nay!" She grabbed for the reins. "I must get back!" She could not afford such a long absence. And certainly not all the way to the harbor.

His expression hardened as he tore the leads from her hand. "I do not care, Michaela." She tipped her head and gazed into his crystal pale eyes. "I will not make it to my ship afore falling, and though it distresses me to admit it, I need you."

He did not look the man in need of anyone's aid, least of all hers.

"Let us be about it, shall we?"

The horse moved faster, deeper, into the city by way of alleys and back streets, and she wondered who he was avoiding to travel this route. People paid them little notice, most making a wide berth for the huge horse. Behind her, she felt movement and suspected he was reloading his pistols and recalled the display of jeweled knives and hooked blades in various sizes. An elegant barbarian, she thought, wondering from whence he'd come. They neared the wharf, the scent of the sea coming with the odor of well-used fish barrels, and Michaela brought her cloak to her nose. It smelled of his blood, and she looked at him in time to see his eyes roll back in his head. He tottered. She gasped, scrambling to catch him, his weight nearly taking them both down. She grappled for purchase, forcing him upright and he slumped forward in her arms.

"Oh, do not die," she quietly begged against his soft hair.

"I shall endeavor not to . . . disappoint you." Was that a smile she heard in his voice?

"Do try," she encouraged, forcing him upright. "I really become unbearably peeved when my victims die on me."

"Put a crimp in your dance card, does it?"

"If I had one," she muttered, swinging her leg over the horse's neck to straddle the beast. Taking the reins from his tight fist, she wrapped his arms around her waist. He fell heavily against her back.

They rode for only a mile before he whispered, "Cease," then pointed. "Head into the alley."

"I will not," she snapped, and even in his weakened state, Rein heard the alarm in her voice.

"Madame," he slurred with impatience, "I am hardly in a condition to ravish your pretty little hide."

Michaela's gaze slid to the side, to the dark head propped on her shoulder, mulling that one good punch would likely lay him down, not that she wanted to hurt him further. With a quick look about and a hope that he behaved, she steered the horse between two buildings and toward the rear of an inn. No sooner than they'd met the shadows of the structure, he tumbled from the saddle, slumping against the mount. The horse did not move, thank God, bracing his fall. Michaela scrambled after him, forcing his weight to hers, her legs nearly buckling under the burden.

"My heavens, you don't look that heavy," she gasped, and he snickered, gesturing to a stack of barrels. She walked slowly, lowering him to the ground, wincing when his head hit the barrel.

"My saddlebags, there is"—he paused to draw air—"a black pouch and a skin of water."

"Aye, aye, I will get it." She checked beneath the apron, her eyes widening at the clean hole in his skin fountaining blood. She folded his hand over the wound, then hastened to the horse. The animal stomped and sidestepped, refusing her nearness. "Be still, you big ox," she hissed impatiently, hands on her hips. "Your master needs help." The mount stilled suddenly, blocking their presence from passersby, and Michaela immediately rummaged in the saddlebags, finding the articles and returning to his side. She knelt. He was so still she thought him dead, and a little squeak escaped her throat as she touched her fingertips to his neck. His heartbeat hummed against her skin and she released a captured breath.

"Rein?" It felt odd, addressing him so.

"Open the sack," he said without cracking a lid. "A vial, blue powder." He licked his lips. "On the wound."

Untying the lacings, she dug inside and found five vials, yet in the shadows, could not tell which was blue or nay. She twisted toward the light and saw strange markings on the glass, written in silver. She'd never seen the like before and rose to move beneath a shaft of light.

"Michaela . . ." Her name came heatedly.

She hurried back, the blue vial in her fist. "For pity's sake, I would not have left you here," she said, staring down at him, arms akimbo, the sack swinging. "What kind of person do you think me?"

His eyes fluttered open. "A wickedly good shot." His lips quivered with amusement and pain. So righteous, he thought. "Am I to trust you?"

"You haven't the choice now, do you?" She knelt, meeting his stare. "And I was aiming for your heart." A choked laugh came from him before she peeled back his cloak, then his shirt and her apron, telling herself to remain calm and do as he bade. She sprinkled the powder on the wound, then jerked back when it smoked like a tinder.

"Dear God!" She set fire to him!

He tipped his head to judge the wound. "Excellent."

Her gaze swung to his, eyes wide.

" 'Twill stem the bleeding for now."

"Thank the Lord," she whispered.

Somewhere glass shattered. Feminine laughter spilled through the open windows above with the odor of ale and ripe sweat.

"Feeling guilty, Michaela?"

She liked how he said her name and almost confessed until the rhythmic squeak of bed ropes vibrated through the inn's walls. Michaela's stomach yanked in a hard knot. "Are you ready to leave?" Impatient, brisk. She endangered more than her meager reputation delaying in this place with him.

Rein frowned, searching her pinched features. She looked suddenly quite pale. "In a moment."

Each telling grunt from the inn made her flinch, and she cast a speculative glance toward the exit.

"Must I tie you to me?"

Michaela met his gaze, swearing he'd the ability to read her thoughts, yet knew she could not abandon him and sleep nights. "That won't be necessary. I promise to get you to your ship—if you will tell me why those men were after you."

"You have little room to bargain."

She folded her arms over her chest and cocked her head, arching a brow. "Neither do you."

His lips curved and he nodded good-naturedly. "Robbery."

Her gaze swept him. "You don't have the look of a thief."

"Because I am the victim. An unfortunately frequent occurrence today." Guilt tightened her features as he shifted subtly, wincing, and she immediately reached for him. He waved her back, the area around his lips gone white.

"They took your purse?"

"They tried," he said, staring at the entrance. "But I shot one."

"Two," she reminded primly.

He looked at her then, arching a brow, a strike of black against his bronze skin. "One more than you . . . or is it common for a country lass to go round putting holes in unsuspecting riders?"

She made a sour face, uncapping the water skin and offering him a drink. Water trickled into his open mouth. "You were hardly unsuspecting." He surprised her by smiling, and the sight triggered a wash of warm sensations she did not care to examine.

He swiped a drip with the back of his hand. "Looked like your worst nightmare, did I?"

Nay, she thought, *not my worst. "You* should have called out a warning," she said in her defense, corking the skin.

"Mayhap." He shrugged, then winced, clutching his wound. " 'Tis done now. Shall we leave this dank place?" He struggled to rise and she darted forward to assist, her head hitting his chin. His teeth clicked. He groaned over her apology, accepting her aid to stand, her hair catching under his arm, jerking her head back. She yanked mercilessly, and he gripped her, stilling her. He lifted himself away, flung the stone's worth of her hair at her, then braced against her. *By the gods, she was entirely too soft,* Rein thought, walking unsteadily to the horse. She stepped on his foot twice, her warm hand flattened on his stomach and sending a sweet sensation lower. He gripped the bridle, pressing his forehead to the animal's neck, whispering to the beast.

Michaela lurched back when the black stallion folded down on his forelegs, lowering his head between in a deep bow.

"Your chariot, madame." He gestured sluggishly, loving her stunned expression.

Michaela approached slowly, casting glances between master and horse, then seeing as the beast wasn't going to move, she hitched herself into the saddle with horrible inelegance, landing astride. She hurriedly yanked her skirts down over stockinged calves, her thorny glare daring him to comment.

She looks as if I'll bite that supple limb, he thought, dragging himself atop the rump. Naraka rose, rocking them back before settling straight.

"Bloody amazing," she whispered, shaking her head.

Auburn curls ticked his nose. "Felicitations, old fellow, you've impressed her enough to swear."

She looked back over her shoulder, prepared to remind him that a gentleman did not mention a lady's indiscretions when she noticed the gray cast of his skin.

Rein's vision blurred, the herbs working their power, yet he recognized the question in her eyes. "Aye. Quickly, lass."

She clucked her tongue, urging the horse out of the alley and into the flow of life.

"Your ship, the name?" she asked, too aware of the looks they garnered from gentry and servants, vendors and seamen milling in the street. A squad of soldiers rounded the corner near a tavern, their steps uneven with liquored cadence, and she shielded her face in the folds of her hood.

". . . *Empress* . . ."

Michaela dug her heels in and headed down the quay, not uncertain of her destination, yet aware of her need for expediency. Wind whipped at her clothing, the ocean's mist dampening her face. Men stared, the lurid looks driving a chill through her already cold skin and she bowed her head. The cloud covered sun lowered in the sky and she knew that soon, her absence at home would garner notice. Millie or Argyle would offer a plausible excuse for her truancy, she assured herself, yet it would stay her uncle only so long. Time was crucial, and she prayed her father's brother did not come searching for her. Nor send troops to do it for him.

Hurriedly, she stopped a boy selling chestnuts on the edge of the wharf, his face smudged with dirt, his fingers protruding through gloves with missing fingertips.

"Know you a ship called the *Empress?*"

The young boy's gaze narrowed and he took a step back. "Ye ain't dumb 'nuff to go on there, are ya?"

Trepidation magnified through her, prickling her skin, but Michaela was without options. He would surely bleed to death.

She fished in her pocket, holding up a penny. "The location, boy." She tossed it.

He pointed, and she followed the direction of his attention. Michaela inhaled sharply. Docked a few yards away, the ship was huge, painted pristine white but for the wood mast and railing gleaming in the light. The tide brought the fog, the mist enveloping the ship, curling around its brass fittings and lanterns. It was ethereal, a ghost ship of white and gold, and the deserted sight of it brought a mix of fear and curiosity. Surely naught like it existed elsewhere.

Rein moaned, muttering unintelligibly, and she kneed the mount, riding toward it, thankful she could feel his breathing against her neck. Yet it offered little comfort, for as if she were inside his body, she felt his life slipping away. At the pier's edge, she called out. No sound responded but the slosh of waves beating the hull. Unguarded? Impossible, for the character of the local rapscallions would loot this floating palace for every scrap of wood.

Impatient for aid, she shouted, bringing the horse closer to the gangplank. The stallion moved up the narrow wood walk. "Nay, nay! Rein!" came with tense impatience. "Stop this creature!" He didn't, and she pulled back on the reins, yet the horse continued on his way toward the deck. She peered at the black water, envisioning them tossed in the sea and crushed beneath the horse's weight.

She did not dare shout again or startle the horse but made her throat raw with loud whispers.

"Aye, aye," a masculine voice snapped back, a figure moving on the quarterdeck. "Judas!" He called out a sample of names and men appeared from various spots in the mast and deck, clambering to the gangway.

Oblivious to the rumble of footfalls, the great black stallion delicately picked his way closer, the bowing plank having little effect on the crewman.

"What're you doing with the captain's horse?" Baynes demanded from the rail.

Captain. Cracking good fortune, she thought bitterly. He couldn't be a simple bo'son, or even a first mate. Nay, her first victim was the lord of the vessel. "He's shot."

A round of curses, and when the horse stepped onto the deck, Michaela struggled for balance as the steed folded down on his forelegs. A trained puppy, she thought, sliding off in time to see Rein fall against the support of a crewman.

"Sweet Christ, Capt'n, what have ye gone and done this time?" Baynes nodded to a mate and, together, they helped him toward the hatch. Michaela took a step backward, toward escape, but a huge dark skinned man with beefy arms and a turban-wrapped head caught her wrist.

She struggled helplessly. "I must leave." It would take hours to get home on foot.

The man shook his head, ushering her toward the open passageway. Michaela stalled, bearing down on her heels. Panic swept her like an oil fire.

I can't go in there. Not with all those men.

The dark man clapped a hand to her head, forcing her through the hatch. A few steps and she stumbled into the captain's quarters. The guard released her and she glared at him.

"Do not attempt such again, sir." She shrugged deeper into her cloak. "I am armed," she lied, tipping her chin.

He smirked, studying her, and she returned the perusal, her gaze wandering over his ballooned breeches, the shoes with curled toes, to his bare chest with only a sleeveless leather vest shielding him from the cold. He folded his arms over his chest, gold bands strapping his biceps, a fortune in gems adorning his fingers. What an interesting looking man, she thought, just as a howl of pain rent the air.

She crossed the room, tripping on the edge of the carpet and barreling between crewmen. She stopped short at the side of his bed, unmindful of its opulence, its grand size, her eyes only on the man she'd shot. Without the sinister darkness of his tricorn and cloak, he looked suddenly vulnerable lying on the coverlet, his shirt torn from his shoulder, her apron gone sticky red with his blood. A crewman pulled at his boots, dropping them to the floor with a thunk as the first fellow straightened, barking out orders for hot water, soap, bandages, and some particular box.

Rein moaned, whispering something to the seaman.

"Aye, she is here." Baynes glanced at her. "I'm Leelan Baynes, the captain's helmsman and first mate."

Michaela acknowledged the thick-chested man with a nod, inching closer to the bed and staring down at Rein. "He's lost a lot of blood."

"And will lose more to get that bloody damn ball out."

Rein muttered again, and Baynes bent to him. His brows shot up and he cast a look at the girl. "He says you're to take it out."

Her gaze flew to Rein. He stirred, his indecently long lashes sweeping upward. He met her gaze, the corner of his chiseled mouth lifting. Dastardly man. He had a look about him, that don't-I-look-pitiful-and-you-are-the-cause smile. And she knew one whispered command from him and his crew would shackle her for his bidding. *Best get it done and be gone,* she thought, shoving her hair back over her shoulder and moving closer. Baynes brought her a stool and she sat, shrugging out of her cloak and laying her pistol at her feet before tearing his shirt further open.

"The price of your crime, slayer," he said for her ears alone.

She scoffed. "Think you I will faint or such silliness?"

"You do look a wee bit pale."

She leveled him a superior look. "Preferably to your pea soup pallor?"

His smile widened a fraction, and she did not want that flash of white teeth to affect her so deeply.

"Be still," she snapped, even though he was.

Through slitted eyes, Rein watched her probe the wound, concentrating on her and not the pain as Leelan brought the teakwood

chest, opening the lock and flipping the catch. Pushing back the
lid, he withdrew long-tipped tongs and dropped them in a bowl,
pouring boiling water over them.

"Wash yer hand before touchin' him again," he growled to her
in a tone that said she was stupid for not doing so before, and over
her head Rein sent Leelan a quelling stare.

Covering the wound, Michaela obeyed and rose, turning back
her sleeves and cleansing her hands whilst Mr. Baynes opened vials
and pouches, sanding powders and herbs into a cup of steaming
water. He crossed to offer his captain a drink. Even as he drained
the wood mug, he held her prisoner in his pale gaze. *He traps me,*
she thought. *With a single look, he traps my very breath.*

Rein saw the uncertainty in her lovely eyes, and for reasons he
did not have time nor the mental capacity to examine just now, he
wanted her near a moment or two longer. Even if it meant her
digging in his torn skin for a ball. The lass could not know this
was minor compared to the wounds he'd suffered over the years
and he was not about to inform her of such. Let the chit suffer a
bit.

She came to him, the still-steaming instruments rolled in a clean
cloth.

"I am not certain as to—"

Rein scooted up on the pillow, suddenly alert. She frowned at
him, then the empty cup on the commode aside the bed. *Do not
ask,* she thought.

"You search for the ball and remove it."

She dropped a hand to her hip, cocking it. "Capital idea," she
mocked, batting her lashes. "Why did I not think of that?"

He smiled.

She ignored it, plopping to the stool and leaning close, prying
back the stained cloth. The blue powder was gone, absorbed into
the skin, she assumed, and the bleeding had stopped. But the hole
was clean, and she feared she would have to open it wider to get
at the shot. She'd done such for her father once or twice, yet she'd
never inflicted the wound herself. And Papa had been heavily
drugged at the time, not staring her down like a bloody vulture.

"This will hurt."

He scoffed lightly. "No more than going in."

"Certain you would not prefer to be unconscious?" she asked with the smooth lift of her brow, her attention on cleaning the area.

He studied her a bit. "And how would you render me so?"

Only her gaze shifted. "Cuffing you with my pistol seems like an excellent idea."

He laughed, the low, sultry sound tumbling like butterflies in her belly. Rich, she thought fleetingly, his laugh was rich and without malice.

"Here comes the hurting part," she warned before inserting her finger, digging about for the sphere. He made not a sound. When she felt it, she immediately picked up the tongs and dug. He watched her, his gaze weighing, yet he did not move a fraction, his breathing slow and regular, and Michaela marveled at his show of strength. Mr. Baynes hovered close, offering her cloths to blot the fresh blood.

She gripped the ball, then lost it. Twice more she tried and the gush of cherry-red liquid told her he could not take much more and survive. *Lord help me, I will kill him here instead of on the road.* After her failed attempt, she sighed, her head bowed. "Do not make me do this."

Rein leaned close. "You put it there," he challenged in an intimate tone. Behind them, Baynes frowned as Rein slipped his hand over hers, feeling the tremors and willing her into calm. In his mind, he chanted ancient words, drawing her fear into him.

A wave of heat and serenity coated her as if she were suddenly in a warm, soothing bath, the stiffness leaving her limbs, her shoulders, and she stared at his dark hand covering her pale fingers. His fingers were long, and bronze as a toasted biscuit. The thought made her smile a fraction and she lifted her gaze to his.

My lord, he was a beautiful man, she thought, slashing dark brows over so pale eyes, his features exquisitely carved and softened with the warm hue of his skin. He appeared the lazy cat lying in a lake of deep blue down, his body outlined only by the white shirt he still wore. Yet Michaela could sense him, an undercurrent that told her no matter how still he was nor how relaxed, he was prepared for the slightest change. The knowledge magnified her perception of him, offering tiny details, a scar on his brow, the chain looping the curve of his throat, the sculpture of his hairless chest. Lantern light skipped over hair so black it was nearly blue, the gleaming locks not queued like most Englishmen, but sheared into short layers at the crown to fall in waves to his shoulders. It spoke defiance and efficiency, a man who did not bend to fashion. *He bends to no one,* she thought fleetingly, letting her gaze wander over his face, and her only thought was . . .

"Do it," he whispered softly, seeing the warm turn of her thoughts in her eyes and not caring for his fierce response.

She blinked at his harsh tone, then nodded, probing. The shot came out with the tongs on the first try. Immediately she covered the wound with a fresh cloth, holding it tightly.

"A needle and thread," she asked of Mr. Baynes, then dragged her gaze from Rein's to the mate's.

Leelan shook his head, handing her only the needle. "Use a strand of his hair."

She frowned, glancing between the two men. Rein nodded, and she rose, first washing her hands again, then hovering over him.

Bloody damn and thunder, I should have had Baynes do this, he thought as her fragrance enveloped him in a warm mist. Lemons, he realized, inhaling and aching to pull her down onto his lap. God above, he'd no time for females, and especially ones who were wont to shoot first and speak after. Yet she enchanted him, her candor, her unflinching stares even when he knew she was scared. Good sense did not fail, and he dug his fingertips into the coverlet to keep from shaping the bosom nearly pushed in his face. He scarcely felt her pluck the hairs from his head.

She sat, unaware of his turmoil, and Rein sagged into the bedding. His lust was a dangerous thing, he thought, focusing on her, his lips quirking as she screwed up her face to thread the needle, loving the adorable way her tongue lined her lips with her efforts. She knotted the end and began stitching.

He looked at the wound, then to her. "A nice herringbone, if you please."

Her gaze collided with his and found laughter spilling there.

Michaela shook her head ruefully. "How can you make light when your flesh is open like this?"

"Would you prefer I curse you to perdition?"

" 'Twould offer satisfaction, I suppose."

He mumbled words she suspected were Gaelic and she scowled.

He laughed. Such a fierce look, he thought, wincing at the fresh burst of pain.

"What did you say?"

"I wished you hairy arms and warts."

"Oh?" Her thin look was bone dry, yet her tugging stitches gentle. "A few 'damn you, impulsive woman' would have sufficed, you know."

"And waste a good curse?" When she furnished him with a wholly speculative look as to his powers, he said, "Shall I remove it?"

She shrugged and stitched. "I do not believe in curses anyway."

His chiseled mouth quirked. "Tell me thus when your comely face is ruined."

I will be ruined regardless, she thought, *if I do not escape soon.* She leaned forward to bite off the thread of hair.

He caught her chin between forefinger and thumb, and she met his gaze. "Leave it." Without will, his thumb rasped over the seam of her lips, the curves.

Her breath shuddered softly against the tip, and the air between them changed, grew heavier, warmer. His gaze swept her delicately rich features, her hair flowing in long spiraling curls over his uninjured arm. Without notice, he caught a thick lock between his fingers, sanding it gently.

"Goddess of light, you are lovely, Michaela."

Her cheeks stained pink, yet her hazel eyes glossed bright with guilt. "I am sorry, Rein."

"I know, little slayer. I know." He neared. And in an instant, he wanted, hungered down to his heels for her, all of her, the touch, the taste, the smell—ahhh, the sweet smell of her was a drug of its own. And when she remained close, waiting, his appetite flourished, his groin filling and throbbing with amazing swiftness.

Desire flickered wildly through her body and she wet her lips. His eyes flared, the irises gone wide and black and he angled his head, neared. Michaela's lashes lowered of their own volition. A hard, palatable yearning filled her like a goblet poured too high, spilling over her with thick heat and ravenous tremors she'd never experienced before.

She forgot the audience behind them. Forgot that she was aboard a ship loaded with randy men and how easily this one could bind her and sail away.

His thumb mapped her moist lips, peeling the bottom one down.

His breath brushed her mouth and she could smell the wind in him, the earth and fire, and she knew nothing but that in this one moment, she risked more than the touch of his mouth on hers.

She risked her freedom.

Instantly, she jerked back, shooting to her feet so fast the stool tipped over. She glared accusingly at him, her fear so palpable it left a bitter taste in his mouth.

The notion warned him that although she might be as bold as a brash servant, she was untried. An innocent.

And Michaela watched his expression close to her, his features so lacking in emotion, she felt a chill grate her spine. Her eyes swore to her confusion, yet before she could speak, Baynes moved, blocking her view as he made to bandage his captain. Rein called for her, his tone harsh as he demanded Leelan to move aside. The helmsman ignored the command, and Michaela took little note of the sumptuous cabin still filled with crewmen worried for their captain and inched toward the door.

"So, who did this to you, sir, so's we can go hunt the cur down?" Baynes asked, and Michaela immediately bolted, hiking her skirts and running through the passageway. She hit the deck in all haste. The ship heeled on the roll of waves as she skittered to the gangway, overtaking it in seconds.

Her feet met the pier as a dark howl ripped from the vessel, her name vibrating on the night air and bringing heads around. She stilled, her heart slamming against her ribs, and she warred with returning to his side to see him healed of the damage she'd rent, or home before she was missed. She bolted into the crowd. People gawked as she tore down the wharf, pushing her way between the swarms of sailors and fishmongers, her cloak forgotten with her pistol.

And the dashing sea captain with forbidding blue eyes.

Two

"Cabai! Send four men," Rein ordered when crewmen crowded after her. "But you stay." The big Arab froze, his smooth face twisted in a frown. He attracted far too much attention. "Warn them to be discreet, simply see that she arrives safely at her door. No more." Rein did not wish the lass punished for her crime. Nor did he want her trail traced back to the *Empress*. Cabai pointed out his selection and the men departed in all haste.

"She'll be dead afore she reaches the end of the wharf," Rein gnashed, swinging his legs over the side of the bed and reaching for his boots.

"You can't be going after her, too?"

Only Rein's eyes shifted to the helmsman.

Leelan threw his hands up. "Fine. Rip the girl's stitches, but if you bleed to death and yer mother starts castin' spells on me fer not stoppin' you, then 'tis your hide I'll be handin' over to her."

Rein dismissed his threats. "You want your conscience weighted with her death? Great thunder, man." He plowed his fingers through his hair. "She's a woman. And a little one at that." And unarmed, he realized, picking up her cloak and pistol. She would freeze this night.

"She was big enough to put a bullet in you."

Rein arched a brow.

"Why else would ye have her take it out? Made yer brother remove the dart he plucked in you." Leelan laughed to himself, shaking his head and gathering up the soiled linens.

Teaching her a lesson in recklessness was not his intention, Rein thought, unwilling to admit he'd untoward designs on the girl. "Stopped him from shooting unsuspecting passersby, did it not?"

Rein stood and staggered, dropping his boots and catching himself on the bedpost. He cursed the green-eyed woman and her marksmanship. Leelan crossed to him, holding out a fresh shirt as if he were his handmaid and not a helmsman with thirty years experience. His know-it-all smirk incensed him, and Rein snatched the garment.

Leelan's shoulders fell with relief, and he hastened out the door, calling for the cook.

Rein shrugged into the shirt, foregoing the strength it took to fasten it. His head reeled with the blood loss, yet he felt little pain. With her pistol and cloak in hand, he crossed the cabin, shifting carefully behind his desk and gently sliding into the chair. He laid her possessions on the cluttered surface, resting his aching head on the leather chair back. After a moment, he flung his leg over the arm and fiddled with a protractor, poking the sharp tip into the wood with impatient jabs. He stared at her possessions, his worry far greater than he preferred.

She thinks I will name her to the authorities for shooting me.

He'd given her no reason to believe otherwise, kidnapping her like he had, and he hated to think she was running for her life right now. The faint engraving on the stock of her pistol made him frown.

R.A.D., Captain H.M.L.D.

His Majesty's Light Dragoons?

The pistol was a later model, ten years old, if that young. And how would Michaela come by such a weapon? Stole it, he thought, his lips quirking. For no honorable soldier gave up his weapon willingly, and though it was prudent he dismiss the woman from his thoughts, he could not.

As if to taunt him, her image tumbled behind his eyes, her slight frame, her delicate, pale features, the sharp arch of her brows over greenish-brown eyes. And that wickedly lush mouth, the taste of her held a feather's touch away from him. He'd never wanted to kiss a woman—nay, lay her down and ravish her, as he had then. He rubbed a shaking hand over his face. Ahh, Goddess, to be touched by such a female, he thought, his body answering the fantasy.

Rein shifted in the chair. "Damn me," he muttered, tossing the instrument aside, shielding his eyes and massaging his temples. But the image of her would not fade, details coming to him, her sarcastic glances, her impertinence with him. His lips quirked and he fell deeper into her image, the dark, coppery curls, the tender look in her eyes when she apologized for gunning him. She's an

innocent, he reminded himself. Forbidden. Not that he'd the time
to go sniffing her out.

He jolted as something wet nudged his hand, and he lurched
upright, her image dissolving into oblivion with the onset of fresh
pain. He glared at the intruder.

"Goddess of light, Rahjin, I've taught you better!" Fat paws on
the edge of his desk, the black leopard tipped her head and slathered
his hand again. Rein jerked back, furious. He stared at the leopard,
then inclined his head for her to be gone. The cat stretched her
jaw, showing razor-sharp fangs before dropping to the floor. She
sauntered to the bed, velvety muscle rippling as she leaped to the
center and stalked the sheets. Her growl was low as she scented
his blood, then raised her head. Green-gold eyes stared, unblinking.

"I am fine. Go to sleep."

Rahjin plopped inelegantly to the cushions.

"Not in my bed!"

The cat did not move, looking entirely too regal. Rein sent the
creature an arched look. "Kill you some rats today?" he asked.

Like a punished child banished to the corner, Rahjin slithered
quietly from the mattress and found her bed beneath the bench
before the aft windows. She vanished in the dark shadows, only
her long, slim tail visible as it swished rhythmically across the
carpet. Rein tipped his head back and sank deep into the leather
chair, his hand closing over the medallion, its dark fortune proving
itself this day. He slammed his eyes shut, his twisted emotions
working through his weakened blood, his thumb rasping over the
engravings. In the last three years he'd done the like a thousand
times, enough to wear the carving smooth. He'd no need to look
to know it was the image of a ship, a dead ship, thirty or so years
decommissioned. The name was inconsequential, the award of the
emblem even less. The accursed thing held only one purpose—a
connection to his past, and if this day was any indication, he suspected, it was a deadly one.

"See what happens when you do not accept my invitations?" a
male voice called.

"You have my permission to remind me next time," Rein said,
his eyes still closed, and heard Temple Matthews step inside. He
cocked one open, looking at Rahjin, snoring beneath the bench.
"Fine protection you are."

Temple frowned, his gaze moving to Rein's bandaged shoulder, then the medallion clasped in his fist. "She only got in one shot?"

Rein's lips curved. "Aye. Had she more weapons, I think she would have . . ." Anger sharpened his features. "By God, I'll have Leelan's hide for flapping his jibs!"

"I beat it out of him," Temple laughed softly, striding into the cabin and crossing to the settee positioned near the desk. He dropped lazily into the cushions, stretching out his long, booted legs and yanking at his cream-colored neck cloth.

"You reek of perfume, man. Several varieties." Rein waved his hand in front of his face, noting the day's growth of beard, the lip rouge painting his chin.

"And sex." He poked the air. "Let us not forget the hours of riding atween some very willing thighs. Scented ones, too." He grinned, flashing deep dimples. " 'Twas a carnal delight getting this disheveled," he remarked with a flowing sweep to his elegantly rumpled velvet garments.

A debaucher of the first order, Rein thought. "Are you not afraid of catching some disease?"

Temple blinked owlishly. "I fornicate with only the finest ladies, Captain," he said, looking affronted, then reached out to snatch an apple from the bowl on the desk, tossing it twice before taking a noisy bite.

"Ladies do not fornicate."

"Nay," he replied with a rascally grin laced with lush memory. "They turn into imaginative little strumpets, howling in all the proper moments, of course." His smile turned sly. "Lady Katherine sends her regards, by the by."

Only Rein's gaze shifted to his.

The man was not the least bit envious that he'd bedded the widow, though the fact did not surprise Temple. Rein had spent one evening with the young woman, and after such, she'd considered him her personal paramour. By God, the chit even had the nerve to arrive by carriage at the wharf. Only to be summarily dismissed without laying eyes on Rein. Temple was certain the singular liaison did her reputation well, to have survived a night with Rein with her arteries intact, was the last rumor he'd heard, yet both men knew her game. She sought a new protector, plentiful coin to fill her purse and maintain the lifestyle she was accustomed to whilst wed to a duke or something as blue-blooded. And, in turn, the bitch repaid it on her back.

"Can you afford the woman?"

Temple scoffed, chewing a bit of apple. "Of course not." Gambling was coin better spent, he thought.

The captain's brows rose, questioning the assignation.

"I only wanted a sample of what you so easily discarded." He tsked softly. "Such a waste, Rein." Katherine was a passionate creature. Trouble was, she demanded more than she gave. And she demanded sex like a disease.

"Careful, old man, the lady—"

"Is a whore." His tone bit harshly in the quiet room. "I know. But what can a lowly South African hope for?"

"Respect for yourself would be an excellent start. You are going to find your life ending in a duel, if you are not circumspect."

Temple waved him off, his dark eyes clouding a bit. "I am discreet enough. See, I left under the cover of night." He waved a long-boned hand toward the slanted windows, the twilight just beginning to prick the sky. "And I respect myself, Rein, my past and those around me. Which is why I chase after lightskirts and leave the virtuous ladies to the gents." He stared at his friend, tapping the unfinished apple against his kiss-bruised lips. "And so do you."

Rein stiffened in the chair. "You would not know what to do with a real lady, Temp. Should you ever find yourself in their company, which is moot." His tone sharpened. "And I chase no women." Michaela's image burst in his mind. He shook his head as if to clear it.

" 'Tis the problem," Temple said with a thoughtful look and a pointing finger. "Your disposition would not be so sour if you took a wench once in awhile." Rein's expression darkened, threatened, yet Temple simply stared back. "What about this shooter?" He nodded to his bandaged wound.

His look said the matter was not up for discussion.

Temple, as usual, ignored it. "Leelan said she was a beauty. Surely the wench—"

"Nay."

"You are certain?"

"Nay!" Rein exploded, his gaze shredding him. "And you push the line, Mr. Matthews. 'Tis done."

Not from the look of it, Temple thought, smiling only in his mind. As if Rein sensed his thoughts, which he likely did, he glared at him.

"Rahjin, earn your keep!" he barked, rankled by the curl of emotions moving through him.

The black leopard rose, her coat like velvet brocade as she strode across the room. Rahjin paused at Temple's elbow, eyeing the apple. She nudged his arm, smacking her lips.

"Do you love me?" Temple asked, smiling his best.

Rahjin nuzzled her big head against his sleeve, growling when she scented the woman on him. "She meant naught to me, I swear," he crooned, and Rein shook his head, his smile rueful. Temple and Rahjin played this game often, and each time, Rahjin's jealousy offered the chance of sharp claws across tender skin. But Temple Matthews chased danger in all forms, and, of late, Rahjin was the least damaging route.

"You are being possessive, my kitten." Temple leaned closer, offering his cheek for Rahjin's claws. "You know how that vexes me." Rahjin growled low, scenting Temple, the apple in his hand. "She was an amusement. They all are." The truth of his words rang in the cabin. "Love me forever?" He tipped his face, and Rein held his breath, a warning in his eyes. Rahjin's growl grew louder, and when Rein thought she'd strike, the cat slathered her pink tongue across his face, the sound rasping in the tense silence. Temple chuckled, rubbing Rahjin behind the ears, then giving her the apple. She devoured it in seconds.

"Go to work, my lovely." He scratched her some more and Rahjin purred before sauntering out of the cabin.

"Goddess of light, even I would not tempt such and I raised her."

Temple shrugged, then swiped the slobber from his face with his sleeve, leaving a stain on the brown velvet. "You are simply unhappy because she loves me best."

Rein smirked, unable to hide his amusement as he took a piece of fruit from the bowl and a knife from his waist belt. He frowned down at the array, realizing one was missing. Crafty little cutthroat, he thought, smiling privately as he methodically pared the mango. He brought a slice to his lips, savoring the sweet juice before popping it in his mouth.

"So tell me how you managed to get shot by a woman?"

"Nay."

Temple arched a sable brow. "Nay?"

"Ahh, so you are only thickheaded, not deaf."

Temple grinned hugely and sank his teeth into the crisp fruit, crunching loudly.

"I will find out, you know," he said around the food. "I did about Katherine."

Leaning back on his elbow, Rein spared him a mild glance. "Only because I let you." Nay, Michaela he would keep to himself, an isolated memory left undefiled by the stigma of his meager pedigree, his vulgar past. Though there could be no more between them but assailant and casualty, Rein felt if he did not speak of the moments to any soul, the fragile images would never shatter.

Michaela hopped off the back of the peddler's cart, running toward Argyle. He skidded to a halt, his horse's bridle jingling noisily. "God be praised, lass! I thought I'd find ye dead."

He pulled her into the saddle and wheeled the horse about, bolting.

"Has he asked for me?" A hard shiver wracked her body and she hugged his warmth.

"Aye," he said out of the side of his mouth, tipping a look back at her. "Millie told him you were feeling poorly, but that was earlier." A pause and then, "The major's with him. Been locked up in his study with 'im all afternoon."

"That means he'll stay for dinner. Damn and blast." She did not need her Uncle's lap dog sniffing after her again.

Argyle's lips curved at her cursing and he shifted around a strand of trees, then brought the horse to a stop on a knoll of grass to avoid the clatter of hooves and notice.

She flung herself from the saddle, racing to the door and shoving it open. Servants stopped their work, gasping collectively. Mrs. Stockard rushed to her side, hushing everyone. "Oh, lovey. Look at you," she crooned, then called quietly for water and rags.

" 'Tis not mine," she said when the woman gaped at the blood covering her shoulder and the wrists of her blouse. Her look said she'd not offer an explanation and Michaela had no time to think about him. She'd done her regretting during her race from the city, evading the horde of seamen he'd sent after her. Their chase told her he wanted her back for more reasons that seeing her pay for filling him with lead. And Michaela could not bear the thought of a man touching her.

Until him, a voice called. *You let him touch, let him get close enough . . .*

"I've water warming," Mrs. Stockard said, interrupting her thoughts. "Go on up to your rooms." She bustled with her toward the servants' staircase.

Michaela gripped the cook's arm. "My thanks, Agnes," she said, bussing her cheek with a kiss, then looked beyond her to the maid. "You, too, Millie."

The maid bobbed, smiling, and Michaela mounted the stairs, quietly, measuredly, her feet blistered from running. For half the distance, she imagined the sea captain was following her, but knew he was too weak to travel. Guilt pressed and she forced it aside as she tiptoed down the hall toward her rooms, not breathing till she slipped inside and closed the door.

Quickly stripping out of her clothes, she stuffed them in a basket, handling the blade she'd clipped from him, her only protection during her trek home. Turning it over in her hands, she smoothed her fingertips across the carved bone handle. It was the least finest of his collection, and although she knew he'd miss it, she prayed it was not enough to come looking for it. *I am a thief now, too,* she thought with regret, storing the knife in the base of the basket before crossing naked to the tub near the hearth and climbing in. Briskly scrubbing the blood and grime from her skin, she buried her thoughts of him with the desire she recognized in his beautiful blue eyes. Vigorously she soaped the cloth, lather foaming as she dragged it across her throat, her breasts. The entire journey home, she thought of nothing else but the way he looked at her before he tempted a kiss, as if she were a cherished and fragile creature he dared not touch. She scoured harder, attacking her sore feet, yet the image of him chasing the hatchlings for her and the way his eyes crinkled at the corners when he smiled blossomed in vivid splendor. With a single look he created sensations that were wholly new and bright. And she could never explore.

It was the same with all men. They were sweet and cunning until you crossed them. Then they showed their power with their fists.

Except Papa. Papa never hurt you, she thought, grinding the cloth over her skin till it was red. The death of her father had brought more than the loss of a beloved parent. It stole her future. In the privacy of her bath, she mourned the children she would never have, the home she would never tend, the loving husband who would never offer for her. Tears dripped into the bathwater, unexpected, hot, and she angrily brushed the back of a soapy hand across her cheek.

Buck up old gell, she thought. *I've a roof over my head and food to eat,* she reminded herself and swore she needed no more. And she swore and swore.

Then the image of bronze skin and a challenging smile filled her mind again, and she sobbed helplessly. He'd rejected her with only his expression, cold and closed when she refused his kiss, offering proof enough that even a handsome face and the consideration for her life were no match for a man's will when they wanted to bed a woman.

And if he knew . . . he would not want even a kiss.

No man would.

She sank beneath the hot water to lather her hair. Aye, she never wanted to see him again, for if she did and he told a soul that it was she who'd shot him, Michaela could very well dance from a gibbet for her crime.

A knock sounded, and Michaela sat upright. Millie popped her head around the curve of the door, her look questioning. Michaela motioned her inside, and after the girl helped her rinse her hair, Michaela left the tub, drying and dressing with a speed that surprised her. "Oh, Millie, hurry," she said, as the girl fastened her gown. "I hear him."

"I'm sorry, but 'tis worn and frayed." Her tone sharpened. "You should not 'ave to wear such a thing."

Michaela knew the garment was out of fashion and faded from laundering. " 'Tis the best I have." And more than most, she thought, drawing her hair in a braid.

The maid shifted from foot to foot. "Be still, miss, please."

Michaela ceased trying to braid her hair into control. Curls escaped, and she smoothed and tucked. Millie finally finished, then hurried to clean up the mess from the bath.

A pounding rattled the door, startling them both. Michaela shoved a pin into her hair as she crossed the room, and for the breath of a moment, imagined the magistrate on the other side, prepared to lead her out in shackles for shooting the sea captain.

"Go, I shall be fine," she assured Millie, but the woman's reluctance to leave her alone showed in her face. She shooed her on and Michaela swung the door open. She met her uncle's hard green stare.

"So, you are finally up and about."

"Aye, and feeling much better, Uncle. Thank you for asking." Her sarcasm was wasted on him.

He did not cross the threshold and Millie waited patiently for her uncle to step back and allow her passage. The man did not spare the servant a glance, his gaze raking over her as if inspecting one of his troops. He nodded his approval of her demure gown, his balding pate gleaming in the candlelight. Absently she wondered if he expected her to come below stairs in her stays and stockings, and almost said as much. But he accepted no insubordination for his troops, and even less from her.

"Well, get down there then. We're famished."

And you, of course, could not lift a fork without me? "We?" she feigned innocence.

"The major is dining with us, of course."

"What a delight." It was too much to hope he'd dropped dead in the last hour, she supposed, slipping her arm through her uncle's. He looked down at her as if her touch fouled his coat, yet Michaela did not retreat.

If her father had taught her anything, it was to remain vigilant in the face of the enemy.

Three

Temple frowned down at Rein lying on the bed. "One would think he'd thrash out or something. Mumble a word or two. By God, he is still."

"Then you do not know him as well as you believe," Leelan said.

" 'Tis a fever, what else is to know?" If not for the sweat gleaming on his bare chest, he appeared to be on death's threshold, Temple thought, worried.

"He's healing himself," Leelan said, wondering, as he always did, where he went to do that.

Temple looked at him, uncertainty in his eyes. He'd known Rein only a few years, and though their paths seldom crossed, for he was usually sailing another of Rein's ships for him, Temple found the man a bit odd. He was not without tremendous honor and unfailing loyalty, yet there were things, strange things, about the man that could not be explained. And this was one of them. "I know he dabbles in the Wiccan arts."

Baynes's snort cut him off. "One does not dabble," he said with all the eloquence of the gentry. "You simply do not understand."

Temple leaned his shoulder against the bedpost, drawing his coat back with a fist and dropping it to his hip. "Well? Explain, man. Rein certainly does not speak of it."

Leelan stared at the young man for a moment, indecisive. "He'll tell ye if'n he wants."

Temple looked back at his employer. Rein had shared a bit of his past over a bottle of madeira, yet rarely mentioned this aspect of his life.

"Leave 'im be," Baynes said, nodding to the door and making his way there himself. Rahjin guarded at the foot of the bed, curled like a kitten, her head resting on her fat paws. " 'Tis but a matter of waitin' it out." Temple left, and with one last look, Leelan closed the door behind him.

Rein did not hear, a cocoon of light enveloping him, holding him weightless, ancient words chanting through his mind, filling his spirit, buffeting his skin. Heat spread unbroken in his blood, pushing against the wound with the beat of his heart.

A street appeared in his mind, several avenues spindling off in all directions like the spokes of a wheel. Three were dark and shrouded. He moved toward the light. Suddenly, the image of his childhood materialized, of a rawboned child lying on the skin of the earth, his hand clasped in his mother's. He turned his head to look at her misty image, yards of black hair rivering the green grasses of Sanctuary. Her lips moved, yet he could not hear, but knew the words.

"Can you feel it? 'Tis the energy of the earth. Capture it, Dahrein, hold it close, for 'tis very precious."

He beckoned that power now, the spinning taking him deeper into the healing sleep. Energy seeped into him like hot wine, drenching over his body, and he welcomed it, let it absorb into his wound and destroy the impurities.

A null e. A null e. Slaintè. He heard.

Aurora?

Aye, my son. I am here.

In the stillness of the cabin, his lips curved.

Brigadier General Atwell Denton eyed his niece as he forked a slice of boiled beef. "Have you seen to the guest list?" he asked.

"Aye."

"Have the invitations been delivered?"

"Half are. Argyle will tend to the remainder in a sennight," Michaela said, poking at her meal, annoyingly aware of Major Winters sitting directly across from her, staring like a mouse before a cube of cheese. The tall, blond aide-de-camp possessed the likings of a broken fixture in the house, loitering about without use and forcing Michaela to look upon his deceptively handsome face at least once a night in the past days. "The food has been ordered, even now Mrs. Stockard prepares." *And prepares and prepares,* she thought. Only the Brigadier would throw a party for himself, celebrating his recent promotion.

"I've sent for a gown for you. That"—he gestured to her throat clipping gray dress—"will not do."

Then give me back my stipend and dowry and I will see myself fitted properly, she thought, yet did not expend the breath. Since her uncle sailed into her life after her father's death, she'd lost control of her own purse strings. It would not matter if she were marriageable enough for a man to offer for her, she would have nothing to take to a husband. He was spending it on his bloody ball.

"Nay, my thanks though." Her tone was cordial enough, was it not? " 'Tis too late to have one altered."

"Then you may wear it as it arrives. Should fit well enough, I think."

He thinks? Michaela ground her teeth and nodded, the need to scream at him clawing through her body. What did a man whose life was nothing but troops, ordnance and battle know of the hours undertaking the fit of a ball gown?

"My thanks, Uncle Atwell," she said, sampling the poached fish Cook had prepared just for her, the succulent taste waning with her appetite.

"Need you hire more staff?"

"Nay." Her voice sounded tired she knew, but the man was being tedious. She lifted her gaze to greet his at the head of the table. "I have seen to the running of a house since I was four and ten. Homes twice this size when my father was assigned to the rajah. Papa was renowned for his splendid affairs. The Spanish king said as much." She took immense pleasure in the tightening of his lips. He did not like the reminder of his brother's accomplishments, and she'd be wiser, and healthier, if she'd keep her mouth sealed. But the opportunity to exert her true feelings was so rare. "One ball is hardly an effort," she finished in a matter-of-fact tone.

"But this must be the very best." When he postured, it was much like a fat bear, she thought, hiding her irritation in a sweet smile.

"Have I failed you yet?"

Instantly she wished the words back when he tipped his head to the side, then swung his gaze to Major Winters. Shame stained her cheeks, her fingers white knuckled around her utensil. It took every ounce of willpower to keep her features schooled in a mask of remorse. She looked down at her plate. Oh the cur, the insensitive, unforgivable cur! It was arduous enough with her mistakes sitting across from her, did he have to remind her of his foul victory?

"Nay, not lately," he conceded, intent on shoveling boiled potatoes into his mouth. He did not see the major's gaze roam her figure, his lips curving in a predatory smile.

Michaela's stomach churned, threatening to empty the contents on the table as his stare deepened. It was a look she recognized in her dreams, and she reached for her wine goblet, trembling fingers hitting prematurely and tipping it over. Dark-red liquid bled on the creamy Irish linen.

"Now look what you've done," her uncle growled as she blotted hopelessly. "Bungling female."

A faint snicker rose in the candlelit room, and she could withstand no more of Major Anthony Winters's perverse pleasure in her shortcomings. She stood abruptly and, with a muffled sob, quit the room, ignoring her uncle's calls to return.

Outside the dining room, she stopped, bracing her hand on the sideboard and commending herself on holding her temper around them. Convincing them she was no more than a carpet they could trod upon without notice had been simple. Maintaining it now was crucial. And, as she glanced back over her shoulder, she noticed the two men in deep conversation, her presence already forgotten. Predictable. She headed to the kitchen to confess to Mrs. Stockard she'd ruined yet another tablecloth.

I am surprised the wine did not leap off the table to soil my gown, Michaela thought with a disparaging smirk, and wondered how she'd managed to survive this long without killing herself. Even as the thought took shape, she tripped on the edge of the carpet and went flying forward only to land in Argyle's capable arms just as he came around the corner. Without a sound, the brawny Scot set her to rights as if he were merely passing by and adjusting a painting on the wall, then moved on. Michaela sighed, smoothed her hair, then continued on her way, yet a little laugh escaped when Argyle, who was nearly at the opposite end of the hall, tsked softly.

On stocking feet, Michaela padded down the darkened hall, waiting outside her father's old chambers, listening for her uncle's nightly creaks and groans that signaled he was abed. When the light extinguished, she turned back to her chamber, throwing the locks and stripping out of her clothing, tossing them hither and yon as she crossed to a large, lidded basket. Flipping the top back, she removed the garments hidden beneath layers of family mementos, jamming her legs into boy's breeches and her arms into shirtsleeves and a heavy woolen coat. Pulling on her jack boots, she straightened, tucking her hair in a cap, then dug in the woven chest for the boned-handled knife.

She stared down at it, her thumb rubbing the intricate carving, the hours in his company a lifetime away, instead of two days. An ache stirred in her breast, the unforeseen strength of it, the memory of his smile, intimate and cherishing and leaving her unexpectedly breathless. She clapped a hand over her heart, the rapid beat humming skin to skin.

No one made her feel her carefully guarded emotions like he did and she did not want to feel them. Yet for the sake of his charming smile and ripping good humor over the whole incident, she prayed he survived. Bending, she secreted his knife in her jack boot, and for justifications she'd rather not probe just now, felt a tiny bit safer than she did the day before her father died.

Dusk had long since fallen on the wharf, the odor of dead fish and the freshness of the sea mingled, the moon glowing high in the pithy darkness above him as Temple leaned against the rail, arms folded. Hidden in the darkness, he watched his employer bring his mount from his private stall, clean his hooves, brush him down, then offer a sack of feed as he flung the Spanish saddle on his black back.

"You pamper him like a child."

"He's only three," he said without looking up, and Temple decided Rein could see in the dark. He rubbed Naraka behind the ears like a kitten.

Temple swore the animal purred. "You can't think to travel. Your injury."

"Two days of Cabai's hovering is enough. I'm in need of a little exercise," he said, adjusting the girth.

Rein's idea of fun was climbing a mountain or daring some deep-buried need to swim in shark infested waters. He hated to think what he had in mind for this evening. "Tell me you're venturing to Madame Goulier's and I will join you."

Rein met his gaze over the back of the horse, the look dry. "I think not."

"Nay to Madame's, or a partner?"

"Both," he said, and mounted. Temple caught the arsenal of weapons tucked in his waistband and frowned, his look pointed. "Stay out of this, Matthews. Are we understood?"

Captain Montegomery did not wait for a response and swung

Naraka around. The horse picked his way down the gangplank,
drawing the attention of several sailors lounging on the pier, yet,
as painted hooves met the wood surface, Rein dug his heels in.
The pitch-black stallion bolted, sending pedestrians flying for shelter during his mad ride down the quay. Temple watched for a moment, then pushed away from the rail and headed toward the
passageway.

"Don't think to follow, laddie."

Temple looked up and met Leelan's gaze.

The old man munched on an apple, gesturing toward Rein's retreat. "He don't need motherin'."

Temple's lips twisted wryly. "Mayhap just a friend?"

"Ain't likely. 'Sides, the lad's got demons you ain't even imagined."

A hard look passed over Temple's features. "I bet I can."

Argyle sat astride his horse, hidden in a cluster of trees as he
watched her carefully pull her mount from the stable. He had to
hand it to the lass—she did so without waking the boy sleeping
there. He waited until she mounted and rode some distance away
before he urged his horse forward. He'd no notion of what she was
up to and it mattered not, but with Michaela, it was oftimes a good
bit of mischief. His lips curved as he ducked beneath a low slung
branch, remembering the little girl in aprons and braids who'd taken
a camel out for a ride, her disappearance leading an entire brigade
to believe she'd been kidnapped by Bedouins. Argyle had fetched
her then, dirty and sobbing, and the poor child could not sit for a
week for the bruising jolt. Yet even when her father scolded her
for her behavior, she interrupted his tirade to inform him that camels could smile and didn't he find that odd, since they'd little to
smile about, being lumpy and ugly.

Her father had lost his steam then, dismissing her with a tender
smile. Little Michaela had rubbed her sore behind and trotted to the
door, pausing to tell her father that he needn't have worried
that the desert people would have ever taken her. She was his
daughter and none dared touch her. So trusting and innocent, Argyle thought, urging his mount to a brisk pace. Nothing could harm
her whilst her father lived, yet now that he was dead, Argyle shoul-

dered the precious trust. Even if she was unaware. He would not forsake her, for as her father lay dying, he'd sworn an oath to it.

And he'd already failed her once, he reminded himself grimly, keeping his distance, yet maintaining her in his sights. And the price she paid for his dereliction would haunt him till he took his final breath.

Four

In a darkened corner of the Boar's End Tavern, Rein nursed a drink he didn't want, his gaze moving over the soldiers enjoying rum and women. He'd fed their drunk half the afternoon, trying to garner information, and when a burly man, older than the rest, moved toward him, Rein kicked out a chair.

"A drink for His Majesty's finest," he murmured, and the sergeant major frowned, wary.

"Aye, if ye're buying?"

"I am. Rein Montegomery," he introduced himself.

The man's expression showed recognition, and Rein hoped it would not keep him from joining. After a short study, he sat, and Rein nodded to the serving maid. The full-hipped woman hustled to the bar and returned with a mug of ale, smiling sweetly as she set it all too carefully before the solider.

The soldier's gaze followed the woman to the bar, then turned to Rein's. "You've caught the girl's eye, sir."

Rein scoffed. "Hardly. 'Tis you and all those medals that's impressed her."

He glanced down at his chest, his smile sad. "Can't spend them, or eat them, gov. Ain't much use after that, 'cept makin' my coat heavy."

Practical man, Rein thought, leaning forward. "Where have you served?"

The soldier eyed him, judging his genuine interest. "Colonies,

Morocco, India, Cape Town." He shrugged lightly. "And a few others."

"Do you mind talking about them?" Rein did not care to speak of his own past, and whilst searching for information on his father's identity, he was not willing to pry from those who'd rather keep the ugliness of war buried. The battle-worn sergeant major wasn't a man he'd have customarily sought out, the ones who'd reveal all for a bit of gold and fabricate more for the fattening of a purse. Yet this soldier looked as if he needed to bend an ear.

"You really want to hear it?"

Rein's shoulders lifted and fell in a careless gesture. "If it would not cause you grief, sir. I've seen much of war and care not to be in the thick of it again." Aye, Rein thought as horrible memories of the mines, the sultan's prison and battling slavers clouded his thoughts. He'd experienced his fair share of fighting for a noble purpose, and he was done with it. Nothing, he decided long ago, was worth the carnage in taking up arms in battle and seeing blood run red over his decks.

"Begin at the beginning if you like, Sergeant Major . . ."

"Edward Townsend," he supplied, and shook Rein's offered hand. "Most call me Rusty." One hand braced around a mug, he pushed back the white wig to reveal flame-red hair. Rein grinned, motioning for the maid and ordering dinner for them both.

It was in the wee hours that Rein helped Townsend up the staircase, the man's weight and intemperance nearly toppling them both backward. He shoved open the door to the room he'd rented for the valiant soldier.

"You're certain you do not have to return to a barracks, sir?"

"Stop callin' me 'sir,' Rein." Rusty elbowed him. "Gads, you're a tight-assed fellow."

Rein's lips quirked. "Of course I am."

"Odd, too."

Rein shook his head and dumped the huge bear of a man on the bed, then turned to the tavern maid who'd catered to them all evening. "I want him to have aught he needs. A good breakfast . . ." Rein briefly glanced at the man, leaping forward when he was wont to slide off the bed. "If he can handle it." Rein swung Rusty's feet onto the mattress, then pried off the boots, setting them neatly aside.

"A bit of the hair of the dog, if he can't. Tell him the room is let for two days if he chooses to simply sleep it off."

The woman nodded.

"I ain't deaf, Rein."

"Nay, only thoroughly saturated."

Rusty smiled, his eyelids heavy. "Drank you under the table, didn't I?"

And over it, too, Rein thought, turning to the maid. "You tell him this . . ." He eyed her, assured of her complete attention. "Word for word . . ." She nodded, her eyes round as the neat stack of coins he pressed into her rough palms. "Should he require aught of me and mine, he need only ask."

She nodded, repeating his words, and, satisfied, Rein bent and bussed her cheek with a kiss and whispered, "It would do the man well to see a pretty face over his meal when he manages to stir below stairs in the morn, miss." She blushed like a girl half her age.

The sergeant major was a lonely man, refusing to wed to spare a woman the rough Gypsy life of the military. But he was near the end of his career and feeling the loss of his vow. Rein felt a kinship he'd not expected, leaving him feeling more isolated than when he was but four, kneeling on bloody knees and chipping away at stone for little sparkles that the wealthy needed so badly to feel content. Yet, regardless of the information Rusty had offered, Rein sympathized with his pledge to remain alone.

Leaving Rusty, he headed quickly below stairs and to Naraka lashed to the post outside. He mounted, wheeling about and racing off into the night without destination, without purpose, the hard ride burning the liquor in his blood and clearing his head.

Later, he would consider Rusty's tales and how they linked to his past, but now he only wanted freedom, to escape the memories crowding his mind. He pushed them out, slowing his ride down the dank, isolated streets toward the wharf.

A noise caught his attention, a scuffle, a yelp of pain. A returning slap. Rein halted, listened, withdrawing his pistol, then urged Naraka toward the alley. As he reached it, a man darted from the narrow passage, clutching his side, pausing when he saw Rein, shrieking as if he were Lucifer come to snatch his immortal soul. Naraka reared, pawed the air, and the man sped off into the night before Rein could bring the horse to heel. He took aim into the alley.

"Come out."

"Gaud, gov, already busted me way round one bloke. I ain't no fool to be mixin' it up wit' the likes of you," a voice replied, and Rein smiled at the attempt to cover the lightness of tone.

"I will not harm you, laddie. Come. 'Tis well and clear."

"Am I to be trustin' *you?*"

Rein moved beneath the streetlamp's flicker. "I could come in after you."

A long moment passed before a figure shuffled in the shadows, stone crunching beneath heavy, plodding steps, and Rein waited until the boy moved into the light. A small thing, no more than four and ten, if he hazard a guess.

"Need you a ride home, son?"

The boy stiffened, silent, shoulders hunched, capped head down. He shook his head, edging toward freedom. Naraka nudged the lad's shoulder with his nose, pushing him back. The lad muttered something unintelligible, and without fear of the animal's size, shoved the stallion's head away. The horse lipped his hat, taking it with him, and as the lad scrambled to retrieve it, long, dark hair spilled over narrow shoulders. Rein's brows shot up.

"Damn you, beast." She battled for her hat, but the horse thought it a game and lifted it out of her reach. It was then Rein caught the scent of lemons and ducked to catch a look at her face.

"Goddess of fire," Rein groaned miserably. "Please say 'tis not you."

"Fine. 'Tis not me." He sounded far too put out, as if she were suddenly *his* problem, *his* bother. What swill. "Make him give my hat back and we'll call this settled."

"Look at me, woman."

Michaela did, hands on her hips, a quick toss of her head to send the unruly mass of curls back over her shoulder. It was a futile gesture, a bit of imaginary armor against seeing him again, against those translucent eyes and the leaded sensations trudging through her body. How could he do that with just a look, she groused, ignite her insides, make her stomach flip and her skin heat. And why did he have to be so handsome? Could he have not uglied up a touch in the past days? Though she was terribly glad to see he'd survived the gunshot. Guilt assailed her, yet she smothered it quickly. She'd little time to spare, *again,* and needed to escape. Yet, as if sensing her thoughts, he moved the horse forward, the black beast forcing her to backstep. He pinned her against the wall.

"If you'd wanted my company, Rein, all you needed to do was issue an invitation." Gazing down from his high perch, he had that smug, Ah-ha-I-have-you-now look about him. She'd dealt with three of those already this evening, one man recently leaving her side with a cracking good hole in his, yet Rein's expression angered her the most, though she couldn't understand why just yet. Would he drag her to the magistrate, shoot her himself? Call out and claim her a killer, a thief? What? *What?*

" 'Tis awfully late, Michaela."

"Shhhh." Good God, if she were found out now . . . She shifted to the side. The horse covered her motion. She inched to the right. Naraka danced, pushing her harder to the wall. Her breath squeezed out and her hand went to Rein's thigh, the other on the mount. "Enough. You'll crush me."

His body responded, warmth under her touch, rising to blend through his blood with a fierceness that made his groin clench. His lips tightened. Sweet thunder. He did not want to feel this for her. Not now, not ever.

"You will answer me."

"Not if I cannot breathe, you nosy oaf!"

He maneuvered back a fraction, yet her hand remained on his thigh. She stared up at him, locked in his icy gaze, and for an instant, the sounds around them grew distant and foreign: the drunks leaving nearby taverns and stumbling home, the scrap of something being dragged across the pier, the soft talk of sailors relaxing on the prows of ships moored close.

Her fingers flexed, corded muscle hard beneath, the fabric smooth and tight, offering indentation and contour—and familiarity. She jerked her hand back, rubbing her damp palm on her coat and silently insisting she did not enjoy that. She did not.

"What the in the name of the goddess are you doing out at this hour? On the quay? Alone?" His voice strengthened with each word. "And dressed as a *boy?*"

"Snipe fishing." He smirked, so insolent, so male, and it irritated her further.

Naraka swung his head around to look at her, and she yanked on her hat. It tore a bit and she gave up, shoving him away.

" 'Tis far too dangerous out here for a man, least of all a woman."

The concern in his tone touched off a little spark of warmth inside her. "Obviously." She gestured to him.

"Come." He held out a gloved hand. "I will take you home."

It died a quick death. God forbid he knew where she lived, she thought, and she had a horse tethered beyond the next building, if he'd just let her pass. "I got out here, I can get home," she said, smothering her panic. The childish beast waved the cap in her face. "Make him give it to me." She needed it to cover her hair and started rebraiding the mass. Her chin tipped, belligerence in her every fiber. "Make him give that back, Rein, or I will cry out."

"Be my guest." He waved as if they had an audience.

Her body screamed vexation, even if she did not. "Your attention is *quite* enough, thank you." Her lips scarcely moved, her eyes darting for escape.

He smiled indulgently, telling her without words that he was going nowhere until he received answers.

"Fine. Keep the cap. He obviously has little enough wool in his diet as it is." She slid down the wall and ducked under the horse's belly, bolting into the street. Michaela smiled, arms pumping, almost wishing he'd come after her.

Rein blinked, twisting, glancing about for her, stunned at how fast she moved.

"Give me the blasted thing!" Naraka swung his head around, and Rein snatched the cap, then wheeled about and gave chase. She darted into an alley.

A cat shrieked. Something crashed, and he suspected it was his slayer. Rein followed, the brisk clop of hooves echoing in the narrow corridor. Yet she ran, hair flying wildly, coattails flapping. He heard her bump into crates, slop through rubbish. He called her to halt.

A woman shouted for silence from a window above.

Rein slowed, cornering her against a fence. "Ask for quarter, lass, and let me take you home to your father."

Michaela stared at him, his striking figure silhouetted against the streetlamp. "I have none and nay you may not." Yet, a desperate, lonely part of her wanted to swing up behind him and ride off into the night.

Optimism painted his voice as he asked, "A husband?" *Please, Goddess, let this lass be well and truly wed.* Yet she scoffed, enough disgust lacing her tone to make him raise a brow. "You are trapped." She was but a blotch in the dark, rancid-smelling alley.

"Am I now?"

Rein squinted into the murkiness, wishing for the shift of clouds and the offer of moonlight. He heard the creak of wood, the kick of broken crockery, then his gaze rose, following shadowy movement as she clambered over the top of the fence, teetering for a heartbeat to salute him or likely snub him, before losing her balance and tumbling to the other side. Wood shattered. She groaned.

He fought a laugh and looked to the sky, smiling and shaking his head. "You are the victor, lass."

"It would appear so," came from the opposite side.

"Good night, manslayer."

Michaela looked up as her wool cap came sailing over the fence. She caught it before it landed in the mire and rubbed her fingers where the warmth of his touch lingered. She tipped her face toward the celestial sky and smiled. "Good night, Rein."

Argyle backed his horse into the shadows, observing her and her easy rapport with Rein Montegomery. He'd never heard her speak so freely, nor sharpen her tongue on so dangerous a man and he regretted losing sight of her and failing to hear more than snatches of the conversation. When she rolled over the fence and crashed to the ground, Argyle winced, shaking his head as he rode into the street. The lass was going to get herself killed purely by virtue of her graceless daring, he thought, determined to catch up with her. He passed Montegomery on the wet street, yet the man did not acknowledge him, his attention still on the spot where he'd cornered her in an alley.

Argyle was relieved the pair exchanged some odd familiarity, and though he was curious, he would not pry. Michaela would never tell anyway, he thought, and counted himself fortunate that he'd let the girl go unharmed. He was too old to do battle with the likes of Rein Montegomery. Not and live to speak of it.

Five

Michaela adjusted the deep blue gown and lacy funnel sleeves, plucking and shifting herself inside the stiff fabric. She stared at her reflection with a critical eye, then sighed, dispirited that nothing would make the gown fit better. She'd hoped to have the seamstress tailor the dress, but her uncle refused the expense. Twice, she thought, touching her tender jaw. It was fortunate she had a new garment a'tall. At least it covered her scraped elbows.

Dipping her toes into her slippers, she gathered the cumbersome skirts and swept to the door. One ill-fitting shoe fell off and she darted back, jamming it on and hopping toward the door. Suddenly, without benefit of a knock, her chamber door swung open and, looking up, she lost her balance, falling to the carpet in a heap.

Her uncle's polished stare sliced down at her.

She felt no better than a bug about to be squashed by a giant. He did not offer a hand up, keeping both of them clenched at his side as if touching her would soil him.

Michaela gathered her dignity and her skirts and climbed to her feet.

"Try not to do that in front of our guests."

She nodded. Did he think she preferred her clumsiness to grace and elegance?

His gaze swept her jaw, his expression emotionless as he assessed the damage and her attempts to cover it with powders. His lack of remorse stung deeper than the blow.

"Most of the guests have already arrived." His tone blamed her for not greeting them properly in his house. "Get yourself below-stairs, child."

I am not a child, she thought waspishly, and he knew that better than most. Sweeping past him, she headed down the curving staircase, managing not to catch her skirts on the carved banister and blessedly met the bottom step. She moved forward, her smile so tight her cheeks hurt, and, as guests filed in, the musicians layering the air with sweet melodies, Michaela wished she were anywhere but in this house.

'Tis your duty, she reminded when the urge to flee made her steps falter.

Guests greeted each other in high abandon, members of Parliament, wealthy merchants, decorated generals, and the Secretary of the State of War, the very heartbeat of England's government gracing the Denton threshold. Michaela might have been impressed had their presence not been a commonplace in this household. Over the years, she'd seen these men in various states. Her lips curved in a mischievous smile. Most of them, terribly unflattering.

Her thoughts were blunted when she felt the warmth of a presence behind her.

Turning, her smile slid off her face like icing in the warm sun. "Good evening, Mistress Denton."

Her spine rigid, she tipped her head slightly. "Major." Her lips scarcely moved, her features froze with politeness.

His gaze roamed over her with a feral quality she recognized in men. Especially in this man. It made her stomach clench and she swallowed, fighting the wave of nausea rushing up to her throat. Her fingers tightened on her fan, and in the silence reigning between them, she heard the delicate sandalwood slats fracture.

"You look enchanting, my dear."

She looked like a child in her mother's gown and she knew it. "My thanks, sir." She bowed her head gracefully. "My uncle, I believe, awaits your arrival. Would you like me to announce you?"

"There are servants for that, Michaela."

She inhaled, and her head jerked up. His tone caressed and condescended in one stroke. "I have warned you. Do not address me so."

"I think I have the right." His smug expression was like a blade to her heart, killing all semblance of politeness.

Her posture so inflexible it ached, she leveled him a courtly smile. "Think? Surely 'tis a strain?" She tipped forward slightly, her hazel eyes glittering with contempt. "Please continue, Major." Her voice dripped venom. "For it makes you a grander horse's ass than you already are."

His eyes widened a fraction, then his expression reshaped to a mask superior enough to put the king to shame. "Calm yourself."

"Go leap in the bloody Thames," she muttered as she moved around him, evading his touch. Wisely, he did not follow, yet she felt her uncle's scowl pinning her in the back as she walked around the ballroom and headed straight for a table overladen with comfits and silver tureens of sweet punch. She reached for the ladle. Her hand trembled and she drew back sharply, gripping the table ledge and battling rage and festering wounds. And the loss. Oh, Lord, the loss of so much more than her ideals was the worst of it. Her trust was gone. Her certitude in family, bloodlines, in justice and fairness, beat to death in the last three years. She refused to let it fall into complete decay, and in her own insignificant way, struggled to keep her ideals and allegiances alive, counting her fortunes as they came to her in simple friendships and risking her life to preserve a tiny thread of justice.

She glanced over her shoulder, scanning the crowd, and knew the danger lay in not recognizing her enemies. *Trust none and you will survive.* Pouring a cup of punch, she drained it swiftly, allowing the rare illegal champagne lacing the drink to buffer her frayed nerves before setting the cup on the tray of a passing servant.

Please, she prayed, strolling around the grand ballroom, smiling. *Let this evening progress without incident.*

Rein strode into Christian Chandler's house, pulling off his cape and tricorn, scarcely noticing the servants scattering like mice the instant he crossed the threshold. He flung the garments at the attending butler and continued toward Christian's study, ignoring the fact that no one met his gaze. Most rarely did. And not for the first time in the last days Michaela's image blossomed in his mind, her unflinching stare despite her fear.

His precise steps broke, and he slowed, frowning. And hating that he was moved by one so innocent.

"Good God, man. Try not to look so hostile. My servants are terrified enough of you."

His head jerked up. Christian Chandler, sixteenth earl of something, Rein could not recall exactly what at the moment, stood in the doorway of his study, his sandy hair mussed, his shirt open as well as his waistcoat. Rein's gaze narrowed at the rare state of dishevel. A woman, he decided easily, noting the telltale mark on his throat.

Uncomfortable under his scrutiny, Christian plucked at his shirt to cover the staining kiss, cupping a snifter of brown liquid, jiggling it into a swirl as his gaze lingered over Rein's high color and wind blown hair. "Must you always dress so dark?" he said, waving at his clothes. Though well tailored and rich in fabric, the midnight-dark garments made the man appear the devil incarnate.

"Contraband?" Rein arched a brow, a strike of black against honey-dark skin as he nodded to the drink. French brandy was rare, especially when England was at war with the Colonists and France was their ally.

Christian smirked, glancing at the glass. The man reveals naught, he thought, and always turns the tables. "Quite the thing, eh? Makes me feel as dastardly as you."

Rein's lips twisted wryly, loneliness in his tone. "You could never be that, Christian. Impeccable lineage and all that rubbish."

Christian made a face as he stepped back to allow Rein passage into his private study. "Do not credit me with that." He gestured to the sideboard, emploring Rein to help himself. "I try very hard to make a complete ruination of my ancestors' puritan bloodlines."

"Pity you do not enjoy the task well enough," Rein murmured as he moved to the sidebar, sloshing liquor into a glass. He brought it to his lips, pausing briefly, scenting it, forcing her memory aside before draining the glass. He'd not time nor the energy to spare on women, especially that one, he thought as the smooth fire of aged bourbon burned in his stomach, veining through his cold body to warm his chilled skin. He cocked a look over his shoulder.

"Shouldn't your valet be dressing you? Powdering your hair? Filling your snuff?"

Christian saluted the jibe with his glass, then moved to the settee, flopping onto it with all the decorum of a dockside shoreman and eyeing his friend's broad back. "Certain you are prepared for this gala?"

Rein's straight shoulders lifted and fell in a careless gesture. " 'Twill be as every other occasion." He faced him fully. "My presence will cause a complete stir, you will have a delightful time shielding the respectable English roses from my pagan soul and come out smelling"—his lips quirked—"far better than you do now."

"Then why attend and subject yourself to such impudence?"

The means to the end, Rein thought, his expression hardening. *And I must find it.* "You ask that far too often, Christian."

Chandler ignored the warning in his tone. "And you never respond. Terribly irritating, you know."

Rein's lips curled a bit. His Grace looked much the sulking child. "Good of you to tolerate me," he said, as he moved to the fire, inching his booted toes close to the warmth. Bloody damned cold in this country, he thought, missing the balmy heat of Sanctuary.

"Do not lop me with this fickle government, sir," he said, a little offended. "What with the Guardian making a muck of it, I take my pleasures and leave the world alone." He sipped his drink. "And I endure the peerage. You are my friend."

Rein twisted, meeting his gaze with an amusement that was both real and distant. "This wretched soul thanks you for your kindness, sahib." Rein tipped at the waist and salaamed with a long, elegant hand.

Christian blinked, taken aback by the easy gesture, almost forgetting Rein's strange background.

"You enjoy taunting me."

Rein stared at his glass. "Perish the thought."

Aye, Christian mulled. *He toys with us all and does not give a fig's weight of opinion.* Christian envied Rein's tolerance for gossip and innuendo. Whilst all of English society struggled to keep their reputations pristine, Rein went about in his own formidable manner, the veiled barbs sliding off his broad back like water against the hull of his damned ships. He knows what they want and holds it at bay, he thought. The White Empress Company and its invincible fleet. And tea. The Crown wanted him under its rule, for his ships carried crates of damned stuff everywhere England had not yet reached. He was beyond their touch, their power, and English society subjected themselves to his presence quite willingly, for with the war in the Colonies, Rein Montegomery could break the British Empire and its sanctions.

If he chose.

The Crown was bloody fortunate the man did not give a rat's arse if the Brits and Americans blew each other to pieces.

And Lord Stanhope, Christian Chandler, could not wait to see the hierarchy of the British Navy and Parliament bow and scrape to a man they considered a pariah. 'Twas a most enjoyable evening ahead, he thought, pushing off the settee.

Rein spared him a quizzical glance.

"Take liberties with my home as if 'twere yours, Rein." He sent him a droll smile. "Do leave the servant girls alone, though." The corner of Montegomery's mouth quirked. Not a smile. Never a smile, more like a panther entertaining himself with his prey.

The look drove a hard chill over Christian's skin and he wondered if anyone knew exactly who Rein Montegomery was. There were far too many rumors about the man to discern which was fable or nay, and Rein would not gainsay a single one, blast him. And Christian considered himself a close friend.

Rein felt the sympathy in his stare and smothered his vexation with it. "Get yourself properly attired, your lordship—" The title bit on the edge of insulting. "We are already late."

Christian did not spare the water clock a glance. "They know you are coming."

The man was fairly sanding his hands together, Rein thought, and would not doubt if his friend had planted the seed of speculation simply for excitement's sake. "I am delighted to be such an amusement for you," he said, not unkindly.

Christian grinned. "Adds a bit of fun to these rather dull obligations." He left Rein alone with his liquor.

Fun, Rein groused, then drained the remnants of his drink and set it aside. He expected nothing this evening but sumptuous dining, soothing music, and courtesy thinly veiled in icy contempt and vulgar curiosity. Yet he'd suffer more nights like this to uncover the truth.

Bracing his forearm on the mantel, he stared at the crackling blaze. A glowing red ember popped and he toed it back before it seared the expensive carpet. It took only one visit to England to remind him of his incompatibility with this society and he longed for the roll of his ship beneath his feet, the warm breezes and carefree life of his island home.

Turning away from the heat, Rein dropped into a chair and stretched out his long legs, pausing to efficiently unfasten his black velvet waistcoat. His hand passed briefly over the medallion suspended from a chain and hidden beneath his shirt.

It was cold against his skin, heavy.

And Rein felt the weight of his deeds.

The hardness of self-disgust coiled in him and he sat upright, bracing his elbows on his knees and raking his hands through his hair. He rubbed the back of his neck. This evening was more than an officiously opulent ball for a decorated British commander. It was the next step to destroying the faith of the two people who loved him, cared for him when he was lonely and alone. Ransom and Aurora breathed life into his existence twenty years ago.

He owed them his loyalty.

And this evening, he would butcher it like a gentle lamb in a pagan sacrifice.

They will never forgive me for this.

And Rein did not know if he could ever absolve himself for betraying the only family he ever knew.

But he had to.

His sanity demanded it.

The din of chatter, tinkling crystal and china rose around her as she mingled from one pocket of guests to another. Michaela directed the servants, saw to the replenishing of the buffet and kept herself occupied as her uncle's hostess and out of the reach of the officers begging for a dance.

"We're running low on wine, ma'am," a servant whispered from her side.

"Send James to the cellar to bring up another two dozen bottles," she instructed, then leaned closer. "If worse comes, there is a comfortable stock in the Brigadier's study."

Horror colored the servant's features, yet Michaela simply smiled, a little devilishly, and urged him off. Her uncle would approve if the sacrifice saved him from embarrassment, and he'd never admit his comrades were wastrels out to embrace as much of his food and drink as they could in the few hours, she thought, glancing in his direction. He and Major Winters had their wigged heads together in a discussion she assumed was about her, if the major's covert glances were any indication. Her gaze narrowed on the man, and she gave him her best get-thee-to-hell look she could muster without notice, yet he returned it with an amiable smile. *It will take cannon fire to penetrate that dense skull,* she decided, turning away and wishing she hated someone enough to redirect his affections toward, yet could not wish such a sapless man on another woman. The consequences would be too damaging to repair.

Someone touched her arm and she flinched, whipping around.

"Duncan!" she gasped, her glare immediately softening as she stared up at the familiar face of her father's former adjutant.

Duncan McBain continued to scowl, his gaze searching hers. "Are you well, lassie?" Was that a bruise on her jaw?

"Of course." Clearly he was not satisfied with the response, yet too much of a gentleman to press her. " 'Tis good to see you. Enjoy yourself, Captain." She started to move away, then stilled.

Duncan watched her smile vanish, her features go slack. "Michaela?" When she did not respond, he followed the direction of her gaze.

"Your uncle invites an interesting sort, eh?"

Michaela wasn't listening, the blood leaving her face and draining to her feet.

Her heart slipped an entire beat, then quickened with fear.

Raven dark as twilight, he stood out from all others, his piercing gaze scanning the crowd with bored insolence. For the space of a needed breath, Michaela thought she would escape without notice as his gaze passed over her.

Until it jerked back, pale blue eyes locking her in a cageless prison.

She needed help escaping and boldly whispered, "Dance with me, Duncan." She jerked on his arm. "Now. I beg you."

Six

Goddess of light, how could he have ever taken her for a servant?

And who was that man, he wondered anxiously, his gaze dropping to her hand on the gold braided sleeve of a British officer. Did he leave the barely concealed mark on her jaw? *I will beat him for it,* he thought fleetingly, his fingers tightening into fists as her escort swept her into the steps of the dance. He watched, smothering his pleasure at seeing her again, trying to push it into a safe, forbidden place in his mind as she moved in a circle to face him. Her head tipped back a fraction, her lashes sweeping upward.

And Rein experienced the unquestionable connection crackle across the grand room.

And she felt it, her eyes flaring, her steps stammering.

By God, she's damned lovely, an unfamiliar thrill stirring deeply through his blood. Clad in midnight blue, she contrasted like a glittering sapphire in a sea of colorless gems, her lustrous deep auburn hair striking a slash of defiance amongst the powdered heads of the other woman. His gaze raked her features again and again, as if she'd turn to mist before his eyes and he'd forget the dark brows arching over her feline eyes, or the lush mouth shaped to torture a man's dreams. Yet he knew another Michaela, a woman of subdued strength, the depth of it he'd but glimpsed. It emanated like a fresh fire neatly banked. Stroking him, heating him like dry tinder about to ignite.

She almost dared him to come to her, and if experience hadn't taught him that a simple dance would destroy her reputation, he'd have the woman in his arms now. His focus narrowed to her, reaching for her until he could feel her breath move in her lungs, the heat of her skin simmering with her perfume. Her citrusy scent washed over him in hot waves and he did not question the distance separating them and simply—absorbed.

Her eyes flared, as if sensing the unworldly energy ruling between them, and he recognized her fear, her sudden unnamable discomfort an instant before she broke eye contact, severing the line. Rein looked away, his chest intolerably tight, his breathing a bit labored. Clenching his fists and banishing the swelling sensations into a calm sea, he cursed his Wiccan mother for teaching him to cultivate his senses too well, then cursed the ugly past that put the soft beauty so far from his reach.

She was a lady, forbidden, and though he'd suspected thus from the moment he'd met her, he could no longer hold even the thread of a dream. The crush of unjustness left him barren, vanquished. It was clear he needed more than chains of his past to keep his riotous thoughts harnessed and away from her, and after a few seconds, he turned toward Brigadier Denton, all too aware of Christian's probing gaze on him. The suspicion alone was warning enough.

"Brigadier."

His spine stiff, Sir Atwell rocked back on his heels, his hands clasped behind his back and making his barrel chest appear even larger. "Glad you could join us, Montegomery." His heavy jowls jiggled, though his lips scarcely moved.

Rein's brows shot up. "In need of fodder for gossip, Denton?"

Denton reddened and Christian coughed, covering a snort of laughter.

"There would be little of it, if you were loyal to the Crown."

"I am loyal to me, my employees, and my family. Not necessarily in that order." His chiseled lips twisted. "Have I done something to offend the Crown?" Chandler was nearly busting a seam, Rein thought.

"You have gunned ships and sailors to man them. Every able bodied Englishman has offered his service to the war."

"Now there is your failing," Rein said, selecting a goblet of wine from a servant's tray and dispatching half of it in one swallow. "I am neither a British subject, nor do I care about your war. Oppress whoever you desire." Briefly Rein eyed the goblet as if judging the clarity of the vintage. "My ships carry tea, coffee, a bit of sugar and profit, not troops." He held Denton's gaze trapped in his own over the rim of the glass. "Nor will they ever." He finished off the wine.

"One could expect such from a Montegomery," came from a distance.

Rein twisted slightly, his expression merely quizzical as a slender officer approached. His eyes thinned. "Have we met?"

"My aide-de-camp, Montegomery, Major Winters," Denton introduced. "My most trusted officer."

Rein bowed slightly.

Winters did not bother to acknowledge it. "The titled care only to feed their pockets."

Beside him, Christian stiffened. "You dare much, Major."

Winters spared him a dry glance. "Do I? When will you purchase a commission and serve, Your Grace?"

"When there is an heir to name the next earl," Christian snapped out.

Rein inched forward. "You obviously are misinformed, Major

Winters," he said politely, yet none mistook the razor's edge in his tone. "I am neither the blood heir, nor the only son. Ransom Montegomery has several children."

Winters snorted rudely. "Then the bastard lord has followed in the shoes of his father, Granville."

The empty crystal flute shattered in Rein's grip, spraying the area with glittering fragments.

The men surrounding him inhaled collectively, stepping back, gawking.

Yet Rein's cool gaze remained fixed on Winters as he shook the pieces to the floor, his hand unbloodied. He'd tolerate slander on himself, but not on Ran and Aurora. Never. Yet he would not defend them here, in public. That Winters dared such told him the man thought himself well protected. 'Twill be a reckoning, soon, he thought and nothing in this life will protect him.

"Ransom Montegomery is wed to a Slavic empress, is that not so, Rein?" Christian piped into the straining silence. Damn Winters for treading on sacred ground.

"Aye," he said, his pale eyes burning into the major's.

"I heard she was a witch," Winters said. "Practices the black arts."

Rein arched a brow, his smile more cunning than amused. "Do not believe every word repeated, Major." Casually, he dusted his fingertips, then sucked the tip of one to remove a crystal sliver. " 'Tis rumored that I sacrifice vestal virgins on the eve of a full moon, dine on the hearts of my adversaries," his tone shaved the edge of steel and he played this hand for all its worth, "and would cut the throat of those who speak ill of my family." He took a step back. "I assure you the former is not true." With that, Rein salaamed a bow and strode away.

Winters stared after him and Christian noticed the man's Adam's apple working furiously. "Test those waters again, Major and you will find yourself without a commission."

Winters drew himself up, his gold medals and ribbons flickering in the candlelight. "He dares much, even showing his face here. The man lacks good breeding—"

"I invited him personally, Major." Denton eyed him into silence.

"And we need him to be our ally or remain neutral," Christian said before the major could comment. "The man could sail cargo to the Colonies through a British blockade or around the four continents if he chooses and 'tis naught we could do to stop him." The officer's eyes widened. "Aye, Major, you'd best, for the Crown's sake, be amiable to Rein Montegomery. We need him." Christian turned to Sir Atwell Denton. "Harness your minions, Brigadier," he said in a tone he'd heard his father use, and Denton's small eyes grew sharp with indignation.

Denton looked down his nose at the earl. "He is a bastard's bastard. A disloyal blackheart who cares for naught but idle pleasure and lining his pockets."

"And what is this?" Chandler inclined his head toward the swarming guests. "Would you have everyone in England melting teaspoons for bullets and cutting drapes for uniforms? Or would you prefer we all line up and be shot for a war draining far too much from England's coffers."

"You tread the line of sedition, Your Grace."

Chandler admired the man for keeping just the right amount of respect in his tone. "I speak what you do not wish to hear, yet is bandied about right under your nose. One man defending his home and the right to rule it is far stronger than a thousand defending a king's declaration."

Denton reddened, his brown eyes flaring with outrage. "The Colonists will submit!"

Chandler shrugged carelessly. "I wish to see this country survive, sir. And how will the colonist submit with Howe commanding? And how many British soldiers will perish to keep that wilderness unfit for English subjects?"

"None, if it wasn't for the Colonists' Guardian," Denton said, nodding so that Chandler followed him to a more secluded spot where they wouldn't be over heard. "Damned infiltrator is too bloody accurate, fouled an attack that took weeks to plan!" When Winters was wont to follow, Denton shooed him away like a punished child and kept talking. "I was fairly marooned in that godforsaken country, half frozen whilst that damned Virginia tobacco planter gathered nine thousand troops . . ."

Of all the brass. He'd arrived with the earl and Michaela realized he'd known all along that they wouldn't be ousted from his lordship's land, the scoundrel. And how did a sea captain come to know Lord Stanhope, she wondered, trouncing on Duncan's foot again.

"Michaela," Duncan said. "You've never ruined the shine on my boots in a dance afore." She met his gray gaze and shrugged, sheepish. He grinned. "Tell me what has you so flustered?"

"Fatigue, I suppose."

He eyed her from the side, his arm out, her fingers clasped in his. "You do not make a convincing liar. You never did."

If he only knew, she thought. "Uncle keeps staring."

"Likely thinking of another duty to give you."

At his bitter tone, she shifted her gaze and saw anger in his eyes as they lingered on her jaw. "Swear to me you will not interfere on my behalf."

"If I had enough rank on my shoulder I would," he groused.

"And if you had any more starch in your step," came from close behind, "you'd snap in half."

Duncan turned, his gaze narrowing on the young woman.

"Cassandra!" Michaela said, delighted to have an ally in the sea of men.

"Hullo, Michaela," she responded, giving her a warm hug and an invitation to lunch in the following week, then smiled impishly at McBain.

"Where are your brothers?" he demanded. "Shouldn't you be on a tether or a leash?"

"Duncan!" Michaela gasped.

Cassandra waved her off. "Captain McStiff thinks I should be locked in a tower. Isn't that right?"

"Aye, often. With no chance of a pardon."

She only smiled. "My brothers are watching." She waved to the three men standing like sentinels before a row of giant potted plants. "You aren't a threat. They know you are too sanctimonious to be a bother."

Michaela snickered and Duncan's complexion darkened. *"You* are a bother," he said, as they passed each other in the dance.

"Duncan!" Michaela scolded, aware of Rein edging with her around the room. "Please. Be civil."

Briefly, they traded partners in the dance, and Duncan found himself staring down into Cassandra's china blue eyes filled with excitement and challenge. "To her? The girl doesn't ken the word."

Cassandra tipped her head, thoughtful, black curls brushing her bare shoulders. "You are terribly handsome when you are angry, Duncan."

"Behave yourself, child."

"Now you can see I am no child," she said in a sultry voice that momentarily robbed him of thought as they backed away and came together. "And what pleasure is there in behaving? You should try it." Her look was direct, gripping him where it shouldn't. "Pleasure, I mean. Risks. Chances."

"By God," Duncan growled. "You need to be tamed."

She scoffed, eyeing him from head to boots. "You would not *ken* where to start."

"I would have to want to, which I do not." He turned her toward her partner, giving her an unnecessarily hard push. "Have a care, Lieutenant. This one is too brash for polite society."

Cassandra's laugh grated as he turned back to Michaela, ignoring her smirking smile and continuing with the dance.

"Randi is lovely, isn't she?"

"Randi?" he scoffed, disgusted with the nickname. "That girl is a hoyden."

Michaela smiled privately, thinking he looked like an angry little boy just then, and over his shoulder, her gaze fell on Rein. "That man who arrived with His Grace, the dark one, who is he?"

Duncan glanced over his right shoulder, the motion scraping in the tight collared uniform. "Montegomery?"

Montegomery.

Wonderful. She did not dare ask if he was certain and bring attention to her interest. She already knew. Everyone knew the family, the man, by name, by reputation, yet rarely by sight. That he was here spoke of more than an evening out. It spoke of motive, and Michaela feared she was it.

Duncan looked at her. "In shipping, I believe. Tea and coffee, if I'm not mistaken." He refrained from adding to the unfounded rumors sailing about the man.

A short little laugh escaped her, bordering on hysterical, and she was thankful when the music ended. Nay, Duncan, she wanted to say. You are not mistaken. But his assets were not simply in shipping tea and coffees and fruits, but in ships. Heavily gunned, rather swift ships. Over a dozen, if memory served. But that was not what disturbed her. Nay, that she'd shot a man of such notorious means did.

"Michaela." Duncan frowned. "Mayhap you should rest. You look a wee bit pale."

Mayhap I should get to a nunnery—in Spain, she thought honestly as Duncan led her from the dance floor. He would point her out and claim her his assailant, a thief, and her life would be over. Her uncle would toss her to the streets, and all she'd worked for in the last years would be for nothing. He had the contacts to do it. She'd heard her uncle and his cronies curse him, his influence outside their touch. He was allied with the king of Spain and Portugal, the emir, the shah, and half the rulers of the Ottoman Empire. He had contacts and connections people only whispered about. Michaela feared that if he chose, she would be strung from a rope in the west garden by nightfall.

She prayed her inner instincts about him were true, and the fabrications of her tired mind were unfounded.

Oh, please, Rein, don't speak of it, not here, she thought, dropping numbly into the seat. She stared at her hands. Mayhap he won't. He appeared to be well healed, she thought guiltily, and he hasn't spoken up yet.

"Michaela?"

She lifted her gaze to find Duncan holding out a cup of punch, several soldiers, a few on bended knee around her, one offering a china plate of food as if she were some deity. Cracking good. *Just bring more attention to myself,* she thought.

"Cease this nonsense." She refused the punch and tried to stand. "I am fine."

Gently, he pushed her back down. "You do not look fine."

She cocked her head and delivered her pardon-me-but-that-borders-on-an-insult-look. "Stop coddling me, Captain."

He smiled, handing her the cup of punch anyway. "Then sit and entertain them."

She looked at the young dragoon soldiers, feeling so much older than they, then, over the tops of their heads, caught her uncle's gaze. It narrowed and forced her to remain in the chair. She accepted the plate of food. Duncan moved behind her chair and she turned her attention to the soldiers whose greater intent was usually a decent meal that did not come at a cost to their purse and wondered with all the lovely young girls in attendance, why they bothered wasting time flirting with her.

Unwillingly, her gaze lifted to where Rein stood on the opposite side of the ballroom, his figure shrouded in shadows. Even from her position, she heard the flutter of whispers, words like "pagan" and "uncivilized" catching on the fragrant air, and noticed that he took an almost sadistic amusement in spearing a plump woman with a look and watching her nearly swoon into the nearest chair or pair of masculine arms.

He plays them all like fools, she thought, and knew few women were bold enough to actually approach him without a protector. Yet Katherine Hawley, Lady Buckland, was bolder than most, she thought, watching her ladyship's prowling advance in the company of three men, none of whom Michaela knew. *Close your mouth Katherine dear,* she thought acidly. *Lest you drool on that expensive gown.*

Rein watched Michaela, unaccountable emotions bucking through his blood. He wanted to ask questions, find out who she was, why she was here, then, in the next breath, told himself the answers didn't matter. She was forbidden. But seeing her in the midst of those young stags made his chest clench, his teeth hurt, and it took every effort to tear his gaze away.

"Madame," he said, tipping at the waist. Lady Buckland acknowledged him with a nod. "You look radiant this evening." Aye, he thought, never having seen such artfully placed paints to cover her well-used appearance. She moved closer, her dark eyes sliding over him from boots to hair with undisguised desire. Any other time he'd welcome the invitation, yet tonight, the look served to no end but mild repugnance.

"As do you, Mr. Montegomery."

A single black brow arched. "Mister? So formal, m'lady."

"You are bold, sir." She tapped his arm with her closed fan.

"In your company, I could be no less." He accepted a glass of wine from a servant. "Carry you these saplings for armor, Katherine?" His head inclined ever so slightly to the men flanking her. "Or have they what you desire?"

She snubbed the air, yellow curls bouncing on her shoulders. "As if you could claim to know."

"Ahh, but I do, Lady Buckland," he said, the glass poised at his lips. "A full purse is more precious than your body." He sipped.

She gasped, her skin flushing. "You dare insult me!" she hissed, all coyness vanishing, her gaze darting about for eavesdroppers.

He shrugged. "Speak plain to me and I to you, lady. I have never done otherwise."

Lady Katherine stared up at his handsome profile, remembering his parting words, to never expect more than one night with him, no more than what he offered in a few hours. His cool dismissal irritated her, and the very prospect of feeling his touch again made her body flush with heat. Rein Montegomery was unmatched, mysteriously aloof and tender, yet restrained like a raging beast held in tight bridle. She wanted the leading straps in her hands.

"Your eyes betray you, woman," came for her ears alone, harsh and brittle. "Have a caution."

She blinked, then immediately cast a glance about before meeting his odd gaze. "You are cruel to discard me, Rein," she pouted.

"I never *had* you, Katherine." His murmured words circumvented the boundaries of politeness, sparing the vulgarities. "We both know that."

The woman was without pride, and selfish, sex with her leaving an acrid stain in his memory. His gaze dismissed, even when she was wont to introduce him to her companions. Rein did not fool himself to believe she or any one of the guests desired a friendship. Nor did he want it. He chose his friends carefully, and over the tops of their heads, he scanned the crowds for his slayer.

"Looking for someone in particular, Rein," Christian asked as he approached.

Katherine's eyes immediately sharpened on him, her neck twisting as she attempted to glimpse whomever he was routing out.

Only Rein's eyes shifted to his friend. "Nay." Goddess of thunder, could he do nothing without scrutiny?

"Well, I am. Introduce me," he nudged him, his eyes for Lady Katherine. Rein glanced between the pair, then decided if Christian was foolish enough to venture into a relationship with her, then he deserved the repercussions. He made introductions, then stepped back from the group, easily spotting Michaela's dark hair in the crowds. The sight of her still surrounded by red-coated men drove the urge to cross the room and rip the slobbering sots from her side down to his boot heels.

Damn me, he thought, taking a gulp of his drink. Annoyance replaced jealousy, and Rein wondered how she managed to gain such a fierce reaction from him when women like Katherine could garner no more than a hard cock and mild amusement for a few hours' time. Yet just the same, he surveyed her, her demeanor finally penetrating his possessive fog.

She had a glazed look in her eyes, like staring too long at single object until you no longer saw it. Her smile was brittle, and though any woman would count her fortune over so much attention, Rein sensed complete boredom. His gaze narrowed, senses seeking beneath the delicate veneer. *She is uncomfortable,* he realized, his gaze taking in her demure pose and poorly fitted gown. A strand of hair escaped her coif, tumbling down to dangle on the swell of her breast, and he ached to twine it in his fingers again, feel its silkiness against his skin. Her gaze flashed up suddenly, startled—clashing with his. Her skin pinkened becomingly, yet her smooth brow furrowed softly as she fingered the curl, staring.

Rein's muscles tightened. *Do not fear me,* he whispered in his mind.

Her eyes flared in response, her gaze darting about as if someone had spoken aloud, then swung back to him. She tipped her head, studying him more closely.

And Rein felt unreasonably vulnerable just then.

One of her admirers turned, following the path of her attention, and mindful of her reputation, he immediately looked elsewhere, calling himself a fool. He was a half-breed, a motherless bastard, presentable enough for women like Katherine and only then in the darkness of her bedchamber. He'd no right to entertain a single thought of Michaela.

Defeat spoiled through him and he released it with a long breath moments before two wealthy merchants whom Rein dealt with in seasonal regularity brought him into their conversation. He was thankful for the distraction.

"You wish an admiralty court deciding the fate of merchants?" he said into the discussion. "What know they of shipping and lading bills, accounts?"

"You sound as if you have English interests, Mr. Monte-gomery?"

Rein looked at Burgess, a tall, slender man he judged to be nearly three score at least.

"Why ask, when you know I do not?"

"Why comment when you mean naught by it?"

Amusement lit his dark features. "Because, sir, I enjoy seeing you lose several pounds sterling and find it in my pockets." Burgess looked ready to shriek, Rein thought, becoming a most interesting shade of purple. "Do not say you would act otherwise. For if England could rule the world, she would."

"We do try, sir." That brought a round of chuckles, and Rein was introduced to Lord Germain, Viscount Sackville, the Secretary of the State of War.

Rein's body went instantly rigid, his gaze searching the man's features. As the conversation rolled to the state of war, Rein noted the man's scorn and insurmountable arrogance. He was the epitome of English aristocracy, spouting his high moral values, his choices, as if he possessed the king's unrestrained hand to rule.

Yet at this moment, he ruled Rein's every sense.

For the viscount was one of the men he suspected to be his natural father.

Seven

Rein's gut twisted in a hard knot as he scrutinized Germain's features, seeking a hint of similarity. He could find none, yet knew years of breeding gambled on the outcome of appearance. And the longer the conversation drew on, the more Rein prayed he'd none of this man's blood running in his veins, the viscount's extreme insolence, an arrogance borne of centuries believing his birth gave him power over those less fortunate, howling from him without a sound.

Rein was still undecided as to what he would do when he uncovered the truth of his past, or if Germain was part of it, yet the man who'd taken his mother's body, promised her faith and marriage, then discarded her like a rag, was in this room tonight.

Unnoticeable to watchful eyes, Rein took a slow, calming breath, casting his emotions into a cavern fashioned when he was child in the streets. A place they could not touch him until he chose to relive and disband them. He carefully culled the conversation toward past exploits, and Germain, drinking steadily, was most willing to offer dates and places, even names of conquered hearts.

And when male conceit turned to less stellar exploits with the maharajah's household, Rein's jaw clenched.

His mother was a handmaiden to one of the princesses, one of over a dozen siblings.

Which one and at what particular time was the mystery Rein had yet to unfold.

And because of Sergeant Major Townsend's help, the constant influx of British ships and brigades back then was finally narrowed.

"There was a sweet thing, of no more than six and ten, doe-eyed with dark, lustrous hair and teaberry skin," Germain was saying, and Rein steeled himself against the need to thrash the man right then. "She was made a gift to my commander, but he'd been wounded on a safari and could not take the girl. So . . ." He let the words hang.

Impatience rode down Rein's spine. "Surely not a daughter of the maharajah? The repercussions would be insurmountable."

Germain furnished Rein with a superior glance. "Repercussion upon whom, Mr. Montegomery? Certainly not England. And the gell was a maid." He flicked a thin hand as if waving away an insect. "Of no consequence."

Bitterness filled Rein's mouth. "Could you speak so to her father?"

Germain stiffened, a tinge of conscience showing. "Her father gave her to my commander."

Rein's shoulders dropped a fraction and he listened, the other men picking up the conversation and doing the work for him, prying secrets whilst the viscount was besotted. A name, Rein thought. He needed a name. Then it came. Varuna.

The woman who gave Rein life was Sakari.

The rush of relief drained through him like hot wax. He felt boneless and lost as he stared at his glass, the air gone dank with smoke and sweat and the thick aroma of food. His throat tightened, the trap of memories flooding through his mind. Suddenly, he was a lonely, hungry child, staring at the women serving food in the mines and wondering, *Could she be my mother?*

Quickly, he excused himself, moving toward the doors open to the night breeze. A hundred pairs of eyes followed his departure into the gardens, yet he didn't notice, didn't care. As he neared the doorway, unwillingly his steps slowed, his head turning as he scanned the crowd.

His gaze sought her, hungering for a simple glimpse, and when he found her, gazes clashed and locked. A heavy sensation shot down his body, so solid and warm he thought his knees would fracture. A mix of emotions played across her features: wonder and curiosity and a touch of resentment.

She swallowed visibly, and before anyone noticed the exchange and put a name to the familiarity, he headed out the doors. Once outside, he sagged against the stone wall, taking long, deep breaths of cool air. *God of thunder, to what end is this torment?* he agonized. What did he hope to accomplish?

A release, he thought.

Aurora would advise this was not good for his earthly spirit.

Karma to karma, he thought. *What I do not solve in this life, I will solve in the next.*

Against his stomach lay the careless gift his father had tossed his mother, a simple memento of the loss she'd suffered for one night with him. Inside, Rein hurt for the woman he never knew, and in the depths of his soul he believed Aurora carried her spirit, for no boy could have felt more loved than in the comfort of Aurora's care and Ransom's guidance.

And you dishonor their love each time you hunt.

Regret sliced through him and he tipped his head back, staring at the pinprick of stars. He let his soul open, focusing his thoughts to sweeter days, to secret treats brought to him before bedtime, for tales of valiant Pict warriors to believe in, to laying on the earth and feeling it spin, his raw boned hand clutched in the grip of his rightful mother, Aurora.

His throat worked, outrage seeping from his limbs with the pleasant memories, his world gone misty and cool with the images of the sea, its unfailing heartbeat. He remained so, his back braced against the cold stone wall, a drape of vines shielding him from view. He glanced to the side, catching a look into the ballroom, the hover of smoke in the air, the glow of candlelight flickering against crystal prisms of the chandeliers. The world seemed so untouchable to him then, as if he lay too far outside the realm. His gaze lingered briefly on Christian as Katherine discreetly touched and petted him, drawing the snare of her trap. Poor fool, he thought, then, against his own volition, he looked for Michaela. He frowned as the Brigadier gestured heatedly to her.

Whyever was she carrying a tray? And catering to the old man? Rein rolled around the edge of the wall, remaining hidden as he watched her. The fit of that gown was horrendous, he thought sympathetically as she moved across the room, the unstable glasses on the silver tray teetering precariously.

Michaela's untailored hem threatened her every step, and regardless of her uncle's impatience—one would think he was in a desert dying of thirst the way he was motioning her to hurry—she could not move any faster. She lurched back to allow a guest to pass and lost her slipper for the third time this evening. Uncle Atwell scowled darkly as she jammed on the shoe and clomped inelegantly toward them. The hem caught in the loose heel and she stumbled. The tiny, thick glasses sailed from the tray and the sound of shattering glass burst through the air as she fought for balance.

Duncan McBain darted forward, catching her elbow to keep her from falling on her face. "Are you well?" he rushed to say.

"Aye, Duncan, my thanks." She blew a curl from her mouth, offering a weak smile, then looked at her uncle. "Oh, dear," she said, as she realized the entire tray of port had landed on Major Winters. Claret-red liquor dripped from his angular nose, and with his angry gaze pinning her, he snapped a cloth, blotting it meticulously.

Her uncle stormed toward her, and Michaela covered the impulse to flinch.

"You idiot," he hissed, and Duncan straightened protectively at her side. Denton did not acknowledge him, his intent on his niece. "Can you not do a bloody thing right, child?" His breath reeked of liquor, his features twisted with subdued fury.

"I apologize, Uncle, but the gown is too long, and if you had allowed—"

"Silence." By God, she was not going to blame him for this! "You're a disgrace." The conversation immediately around them suddenly hushed and he lowered his voice. "Your incompetence is humiliating. That such a blundering, inadequate female carries my blood, is a . . . dishonor!" People gasped, several stepping back and whispering amongst themselves. "Look at the major." He lashed a beefy hand to his aide-de-camp. "His uniform is ruined."

Only a pistol shot would ruin it, she thought maliciously, but did not think her uncle wanted to hear her opinion just now.

Uncle Atwell stepped closer, glass crunching beneath his shoes, his small eyes threatening retribution. "You did this a'purpose."

Her eyes widened, her gaze ripping between the two men. "Nay—!" *Please do not hit me—not here.*

"Do *not* question me," Denton growled nastily, his fingers working into a fist, crushing the urge to beat some sense into the gell. "Get someone to clean this mess." He would deal with her later, and his look said as much. "And repair yourself from my sight!"

Michaela stared at him, biting her lower lip to keep from lashing out at him and didn't dare look at another soul and see their pity. She shoved the tray at him, forcing him to take it, then gathered her skirts by the fistfuls.

"If you will excuse me then," she murmured softly, and with all the dignity of a queen, headed to the garden doors.

She stepped into the moonlight, the glow streaming over her like silver threads. Compassion swam through him and Rein ached to go to her, comfort her, a sensation so foreign it left him weak with anger. Denton's behavior was abominable, and though Rein knew she was not a servant, he wondered how he justified treating her so hideously. A ward? For he knew the Brigadier had never married.

His gaze followed her as she moved deeper into the garden and he frowned, searching her face. No tears, no sobbing over her humiliation. She'd likely spent a lifetime suffering such, he thought, and was about to make himself known when she cast a look behind herself, into the ballroom.

What is the lass up to? he wondered, melting into the shadows to watch and listen.

Michaela stretched her neck to be certain her uncle was still inside. The reverie, she noticed, was slow to return. Good. It would give them something to talk about, she thought, and knew she'd not be missed until her uncle needed something.

Argyle approached, and she moved to him, smiling sheepishly. "I've broken some glasses."

"I heard."

"Know you anyone who did not?" She peered, her tone cheeky. "Hurry, for we must certainly tell them, lest they hear the gossip secondhand."

Her humor fell on deaf ears as his brows drew down. He held out her shawl and obediently she turned and let him drape it over her bare shoulders. " 'Tis cruel, the way he speaks to you, lassie," he said softly into her ear. "And in public."

Long ago, she learned she held no special place in her uncle's heart and ceased trying to make one. "He shames himself when he does, Argyle." She smiled. "And is too pompous to realize it."

Grunting a laugh, he offered his arm and she threaded hers around it, smelling his familiar woodsy scent of the outdoors as she rested her head on his broad shoulder.

"He is right, though." She sighed, dispirited. "I am a clumsy, inelegant woman." Even as she said it, she hated the self-pitying words.

"The gown is too long, missy."

"Yet another woman would have managed."

"Any other female would not have a too big gown."

"Mayhap I should simply eat my way into it?" She plucked at the bodice she did not come close to filling.

He chuckled shortly, then stepped away. "I'll be gettin' someone to muck off the major now, lass."

"Try a dunk in the horse trough."

"I say we leave 'im soakin' for a wee bit longer. Since he wears his port so well." He turned away. "Afore the braggart wears me bloody fist," he muttered under his breath, leaving her alone.

Michaela checked the time, her father's watch heavy in her skirt pocket. Glancing about, she strolled down the short steps to the pavilion, moving around the fountain to a strand of trees planted in perfect alignment. She paused to pluck an early bloom from a bush, holding it beneath her nose as she scanned the area to be certain she was alone. With a casual step, Michaela strolled, stopping before a granite statue of Persephone. She checked her watch again, and a moment passed before a man in ragged clothes darted onto the stone path. She moved to him, their figures shaped within the shadows.

"This is not wise, girl."

Gripping his coarse wool coat sleeve, she pulled him deeper into the branches of shrubbery. " 'Tis the only occasion I had to leave without suspect." Michaela thought of how fortunate she was to have spilled the port.

"Is he watching you?" Concern laced his tone.

"Nay."

The man's eyes narrowed with doubt.

"If not for running his household, my uncle would rather I disappear altogether."

"Do not underestimate him, girl. He would offer you to the dogs if 'twould save his hide."

Pain flickered in her eyes just then as she stared at him. "He already has."

Rein moved silently within the trees and stone pillars of the garden, seeking and finding a spot beneath a cluster of trees. He concentrated, trying to hear their conversation, but the man vanished into the trees before he had the chance. Then she moved toward him, unsuspecting of his presence and Rein wondered what the woman was doing meeting men in the dark like this. A smile turned his lips. The old man he recognized as a servant when he'd first arrived, the other, well, he admitted he'd failed to gain a decent look at the fellow and did not care.

For over a fortnight he told himself what he felt was purely his undernourished imagination, that the tightness in his body whenever he thought of her was no more than unsatisfied lust. He'd lain witness to the same in many men, had seen the powerful sensation tear a man in two and leave him miserably discontented. But Rein had not reached this age by succumbing to his emotions. Or to the sensations that were purely physical. But they were ruling him now, he admitted, the unquenchable tension, the wickedly hot blast through his veins, and the sound of his heartbeat thrumming in his ears. It was almost too glorious to ignore.

All there was of her impressed upon him, the shape of her in the gown, the drape of curls on her shoulders. The fragrance of lemons filled his senses and he inhaled deeply, like a draught of fine fruit wine. She moved with aimless steps, plucking a flower here and there, tearing it to shreds.

Then she ducked under the cloak of leafy branches and slid to the bench a few feet away.

He clenched his fists and felt at once alone and obsessed. For reasons he could not understand, he was vulnerable to her, only her, and knew if he so much as touched her, he would be well and readily trapped. And Rein admitted that, poised on the stone bench, was a woman who could destroy him.

And she was oblivious to his hunger. Aye, a hunger, to be touched and looked upon with anything but that damnable distrust. An arm's length from her, his dark clothing shielded him from the light and interested eyes. He watched her peer around the edge of the trunk and knew she searched for the Brigadier, nearly positive she was a relation.

She relaxed back, folding her hands on her lap and breathing slowly.

Rein simply stared, the shadows painting her features in silver and gray, giving her an almost bluish cast. She was a vision of serenity, yet he could feel her heart beat as if he owned it. A thousand thoughts collided in his head. Was she betrothed? What was she doing on the road that day, or out last night in an extremely dangerous part of the city?

And did the taste of her mouth match its rosy hue?

He stood perfectly still, letting his senses find her, her perfume lure. And like a string attached between, he tugged it.

Michaela blinked, a strange sensation running over her skin. She straightened. "Who is there?" She felt it, like a warm breeze mixed in the cool night, a presence surrounding her. "Who's there?"

"Good evening, manslayer."

She gasped and shot to her feet. "Rein."

The sound of his name on her lips lingered sweetly on the air. He slipped around the curve of the tree, gazing down at her.

Michaela stared like an idiot, relishing being near him again, but then her girlish fantasy quickly waned to suspicion. She eyed him. "How long have you been there?" She prayed it was after her man had left.

"Long enough to know you are related to the Brigadier."

"His niece," she said sourly.

Her gun, he recalled. "So then your father was Richard."

"You knew him?"

"Nay, lass," he said with sympathy. Her energy wilted and she sat, slumping back against the tree. "My father mentioned him on occasion."

She nodded, her gaze sweeping his handsome features. Except for his face and the pristine white of his shirt, he appeared a spirit hovering in the dark, without substance, and, as in the ballroom, she felt at once frightened and intrigued, as if he could speak to her without benefit of words.

"You did not fear me afore, Michaela."

Lord, she loved the way he said her name, so musical. "And I do not now."

"Yet you tremble."

She reared back a bit, looking him over end enjoying the moment. "My, aren't we awash with ourselves this evening," she said regally. "I am cold, you dolt."

Immediately he shrugged out of his coat, bending close to drape it over her shoulders, holding the edges. He searched her gaze. "I see fear still." God of thunder, he did not want this woman to quake in his presence, too.

"Your reputation precedes you."

He looked sheepish. " 'Tis a bad one, eh?"

"Aye." She smiled. "Deplorable."

"I am not so notorious, little slayer."

Hah, she thought. "Not according to Lady Buckland. She bandies your name about like a tournament pennant."

He released his hold, straightening suddenly. "Katherine should mind her tongue." His tone was soft, yet bit into her like teeth. And Michaela bristled at his easy use of the woman's name. It spoke of an intimacy she did not want to explore.

"I am but a simple planter," he said in a tone unlike moments ago.

She slid him a high-browed glance. "You expect me to swallow such swill?"

His chuckle rasped seductively around her like a warm cloak. "Believe as you wish, Michaela. I already know you will."

"You know naught of me, Rein Montegomery."

"You skulk about in the dark wearing boys' garments, dicing bandits. With my knife, I suspect."

She stiffened on the bench, and he watched, entranced, as she reached between her breasts and pulled something from hiding.

Leaning out, he peered. "What else have you in there, lass?"

"Rein!" she hissed, a blush warming her cheeks as she covered her bosom. "Have you no shame?"

"Shame is when you regret an action."

Michaela smiled at his logic.

"And looking at you I could never regret."

"The swill rises," she muttered. "Hurry, get buckets."

He grinned hugely, his sultry gaze smoothing over her like the brush of velvet. An uncomfortable silence reigned between them, then quickly she thrust her arm up, her palm open, the razor-sharp blade lying innocently across.

Rein stared at the knife, trapped. Memory surfaced, like a crack of lightning, of a blood-soaked hand, a blade lying in lax fingers. Agony and loss shot through him, making him flinch. He blinked, realizing she stared intently. For a woman, any woman, to hand him a knife in the dark as if sacrificing herself to his will knew nothing of the ugliness still clinging to him like a worm-infested skin.

Rein bent and folded her fingers over the hilt.

"Keep it." That she felt it necessary to carry it now told him she needed more than a slender knife to protect herself, and the fact made him ache to champion her.

"You will not cast me as a thief?"

He frowned, taken aback. "Of course not."

Her shoulders sagged, the back of her hand smoothing shakily across her forehead. "Rein, ah, I must ask . . . though I'm without the right to even assume that you would—"

"I will not drag you by the hair to the magistrate for shooting me," he cut in. She nodded, staring at her lap, the blade. "Michaela. Look at me."

She did, and Rein was struck in the gut by the unguarded sheen in her eyes.

"If I wanted to see you pay for the wound, you would be in the gaol now."

Her eyes watered, her relief driving her back against the rough tree bark. "I suppose I knew that."

"Trust me?"

She scoffed, her gaze on the blade. "Hardly."

"I didn't rat on you for being loose in the city," he said in his defense. "Which is a matter we need to discuss."

She looked up. "Will you tell?"

"Seems I have the advantage here."

"And you will use it, men always do."

He scowled, digesting her bitterness. "Your secret is safe." He crossed his heart. A moment passed and then, "Who hit you, Michaela?"

She inhaled a quick breath, her hand flying to her jaw. "My uncle."

His gaze shifted to the glass door and the Brigadier within, surrounded by his peers, laughing uproariously as if he had not scorned his niece before the cream of London society. He wanted to pound the man into dust.

Mercy, the look of retribution in his eyes was enough to chill her skin, and she wiggled deeper into his coat, her cheek brushing the soft fabric. She inhaled his scent, wind and spice and a bit of the sea.

"Why?"

Only her gaze swung to his. "Does it matter?"

"Nay. Do you wish to leave this place?"

There was a long moment before she said, "Nay." She could not. That she was alone and penniless was the least of her concerns.

"Yet you subject yourself—"

She replaced the blade in her bodice, giving it a pat. "I do as I must."

"Why were you on the quay at midnight?"

She furnished him with the same belligerent smirk as the night before and he released an exasperated breath. Intractable female. Accepting her need for privacy and laying his concerns aside, he did what he knew would make her uncomfortable. He stared.

Michaela fidgeted, unaccustomed to any man's close regard. "So," she squeaked, then cleared her throat. "So. Are you enjoying the ball?" *Wonderful, Michaela, prove what a failure at polite conversation you are, too.*

"I am now." Her breath caught. "The honor of creating a spectacle usually befalls me."

She made an indelicate sound. "I shall endeavor not to act the buffoon again. Giving you the floor." She gestured to the stone at his feet.

"You did not deserve that, Michaela."

Elegantly clad shoulders moved restlessly and she refused to look at him. "Spare me your pity, Rein. Please." To have him see her ridiculed like that, however unintentional her motives, left her feeling cloddish and ugly.

A silence that was almost pungent hovered between them. Suddenly, he slid to the space beside her.

She cast a quick look about, too aware of the scandalous position should they be spotted. "Rein?"

"Aye."

"You seek to ruin what is left of my reputation?"

His expression changed, eyes glittering, and she regretted her choice of words.

"I promise not to devour you whole."

Her lips quirked a bit and she eyed the fine cut of his garments, his broad shoulders, and how fierce he appeared just now, hovering in the bands of the silver light. Like a dark dragon peering from his cave. "Only in small bits?"

"Say the word and I shall leave you."

"And what word is that?"

Cheeky lass. "Vanish." She did not speak it. Her lips pressed in a tight smile and Rein let his gaze wander her face, her wide, feline eyes. So expressive. "I knew you were a brave girl."

Those eyes narrowed, her tone caustic. "I am no girl, Rein."

His brows worked for a heartbeat. A wealth of meaning came in that statement. "Oh, nay," he said with silky look down her body. "You are a lovely manslayer, prettiest one I've clapped eyes on yet."

"Ahh! Ah!" she whispered in a stage shriek. "The swill, the sludge! Take cover." He grinned. She did not. "Come now." She rolled her eyes, distrust in the silly motion. "I have seen you in the company of beautiful women this night, which assures me you are only thick-witted, but not blind."

His gaze shifted over her, creating a tingling path on her skin. When he spoke, his voice was rough. "My sight is fine, Michaela Denton."

Michaela gazed into his pale eyes, sinking, trapped for an instant, for an eternity. His sincerity sank home, and a blush stole up her features.

Her mouth fought a smile so genuine, Rein thought he'd rupture just waiting to see it. When it came, it pierced him like an arrow. He reached out and she did not move as he touched a curl at her temple, the back of his fingers trailing softly down over her cheek.

"Rein?"

He tangled his fingers in a coil of auburn hair, the curled end brushing the swell of her breast.

Her breath seized. "You will not kiss me, say you won't."

Panic, he thought, his features shifting into a soft frown. She is unconditionally panicked. "Why do you ask?"

"You have that look about you." His brows arched quizzically. "That I-will-kiss-her-and-she-will-melt-for-me look. I assure you I do not melt."

He shook his head slowly, his gaze never leaving hers, his lips ghosting with a smile. "I have that will-she-*let*-me-kiss-her look. That 'will she allow me a taste of her mouth, for from the moment she caught her lip between her teeth when she took a bullet from my body—I have been rattled with the prospect.' "

Her heart skated to her throat and stayed there. "Have you?" came a little breathlessly. "That long?"

"Aye." His eyes turned soft, a little darker, and his face neared.

"What? No tea to plant . . . ships to sail . . ." Her gaze flicked between his eyes and his beautiful mouth. "Rein." Half denial, half plea. She swallowed, and her tongue slid across the seam of her lips.

His breathing increased. And he angled his head, his gaze locked with hers. A tiny sound escaped her, fear and premonition biting the air. He paused, his mouth a fraction from hers, so close the heat of their lips blended and teased. He waited, unable to press further and not understanding why when he was cleaving in two to have a taste of her. Still he waited, his throat working, impatience riding through his body in a hard surge. Her gaze rapidly searched his face, absorbing him.

He lingered, anticipating. Her body moved an increment closer, and Rein shifted, pressing his mouth to hers.

She whimpered, her lashes sweeping down. Her lips trembled as he tasted them delicately, patiently, a voice inside him telling him this woman would run if she knew the desire he checked for her. Goddess of light, it was sweet, gripping him deep in his vitals, and he knew he'd never felt anything as potent, a power he could not define, and as her mouth shifted over his, tentatively sipping at his lips, giving of their lush fruit, Rein felt years of discipline crumble.

Fleetingly, Michaela wondered if she were still sitting, still on this earth.

And she had lied.

She did know how to melt.

Eight

He tasted of red wine and darkness, the wet touch of his mouth offering incredible heat and exotic pleasure. Yet painful, ugly memories crowded for supremacy with the languid feelings he created, with the tightness of desire tensing through her, and Michaela felt bittersweet tears form behind her eyes. 'Twas silly, she knew, to be so moved by a kiss, yet his touch was infinitely tender, almost reverent, making her feel truly desired and cherished.

It made the kiss all the more poignant, for she could never, ever, have more than this moment. With him. With any man. The denial struck her like a mortal blow and she wanted to scream at the injustice, the cruel cards dealt her, yet instead she absorbed the delicious crazy spinning in her blood, the heat wrapping around her middle and driving lower. He gave with gentle persistence, stealing her very breath, sending one sensation after another to tumble through her body. Only his mouth touched her, his body held inches away, a layer of heat simmering between them, a part of her aching for his strong arms around her, and another, terrified of what that touch would bring. Yet when he angled his head, his slick mouth torturing her lips, tasting, licking, his tongue sweeping the outline of her mouth, over and over, slowly, until she gasped for air and heard the beat of her own heart in her ears, she knew he could defeat her misgivings if he just kept kissing her, kept the world at bay.

"Michaela," he whispered against her lips. "Taste me." And like spilling wax, she yielded, opening her mouth wider, pressing closer, and when his tongue pushed past her lips, sinking into her mouth, Michaela felt her entire body clench down to her toes. Her skin flushed hot. Her breasts tightened beneath her bodice, taut nipples rasping against her loose clothing. Her tongue stroked his.

A sound trembled between them. A whimper, a groan, blending into one.

Her hands bunched in the folds of her gown and she pressed her thighs tightly together, forcing back the uncontrollable throbbing building between. As if sensing her anxiety, his warm hand covered hers, his thumb moving slowly over the back in tiny circles. Her fists unfurled and he brought it to his chest, laying it carefully there. Her palm flattened, the vibration of his heart running through her fingertips. The strength of it left her defenseless and without pause, her hand slid up his chest, curling around the back of his neck, pressing him harder to her mouth.

Rein moaned darkly, savoring the lushness of her, her acceptance stabbing like a waiting sword through his chest. She offered and he took, aware this might be his only moment, his only opportunity to touch her innocence. He wanted more of her, to feel the satiny length of her against him, bare beneath him, and though he knew this tryst in the darkness would haunt him, torture him with its forbidden lure, he slid his arms around her waist and stood, pulling her up with him. His jacket fell to the bench with her shawl, yet he never broke the kiss, fearing she would evaporate into mist if he did. His head reeled, his body trembling with her untutored response. He pressed her tighter, soft to hard, and he felt her tense, retreat—grow frightened. Instantly he loosened his hold, yet he deepened the kiss. Probing, liquid heat and uncapped passion. And she clung, molding her lips to his, her fingers sifting the hair at his nape, soothing and stirring him more than before.

He craved and did not deserve the hunger.

He pulsed, a merciless greed escalating through him, and he forced himself to let her go, afraid the desire unchecked would scare her, yet he could not cease touching, his broad calloused palms cupping her small face. And still he kissed her, trailing his mouth to the corner of hers, her cheek, her jaw, to soothe the mark left by her uncle's fist. His breath scattered across her face as he lay delicate kisses over her eyes, her temple.

"Michaela," he growled on a heavy breath. "Goddess of fire, you are so sweet."

She tipped her head a fraction, her dark lashes sweeping up until she met his pale-blue gaze. She was nothing as he imagined, and the sorrow of it collapsed the longing flickering to life inside her. She was tainted, and to entertain untouchable dreams wounded her to her very core.

Rein's brows furrowed a touch. The unmistakable sheen of tears glossed her eyes, and he brushed the backs of his fingers over her cheek, his voice low and haunted. "Did I hurt you?"

She shook her head, yet before she could speak, the sound of voices came to them, her name on the air. She gasped, panic striking across her features.

"Nay, none saw us." He caught her close when she tried to leave, shame in her eyes, and the sting of it burned through him. "And none can see us now," he assured her.

"He summons me." She pushed at his chest.

"Let him bloody well wait," he rasped, his need to keep her close, protected, making his voice harsh.

She met his gaze, her desire mirrored in her luminous hazel eyes. "I cannot." Did he not care for the repercussions? "If I am found here with you, I will be completely ruined." Her own welfare was not her uppermost concern, although if her uncle discovered them, she would be tossed in the streets before the last guest departed; yet far greater consequences teetered in the balance and depended on her remaining in this house. Inasmuch as she would like to hide here, she could not risk it. "Please. Let me go."

He did, instantly, taken aback by the sudden harshness in her voice. She stepped quickly out of the shadows, her body showered in moonlight.

From across the murky expanse they stared, his pale eyes glowing like a wolf's in the black shroud of tree branches.

The wind rustled the leaves.

A tear escaped, rolling down her cheek.

The sight of it unmanned him.

"Michaela."

Did he have to look at her as if he was at fault, as if she were innocent and precious? The splinter of hope and the denial of it was too hard to bear. "I should never have allowed that." She brushed the tear with the back of her hand. "You should never have touched me." He could not want her like that. He could not.

His jaw clenched, the division between them acutely more cavernous, and the cruel physical existence of it punctured his usual calm. "You enjoyed it as much as I." His tone bit for the truth, and she made a frustrated sound, unable to lie.

"You need ask that? Now?" she said, her voice wavering. "Of course I did." What did he want? To hear how her blood was still singing, that her body was screaming for the heaviness of his touch, that for the first time in years she felt no revulsion, no shame, no anger when he—only he—touched her? And that it terrified her? She couldn't, not without revealing her hideous secret, and she'd so little pride left, debasing herself for a man she scarcely knew, was the last crumb she refused to give. "How could I not? 'Twas obvious you are a master at stealing kisses in the dark." Beyond the pleasure of his touch, his ease at seducing her reaffirmed how easily men manipulated. And how weak she was to it.

His chuckle was dark, bordering on cynical. Her words were proof of her naïveté, for he'd scarcely scraped the surface of his desire. "I would steal more, make no mistake, Michaela."

Her body instantly responded to the softly growled words, climbing with heat and pulsing madly. *Do not want more,* she warned herself, *for with such a man, outcast or nay, you cannot have it.* Her private poison spirited through her, driving regret and anger to the surface and coloring her voice.

"I have no need for a man like you in my life, Rein Montegomery." Any future was long ago ruined, and a man of such visibility would surely destroy her meticulous plans, she kept trying to justify, wincing at the bruise left in his eyes.

Reality slapped him, hard. He hated that a well-chosen word could wound him still, and he schooled his features, swearing he would not leave himself so exposed again. "You are assuming, of course, that I have more than a fortuitous interest, then?" His hard gaze roamed her from head to toe, insolent, chilling her, his next words snapping like breaking bones. *"Don't.* 'Twill be your undoing." His caustic tone clawed her with its contempt. He grabbed his coat off the bench, his face near, pale eyes glittering. "Good life, manslayer."

He receded into the darkness like dissipating vapor, and Michaela remained there, her feet frozen to the stone floor. He wanted no more than the others . . . *oh, this should not hurt so much.* She'd so wanted him to be different than the others, she realized, closing her eyes and willing the knot in her throat to unwind. But was this not what she wanted, needed to complete the tasks ahead? she asked herself. To be exiled, unnoticed? Then why did she want nothing but to find him and demand he not be so damned indifferent and ruthless and contriving. Her throat tightened again. *A fine ugly mess you've made now.* She started toward him, yet the insistent summons came louder, and she had no choice but to snatch up her shawl and turn away and race after the servant.

Rein watched her leave, throbbing for her, his desire at dangerous levels, his emotions joining the catapult to the surface. His fist clenched, his mouth flattening with self-recrimination. If she were any other woman, he would have lain her to the cold bench, seducing her to passion's end. But Michaela was a lady, virtuous, and she was right, he should never have touched her. He ought to be grateful she understood little of his failings or she would not have given him even a second look, he thought, jamming his arms into his coat sleeves and shrugging it on. Her scent immediately filled his nostrils and he groaned, raking his fingers through his hair and rubbing the nape of his neck. His mouth still burned from her kiss, her taste permeating with the warm memory of her body lain to his. Damn her for becoming pliant and seductive in his arms, for making him crave the forbidden!

His groin throbbed mercilessly, and he knew he could not reappear in the ballroom in such a state of readiness and leaned back against the tree, withdrawing a cheroot from inside his coat. He bit the tip and spat it aside, rummaging for a flint, then lighting the thick cigar. He drew deeply, knocking out smoke rings and letting the night air cool his body, yet the chill did nothing to ease the fullness in his breeches. Naught would, he realized, even as he recognized the damage he'd done. To himself and his purpose. She wielded power over him and he despised it, chose not to examine it further than this moment. He tipped a look toward the house in time to see her skirts disappear around the edge of the doorjamb.

Run, manslayer. Hide. For if I find you in the dark again, I might succumb to my madness and refuse to let you go.

Michaela escaped to a side door and paused long enough to look back. He was nowhere in sight. The loss struck her harder than she imagined, and she touched her fingers to her lips, still warm from his touch. Closing her eyes briefly, she willed the heat to leave her body, the sensations only he created, and focused on moving through the house toward the kitchen, several yards behind James.

All thoughts of the man fled when she found servants scurrying wildly from table to table, dishes clattering, their haste to prepare and serve making them harried and clumsy. A bowl hit the floor, heavy cream splattering the walls. Someone cried. Another cursed, and Michaela caught one girl as she passed.

"Millie, do calm down."

"But they are gobbling it up as fast as we can prepare it, ma'am."

Michaela smiled softly, straightening the girl's cap. "They will avail themselves of drink till you arrive." Millie gave her a doubtful look and Michaela arched a tapered brow. "None would be so rude to mention 'twere too little food when those tables are fair sagging under the burden. 'Twould prove them gluttonous." Michaela's nose tipped the air and she effected a rather good imitation of her uncle's nasaly tone. "Especially when we are at war and should all sacrifice."

Millie giggled. An instant later, her smile fell. "Them royals and such don't give a wit," she said sourly.

Michaela plucked a ripe tart from the girl's platter and poised it at Millie's lips.

"Then we shall avail ourselves of a sample or two. Good for those expanding waistlines, aye?" she said, and shoved the cream puff of fruit into the girl's mouth. Agnes glanced her way and grinned, and Michaela chanced a look at the door, not that her uncle would ever find his way into the kitchen, then swept around the hot, steamy room, offering a sample of the wares they'd slaved over since dawn this morn. In moments, the mood was a bit less chaotic as they finished sampling and went back to work.

Except Agnes, who touched her arm and motioned to her the side. "Where have you been?"

"In the garden. Why?" Her eyes wide, she gripped the older woman's hand. "Did he come in here looking for me?"

"Nay, but 'tis obvious you've been . . . occupied." She lifted a platter and Michaela stared at her reflection in the silver. Her hair was in place, yet her lips were slightly swollen, the surrounding skin left red by his beard. Embarrassment fled up her cheeks.

"Did ya like it?"

"Agnes!"

The cook eyed her. "Aye, ye did."

"Hush!"

"Mistress Denton!" James called softly, quickly, his gaze darting into the kitchen and down the hall. "Come."

Michaela recognized his look. Her uncle had discovered she'd not returned to the ballroom. Cursing Rein and his kisses, she'd not time to return to her room to apply powders and shifted past Agnes, scooping up flour, patting it to her face, then brushing the excess as she judged her appearance in the silver platter. Agnes snickered. 'Twill have to do, she thought, and was about to set the platter down when she spotted a dark, familiar reflection in the silver. She gasped, whirling about, searching the open kitchen door, yet it was empty. Her brows drew down, her skin prickling. Surely he was not there. A breeze and the scent of smoke wafted and she stepped closer to investigate, but James called again. She handed over the tray, hastening out of the kitchen and toward the ballroom.

In the lower hall, voices came from her uncle's offices, and she slowed her steps.

"We sail in a fortnight. Evening tide."

The door ajar, Michaela did not dare to look and tried to decipher the voices. She cast a furtive glance about and listened. Lord George Germain, she realized, the Secretary of the State of War.

"The colonists will find his arrival well met with nearly seven thousand troops."

"Good God, the cost! Is there no other way?"

"None. Never mind the cost. The king is long past the point of a gentle hand, be assured. And 'tis time we gave them a good rousting."

Someone scoffed, and Michaela struggled to put face to voice. "As we met at Tighcondaroga?"

"That was a misjudgment of numbers."

"Spain is entering the fray now."

Another rude sound. "The Spanish know naught of fighting in the wilderness."

"The colonists do. 'Tis their lands."

" 'Tis the king's lands!" By God, Germain was pompous, she thought.

"Armaments?"

"A full garrison's worth, and four ships with full complement."

Michaela repeated the words in her mind. Fortnight, four ships, seven thousand, and even catching the names, yet when the conversation turned to past victories, she hurried toward the ballroom, glancing back to be certain she was not seen.

She stepped into the ballroom to see her uncle speaking with Rein and her heart did a strange hop in her chest. Holding his tricorn and cape, he shook his head, and though her uncle called to him, he headed to the door.

He brushed past her, snapping off, "Good evening, Mistress Denton," without meeting her gaze, and her last look of him was his punishingly straight spine and long, easy strides.

And the path the guests cleared for the lone dark dragon.

Nine

Forgoing the politeness of a glass, Rein tipped the bottle of rum to his lips, head back and his Adam's apple bobbing as he drained a healthy portion. It blistered down his throat, slamming into his stomach and channeling through his blood. The liquor's effect was quick and poisonous, heating the anger left alone for so long. He smirked, taking another short sip. He prided himself on control,

with his company, his ships, and mostly himself. But tonight, his
ability to master his emotions had vanished.

I've little need for a man like you in my life, Rein Montegomery.

He snorted a scornful half laugh. Little need. Ahh, lass, you
have none a'tall, believe me.

That he knew she was accurate in her condemnations did not
soothe the denial bending through him, threatening to snap his
bones. *You will ruin her for a good match, for the sake of another
kiss, a secret chat?*

And will she have her respectable match with the blackguard
Winters?

The very thought drove a bitter-tasting sewage up to his throat.
He rarely associated with anyone so pure. He'd always preferred
whores to satisfy his appetites. They came without obligation—
without expectations, where the color of his skin or the branches
of his heritage didn't matter. And touching them never left a mark
behind.

He stared down at the colored glass vessel for a long moment,
then hurled it across the cabin. It hit the wall, the thick glass shattering into chunks and falling to the floor. He raked his fingers
through his hair, rubbing the back of his neck, then staggered toward his desk.

A knock sounded.

"Go the bloody hell away!"

They didn't, and Temple peered around the edge, frowning when
he found Rein coatless, his waistcoat unfastened, his shirttails bil-
lowing from his breeches.

Rein glared at him. The man, he decided, was too dense to see
it was not a good time for a visit.

"I thought you were staying the night at the earl's?"

Rein dropped into the chair behind his desk and propped his
boots on the surface.

He cracked open a second bottle and swilled back a gulp, swiping the back of his hand across his mouth. "Spending the night in
a house whilst a member of the realm rogered your last whore
was . . . I don't know . . ." He shrugged minutely. "A shade off of
proper." He had some pride, he thought. Ahh, what good does it
for you? What good does money and power do you when you are
still alone?

Temple's brow shot high. "Good God, you are certainly feeling little pain."

Rein eyed the contents. "Not quite."

Temple stepped inside.

"Get out."

"What? And let you wallow alone? Wouldn't dream of it, mate." Rein's gaze slid to him, his eyes thin and pale with hostility. "Then again, wallowing alone has its merits." He backed out and shut the door.

Rein rested the base of the bottle on his stomach, the glass clicking against the medallion beneath his shirt. His scowl deepened. The only fortune this evening was that Germain, the top-lofty bastard, was not his father. His relief should please him, and in the recesses of his mind, Rein loathed the need to seek out the man whose blood ran in his veins. Yet, after his encounter with Michaela, the need to end this unholy torment made him more determined. *I will find you, Father. And mayhap,* he thought drunkenly, *I will run you through.*

Rein's gaze fell on his coat flung carelessly across the desk. His eyes narrowed, remembering how her slight frame swallowed the heavy fabric, and knowing he should not, he reached for the garment and brought it to his nose. He inhaled, her scent still lingering in the threads, hating and hungering for her in one sharp breath. But he would not go near her again, for he understood the power of speculation and innuendo better than any man, and he, to his constant vexation, was bloody well swimming in it.

Nay. He would not allow the taint of actions to kill another woman.

He would gladly die first.

Alighting from her carriage, Lady Katherine paused at the gangway, biting her lower lip as she glanced at the men lounging on the pier repairing sails and drinking gin. They cast her an admiring glance, and though her stomach knotted at the thought of them touching her, she responded with a polite nod, then moved up the plank. The *White Empress* was at rest, her sails lashed down, the decks barren but for the mount stalled in the corner. It was annoying that the man pampered the four-legged beast, yet refused her. She was here to change that, yet no sooner than her slippered toe touched the freshly swabbed deck, he appeared. His hair amuss, his clothing wrinkled, he looked well into his cups. And defenseless, she thought with a smile.

"Rein, you poor dear."

His head jerked up, and Rein squinted against the sun. "Sweet Mercy," he growled. "Get out of here, Kat. I'm in no mood for company."

With only the slightest hesitation, she swept forward, cooing softly. "Oh, but look at you." She reached to brush her fingers over his furrowed brow, but before she met her mark, he snatched her wrist.

"Don't." Her lips mooed and Rein's irritation mounted, his eyes sharpening on her. "Get off my ship."

"But I've come to see you."

"I do not wish your company, Lady Buckland. Apparently I did not make that clear the last time."

Cupping her elbow, he propelled her toward the rail, but she twisted, immediately pressing her plump body to his. Rein went absolutely still, his need reacting to the feminine curves, his desire born in a red-haired lass with a sharp tongue and guileless eyes. God, he'd like nothing more than to take this heated bitch beneath him, pound into her and obliterate the image haunting him all night. But he could not. Aristocrat or nay, Katherine came with tethers attached.

"I've missed you, Rein. Can't you see how much I love you?"

He scoffed meanly. She loved money and power. "Lost the earl's support after one night, have you?" His lips twisted in a snarl.

She huffed, pouting in a way that did nothing to enhance her appeal. "He was dull and boring. Not like you."

Her free hand slid downward, toward his aching groin. He grabbed it, jerking it away. "Men prefer the chasing, Katherine. And only those less than a gentleman prefer to be pawed in public." He ushered her to the rail.

Katherine rounded on him. "I will not beg."

He chuckled sadistically. "Then I suggest you learn to satisfy your desires yourself. I'm sure you'll find more love there."

She inhaled and slapped his face.

He arched a brow. "Go home, Lady Buckland. And be more circumspect of the men you bed. It could be your undoing."

Katherine saw all hope fall to ruin. "Is that what you said to her, Rein?" His expression went black as night, his pale eyes glittering with savagery, and Katherine knew terror. He looked as if he'd take pleasure in snapping her neck with his bare hands.

"Mind your tongue, my lady." The words rasped like the grate of flint to stone.

Her spine stiffened. "Is that a threat?"

"I haven't the time for threats."

Her lips tightened, her eyes gone hot with anger. "You will regret this, Rein. I will see you in hell."

"I await your arrival, m'lady." Out of patience the instant she arrived, Rein thrust her off his ship.

Katherine stumbled, then caught up her skirts, jerking a glare over her shoulder. "You'll pay for this." She walked down the gangway.

Sailors snickered, several calling out that they'd be happy to accommodate her if she was hurting for a bit of salmon in her bucket, and she flung them an ugly look, eliciting several glares. A few started toward her. She chanced a panicked look at Rein, but he remained on the deck, arms folded, legs braced against the heel of the vessel. Unsympathetic. Utterly ruthless and icy cold. The sight of him made her heart pound, and she started toward him.

"Sweet thunder, what must I do, woman?"

"Want me." Her eyes lit with an unnamed emotion. "Or kill me."

Rein issued the air with foul curses as she climbed into her carriage, his gaze following the conveyance down the quay.

Lord Heyward frowned when Montegomery scraped the coins and markers into his palm, then stuffed them in his pocket as he stood.

"Sure we can't entice you to stay, and let us win a bit back?" He received an arched look as cool as the London spring.

"You are already in my debt, my lord. Sure you do not want to dive deeper?"

Nay, Heyward thought, sighing resolutely. The man was far too good with a card. All that time at sea with nothing else to do, he supposed.

"Damn, Montegomery," Sir Sheppard said. "My wife will have my head."

"Broke a promise, did you?"

Sheppard reddened, and he glanced about to see if unreliable ears were listening. He looked back at the privateer as Montegomery casually fastened his waistcoat, straightened his neck cloth. He didn't look as pleased as he ought, Sheppard thought, especially since his pockets were full of his monthly stipend.

"Never make promises to women, Randal, the price of breaking them is too great." A servant approached, holding out his cloak and tricorn. He accepted them, Sheppard's brows flicking in surprise as Montegomery discreetly pressed a thick stack of coins into the old man's palms.

"From what I hear," Heyward put in, "Katherine thinks otherwise."

"My point exactly," Rein said with a disgusted twist of his lips.

"This is what we get bringing his kind into polite society," came from the fourth, Lieutenant Ridgely, as he tossed his fouled hand on the table. The others looked at him.

"Christ, Ridgely," Heyward groused, tensing. "Watch your mouth."

Ridgely spared the peer a glance, then focused on Montegomery. The heathen shouldn't be allowed inside respectable gambling houses, he thought, tugging at his uniform coat.

"And what kind is that, sir?"

For all the world, Heyward thought, Montegomery appeared unaffected, adjusting the fit of his gloves and staring down at the immature lieutenant from beneath hooded eyes. Heyward knew better. That calm was a prelude.

"A cheating half-breed bastard."

Around the foursome, people collectively gasped. Sheppard glared at the young man. Heyward swore under his breath and covered his face with his hand.

Rein furnished the soldier with a bored glance. "You have deeds to back such an accusation, am I correct?"

"How else could you win all our money?" He flicked a hand at the barren table.

Rein shrugged, his body tense for a fight he did not want. "I am better at the game. Mayhap I should take my coin elsewhere in the future." He looked down at Lord Heyward. "The English, it seems, do not need it."

Heyward's eyes flared, and he turned a panicked look to a man across the room. Lord North scowled, his heavy jowls sinking over his coat collar, but Heyward recognized the warning. If Montegomery decided to take his cargo across the Pacific, England would be weakened further, and all for the sake of an impudent officer.

"No need to be hasty, Rein." Heyward palmed the air, hands down, praying for tranquility.

Ridgely scoffed rudely, coming to his feet and glaring at Rein.

"Sit down, son, afore he beats the skin off you," Sheppard mumbled, shuffling the discards.

"Ridgely!" The group turned as a tall, dark-haired man moved forward, skirting people and tables, his intention on the young captain.

The man bowed stiffly to the peers, then looked at Montegomery. "Captain McBain."

Rein acknowledged with a nod, remembering him from the Brigadier's party and refusing to allow any other image to develop.

"Forgive the lad, sir. He is newly off the battlefield and full of—"

"I don't need anyone to take up for me, Captain. He cheated."

"He did not and you know it, Ridgely. Take your losses like a man." If anything, McBain knew Montegomery was a man of extreme honor.

" 'Tis a harsh accusation he's made, Captain." Rein looked at the lieutenant, an individual full of hatred, for a disregard of the person for the sake of the land of his birth. And it occurred to him that Ridgely was near the age his father had been when he'd taken his mother—by force. "Would you care to meet on the field?"

Ridgely's eyes flared, and through the fog of liquor, Montegomery's reputation with weapons sprang to mind.

"I assure you, this bastard is capable. Pistols or swords, your choice."

"Apologize, Lieutenant," McBain hastened to say.

Heyward stared up at Rein. The predatory look in the man's usually guarded expression told him Montegomery was spoiling for a fight, if his mood this evening was any indication. "Lieutenant!"

"Please forgive—" Ridgely gritted out. His words faded as Montegomery leaned close, his face inches from the officer's. Ridgely felt the savage look down to his polished boot heels, and for an instant thought he growled.

"You live another day, boy. Do not waste it." Rein looked at the others. "Good evening, gentleman." Rein tipped at the waist, ignoring their beseeching to return with no more than a wave behind his head as he headed to the door, the path cleared by his long strides.

Outside White's, Rein called for his horse, pacing as he waited for the lad to bring Naraka around. Polite company. Rein knew dock workers with better manners. He ought to be bloody amused about the whole incident, he mulled, flipping a coin at the youth and swinging up onto Naraka's back.

Gathering information was not as beneficial as he'd hoped. To be made the brunt of jokes and slurs did not bother him. Nor would he have slain the boy officer; he was a product of his rearing. Or lack of it, he thought with a tight smile. Slowing the mount, Rein let Naraka pick her own way home, his thoughts dressing over the evening and the facts he'd unearthed. Having crossed Germain of his list, Rein had three candidates for fatherhood—his lips twisted ruefully at the thought—remaining. His sire, however, was apparently affluent enough after all these years, for doors closed to Rein the instant he'd made the slightest inquiry.

Naraka stopped suddenly, and Rein stared ahead at the three men blocking his path. Ahh, the devil speaks. He leaned forward in the saddle, bracing his crossed arms on the pommel, the leads loosely wrapping his gloved fingers. "Gentleman?"

"Give it over, gov."

For a moment, Rein suspected Ridgely had regained his courage, but his superior did not look the type who'd allow him out of his sights that soon.

Rein jerked the purse loose from beneath his waistcoat and held it out.

"Not that," came with impatience.

He detected a heavy accent and tried to place the origins. "What then, gentlemen? My shirt? My boots?"

"The medallion."

"What medallion might that be?"

"Don't go bein' a smart ass, gov." The distinct sound of a pistol hammer cocking rang in the deserted street. "It'll get you killed."

"Can't have that now, can we?"

The man in the center gestured forward and his mate strode closer, his long-barreled pistol pointed at Rein's heart. He did not move a muscle, his gaze following his approach.

"Open yer shirt."

Rein leaned back, noticing the man's retreat as he uncrossed his arms and from beneath his cloak drew duel pistols.

His gaze slid quickly between them. "I can take at least two of you with me."

"Then you'll be dead, too."

Rein arched a black brow, the motion hidden in the brim of his tricorn. "Can you be sure?"

The man clad in dark garments moved closer, and Rein swung the barrel around to met his head. "Is our first encounter so faded from your minds?"

All but one started backing away. A shot rang, the flash of light and smoke fracturing the stillness, echoing as the ball whisked past Rein's ear. He returned fire, dropping the man where he stood. Another shot and he repaid the second, intentionally clipping him in the leg. The man's howl rolled with him as he fell to the ground, clutching the wound. In swift moves he shoved the spent weapons into his waist belt, returning with a knife. He flipped the serrated blade over and over his fingers, letting it dance on the tips, flicker in the moonlight.

The sight held the man bewitched, and Rein leaned low, his arm shooting out to grasp him by the coat, fisting the garment and lifting him from the ground. Anger surged through his veins, tightening his grip and turning his knuckles white. "Tell your employer to come for me himself. For I will not cease." His voice edged the side of steel and the man's eyes widened. "Never."

He opened his hand, letting him drop, then heeled Naraka and rode around the wounded man.

Nay, Father, this time. But I will win.

Ten

Hawkers called out for the last time before packing up their wares, yet throngs of people milled about, men and women, dock workers and several enlisted troops tossing back gulps of gin before the night and loneliness encroached. The stench of refuse and bile left the air of East End strikingly pungent and Michaela ducked her head, clutching a sack, her wool scarf drawn across her face for more reasons than disguising her soft features. Sewage ran freely down in the streets toward the quay and she prayed for more rain, yet knew nothing would rinse the filth away.

She shouldered her way between the bustle of people rushing toward their homes, a warm spot in an abandoned doorway. Tall, narrow buildings sandwiched tightly on the avenue appeared to lean on the next for support, the walls stained from the splash of water and grime from passing carriages, old washwater, or the contents of chamber pots tossed from above without pause to who they would hit. Grimy children foraged in piles of garbage for food scraps, and if Michaela had coin, she'd offer it, rather than witness the degradation. But she couldn't and raced down the damp streets, slipping and sliding on the muck-covered stone and catching herself on the sleeve of a sailor. He shouted at her, shoving her, yet his hand found their way into her pockets, seeking a coin. She struggled, batting his hands, turning her face against the foul breath reeking of rotten teeth and liquor.

She batted him in the head with her burlap sack, then scrambled down the street, his laughter following her as she darted and paused, hid and strolled, pulling her blade from her boot when another man tried to take her nonexistent purse. Deep in East End, she held close to the structures, counting the buildings, then slipping between two. The alley was scarcely wide enough for a horse, yet Michaela did not notice and continued onward, constantly looking behind to see if she'd been followed. She ducked under a break in crooked wood slats serving as a fence and moved across the courtyard to the carriage house, remaining in the shadows, in the shrubbery, then around rigs and slumbering horses. Stepping into the darkness of the stable, she leaned back against the wall and checked her tracks, licking her dry lips, her fist clenched around her blade. Her heart pounded in her throat, and she realized just how treacherous this adventure was. She closed her eyes, tipping her head back.

'Twould serve no purpose to be scared now, she thought. *You've done this countless times.* She waited until her heartbeat slowed pace and took a deep breath, then pushed away from the wood wall. Her coat snagged on a nail, ripping a bit before dragging her back. Her shoulders slammed into the decaying wall, rattling the rotting structure. She looked up as hay sprinkled the floor, waiting for the damn roof to fall on her head. A fitting end, she thought ruefully.

A hand clamped over her mouth, drawing her back against a hard chest. Immediately she struggled, sliding down and twisting, her blade coming up under his chin.

"Very good, darlin' " came in a deep drawl.

She sighed, irritated. She should have been prepared. He had a nasty habit of creeping up on her like this.

"See my heart anywhere about?" She pricked his chin. "Old man. Seems I've lost it."

He smirked down at her and dug the pistol into her side. "Who are you calling old?"

She pressed her knee to his tender groin. "You, with the gray hair." Her gaze flicked meaningfully to his silver head.

His brows rose, and he tipped the gun to the ceiling and stepped back. "Where's your pistol, lass?" His voice held an edge, laced with the concern of a man who'd seen too much and wanted it to end.

"Lost that, too."

"I've another, if you feel the need?"

She shook her head. He needed it more. He was a rebel leader in his enemy's land.

"Come. You look hungry."

"How does one look hungry?"

He turned, shaking his head. "Pale, I suppose."

" 'Twas rhetorical, sir."

"I know," he said with a rakish smirk over his shoulder. Even at nearly three score, his posture was straight, his shoulders wide with strength, and Lord, he was dashingly handsome. It made her wonder how many hearts he'd broken in his youth. Beside him she waited as he bent, clawing through the mud and hay shielding the trapdoor to grasp a iron ring, jerking the hatch open. He descended in the yawning black and Michaela immediately shifted about to climb down after him. She dropped to the dirt floor and he climbed back up to seal them in.

She looked around at the familiar surroundings, the cot she knew was not long enough to fit his height, to the table and two chairs. "We really must do something about your living conditions, Nickolas."

His lips quirked in an easy smile. "I've had worse."

His tone bore a wealth of bitterness, but she did not press him. "You venture here only when the authorities are close. Are they?"

He moved to the table, sliding into the chair and folding his hands on the tabletop. A candle flickered between them as she settled across from him.

"Nay, but one can never be certain. How did you get out?" He knew her daylight cover of working in a soup kitchen, which she did, had little effect on her uncle's sympathies, and not at this hour.

"I laced their brandy with laudanum."

"Sweet Jesus, woman!"

"Do not scold me, Nickolas," she shot back. "I know what I am doing. 'Twas not enough to do harm, only to assure a sound sleep." She smiled, sheepish. "I have a tendency to make far too much noise than I would like." A pause and then, "I thought you were to work on covering your accent?" He was a Carolinian and it showed in his genteel drawl.

"I 'ave. Ken ye give a fellow a bit of slack in the lines, lass."

Her mouth curved ruefully. "Cockney wasn't what I had in mind."

"Be thankful for that much." He shrugged, and she slung the sack on the table, then tugged at the strings.

"Agnes has been baking." Her gaze flashed up to catch his eager smile. "And I filched." She laid out meat pies with a loaf of brown bread and cinnamon cake.

Nick grinned, looking years younger. "My wife caught my heart with such a sweet," he said, ignoring the meat and bread, and unwrapping cake as if it were gold. Michaela recognized the longing in his face as he sampled the comfit and knew he missed his family. She sympathized. His people were thankfully alive in America, yet with no word whether he was dead or nay.

He finished off the bite and rewrapped it. "My thanks, Michaela."

She smiled and pushed the meat pie toward him. "Eat first, Grandfather." He did, his manners impeccable, and she recalled the comments from the guests at the ball, referring to the Colonists as uncouth barbarians, yet Michaela saw no such point to reference and instead found a strength and dignity in them unmatched in any Englishman. Each time she met with Nickolas, her admiration grew. He'd suffered horrible treatment by British authorities, prison, pressed into naval service, and his back bore the English's opinion of the colonial privateer. He'd struggled for over twenty years to see the Colonies free of British rule. And from what Michaela knew, not a single sanction from the Crown had deterred them from their goal.

Such tenacity had to be admired, and offering counterintelligence to the Sons of Liberty was the least she could do to help them. Michaela wanted some of that freedom, too. Not so much from the rigors of British society, but the hope of a new beginning. She'd lain witness to her countrymen's cruelty in Morocco, Africa, in India, the tyranny and horrors, the bloody damned need to conquer every corner of the globe. Her own people were treated like lepers if they'd no coin to better themselves and no manner in which to gain it. Michaela was no better than the urchins in the street. She'd a bed and food, aye, yet without family or coin to book passage, she was a prisoner as much as every soul in Newgate.

Make the world England, Germain had said.

Swill.

And Michaela knew that spying for the American rebels was her own private retribution to the men who'd dishonored her. And this time, she vowed to hold victory in her hands. And she would gladly die to get it. And kill to keep it.

"Any wine in there, lass?"

She looked up and smiled, then withdrew a bottle from the sack and glanced around for some cups. Finding none, she uncorked the flask. "We drink like Vikings," she said, and tipped it to her lips.

Nickolas smiled, leaning back in his chair as he swiped his lips with a cloth. "You will fit in well with my daughters," he said, affection in his voice.

"I'm flattered you think so," she said, lowering the bottle to the table and nudging it toward him.

Nickolas frowned. She was so private, bloody remote sometimes, and Nickolas knew it was not well for one so young to hide their feelings, especially a woman. God knows he lived in his for far too long. "If you do not tell me what ails you so, Michaela, how can I help?"

" 'Tis of no consequence." She'd lived with her shame for years, but she did not have to revive it with the telling. That she would never do. "And I am here to help you." Looking at him, she reached across and caught his hand. He gripped her fingers warmly. "I've vital information this time."

"You always have vital information. Have I told you our appreciation?"

"Aye," she rolled her eyes, "to my utter annoyance." He smiled, a flash of white teeth and dimples. "Now. You have to contact your man and send him out on the first ship sailing west. If I am correct—"

"You always are."

Her smile was tight and quick, then her brows drew down. "In a fortnight, ships will sail to the Colonies, bringing nine thousand troops . . ."

Nickolas's faced mirrored his deep concentration as he committed every scrap to memory. The world beyond saw a reserved auburn haired woman prone to awkwardness, a bit of trouble. Yet he knew better.

Michaela Denton was the Colonists' finest weapon. Known only as the Guardian, her attention to detail, to parcels of seemingly inconsequential bits of conversation which might pan to something more, was uncanny. And those fractures of gossip she managed to piece together on more than one occasion came in time to save countless lives and quicken them toward freedom. He owed her his life and his country, owed her a debt they could not repay. But Michaela was in the very best position to gather information that was more accurate than any other. And Nickolas's concern for her safety was a constant nightmare, for when he looked at Michaela, with her flowing red hair and greenish eyes, all he saw was his own daughters attempting to accomplish such daring. Which is why he'd seek an old friend's help.

She finished her delivery, leaning back, concern marring her face.

"What is it?"

" 'Tis naught." She waved, her features smoothing.

"Michaela," he warned, "do not take unnecessary risks. Meeting at the ball was hazardous enough."

Michaela mentally shoved aside the memory of that night, of Rein and his wet kisses, and she sighed, pushing out of the chair and adjusting her cap and scarf. Another sleepless night with his memory nagging her, blending with the same nightmares that haunted her for three years, and she'd be a useless pot of bones to the people who depended on her, to the cause.

"I cannot dismiss the feeling that there is something deeper occurring in my house. Uncle Atwell is being secretive. Normally he chats with his cronies without regard, yet lately . . ." She shrugged. "I am not certain. I've discovered them only twice whispering like excited girls." Still frowning, she moved to the ladder, her foot on the lowest rung as she looked back over her shoulder. "The apartments next time? Not that I mind dressing as a boy, you understand." She made a face at his surroundings. "I hate seeing you hiding like a thief."

He smiled. "I am a thief. Are we not stealing information?"

She furnished him a rueful smirk. "We are committing treason, Nickolas."

Her serious tone reminded him that she was in far more danger than he. "Michaela." He cleared his throat a bit, glancing briefly away before meeting her gaze.

Her brows worried. "Tell me."

"Some of the other contacts . . . their information has been found to be compromised."

She tipped her head, thoughtful. None of the operatives encountered one another. It was an assurance that none would have to snitch on a fellow, if any were caught. "Think you there is someone relaying falsely?"

"Aye, that or working both sides."

She inhaled, eyes flaring. A double agent. "You suspect me?"

"Nay," he said, almost insulted. "You are the only one I do not. Yet I am but a single opinion here."

He had superiors, and she understood the Americans were a collective voice of many. If it came down to a crisis of trust, Nickolas would be forced to consider the good of the cause and choose. And she would lose—and die for freedom. "Warn the others, Nickolas, for I answer to you and no other."

He knew that as truth, for she refused to speak with his messenger on more than one occasion. "I will signal you."

Though no one but she delivered and received information, Nickolas managed to have a cloth, each a different color, which signified their meeting place, delivered to her or hung from the bridge. How he managed it, she did not question, but from her rooms, she could see the bright scrap with the aid of her father's spyglass. When she needed to meet with him, she did the same, though she had a devil of a time getting to the attic and the roof without notice.

She considered for a moment telling him about Rein, that he'd discovered her in the streets trying to get home, but the man had better concerns, and she assured herself that she could handle the situation. Michaela looked up at the darkened hatch, praying she could get home before dawn light without mishap.

"Be careful, lass."

"I will definitely try." Michaela climbed, carefully pushing the hatch open a touch. She scanned between the crack before forcing the lid up enough to crawl out. She did not speak as she sealed him inside, thinking it was a dismal place to leave him to spend the night. At least he moved about from house to tavern to inn, she thought, though was never sure where she'd find him, or if she would. Masking her concern, she moved across the stable floor, then flattened against the wall, her knife poised as she moved back into the rank surrounds of East End.

Naraka's hooves sounded uneven and Rein slid from the saddle, bending his leg back to check for stones. Plucking it free, he walked beside Naraka, angry he'd been forced to shoot a man, frustrated at his lack of information, irritated that he'd little control over it, and knew if he returned to his ship, he would not find sleep. Energy raced through him, tightening his muscles, and though he'd tried to harness it, he was losing his grasp on it. He looked up as he passed a brothel, and for an instant, considered hiring the services of a whore to relieve this unbearable tension, then dismissed it and moved on. Drink was certainly not an option, the effects of his inebriation of nearly a week past still lingering enough to warn him off.

And the source.

Damn you, Michaela, he thought, recalling her tears, the brittle look in her eyes when she'd dismissed him so handily from her life. He did not know her well enough to understand anything about her, aware he'd no right to encroach in her circles. Ahh, but she could not lie through her kisses, he thought, sweet and virtuous, banked passion and smoldering heat.

And she'd weakened him, awakened him.

But a little lust is no reason to destroy a woman.

Someone brushed past him, driving him into his horse. He grabbed, and the fellow struggled. A hard boot hit his shin.

Rein cursed, grasping the youth by the shoulders and forcing him to be still. "Have a care, lad— God of thunder, are you following me?"

She stared up into his handsome face, her heart pounding from her run to escape, and in the back of her mind, she knew the moments would could cost their lives. "You flatter yourself far too often, Rein." Michaela glanced back. She heard hoofbeats and footsteps. "Let go!" *The soldiers!*

"Not until you tell me what has you out in East End, for the love of God, at this hour, again." Then he heard them, riders, shouts, the voices familiar. Rein twisted and saw the men who'd threatened him earlier, plus reinforcements coming around the street. Shots rang, plunking into the stone wall several yards before them. He pulled her into the nearest alley, flattening himself against the wall and cupping a hand over her mouth. He held her tight to his side as he peered out. Bullets chipped the mortar walls.

"Not a word," he whispered. "Naraka. Down." The huge stallion folded to the ground like a dog, tucked close to the wall.

Michaela peeled his gloved hand back, but did not move from the safety of his side. She'd encountered the soldiers by accident and prayed her erratic moves through the city hadn't given Nickolas up to the authorities, yet if even one soldier recognized her, they'd drag before her uncle. And he thought she slept soundly in her rooms. She would receive a beating that would defy all others, or be taken to Newgate.

Rein withdrew his pistol, checking the prime. When he leaned out to aim, she gripped his arm and shook her head. Rein didn't think he could resist those eyes.

"Do you want to live?"

She nodded.

"Then do as I say and I will get you home."

She shook her head wildly, and when she opened her mouth to speak, he covered it, pushing her back against the wall with his body.

"Michaela, you do not understand the nest you have fallen into, I assure you. I do not care why you are in this pest hole at this hour, nor do I need aught of yours complicating my life. But there are men out there searching, and a woman clad as a boy in my company will do more than destroy your precious reputation. Savvy?"

She nodded, hating his harsh tone, that his eyes glittered with anything but ruthless determination. He removed his hand and leaned out, then jerked back as riders passed their hiding place. Rein counted the rhythm of the hoofbeats, then ordered her to climb on his squatting horse. She did, and a whispered command brought them right. Rein swung up behind her, clutching her close.

"This will be hard and fast, lass. Hold on."

He wheeled Naraka around and headed farther into the alley at a breakneck speed. Michaela's eyes rounded and she clutched the pommel as the horse leapt, clearing the stacks of empty crates and clattering to the ground. Racing through another alley, crossing an avenue, then swerving to greet another dark, narrow passage. She swore she did not breathe as he maneuvered his mount through the city, away from the soldiers, the black beast beneath them never slowing his wild ride.

He was an expert, his knowledge of the streets better than her own, his evasion without hesitation, and she considered how many times Rein Montegomery had to run for his life.

Lady Buckland stepped close to the carriage, looking up at her driver. The little man swayed in his perch. "Can you at least manage to get me home alive, Clancey?"

He nodded and waved, forgetting the bottle of gin in his hand, then jerked it from sight. He offered a shrug, looking sheepish.

She returned it with an annoyed glance, grasping the leather strap and hoisting herself and her cumbersome skirts into the carriage. Lord, she missed her footman, she thought, falling tiredly against the squabs. But it was an expense she could do without, and it was the going without that had grown tedious. She rapped on the ceiling, and after a moment, Clancey managed to gather the reins and send the team forward. The old coot hadn't bothered to light the lamp, yet Katherine did not care, closing her eyes and enjoying the rhythm of the ride. Her body flushed from lovemaking, she wished her lover were here again, tasting her in the darkness of the carriage. Wonderfully wicked, she thought an instant before something stung the side of her throat. She didn't have the time to wonder when the sting raced across her skin from ear to ear. Her breath choked, lungs filling with blood, and she jerked, trying to get air, her hand clutching at her opened flesh to stem the flow. She stared in horror at her blood soaked-hands.

Oh, God. Oh, God, she thought. *Help me. Help me!*

But no aid came. And as the carriage passed beneath the streetlamps, she glimpsed her murderer, relaxed, arms crossed, watching whilst the last of her silent begging went unheard.

Moments later, the killer discharged a round into the ceiling, and as the driver tumbled to the ground, trampled beneath the wheels, her murderer tossed the knife in her bloody lap.

Eleven

Rein clutched her to him, the ride vicious, the wind biting into their clothes. Their pursuers were unrelenting. It told him they wanted his death, not his medallion. And his troubles had caught Michaela in the crossfire. The Bow Street runners and troops nearly upon them, Rein dragged Naraka back, then loped down a sharp incline and hid under a bridge, frowning as he listened to them pass overhead. The rumble of hoofbeats vibrated down to them, and for the first time since they'd begun, he looked at her.

From beneath her cap, droplets of sweat moved down her temple, the cold air halting their descent. Her head tipped back to stare at the slats above, she was oblivious to the dirt sprinkling her face. He saw no fear in her darting eyes, only determination, and a spark of admiration burst in him. Most females would be terrified, but then, she did not understand the danger in her jaunts through the dark.

"Why, Michaela?"

She twisted a look at him, staring for a moment before answering. "I'm certain you have deduced that no one knows I am not abed, like a good little girl."

He didn't crack a smile, did not cease scowling like a demon. "Aye."

"I work a soup kitchen, much to my uncle's disappointment."

She was lying, he could feel it. "You were not coming from any vagrant's kitchen, lass." There were none in that section, to his knowledge.

She furnished him with an affronted look. "Are you calling me a liar?"

"Aye, and a bald faced one at that."

"I shall not waste time convincing you then." She gestured to the stains on her coat, the gloves shiny with grease.

Rein scowled, still not believing her tale, yet he'd no reason to dismiss the possibility, either. Without asking, he knew she'd encounter more than a scolding with her uncle should she be caught, and the last thing he wanted was to see her beaten for any reason.

"I will get you home and inside you rooms, but—"

"I don't need your help," she cut in. "And if you hadn't detained me—"

He gripped her shoulders, bringing her up to meet his face. "Make no mistake, Michaela, you would have been killed. Men hungering for blood care little about killing a filthy little street urchin to get at their true prey."

"Are you saying they were after you?"

The less involved in his affairs, the better. " 'Tis hardly the matter. I am armed, you are not."

"And you are a man, I am not, is that it? I am helpless—"

"Enough!"

She blinked at his icy tone.

He glanced quickly about and above, praying they did not alert anyone. His pale gaze fell on her like a hammer. "By the gods, you are a troublesome female." He drew a calming breath, resisting the urge to shake her. "I know you are not helpless—I've the scars to prove it—but you cannot risk your life so carelessly." He did not want to ask, damn he would not. He did. "Especially not for a lover who'd leave you to fend alone."

"A liar, stupid, and now a whore? Aught else you wish to call me?"

"You know I meant no such thing," he snarled.

She tipped her head. "Do I?"

"Michaela . . ." his voice held a wealth of suppressed hostility. Did she hide a lover?

"I do as I must. I'm sure you can understand that."

For a damned soup kitchen? "Do not let me find you in the streets again. Or I will not be so accommodating."

He would turn her over himself, she realized, her eyes narrowing on his sharp features. Well, then, she simply would not cross paths with him again.

"And, what might I ask, were you doing so far from the wharf?"

Killing a man, he thought, yet refusing to respond. "Apparently," he said, " 'twas not far enough!" He forced her around, grabbed the reins, and moved from under the bridge and up the hill. A carriage barreled past, driving them back into the trees. He cursed viciously, wishing he'd never laid eyes on the lass.

"There was no driver. Shouldn't we . . do something." His look warned her not to press him. Then the skies opened up, rain drenching them to the bone within moments.

"Goddess, save me from this night," he growled under his breath and burst onto the road.

In silence they rode, the gallop driving her buttocks into his groin. Rein ignored it, ignored that she was brave and enchanting, and how tempting it was to have her near and focused on his anger, that she was reckless and obstinate and could have been riddled with shot simply because she had the unfortunate chance of encountering him. It reminded him that she was beyond his limits, even if his mission put them apart, and he concentrated on maneuvering in the dark.

She fidgeted, trying to force a space between their bodies.

"Be still."

"Your medallion, 'tis poking me."

His body went still as stone behind her. "What?" He slowed the mount.

"Your medallion, the battle reward. I saw it when I was taking out the bullet."

He gripped her shoulder, forcing her around to meet his gaze. "What know you of this?"

She sketched his features, sharp and dark and splattered with rain. "My uncle has one like it."

Oh, God. His first thought was her uncle was a candidate and that they were related. It made his stomach churn. His second was that if she breathed a word of it, the men prepared to kill him for the evidence would kill her.

"Swear to me you will tell none of its existence."

"But—"

He shook her. "Swear to me."

"If you swear to keep my adventure this night to yourself?"

His beautiful lips curled into a menacing smile, sending a foreboding chill down her spine. "Aye. A bargain." He slid the medallion around to fall on his back, then dug his heels in, and Naraka lurched into the darkness again.

The silence was tense and splitting as he cleared the edge of the property and followed her directions to the side of the house. He halted and, through the rain, stared up at the window.

"Well, you cannot get back that way."

"I most certainly can."

He slid her a glance. "I will not have the remains of my evening ruined by the revolting task of scraping you off the ground in a damned puddle."

"Perish the thought, Rein. Wouldn't want to soil those pretty clothes, eh?"

He snickered, then dismounted and looked up at her. Her lips pressed into a tight line, she followed, ignoring his offered hand and dropping to the ground. She slipped in the mire, catching herself on the saddle.

She stared up at him, yet his face wore no expression, showed no emotion. It irritated her.

"Can you get to your rooms through the kitchen?"

"Aye, but the doors are locked."

Grabbing her hand, he moved along the edge of the wall, around trees and shrubbery, pulling her like a child led to her punishment. She jerked free, glaring at him when he looked back. Rein eyed her, then continued. The house was black with silence, their footsteps on the wet ground stunning in the stillness. Rein ducked low and moved to the rear door. Despite their animosity, Michaela hugged his back, peering around his shoulder as he pulled a metal stick from inside his boot. He inserted it in the lock, his fingers scarcely brushing over the latch.

"How do you propose to get it—"

The door sprang softly.

"—open?" She gaped at the door, then him.

He shrugged. "Must not have been locked well enough."

She'd done it herself, she knew it was secure. "A master thief, too?"

He smirked. "No more than you."

"That I highly doubt," she said, moving around him to stand. The door creaked and discreetly he waved his hand near the hinges. The door swung wide without sound. She stood just before the threshold, staring at him, feeling a hundred different emotions and not wanting a single one to pierce her thoughts.

"You'd best get inside before someone feels the draft."

She nodded, yet did not move.

"Leave, Michaela, please."

Her brows drew down. His tone was tight and hissing.

"I will not resist all I must if you do not go. Now."

Her features softened. For all his ranting at her, he was a gentleman, standing there in the rain, his cape limp, his tricorn doing little to protect his face whilst she was shielded under the porch. He'd saved her life this night, again, and though she knew she could have managed, albeit likely spending the night in a rubbish barrel or something as loathsome, she owed him.

"We have a pact then?"

He took the metal stick and poked his thumb, holding up his bloodstained digit. Smiling tenderly, she offered her finger, pressing it into the sharp point. Thumbs pressed, they stared, the rain saturating them and pooling in a river around their feet.

"A silence for a silence."

"Aye," she said. "Someday you might tell me why?"

His features hardened suddenly. "Nay, I will not." Abruptly, he took a step away.

Confused, Michaela slipped behind the open door, peering around the edge as he moved farther away, then stopped, his back to her, his head bowed. Sheets of rain buffeted him, his cloak, his wide back, a funnel of water poured from the curve in his tricorn. Yet still he did not move, hands clenched, one beating his thigh, and Michaela felt her breath lodge in her throat as she waited.

His every instinct screamed that he should keep walking, that to tarry would delay more than his immediate plans. That to remain he danced the thin line between losing the command of his emotions and senses he'd taken years to cultivate—and his complete dive into a hopeless situation. For the sake of one untamed lass with a bit of refreshing defiance. For the simple act of touching her and feeling her touch him back. He closed his eyes, willing his resistance to flourish and protect him, protect her.

Then, suddenly, he turned, and in three strides was upon her, his arms around her, her thinly clad body pressed to his hard length. She gasped at the shock, moaned at the pressure, and tipped her head back. He wasted no time and pushed his fingers under her cap, dragging it off, letting her hair uncoil in a heavy rope, all whilst his pale gaze searched her features as if committing them to memory, and the sensation drove an arrow of longing through her, surrounding her, smothering her, charging her insides with heat and purpose and hunger. Oh, the hunger. It was wild and reckless and ready to be opened, but she could not, not ever.

"I see more in your eyes that you want," he growled in a silky voice.

She scoffed uneasily. "You see naught but your own fancy."

He smiled with tender humor. "Do I?" As if to tell her again without words, an unnamed sensation melted from him into her, warming her cold skin as if he'd touched every private inch of her. Her body felt stroked and coddled, enflamed with fresh passion and tightening down on the very core of her. She gasped, her knees softening.

"A bargain we've struck this night, manslayer. Vowed in blood." His voice was rough. "It dies with me."

'Twas intimate, infinitely so, this covenant pledged and sealed in the dark and the rain. "And with me."

He arched a brow, as if she'd no notion of what it meant to give her life for the sake of honor. Silly man.

His broad hand cupping the back of her head, he angled his own and she knew he would kiss her, knew she would finally feel that power of it again. Oh, again. His mouth fitted securely over hers, possessive and heavy. And she opened. Without hesitation, without fear.

Rein knew this might be his last chance, his only chance to taste her, to match his memory with his reality, and it was more intense than he'd ever dreamed. For a splintered moment, he hid nothing from her, unleashing the capped energy he'd crushed and packed beneath the surface. And she accepted him, tongue driving into his mouth, her hand seeking beneath his cape and coat to the wrap around his waist. He groaned, pressing her snugly, his body pulsing and warm for her, to be inside her, moving gently, then stronger and stronger still. He craved more than a taste, and the opening of her energy gave him a feast. His images fell into her, and Michaela saw them, not knowing from whence they came. 'Twas earthy and rich, the passionate scenes flickering in her mind. She did not want them, fought them, but they came, bodies bare and writhing, mouths meeting flesh, and tongues stroking in places she never knew would bring pleasure. And she still didn't know why, would never know and ceased asking "why this man, why only him?", and in the recesses of her mind, in the hopeful spot that still dreamed, she surrendered.

His lips moved hotly over hers, his mastery coming again. She wanted no man in her life, could not afford any attachments, but stole this one moment, for it came for once without the shame, the revulsion. It came into her purely, without demands, empty of lies or guilt or coaxing, and Michaela arched herself harder, drove her hands up his strong back and touched the medallion.

And she swore, this time, he touched her soul.

His mouth moved back and forth over hers, anxiously, unbroken, as he lifted her, pressing her to the doorjamb, and brazenly she bent her leg to fit him tighter to her. The feel of his arousal spun heat through her, the masculine length detailed against her thread-bare breeches. And still she felt only passion. Sweet and hot and tight. Then suddenly he drew back, groaning at the separation, cupping her face and breathing heavily as he gazed into her eyes.

Something glittered there, for fraction of a heartbeat, making his pale-blue eyes darker, smoldering. "Go inside and to your rooms. Be safe, manslayer. And if you should need me, I will come to you."

"But how would you know?"

His smile was knowing and sad. "I will."

She swallowed, her eyes bright with her passion, and Rein did not think he could tear himself away, wanted only to gather her close and ride into the darkness with her. Instead, he released her, slowly, drawing out the moment. Then he turned her into the house and closed the door.

He stood there waiting and softly whispered, "Go, Michaela, afore you are found with me." And he sensed rather than heard her watery footsteps.

Michaela hastened to her room, stopping only to remove her squishy boots and draw a deep breath.

I am done for, she thought. *I am a wanton, just as Uncle claimed. I am not worth such cherishing, I am not,* she thought, yet found the safety of her rooms, locked the door and padded to the window. She brushed back the curtain, spying his horse in the dark and she found him, under the canopy of a tree, staring up at her. She would have waited the rest of the night, but knew, and did not know how, that he would remain there, too, until her lights burned out.

Bringing a candle close, she passed her hand afore the flame, once, twice, and only then did he take the steps to mount his beautiful stallion. He limps, she realized, then blew on the wick. She stared through the window, fogging the glass, and when his figure moved slowly away from the house and disappeared into the dark, she sagged against the sill. Water puddled on her floor. Her body shuddered, yet she was warm, and inside, in private feminine places, she felt alive and tingling, swollen and aching.

She closed her eyes, holding the moment close, realizing that one man, in a single instance in the rain, showed her how it felt to be a woman again, a woman sought after, a woman desired.

And in her barren room, she smiled.

Argyle scowled, his gaze following Montegomery's retreat. Damn the girl for getting nabbed by the man, he cursed, and blamed himself. He swung his gaze up to her window, then back to the dark man as he disappeared in the rainstorm. So, they were friends, were they? Argyle wondered if Michaela knew that her run through East End was far less dangerous than tangling with the half-breed tea merchant. He'd have to keep a closer watch on her. She was an elusive, crafty little thing, he thought with a smile as he turned his mount into the barn, and was surprised Montegomery managed to harness her for even a moment or two. Let alone kiss the sense out of her like that.

The courier waited patiently at the back kitchen door, stoic, refusing to speak to no one but Michaela. Mrs. Stockard wrung her hands, peering down the hall toward the Brigadier's study, then up the curving servants' staircase in the rear of the kitchen where Millie roused Michaela. Relief swept her as the girl descended in her nightrail and dressing gown, and, like Cinderella, lost a slipper on the staircase. She darted back for it, shoving hair from her face and lifting the edge of her gown to push her toe in the shoe and Agnes nearly shouted at the lass to hurry along afore the messenger was discovered. Himself was breaking his fast, and although she'd just served him, the man shoveled food too fast for them to waste a moment.

"Agnes?" Michaela overtook the last steps, yawning. "Great God, 'tis scarcely after sunup. Millie said there was . . . a package?" Michaela's brow knitted at the sight of the young man resplendent in black coat, breeches, and tricorn, trimmed in silver and white, his costly waistcoat a mix of the three.

"Mistress Denton?"

He's Hindu, she thought. "Aye," she said warily, wrapping her dressing gown to her chin. The young man, handsome and slender, kept his eyes locked with hers as he stepped forward. There was a familiarity in him, the way he held himself, and when she realized why, her breath caught. He did not seem to notice and offered the package as if they were the maharaja's jewels, his head bowed between outstretched arms.

She accepted it, setting the wooden box carefully on the worktable, pulling at the silver ribbon and folding it into her pocket. *What have you done?* she thought, frightened and excited. She lifted the lid and inhaled. Poised in the center was an exquisite

orchid, black as midnight and heavily surrounded by white garde-
nias. So delicate, so rare.

A slip of folded parchment lay on the top. Her hand trembled
softly as she reached for it. It bore a heavy wax seal, the imprint,
a simple line drawing of a woman's profile, head only, long hair
in streamers about her throat. *White Empress,* she thought, briefly
running her fingers over the black wax. Breaking the seal, she read
the bold, fluid script.

> *Because I know you will not behave.*
> *R.M.*

She looked questioningly at the youth, yet his face remained
impassive. How odd. A second aroma blended with the flowers,
and she dug deeper, her fingertips brushing metal and wood. She
need not look to know that beneath the pile of rare fragrant blooms
lay her father's pistol. Freshly cleaned and oiled.

And likely loaded.

She smiled, laughing softly to herself and shaking her head.

"I may tell my employer *mem sahib* is pleased?"

"Aye, that you may."

The lad bowed and salaamed just as the servant's bell chimed,
and Michaela glanced at the board. Uncle Atwell's study. She
waved at Agnes to respond, and when she turned back to the youth,
he was gone, his mount tearing across the lawn and sending him
quickly into the trees.

Twelve

From the floor aside the bed, Rahjin watched her master arch
and thrash, mewling like a newborn kitten with her concern. The
candles and grease lamps sputtered as he tossed on the bed, the
sheets twisting to swaddle him like a child. Images appeared and

receded, colliding in his brain to soothe him one moment and torture him the next.

She was warm and supple against him, their bodied joined, his hardness sliding thickly into her soft, wet flesh. She gasped, calling his name, touching his face, his chest, then grasping his hips to pull him deeper inside her. She was extravagant and hot, and when he bent to take her lips, she choked, her body suddenly covered in blood, thick and dark rivers streaming over his hands. On his knees, her body clutched to him, her head lolling loosely over his arm, he stared into lifeless hazel eyes, then at the blade in his hand. Rage speared him like a dagger. Nay, nay! Not her, he thought wildly. Not her. Like a wounded beast, he threw his head back and howled into the night.

Rein startled awake, blinking, and instantly realized it was his own voice breaking through his dreams. Sweat soaked the sheets and dripped down his chest as he sat up. The grease lamps ceased flickering. Rahjin perched on the edge of the bed, her paw weighting the mattress. Rein ignored the cat and, folding over, cupped his throbbing head in his trembling hands, then raked his hair off his face. He shuddered, hard, forced his mind to put the images where they belonged. Dreams. The free will of the mind. Yet he was not one to dismiss the significance of it. Tossing back the covers, he swung his legs over the side of the bed, his heart still pounding with fear.

By the gods, he'd no energy for this, for the strength of denial, for the want in him. Since kissing her again, he'd tried to put her from his mind, cast his need elsewhere. Success had reached him until she unleashed on him with all the innocent beauty she possessed. He'd wanted it to go forever and he wanted it to vanish, leave him be. His right to it did not exist. Mayhap the dream was telling him thus? That if he pursued even a secret pact with her, it was she who'd perish, not him.

He tipped his head back. Sweat trickled in rivulets down his temple, his throat.

He'd too many people who depended on him for their survival to fall waste to lust now. Rein thought of his business, the people laboring in the fields, the simple homes spread out around his plantations. He held tight to the reflection as he pushed off the bed, padding to his clothes. He washed and dressed quickly, then with the contracts and manifests tucked under his arms, he headed topside.

Strange dream or nay, he'd appointments to keep, goods to sell. A father to find.

Christian Chandler crooked a smile at the big Arab who escorted him into Rein's cabin. "Your cabin boy?" he said archly, with a look at Cabai, and could have sworn the eunuch finally smiled as he backed out of the room.

Rein stood behind his desk, his shirtsleeves rolled back, an astrolabe in his hand. "Of sorts."

"Damn me, Rein," he said finally looking around. " 'Tis a bloody palace in here."

" 'Tis merely comfortable."

Chandler let his gaze move over the rich appointments. A captain's cabin was normally the finest aboard, yet this was decadent in comparison to any other he'd seen. Rein's desk was a teak monument to Japanese craftsmen, the oxblood leather chair worn pale, and he suspected the piece belonged to his father, Ransom. A long table surrounded by several chairs lined the left wall near the door, the port hull was covered with locked cabinets and windowed shelves till it met the commode and the edge of the bed. Hellova bed, he thought, four posted and draped in blue netting. His gaze moved across the room, past the desk and blue horsehair settee to the gleaming mahogany chifforobe. Huge silk pillows were scattered on the floor near a brassier, a copper tub polished clean and tucked in the farthest corner.

Though it spoke of comfort, the heaviest objects harnessed to the floor and walls with bolts and straps, Christian wondered why he resided in the floating room when he had a house and apartments in the finest section of London.

"Good God!" Christian took a step back as the black panther slithered from beneath the aft window bench and prowled across the room.

Rein smiled at his wide-eyed look as the cat curled around his legs. "Rahjin, you're scaring His Grace." Rein ruffled Rahjin behind the ears.

Chandler stiffened, clearly affronted.

"Go to work." The great cat moved past, pausing to stare and bare her fangs at Christian, then sauntered out of the cabin like a princess leaving her royal chambers.

Rein walked to the far cabinets, spreading them open and selecting brandy. He poured two glasses, and with them cupped in his hand, gestured to the settee. Christian still stared at the open door.

"Where did you find it?"

"She found me." He offered him the glass. "What has brought His Grace to the docks?"

Always to the point, Christian thought, sipping lightly. "The Brigadier did not serve on the *Camden*. He was assigned to the *Ogelthorpe,* though there is some question as to whether the man ever set foot aboard. It seems young Denton and the sea did not mix well enough."

Rein slid behind his desk and into the chair, flinging a leg over the arm. "No legs for it, eh?" he said, trying to imagine the Brigadier, a young lieutenant in pristine uniform retching his rum ration all over a freshly swabbed deck. He couldn't, yet the information sent relief easing down his spine and he swallowed a healthy draught of brandy to hurry it along. Living with the notion that Michaela was somehow related to him, be it cousins or nay, had nearly driven him mad with revulsion. Well, now that his mind was at peace, what was he to do about the fantasies plaguing him?

Christian sat on the small couch across from him, balancing the snifter on his knee. "He'd taken to land after that. Should have stayed on the sea, though. Richard outshined him far too much to make his career noteworthy."

Rein cared less of the man's career or his insecurities. The latter he recognized in the man the instant he met him. He bullies to feel strong, he thought, recalling the bruise he'd left on Michaela's jaw.

"Now . . . why did you ask?"

It had taken him two days of weighing the ramifications of involving Christian in his affairs, though the less anyone knew the better. However, this was one piece of information Christian's affluence could unearth without raising curiosity whilst Rein was forced to respond to more questions as to why he wanted to know.

"Moments afore I departed the ball, he'd inquired after hiring one of my ships." Which was true enough, he thought, and likely timed it so none could overhear such a request. "Though he would not say why."

Christian's gaze narrowed. "You refused him, didn't you?"

"Aye." At the time, he was in no mood to grant any request. "Naught moves on my ships without my knowledge." Denton had implied that, upon hiring, he'd sail it himself. The idea was preposterous, and Rein had no intention of relinquishing a ship, at any cost, so the Brigadier could relive his less than stellar sea career. "I'm surprised to find you traveling alone, Chris." He looked at him over the rim of the snifter, and redirected the subject off himself. "What of Lady Buckland? I'd have thought she would be pinioned to your side."

"Odd that," he said with tight brows. "I've not seen her in days. Sent a note by twice with no response. Shame. She was a smashing bit of fun."

Rein shrugged carelessly. "Mayhap she found another protector?"

"She only wanted you."

Rein scoffed, suddenly disliking this discussion. "A fascination, naught more. I've not had so many women as to sport the reputation anyone claims."

Chandler smirked. Forthright and honest as they came, he thought. "I know, I know, but it drives a man's pride all to hell to bed a woman and know she wants another."

"If it makes you feel better to believe that, then do so."

Chandler's lips worked, then broke into a wide smile. "Aye, it does." He finished off the drink as he stood, then set the glass aside. "Better that than thinking I could not satisfy her."

Rein unfolded from the chair. "No man will, I fear." He followed him toward the door, through the passageway and above deck. The late afternoon sun slipped behind the ships anchored in the harbor, giving the wharf a golden glow and hiding the squalor.

"Awful lot of soldiers about, aren't there?" Christian said as they moved toward the rail.

Rein agreed. Since last night, the red coats were bright blotches against the dull gray and browns of the quay. "Searching out rebel lairs no doubt." A bit of gossip sent the entire realm into panic, and though Rein rarely listened, his father's friend Nickolas Ryder was in the thick of it somewhere in the city.

Temple called out as he strode briskly down the long, uneven walk toward the *Empress*.

Rein frowned at the man's unusual haste. "Late for a rendezvous, Temp?"

He waved in front of his face, overtaking the gangway and dropping to the deck. "She's dead."

Rein folded his arms, waiting for the rest. For a split second he thought it was Michaela he spoke of, and his chest clenched.

"Katherine. Lady Buckland. Murdered."

Rein swore and unfolded his arms. Chandler paled, raking his hand over his face.

"You're certain?"

"That she's dead, aye. As to the cause, nay. Happened a couple nights ago, I heard."

"They have a suspect?" Chandler asked.

"Several, apparently." Temple made a circling motion between them. "And all three of us are among them."

Thirteen

The Bow Street runners came for him in the dead of night. Rein thought it rather amusing, this high drama. He'd expected it, of course, warning his crew not to seek retaliation. The entire city wanted to see justice and he was, by virtue of poor timing, a decent suspect. And as he sat, unbound and watching the chief magistrate pace, Rein stretched his legs out.

"If you are unprepared . . . ?"

Sir Henry turned his head, glaring. "You were the last person to see Lady Buckland alive and were seen leaving the area in all haste."

"Hardly accurate, wouldn't you say, m'lord? Since your runners and troops were all over the city then." He arched a brow. "And Katherine's killer was the last one to see her alive."

A couple of rough men in worn dark clothing stepped forward.

Rein spared them a mild glance, looking them up and down, then turned his attention to the magistrate.

"Our sources say you had an argument a few days ago."

"I did."

"Might I ask what it was about?"

"Nay, you may not." He would not speak ill of Katherine, and spared what was left of her reputation.

"Were her last words to you 'love me or kill me'?"

"They were."

"Did you?" a runner asked.

Rein turned his head. "Nay. I did not."

"Yeah, but you were the only one running that night." This came from one of the runners flanking him as the man tapped the blunt end of a club against his palm.

Rein stood, his pale gaze narrowed, glittering. "Seems to me we've been over this before, gentlemen."

"Answer the question!" In a flash, the club came down toward his head. Lord Henry barked a reprimand as Rein caught the blunt end in his fist, wrenching it from the man. He tossed it once, end over end, then, with a thin smile, handed it back. He looked to Henry.

"We have a man outside who says you shot him."

" 'Tis possible. I was fired upon and returned it, 'twas simple as that."

"Why'd he want to steal from you?"

Only Rein's gaze shifted to the runner. "I said naught about thievery, sir."

Henry's gaze swept to the runner, his brows knitting, then looked at Rein. "Why'd they shoot at you, Mr. Montegomery?"

This had nothing to do with Katherine, Rein thought, rising out of his chair. "Mayhap because I'd just won at cards and word got about." The magistrate's brows rose a fraction. "You did investigate my entire evening, didn't you?" 'Twas a bit like prodding the bulls in Spain, Rein thought sadistically. "Of course, you would. You would not drag me in here at this ungodly hour without speaking with those I gamed with that night."

The runner slammed the club against his back, and Rein lurched forward, pain sprinting up his spine. *That will hurt in the morn,* he thought, straightening slowly. Like a snap, he spun, his leg swooping up in a circle, his boot heel connecting with the man's face, whipping his head to the side. Blood sprayed the wall afore he fell to the floor just as the second man lunged, and Rein delivered a sharp slicing blow to his throat that drove him to his knees, then slammed his elbow into the man's shoulder blades. His face hit the floor with a squishy smack.

"Now." Rein picked up his coat, shrugging into it. "If you are not leveling charges, sir . . ."

Just then, the door burst open, Christian Chandler striding in, his clothing haphazard, his skin flushed. He stopped short at the sight of the two runners on the floor.

"Well, Gad, Rein. Dragged out of bed for naught, it appears."

Rein scowled, fastening his coat. How had he known about this?

Chandler's gaze lit on Sir Henry, and Rein saw a feral gleam in the man's eyes he hadn't witnessed before now. "Any more questions, you do so with me present, is that clear?"

Henry bowed. "Of course, Your Grace."

"And my God, man, do it at a decent hour."

"Certainly, Your Grace."

Rein headed toward the door, muttering, "His Grace has his waistcoat on wrong side out."

Chandler looked down and groaned, stepping back to allow Rein passage out first.

"Mr. Montegomery?"

He paused on the threshold, glancing back to find the magistrate staring intently at the runners laid out.

"Have you an alibi for the entire evening?" He met his gaze.

Rein thought of Michaela and said, "Nay. Do you?"

Sir Henry's skin darkened, his lips tight. "Good evening, sir." He nodded. "Your Grace."

The two left, and as soon as they were on the streets, Rein said, "I did not need your assistance."

"I know, but he wouldn't believe me." He inclined his head to the dark, and Rein turned as a figure atop a horse moved out of the shadows. "And he did not comprehend the full portent of ' 'tis late and the earl is sleeping,' apparently."

Rein smiled up at Rusty Townsend. "Apparently."

"Quit yer bellyaching, m'lord. You were done with the gell, anyway."

Rein sent Christian an arched look.

"He strode right into my private rooms. She took the intrusion rather well, I think."

Rein's lips twitched at the image, and swung his gaze back to Rusty.

"Runners ain't known for their gentleness, Rein." He shrugged his beefy shoulders. "Didn't want to see that pretty face ruined."

Rein sketched a bow of thanks. "I don't think 'twas my face they were after."

Rusty Townsend nodded, his smile not quite reaching his eyes as he tipped his head and wheeled about.

"I'd been questioned, too," Chandler said from his side.

Rein cast him a glance. Aye, he thought, and the runners likely came to him with hat in hand and his best manner afforded, certainly not dragging him from his bed in the middle of the night to beat the stuffing out of him.

There was more here than poor timing and gossip. This was his father talking to him without saying a word.

Liveried servants swung open the theater doors, yet their pace staggered the instant they saw the deluge of rain, the slow roll of carriages down Drury Lane. Rein shouldered his way past the attendees, the cloying meld of fragrances and acerbic stares. Sweeping his cloak over his shoulders and donning his tricorn, he skirted the crowd toward the farthest end, toward privacy, away from prying eyes. Reaching inside his greatcoat, he withdrew a cheroot, then rummaged in his pockets for a flint, lighting the tip. He drew a long pull, exhaling, watching the gray smoke curl in the misty air.

'Twas not worth it, he thought, bracing his shoulder against a stone column and gazing out into the carriage-congested street. He shrugged deeper into his cloak, cursing his methods to uncover the truth of his parentage. He'd gone about this as discreetly as possible, yet the admiralty of England guarded her secrets, especially those of indiscretion, and now it was the equivalent of seeking a stone on a shore. Yet he did not consider the threat to his life or how easily it could touch others. Sweet thunder, he thought, if Michaela got caught in it . . . He dismissed the notion, and would do his level best to keep their meetings secret.

Clenching the smoke between his teeth, he pulled on his gloves.

"Well, that was dull as all bloody hell."

Jerking the cheroot from his mouth, he slanted a side glance as Temple approached. "You did not have to remain for the entire performance."

"And miss the stir you cause?"

"You sound like a child with his own sack of comfits," he muttered, unamused.

" 'Tis rich, man, admit it. If they sniveled any more on you, you'd be slobbering wet. Who'd have thought being in the tea business would become so lucrative." Temple glanced at the entrance, watching three members of Parliament leave the theater. The lot was rude enough, and pompous enough, to gesture toward his employer.

"Only since the Colonists dumped theirs," he inclined his head toward the group, "in the Boston harbor." Rein tipped his head a fraction, acknowledging them, and they nodded collectively, smiling a bit too eagerly. He turned his attention to the rain-soaked streets. Theatergoers crowded under the cover of an awning, alighting into carriages to bring them safely home. He was in no hurry. This evening lacked the success he'd hoped, and his disappointment made him poor company.

"Ahh, I won't be . . . ah, joining you on the ride home."

Rein looked at Temple, then beyond to the woman in red, her fan poised to shield the lower half of her face. Yet her eyes were feasting on Temple like a pagan in need of a quick sacrifice. Though she was elegantly clad, Rein recognized the look in her eyes. Desperation. *She will eat Temp alive,* he thought, then leaned close. "Remember the discussion we had about your taste in women."

Temple grinned. "She had her hand in my breeches through the second act."

Rein's look was mild. "And here I thought you'd left my company because I hadn't washed sufficiently." Seeing as his warning would go unheeded, he added, "Mind your purse, man, and take the carriage."

The conveyance rolled to a stop before them, the stark white symbol of the White Empress Company emblazoned on the gleaming black door.

Temple's brows lifted. "You are certain?"

"At least 'twill offer privacy." The way the woman was looking at Matthews, it was doubtless they'd reach the corner before he was well ensconced between her thighs. "I can rent another."

Temple thanked him and leapt to open the door, gesturing gallantly. The woman swept down the steps, pausing before Rein. Her teeth-grinding sweet perfume rose up to greet him, and he brushed his knuckles beneath his nose, thinking of lemons. She went up on her toes and pecked a kiss to his cheek, drawing the attention of more than one person.

The buzz of conversation increased. She left his side, dashing to the carriage, her hand riding mischievously across Temple's chest before she ducked into the conveyance. Slowly it moved into the stream of traffic.

"Frightfully nasty night, Rein. Need a lift?" Lord Chandler said, gesturing to the retreating carriage as he approached, a young woman in opulent gold on his arm.

Rein frowned, his gaze moving between the two. "I'll manage," was all he said, offering the earl a cheroot, then resuming his position against the stone column. Christian introduced his escort, Lady Brandice Coldsworth, accepting the smoke, yet as he made to light it, the lady whispered to him, casting uneasy glances at Rein as she did. Chandler's gaze flew to Rein's, irritation tightening his lips as the woman withdrew and joined a group of her familiars.

"My apologies, Rein."

"I've grown accustomed to driving young ladies away." His lip curved. "She is young, even for you, Christian."

Christian looked as if asked to swallow pins. "Gad, man, don't start a rumor. She's my ward, for pity's sake." He drew on the smoke and glanced her way, a little annoyance in his tone. "She's a timid thing, though. A recent fall from her mount gave her a scare, and with all the rot about Katherine and the suspicion that one of the rebels did her in, 'tis understandable."

Rein swung his gaze around.

"They found her driver. Shot and trampled."

Rein had seen worse in his lifetime, yet winced at the image. "Damn shame."

"Any death is a waste, Christian."

"Any speculations?"

"One must begin with the motive, and the suspect . . . will come."

A sudden tingling swept Rein's skin, his faculties immediately alert. His gaze moved discreetly over Christian's shoulder. His chest tightened. Amidst several men and women, Michaela stared across the expanse of humanity, her bright gaze pinning him where he stood. Never in his life did he think that simply looking at a woman could give him such pleasure.

He nodded cordially. She returned it with all discretion, her hand moving to the green silk of her bodice, her fingers touching the décolletage, and he knew she secreted his blade between those lovely plump breasts. The thought made him smile privately. Her cheeks stained bright, and the sensations he'd fought for a sennight rushed forward, the heat, the feel of her pressed to him, her untamed response in the dark and rain. The moments hammered him in his dreams, through his day, souring his mood, driving him mad with need until short of pounding into a whore, he'd abandoned his work and took to the theater this night.

And now the object of his unsatisfied lust stood only yards away. It might as well be leagues, he thought, yet perversely wondered if she'd attended with her uncle or one of a dozen British officers or gentlemen standing close. He spared them a quick glance, recognizing Cassandra Whitfield and her brothers hovering protectively around their dark-haired sister. Lady Coldsworth moved into the nest of women. His gaze swung back to Michaela, standing a bit off to the side, fidgeting, and he focused on her, sensing her discomfort around so many people.

"Rein?"

He looked at Chandler, praying his expression was bland.

"Who's caught your eye? Cassandra?"

"Mind your own, Your Grace," Rein warned. "Or I will start that rumor." The Whitfield girl was just that, a girl nearly half his age, yet as Adam Whitfield called out to them, offering champagne, Rein's concern was Michaela. Urging Christian on, he hung back, not trusting himself to hide their acquaintance well enough. Not when he wanted to push his way between the throngs of people and kiss her madly.

Rein remained where he was, the rain's mist dampening his cloak. He waved off the champagne and continued to enjoy his cheroot, practically spitting out smoke rings when Major Winters moved up behind Michaela. He wished he could hear the conversation, and ground his teeth nearly to powder when the man placed his hand familiarly on her waist. Then his lips curved when she twisted his fingers back unnaturally and moved toward Lady Whitfield.

Michaela felt the major's gaze as if it scratched down her back, and she accepted the flute of champagne, feeling guilty for even drinking the stuff when she knew there were people starving in the East End. She looked at Winters, then drained the glass quickly.

"Thank you, Randi."

"I saw him touch you. He's insufferable," Cassandra said with a glance beyond her to the major. "Look how he goes after Lady Coldsworth."

Like a hungry goat, she thought. "Mayhap we should warn her?"

"Oh, I don't think so. She looks awfully solemn tonight, doesn't she? And Lieutenant Ridgely looks like a reasonable deterrent. He's so close to Brandice, he will inhale her skirts."

Michaela had to laugh at that. "The major is not above pulling rank."

"What a clod. How your uncle tolerates his insolence is beyond me."

"Me, too," she said, trying to look anywhere but at Rein. Yet she could not, her resistance failing miserably. Through lowered lashes she let her gaze slide over him, his tall physique, and she remembered the feel of that body against hers, that chiseled, hard mouth going soft on hers. He looked dashing in his black evening clothes, his tall jack boots enhancing his long legs. Not a man in the crowd compared to him, his sleek form and dark features. The exotic lingered like a vapor about him, a lazy cat on the edge of his playground. And always prepared to pounce.

"And here I thought 'twould be another evening of horrible acting, incessant talk of the Guardian foiling yet another plot, and too little food." Cassandra elbowed her. "He is intriguing, isn't he?"

Michaela dragged her gaze to Cassandra and arched a tapered brow.

"Montegomery," she supplied in a whisper. "So dark and mysterious. And he's been staring at you."

"That I doubt." At least she hoped he wasn't.

"Sort of sad, seeing him always on the outskirts like that."

"I think he chooses to be there, Randi." He chooses to be anywhere he desires. *Including in your arms,* a voice said, the memory of being there sending a bolt of desire down to her toes.

"I don't think so."

Michaela blinked, praying no one noticed the sudden flush to her skin, and looked at her, waiting.

"He is such an ominous creature. Too misanthropic. Though he has the right."

Michaela's brows knitted. "Speak up, Randi. Clearly I am missing a bit of gossip here."

" 'Tis not gossip, but the truth."

"Randi!" came hotly. She'd no patience for intrigue just now.

"Oh, dear." All teasing fled as she swept closer, lacing her arm with Michaela's, her voice low. " 'Tis sad, really. The horrible mess about his wife."

"Wife?" Michaela gasped, mortified she'd kissed a married man. And furious with him for not mentioning the fact.

"He was very young, I understand. She was found in their bed, blood everywhere. Enough to make puddles. Her throat—"

"I prefer not to hear the grisly details." Michaela paled, her knees the consistency of a Christmas pudding.

"And he was jailed for it."

"You're not saying he . . . killed her, are you?" *Nay, oh, please, nay.*

"Who's to know for certain?" Cassandra shrugged. "He spent quite some time in Newgate until a witness appeared. Most believed he's paid the man to corroborate his story. He was exonerated, my brothers said, but the damage was already done." Cassandra's expression softened with sympathy as she stared at his tall, dark figure in a sea of white wigs. "Poor man."

Michaela swallowed. Murder. She could not imagine it, and tore her gaze away, refusing to hunt for guilt. 'Tis false. Cassandra was notorious for embellishing a tale or two, she reasoned.

Cassandra's brother approached. "You're up to mischief, I can tell, Cassandra."

She leveled him a smirk. "You know . . . had you a wife you would not be in my business so often, Adam."

"How can I find a bride when you occupy all my time?" He tapped her nose, smiling, and Michaela wondered what would it be like to have so many people love you.

"You've done business with Montegomery, haven't you?"

His gaze narrowed. "Aye."

"Well, tell me about him."

"Polite ladies do not discuss gentlemen in public." His gaze bounced between Michaela and his sister.

"She asked, not I," Michaela defended, waving and casting a look elsewhere.

"I'm guilty, yet for tonight we won't be polite." She pinched his side, but couldn't get anything but cloth between her fingers. "Damn."

"Cassandra!" he hissed.

"Is it true, then, that he lives on an2 island somewhere?" she was quick to say. "Owns plantations in Madagascar and Mozambique?"

"Aye. And he eats children for snacks."

She very carefully stepped on his toe. He grunted, gently moving her back.

"If you behave, you may meet him."

Her eyes sparked with excitement.

"Nay." The pair looked at Michaela. "Nay," she repeated. "I do not care to greet him." She couldn't. Not and not blush like a schoolgirl, nor recall the way he kissed her, the way she sank into him like a soft cushion.

"He really is an accommodating fellow, Miss Denton," Adam said, glancing over their heads toward Montegomery. "Well. It seems your uncle has his attention now."

Michaela whipped around, finding Rein deep in conversation with her uncle. Panic swept her, and her fingers tightened in her fan. She felt imprisoned, yet when he shifted minutely, looking beyond Uncle Atwell to her, and he brushed his thumb over his lips, the motion thoughtful, she knew he would keep their pledge. And what kind of promise does one keep with an accused murderer?

"Michaela, you look as if you've seen a ghost."

She glanced away, then at the floor. Cracking good, she thought, alert the entire world.

"You really aren't afraid of him, are you?" Cassandra said, and Adam muttered something about his sister's foolish tales.

She looked at Adam, and knew if she did not attend, all would know something was afoot. "Introductions then." He escorted the ladies close.

Michaela watched Rein greet Adam Whitfield with an open smile and a warm handshake, for a moment completely ignoring her uncle. And she realized she'd missed his charming smile.

Uncle Atwell spared her a glance, then scowled. "My niece, sir. Richard's daughter."

Michaela nodded, holding out her hand. Rein grasped it lightly, tipping over it to place a kiss to the gloved back. She inhaled a breath, her skin darkening.

"Rein Montegomery. Your loyal servant, mistress." His voice was low, a rustle of raw silk sending shivers over her skin. Randi was telling tales, she decided right then. He could not make her feel this way and have committed such a crime.

"A pleasure, sir." She dipped a curtsey, and his lips quirked with amusement.

"Fine, fine." Atwell pulled her hand from Montegomery's, nearly throwing it back at her. "Now, leave us child, 'tis private."

Rein's features tightened with anger. "I beg to differ. This conversation is over."

"Fine, come see me at noon on the morrow."

Rein pulled his gaze from Michaela and stared down the British officer. "I've appointments."

"I order—"

Rein's gaze narrowed, the cutting look silencing him. "It seems we've approached this subject before, Denton. My affiliation with England is in her markets, not her brigades."

"Come now, Montegomery," he said graspingly.

Chandler moved forward. "Enough business." He poised the champagne bottle and glasses appeared. "Drink up. 'Tis Adam's cellar we empty." Soft chuckles responded.

Rain splattered the walks.

Carriages loaded and rolled off, and dismissing the Brigadier's heated looks, Rein moved back, away from the gathering, yet unwilling to let such an opportunity be wasted. He watched her, the little spot at her throat drumming her heartbeat, the flush rising up from her breasts to her face, the pour of wine into her lush mouth. The awareness of her was the same as the day he'd met her on the road, pricking and hot, and when she looked at him on the sly, her lashes lowered as if staring at her glass, Rein felt his body pump to life.

Abruptly, she flinched, sloshing her drink over gloved fingers and startling everyone around her. Red with embarrassment, she turned and found Major Winters smiling at her. She did not return it and carefully moved from his touch.

Rein frowned, smothering the unaccustomed possessiveness swelling though him like breaking waves. As much as he loathed the sensation, it came, beating him with the fact that she was beyond him, that the man beside her would likely share her wedding bed. The thought tore him in half.

He stepped out to hail a cab, catching only snatches of conversation.

"Damned rebels ought to be shot as they find them."

"They usually are," someone said.

"I heard she was strangled."

"Nay, shot."

"Must we have this conversation?" came from Lady Coldsworth, who looked ready to swoon and leaned into Lieutenant Ridgely.

"They've been through her things, talked to her servants, I heard. I understand her coach was seen speeding down the north road without a driver."

Michaela's gaze flashed up, colliding with Rein's, and they both knew they'd seen the runaway coach that night.

"Several people have been questioned. It seems Lady Buckland was last seen on the wharf—" Lieutenant Ridgely swung his gaze to Rein. "In your company, Mr. Montegomery."

Only a single black brow arched. "Have you something to say again, Ridgely?" The question sounded more like a threat.

Very softly, Christian Chandler murmured, "Do not say it, son."

The man bristled at the censure. "Well, I heard this morning she was cut. Her throat. Ear to ear."

They collectively gasped.

"Like your wife's."

Rein's features tightened. And out of the corner of his eyes he caught Michaela's reaction, her skin paling, her step back. Briefly he closed his eyes, wishing he could will back the unfortunate timing. When he opened them, he looked straight at Michaela, but there was only horror in her eyes. She knew.

And any trust she had in him disintegrated.

It seemed, he thought defeatedly as he stepped into the cab, his past had finally caught up with him.

Fourteen

His shoulder braced on the mizzenmast, Rein tipped his head back. The sun finally shining down for the first time in days, he absorbed the heat and rays, cleansing the disease running through his body. Ten years came tumbling back with a strength that left him stripped of gentle emotion. He'd tried to avoid this, this ugly resurrection of nightmares and incrimination. Yet the look on her face, of fear and distrust, refused to dissipate, leaving him raw and bleeding, bringing back the moment when people began to shrink from him, panic when he so much as looked their way.

His lashes swept down, his features creasing with an anxiety even his faith could not penetrate.

So he lived in it, held it close and nurtured it to a festering wound, for the coarse reaction would force the desire to be part of something, part of someone, from building again to torture him in the basest of ways. It was how he survived the last, the prison.

'Twould be simpler, he thought, if there were not so much truth to the accusations. That night tried to materialize in his mind, flashes and sound, yet Rein fought the grotesque images, washing his inner sight clean over and over. If they came, he would be lost, he knew. And it had taken him too long to be even civil company for his mates and employees. He would not let it happen again.

Wheels rumbled on the pier, and he looked up as his own coach jostled to a stop, the footman disheveled and irritated as he climbed down and opened the door. Temple spilled from the conveyance, tripping on the step box. Moving to the rail, Rein watched him make his way unsteadily up the gangplank, and for a moment thought he'd land in the brink.

"Good day, Captain." He swept his tricorn off in a deep bow, swaying like a tall pine with weak roots.

Rein folded his arms over his chest, inspecting him from head to boots.

Temple grinned.

Rein did not. The man reeked of wine and sex and perfume. Again.

"Pray tell, did you exhaust the horses and my driver all evening, or did you manage to find a room . . . ?" Rein's words faded when Temple shook his head.

"So sorry. Will apologize to Fergus later."

Rein's expression darkened. "Sweet thunder, Temp, 'tis unhealthy to be this besotted, this careless—"

Temple angled his head. "You are simply jealous."

Rein leveled him a look of utter disgust. "And you, sir, are no better than a two-penny whore."

Temple straightened, gazing steadily back, and Rein saw the defeat in his brown eyes. "Aye," he slurred. "That I am."

"You do not have to be."

"Keep the righteousness for someone who wants it," Temple snarled. "For we, Captain," he gestured between them, "are two of a kind."

Rein's features hardened, and he stepped aside and let him pass.

Michaela balanced the heavy tray laden with a teapot and biscuits, walking carefully toward the study. She'd been serving on and off like this for hours now, the five men sequestered since early this morn. She stared down at the teapot, lost for a moment in the memory of a tall, striking man, rain soaked and forlorn, their thumbs pressed in a secret vow. A fragile trust was born there.

And destroyed last night.

She inhaled a ragged breath, and continued walking down the long hall.

His wife. He'd killed his wife. Denial of it did not exist, for only he knew the truth. Though she'd had no more details than what Cassandra provided, she wanted to believe, oh, Lord, in her heart she wanted to believe, the accusations were unfounded. But he was running that night . . . yet in the same thought, she did not know

Rein well enough to judge, and knew naught at all of the man of ten years hence. Nor what he was capable of now.

And if Lady Buckland died in the same manner, then . . . well, there would be more evidence to the similarities to suit her.

She paused at the door, prepared to use her foot to knock. She stilled, balancing oddly when she head Rein's name mentioned. She put her foot down and leaned close.

Speak up, she thought irritatedly, but they were on the far side of the room, near the brazier. She inched closer, holding the tray to the far left to press her ear to the wood.

"He refused." Uncle Atwell, she thought.

"Well, you were a fool to ask him."

"I beg your pardon?" She could almost see him delivering that how-dare-you look of his.

"He's a criminal."

Michaela's heart fell a bit, and she wondered what they'd requested of Rein. Though she was pleased, albeit a tiny fraction, that he'd refused, she was equally suspicious that these men felt comfortable enough to approach him, for whatever reason.

"And how do you propose we get one? Steal it?"

"As if you could," a familiar voice scoffed. Winters, the disreputable sot.

"Have you one handy? Any of you? With him, there would be little suspicion. He travels dangerous waters constantly."

"His men do. He's rarely in London but twice a year."

"Then we must take it afore she sails."

It? A vessel or a woman about to sail off?

"Impossible, it will not set to water, then."

Ahh, a ship.

There was a strained silence. And then Michaela heard the words that struck her like a blow to her middle.

"Once we commandeer the gold shipment, we will be done with this war."

The tray fell from her hand, crashing to the floor, splattering hot tea and pots of jam and butter. Biscuits and scones rolled into the hall. The door opened abruptly and she sank to her knees.

"Michaela—!"

"Oh, forgive me, Uncle," she sobbed. "It slipped. I tried to knock but couldn't balance the heavy tray. It's ruined," she wailed.

"All of it." She scrambled to right the chunks of broken teapots and chase rolling scones. Brown liquid spilled over her hem.

Agnes appeared at the end of the hall. Michaela looked at her imploringly, and she raced forward, not sparing the Brigadier a glance.

Uncle Atwell grabbed her arm, hoisting her off the floor with a hard yank. "How long were you there?"

Her eyes darted over his face, wide and scared, her expression confused. "I don't understand?" Did she sound stupid enough for him?

"How long?" he roared, shaking her.

"Here, in the house? Why, all morning."

His hand cracked against her cheek, pain exploding through her face. "Answer me!"

Her face burning, she let the tears come. "I don't understand, Uncle. I did as you bade me, the tray and . . . I tried to knock . . ." She gasped for a breath. "But it fell. What else do you need to know?" she hastened to say over a sob, looking, she hoped, utterly perplexed. Out of the corner of her eyes, she saw Major Winters rise from his chair and move forward whilst the other men in the room turned their backs to the incident. But she recognized Rathgoode's pointed beard, and Colonel Prather.

"If you are lying—" he warned, and with a sound of disgust, he thrust her from him and she tumbled to the floor. She stared up at him and thought for a moment that he might kick her. "Clean this up, bring another tray, and be quick about it." He stepped back and pulled the doors closed.

The discussion that followed was heated and muffled, and as Michaela hastened to clean up the mess, she heard, 'she's a trial' and 'a graceless incompetent creature' and several other colorful names for her conduct, along with sympathy for her uncle and praise that he should tolerate such a woman in his house. Swiping at the tears on her cheek, she gathered the broken crockery.

"Oh, miss—" Agnes said, her low tone laced with sympathy.

" 'Tis all right, Agnes. I am sorry about the pots."

"Never you mind that, lovey. You go on upstairs and get yerself cleaned up. I'll do this."

Michaela looked up, sniffling, then nodded. Placing a cracked lid on the tray, she stood and headed to the stairs, her face stinging with the imprint of his hand. She rubbed the blood back into her skin, racing up the steps and hoping the mark would not show.

Argyle will have a fit, she thought, and voice his opinion to her uncle. That will get him fired, and she needed the few friends she had left. In her rooms, she locked the door and moved quickly to the brazier. The heat from the fire below stairs sent warmth up the pipes and into her chilled room. Kneeling near the little stove, she stirred the coals and listened to the sound of voices carrying upward with the heat. It was not often this worked, nor was it clear, but Michaela needed more information, and short of posting herself outside the room again, this was her only recourse.

With her hem, she blotted her face.

"The *Victoria,*" she heard. ". . . thousands of pounds . . . for the snatching."

Pounds of what? Gunpowder? Munitions? Nay. The *Victoria* was a payroll ship, bringing fresh armaments and pay for the ones already fighting in America. Oh, God, she thought. Pounds meant pounds sterling. Gold sovereigns?

She caught senseless bits and almost screamed at them to cease moving about and talk into the stove. Then one courteously did.

"We will have to submit to their demands anyway. 'Twill be over soon."

Was England prepared to give in to the rights of the Americans? Or just these men? And what a weak justification for thievery.

". . . be sailing in three months, and . . . since none of us are the captain, then we must board her."

Michaela inhaled a sharp breath, sinking back on her haunches. They were going to attack the payroll? How could they even think to take funds meant to feed and clothe their own troops? Why, when those soldiers did only as they were ordered: to serve and die for king and country.

For a moment she weighed giving information to the enemy against stealing pay from troops who'd already gone without proper rations for months. There were five British officers prepared to let their own countrymen go hungry, send their families into the debtors' prison or to their death for their greed when they already had more than most.

And if they attacked the ship, they would kill everyone aboard to cover their tracks. Rage built in her and she clenched her fists.

She wanted nothing but to see them shot for this, yet recognized it was only a plan, a conversation, and, without proof, she could not go to anyone of influence.

Yet until they actually moved on the vessel, she was powerless to stop them.

But Nickolas could.

He was the only one who'd relay this to the right people, the ones who could watch and wait and mount an attack when they moved on this plan.

The conversation grew hummed and low, whispered with the tint of excitement, and she bent closer, straining to hear. The fire in the brazier crackled and Michaela frowned sniffing, glancing about. Her dress was afire.

"Sweet merciful—"

She patted the burning fabric, but it spread, flaming. Cracking good, she thought, leaping to her feet and racing to the pitcher on her commode. The short motion fanned the flames and she grabbed the pitcher, emptying it on her gown. The fabric smoked and dripped and she sighed, rubbing her forehead and leaving a smudge of soot. 'Twas truly irritating, she thought. The way she attracted misfortune like dust, and standing in the murky puddle, she wondered how she'd ever survive this revolution without getting herself killed in the process.

Michaela moved back to the brazier, careful to keep a safe distance, and listened until the men departed. Then she climbed the back stairs to the attic, a colored scarf in her hand.

Fifteen

Michaela felt as if she were sitting atop a ticking clock as she hung over a bubbling kettle, dipping the ladle deep and pouring it into a wooden bowl. She looked up to hand it to the next child, yet this one was dark, his skin the color of coffee with cream, his hair black and long and wild. She gazed into his brown eyes and saw blue, pale and bright and defeated. Something slammed into her heart, bruising it until it ached. It was so hard to imagine the same man who'd held her face in his palms as he kissed her till her knees softened was the same man who could take a knife to his wife's throat.

"We're to feed them, not make them take up floor space," a voice said with an elbow jab to her side.

Michaela jolted and glanced at Cassandra, then the line of poor Irish, Indians, and Jews. She'd no time for this melancholy drivel, she thought, apologizing and serving.

"I feel like a puppy on a leash." Cassandra nodded toward the door. One of her brothers stood close, watching every man who stepped near as if they were a murderer bent on his sister.

"Be thankful you have someone who cares, Randi."

"Caring and smothering are not one and the same." She continued serving. "And what do you call your watch dog?" She inclined her head, and Michaela looked, her shoulders sagging with a groan. Major Winters stood in the doorway, his face wrinkled with disgust as he looked around.

"I call that a boot-licking prig," she muttered under her breath.

Randi paused in handing out a bowl and grinned. "That's one I've never heard."

Michaela blushed, embarrassed. "He's here on his own volition."

"I've seen you set him down, so he must be either in love with you or awfully dull-witted."

"He has no wits to be dulled." And malicious to even come looking for her. She wondered briefly if her uncle had sent him along. After being caught eavesdropping, she considered they'd be suspicious and cover all venues of treachery.

Just then, Father Pete approached, telling them the line of needy citizens was waning and he and the sisters could take over. Michaela swiped her hands on her apron and the two women moved to the washbasin.

Michaela glanced at her father's watch. Though Nickolas would wait at the appointed rendezvous until she arrived, he could not remain in one place for long without terrible risk to the entire network. The double spy threatened them all, and though her life was small in the reality of the rebellion, Nickolas was instrumental. "I must leave for a bit," she whispered.

Cassandra stared at her, frowning. "Without escort?"

"I must, Randi."

Cassandra nodded. "I will take care of it. Go for your cloak and slip out." Her gaze flicked to where it hung on a peg near the rear doors. "I will distract him. My brother will not let him get near enough to do harm," she rushed to add when Michaela's look warned her to be careful.

Michaela dried her hands. Randi caught one, meeting her gaze. "Do not make me regret this."

"I am armed," she whispered, removing her soiled apron and tossing it with the others.

"You are so brave," Cassandra said enviously.

Michaela scoffed. "Or tremendously stupid." Running through the streets again, this time without the disguise of a boy, was an outrageous risk.

"Is Argyle is to come for you?"

She nodded. "The major's arrival is his own problem. Tell him I've shopping to tend."

Cassandra glanced around, finding Winters deep in a conversation with Adam. She met Michaela's gaze. "One day you will confide in me over why you do not simply wed and leave that place and I will listen. Without judgment."

Michaela's eyes watered briefly. She said it out of love and concern, not to pry for gossip. "Thank you, Randi."

"Be careful . . . and I hope he's handsome."

Michaela blinked.

"Whoever you are rushing off to see—"

Let her believe such nonsense, she thought, moving to her cloak as Randi headed to her brother. Good as her word, she faked a stumble and plowed into Winters. He looked startled at Randi's gracelessness, that was usually her forte, his hands immediately going to her slim waist. Michaela didn't wait around for the outcome, slipping beyond the door, rushing out of the alley and into the street, her steps brisk as she headed toward the church. Nickolas had convinced her to entrust herself to the priest there, and though she remained guarded, she kept faith in his decision. She knew Father Joseph, had dealt with him on occasion when he'd gathered clothing and food to be sent to the British subjects imprisoned by the Americans. The British Army would allow the packages past their blockades, and the Americans were generous enough to give them over to the prisoners. She doubted the courtesy was reciprocated, yet it was her only avenue to get much needed supplies into the country, and the Englishmen who sympathized with the rebels would give some of their goods to the ragtag Army.

She reached the church without mishap, entering from the vestibule. A cold pallor hung in the musky air, unwelcoming, and she waited until her eyes adjusted to the darkness. Candles glowed from remote corners, and though she'd not been to church in awhile, it felt sacrilegious to use the hallowed house as meeting place.

She moved forward, whispering for Father Joseph.

From the shadows, the old priest appeared, his movements slow, cautious, as he crossed toward the head of the pews. Michaela dipped, crossed herself, then walked up the center aisle. Father Joseph paused, his hand on the back of a pew as she approached.

"Good day, Father."

"Leave, child." His footsteps dragged as he moved nearer.

She frowned. "I cannot. I'm to meet him here." She glanced briefly around for Nickolas.

His features craggy, his lips pressed to a bloodless white, the priest leaned forward as if to whisper in her ear. She tipped toward him. Abruptly, he fell against her. Michaela stumbled back, grasping his shoulders, and over them, she saw the knife hilt protruding from his back.

"Sweet mercy." She scanned the darkness for his assailant, but his solid weight dragged her to the floor. "Father, *oh, Father.*" She cradled him, wanting to remove the knife yet not daring to injure him further.

"Run, child," he choked against her shoulder, gripping her arm and fighting for his last breath. *"Run!"*

He sagged limply against her and she blinked, inhaling. God have mercy. Michaela scrambled from beneath his weight and ran to the altar, withdrawing her pistol as she darted around it and into the anteroom. Rapid footsteps followed her, and she gathered her skirts, heading for the door. The latch stuck and she jiggled and jiggled, the sound of movement growing closer. She jerked frantically on the handle, her heart pounding. *Oh, please, oh, please,* she wailed silently, and the latch gave. She shoved open the door, busting into the alley and running toward the light, the street, the people, not looking back, afraid of who or what she might see. She met the edge of the corridor, sliding in the mire and gripping the edge of the building. She searched the area, for familiar faces, for troops or runners, then moved quickly into the stream of pedestrian traffic, her head down. She'd gone no more than a block when someone gripped her shoulders. Instantly, she leveled her gun at their stomach as her head came up.

"Nickolas!"

"Megan will be highly upset if you pull that trigger."

She pulled into an empty doorway. "He's dead," she said tonelessly, retucking the pistol. "Father Joseph's dead."

He swore viciously, grabbing her arm and pulling her along the street, away from the church. "Were you seen?"

She thought back a moment.

"Michaela!"

" 'Twas too dark." They moved between the throngs of people.

"Let us hope so." He drew her close, his long strides making her run. "He was after the Guardian."

Her expression did not so much as flicker. She knew the risks coming in. "I can take care of myself. Did anyone know we were to meet there?"

"Nay, but 'tis a rendezvous for others. This changes things, Michaela, greatly. Father was helping me weed out our traitor. If I need to get you out, be prepared for me or . . . the Merchant. No one else, agreed?"

She frowned, perplexed, breathless to keep up with him. "Aye, of course, but you have not heard the worst of it."

A cry hailed, people shouted and wailed, the sound drifting from only a block away. A squad of troops raced toward the church.

"Go. Go," he said when she tried to talk, already pushing her away. "Meet me in four days at the Red Badger."

She and Nickolas fled in opposite directions, darting between people and carriages, ducking under a vendor's cart for several moments afore heading back into the fray of dwellers. She glanced behind. He was nowhere in sight, and she finally slowed her steps, clutching the stitch in her side.

British troops filed into the streets, grabbing innocent people and inspecting their faces. She hastened her steps, running, walking, running again, and once hitching on the back of a moving carriage, the leap off nearly snapping her ankle. She crossed the avenue to the soup kitchen, relief sweeping her. She rounded the corner, and with the edge of her cloak, she blotted her damp throat and cheeks as she walked carefully forward, searching for Argyle. He was nowhere about. She poked her head inside the dilapidated warehouse, scanning the people looking for a warm spot for the night. Cassandra was gone and she wondered if the major lingered to make himself a nuisance. That, she thought, would be the crowning horror for today.

"Been out shoppin'?"

She yelped and whirled about, pistol aimed. She glared. "Don't do that!" She gave him a shove. "Ever again."

He smiled down at her, catching her shoulders and pulling her close. "I dinna ken what you are up to, lass," he said softly, feeling her tremble. "But let's get you home."

She nodded against his chest, then stepped back, concealed her pistol and climbed into the cart beside him. Argyle flicked her a concerned look, then faced forward and snapped the reins. The cart moved forward, and she slumped against the hard seat, staring out onto the passing scenery. Michaela fought the hard tears burning behind her eyes and sniffled, her mind filled with the image of the saintly old priest with a blade in his back. There was no reason to kill him, she thought, and suppressed anger swelled. They will pay.

Yet she might not have the opportunity, for if the killer saw her, she would be arrested within a day. The thought did not disturb her as much as she'd have imagined. Nor did she doubt the murderer was their double spy, the priest likely recognizing the tainted information had come from the killer, yet Nickolas was at more risk than she. He might have met this operative in person, and, to complicate matters, Nick was not the only rebel leader in England, and although he'd never let on to the fact, the Sons of Liberty mingled with the cream of English society. As much as she knew her life was now in grave danger, Nickolas's was, too. And he had much more to lose.

He had a family who'd miss him.

Now, she thought. *How do I get out of the house and to the Red Badger without Uncle Atwell getting suspicious.* Especially when she had no excuse to leave.

* * *

The blood on his hands was unremarkable, yet, just the same, he snapped out a white handkerchief and rubbed the smudges as he walked. Soldiers brushed his shoulders, not pausing on their race to the crime. His steps slowed and he swallowed. It had been a while since he was forced to kill. The feeling, he thought, was not as distasteful as he remembered. Discarding the stained cloth in the street, he pressed onward. He had other duties to attend. And uncovering the Guardian was only one of them.

Nickolas paced the rented room, raking his hair back off his face. He felt frantic, and he failed the rebellion with worrying. He'd had women working for him before, he reasoned, and found females to be much stronger under tremendous pressure than men, his wife a prime example, but Michaela was like his daughter, and though he knew it was unwise to make the association, especially when her life was in peril, he could not.

And the only way to gain distance was to ask for help. With the double agent infiltrating the network, overcaution and less trust were insurmountable to keeping her alive. His best people, America's most loyal sons—whose job was to do no more than watch and listen—were at his disposal and watching her, for a change in Atwell's household, for suspicious behavior that would alert him that the double spy had seen her the night the priest was killed. And even now, Nickolas waited for word.

He moved to the window, brushing back the curtain and gazing out onto the street below. The isolated inn was far enough away from city traffic to lack the filth and less than reputable guests under its roof, and, on occasion, persons of notoriety ventured inside the tavern below. He hazarded much remaining here for so long, and though Michaela was not expected to arrive for two more nights, he would wait. And if his prayers were not answered, he would go find her himself.

A knock rattled the oak door and Nickolas flicked a glance, removing his pistol from inside his waistcoat, and, dousing the candle, he stepped quietly.

"Aye?"

"Damn it, man, open up!"

Nickolas sighed and pulled the door a fraction, pistol barrel first.

Rein looked down at the gun, then to his friend, all semblance of impatience gone. He looked awful.

Nick stepped back to allow him entry, and Rein closed the door. Rein smiled, offering his hand. "Good to see you, Nick."

"Ahh, when I do not want to be seen." Nick shook it.

Rein frowned. "You're in trouble."

"A bit." He gestured to the small table and chairs set near the fire, and Rein swept his cloak from his shoulders, tossing it to the bed. Nickolas relit the branch of candles, then poured a drink from the decanter in the center.

"I need your help."

"I am scheduled to sail in three days, Nick." Rein sat in the chair near the fire.

"I would not ask if 'twere not life-threatening."

The weight of his words sank in, and Rein slumped in the seat. Nickolas Ryder was his father's friend, one of his dearest, and to deny him felt as if he were betraying Ransom. He closed his eyes briefly, regret sluicing over him like ice water. He'd already done that, and though he wanted to be away, distanced from Michaela and the temptation of her, for the sake of the man who'd raised him, he would remain.

He opened his eyes and found Nick staring, awaiting his answer. "I can send another in my stead."

Nickolas sighed, nodding. "My thanks."

"Your fight is costing you much more than me, Nick." He had a family who needed him, a wife who adored him. Would that he had such bounty, Rein thought, naught even a damned war would keep him from it.

" 'Twould go faster if you would join us."

Rein's lips quirked. "Recruiting?" He shook his head. "I grew up fighting Salé pirates and British slavers. I have no desire to climb aboard the slaughter again."

"I have seen much of war, too. And like Ransom years back, 'tis the atrocities and oppression that drives me now."

"Liar," Rein scoffed. " 'Tis bitter memories and retribution that drives you."

Nickolas jerked back. "Impudent whelp."

"Aye and a bastard, and I have more reason to loathe the British than you, my friend, but your quest for freedom will change naught in my life. I can only endure my time here until I am home again."

Nick's gray brows rose. " 'Tis not the man Ransom raised I see afore me. That man would not turn his back on those who needed him."

Rein's features went taut. "Open your eyes, Nickolas!" he hissed across the table. "That boy left his care years ago and, aye, I turn my back on no one in need. If you do not win your battle, thousands who uphold your ideals will lose. And what will England do for punishment? Yet were I to join you, hundreds would suffer for the lack, for I am responsible for the livelihood of too many innocents who know naught of the Colonies and the damned rebellion. I am their survival. Who is to say this life or that one is worth more? And who am I to say that my beliefs must be theirs and at the cost of all they've labored for, the price?"

The corner of Nick's mouth curved with pride. "Now you sound like Aurora."

"A compliment? God of thunder."

In the smoky light, Nick stared at him. "We will win, you know."

"I do not care." He shrugged. "I said I would aid you, Nick. For Ran's sake, I will get you out of the country—"

" 'Tis not me, but one of my own."

Rein's gaze narrowed. "I am not a nanny for your network of rebel spies."

" 'Tis the Guardian."

Rein's eyes flared and he sank into the well worn chair, staring at the blaze. He sipped, and, out of the corner of his eye, saw Nickolas settle into the opposite chair.

"You son of a bitch."

Nick arched a brow. "I say the same to you."

Only his gaze shifted. He smirked. "You'd have me hide this troublemaker, what?"

"Nay. I'd have you protect them."

Rein cursed.

"The Guardian has been perfectly secreted for a very long time. He witnessed a murder and I will not know, nor even have a suspicion of, whether the killer recognized him for another night or two."

"You are certain the Guardian did not commit the murder?"

"Positive."

"If you're certain this fellow is innocent, then what is he doing now? Hiding?"

"Living." Nick raked his hair. "And likely scared out of their wits."

"They could be arrested at any moment."

"Yet there is no proof. None. Only I know who the Guardian is and what they have brought to this cause."

This cause, Rein thought with distaste. The man was blinded to it, and even now did not see the value of getting the Guardian out of England as quickly as possible. There was no other way to protect the spy. Rein knew what freedom meant to Nickolas Ryder and his fellow patriots. He'd experienced the moment of liberation himself more than once. Bloody hell, Rein could not count the times he'd been thrown into a prison cell or come close to losing his head in the past years. He'd seen and experienced enough blood and death, and it was all war brought.

He'd help. He knew it the instant he'd received Nick's summons, yet he was not going to jeopardize the livelihoods of those in his employ for it.

"What need you of me?"

"To be prepared. Should the Guardian be found out, I need to get him to safety."

"And you do not think to risk my ships and crew and my business to do it."

Nick ignored his bitter tone and said, "You will be discreet. If aught I know of you, Rein, no one will find a trail to your door."

"I am justly humbled. But I've been questioned over Lady Buckland's death, Nick, and have a few runners for distant company."

"They won't touch you. Lord North won't allow it. You are too valuable remaining neutral." Nick's irritation showed in the twist of his lips.

Rein flashed him a sinister smile. "Do not make me regret this." He drained the glass of brown liquid and stood. "And be warned, if the choice comes to you and this spy, 'tis you I will choose."

"Nay!" Nick shot to his feet. "Nay, do not. Swear to me here and now, Rein, you will protect the Guardian."

Rein scowled at his vehemence. "And if I do not?"

Nick's eyes clouded, and in a soft voice he said, "Then I will be forced to kill the Guardian myself."

"Surely not."

"Would you want to see a . . . a fellow countryman tortured?

We both know 'tis exactly what they will do. They have, for no reason at all." His tone sang with bitterness. "I could not wish that on any operative, Rein. Especially not this one."

After several strained moments, Rein offered his word of bond. Nick's relief was overwhelming. He slumped into the chair and rubbed his hand over his face.

"Your loyalty is damned strong, Nick."

"If you ever meet the Guardian, you will understand why."

With the cryptic remark, Nick laid out his plan for contact and pulling the Guardian from the clutches of the authorities, if the need arose.

"I must know who this person is."

"Not until it's absolutely necessary. This alarm may be for naught and I cannot risk it."

"Ahh, the truth comes. You do not trust even me."

He reared back. "Don't be absurd, but if you are ignorant to the identity, you cannot reveal it. Would you have not gone to your death to conceal Ram's identity as the Red Lion?"

"I would die for him, you know that." Rein leaned back in the chair, eyeing him. "But what if something should happen to you? What then? What will become of your precious Guardian?"

"I am not the one in danger. No one knows I am even in England."

"I did. I simply could not locate you."

"You are not the average Londoner," Nick defended.

Rein scoffed rudely. "If you believe I have some ear to the goings-on in this city, you, like all the others, are sadly mistaken. Doors are closed to me." Angered that he would risk so much for some nameless, faceless spy, Rein stood and walked to the door. He looked back at his father's oldest friend. "I await word and will not respond if the summons does not come from you."

Nickolas nodded and Rein left. The door closed softly, and Nick sagged into the chair, listening for the sound of his horse racing away from the inn. When it came, Nickolas wondered if Ransom would forgive him for involving his eldest son.

Sixteen

From the quarterdeck of the *Empress*, Rein watched her sister ship, the *Sentinel*, sail into the harbor. The port authorities were already in the water, heading toward her to check her cargo hold against the manifests. Apparently, suspicion of murder meant he was no longer a trustworthy merchant.

His boot on the bench, he bent his knee and braced his forearm across his thigh, gazing through his spyglass. He recognized the two men, yet none of the officers with them. Benson will be fair and just, Rein thought, though times were unsteady in England and the unrest settled more with the ships than with the lawmakers. He did not want his ships and crew caught in the center.

He was not an English subject, nor was his business under the Crown rule, however Rein was not about to destroy his British contacts by angering the proper authorities for the sake of some war.

England was always conquering some poor, unsuspecting country, regardless.

And now he had to find someone reliable enough to make his crop negotiation meeting in Africa so he could keep his promise to Nickolas. Bloody damn and hell, he thought, wishing the world and its chaos would disappear for a fortnight at least.

"Capt'n?"

"Aye." Still Rein watched.

"He's roused hisself."

Rein snapped the glass shut, tapping it against his chin, staring at the deck before lifting his gaze to Leelan.

Mr. Baynes inclined his head, and Rein straightened to see Temple staggering into the sunlight. He almost winced at the man's pain. Matthews dragged his tricorn low on his brow, shielding his eyes from the sun.

At least he has bathed and wears clean garments this time, Rein thought, moving to the forward rail. "Mr. Matthews!" he called down with more volume and good cheer than necessary.

Temple flinched. "Aye, Captain."

"Get yourself ready to board the *Sentinel*."

Temple blinked, searching the water, then swung his gaze to Rein's.

He approached the quarterdeck ladder cautiously, as if the merest movement vibrated through his body. Leelan chuckled softly behind him. Rein did not doubt it was truth. His brow was perpetually wrinkled.

"Sir?" Temple climbed the first few rungs of the ladder, hanging on to the sides for dear life and swearing never to drink again.

"Gather your diddy and get you aboard the *Sentinel*. She rides with a first mate only, so you have no one to usurp. You are her captain. See that she is unloaded, then well stocked for a month's voyage." As he spoke, Temple's frown deepened, his eyes taking on a wary glint. "Take her first to Madagascar for her cargo, then to Cape Towne. I want you to negotiate the crop price of the Darjeeling." Temple's brows rose a fraction, and Rein knew it was concerning the crop. He'd rarely allowed anyone to bargain the price of precious tea, for it represented the salaries of his employees. But his vow to Nickolas gave him little choice. "I trust you will get a fair price?" If anything, Rein knew, Temple was an honest man and, at his job, exemplary. Temple nodded. "Excellent. You sail on the night's tide."

Temple's head turned slowly toward the ship, then back to Rein. His lips tightened. The last place he wanted to be was Cape Towne. And Rein knew it.

"Have you a comment?" His posture was unbending. Admirable. Mayhap the man would find his pride again, Rein thought.

"Nay, sir." Temple hunched his shoulders against the noise from the wharf. "Where to after Cape Towne . . . sir?"

"Return here and report to me alone."

Temple nodded, then groaned, his head throbbing like cannon fire.

"Try some coffee. Has amazing effects."

Temple offered a weak smile, and after he was dismissed, made his way slowly down the ladder.

Rein pushed away from the rail and turned, meeting Leelan's censuring gaze. "Do not even speak of it," he warned.

Baynes nodded, but spoke anyway. "You think a trip will repair a broken man?"

Rein sighed heavily, raking his fingers through his hair, then rubbed the back of his neck. "Who can say? But I'm certain the man has no further down to go." Rein slanted him a glance. " 'Tis one thing to know your station, your prospects in life, and accept them. 'Tis another to disregard even that and sink lower."

"Takin' your own advice?"

Rein's eyes sharpened.

"I ain't seen you pay court to a woman in years."

"This has little to do with females, Leelan."

Leelan jutted his chin toward the *Sentinel*. "You're sendin' him off 'cause he can't control his baser needs."

"Oh, he can. He simply does not wish to." And Rein needed him and knew Temple could be trusted. "If he beds every woman on this earth, he will not forget the one he killed, Leelan. He must deal with it. Or he will be without a job. I cannot tolerate such disorder in my company." His attention shifted as Temple brought his gear topside, then headed below for the rest. "A bit of celibacy will do him good."

"You're judging."

Rein glared. "I am looking out for my company and my friend."

"Then why the hell ain'tcha seeing yerself there." He lashed a hand toward Temple's gear. "He rogers them all to forget, you don't touch a single one to remember."

Rein scowled. " 'Tis hardly true, but, without vows spoken, I touch no *lady.*" Not that a single one found him socially fit, he thought with a bitter smile. " 'Tis a manner which assures that no woman is hurt again, Leelan." *For she will know the consequences an association with me will deliver,* he thought.

The helmsman shook his head. "Nay, just yourself. Temple denies a death and you deny a life fer yerself. Hell, man, you've got more wealth than your father, more than his father. Do you think to take it with you when you die?" Rein opened his mouth, but Leelan cut him off, his tone losing its sharpness. "Ye're a fine man, Rein. Ran and Aurora are bloody proud of you. But I do not think they wanted you to remain alone simply 'cause yer blood ain't pure as English blue."

Rein folded his arms over his chest, staring at his helmsman. "You're awfully philosophical this morn. And I do not care if my blood is white or red or green."

"And that, my lad, is the biggest barrel of bilge water I've heard of late."

Rein's brows rose high.

"Ransom is filled with mixed blood and look how happy he is."

"Credit Aurora with that."

"And you think she is only one of a kind?"

"Aye."

Leelan's lips quirked. "I'll grant you, she's a woman of her own will, but that doesn't mean there ain't another out there."

"Enough." He slashed the air with his hand, then clenched his fist, slowly bringing it to his side. He stared out onto the deck. "Aurora taught me that we are all the same, no matter the blood, the past. I have accepted such." He gestured to the crew working on repairs and maintenance, stitching sail and coiling rope. "I begrudge no man a life he chooses. Nor should anyone begrudge me mine. But that does not change the outlook of others. Nor the ramifications. You know 'tis true."

Leelan sighed, running the cloth over the brass fitting on the wheel. "Aye."

Rein had already experienced the repercussions of his lineage, on friends, on women he'd so much as spoken to, and recalled a young woman he'd danced with at a ball once, her parents whisking her off the following day and marrying her to the next man available. It was then he'd understood. The girl suffered because of him, and though he could do naught about the unfairness of it, he'd come to be more circumspect than ever. To allow rumors and notoriety, cultivated with more lies than truth, to touch a lady, to ruin her, was unthinkable. It had already killed his wife. 'Twas a matter of honor, he thought. And those who sought him willingly knew the consequences. Those like Lady Katherine.

Rein pushed away from the rail and strode to the ladder, turned, and descended hand over hand. Just as his head passed the edge, he heard Leelan say, "Stubborn mule-headed half breed."

Rein rose a fraction. "Ugly crag-faced Englishman," he tossed, and Leelan smiled.

Rein walked to the passageway, slipping past Temple and his

baggage and moving through the hatch to his cabin. He closed the door behind him. He loved Leelan like a favored uncle, but the helmsman dug where he should not.

He crossed to his desk, sliding into the chair and focusing on the mounds of drafts and manifests, matching cargo lading with shipping orders. Rein made arrangements, staffing two of his homes in London, one on the outskirts. Giving the appearance of livability was necessary should the need for the residences arise. Which he did not feel they would. But regulating this spy to the stature of servant or crewman seemed the best possible solution. Unless the Guardian was a person of some notoriety, which Rein suspected was true. Nickolas would not have been so adamant about protection, if they were not.

Neither age nor gender would have any meaning, really, he thought and signed another note to pay for larder supplies. Rein cared less of the expense. He had more money than any sane man needed to survive, but it was the time spent that rankled him. A rap sounded, and he lifted his gaze and bade them enter. Cabai appeared, stepping back to allow a guest to pass.

"Rusty." Rein smiled and rose.

"Have you some nice digs, eh," he said with a glance around the captain's quarters. "Should I be addressing you as sir?"

"God forbid," he groaned, then offered him a drink, which he declined, and a cheroot, which he accepted. Rein hitched his rear on the edge of the desk and gestured to the settee.

Rusty lowered his bulk into the cushions, clenching the cheroot in his teeth. "Got you some news."

Rein's blood started pumping harder, tingling his skin.

"The three are supposed to head to Morocco in two months time."

He rubbed his finger across his mouth. "All three?"

"Aye. Funny that. No need of them to be there, not to inspect troops that aren't doing aught but taking up barracks space."

Two months, Rein thought. Would this mess with the Guardian be over before then? Would his quest fall into ruin because of his pledge to Ryder?

"You gonna kill 'im or what?"

Rein's head jerked up, his eyes narrowing.

Rusty shrugged. "I figure you have beef with one of 'em, can't figure out which or why, though."

"You do not need to know."

Rusty blew out some smoke and nodded thoughtfully. "Aye, you're right. I don't. Don't want to even, if the truth be told."

"I appreciate you doing the legwork for me."

"Raise a bit of suspicion, do you?" he said with a thorough look at his newest friend. Rein wasn't so much unusual-looking with his light eyes and dark features, but it was the way he carried himself, with such dignity, as if nothing in this world could touch him.

Rein scoffed, then leaned back, twisting to reach inside the top desk drawer. He tossed a sack to Rusty and he caught it.

He fingered the pouch. "This is too much. I haven't given you aught to use well enough." He handed it back, but Rein waved him off.

He couldn't find a single scrap since Katherine's death and word got round that he was a suspect. And with his vow to Ryder, he couldn't keep vigilant to the whereabouts of his paternal candidates until this spy was well protected or out of the country. "You have, believe me. You've earned it."

"Good, 'cause I could use this now." The soldier smiled, pocketing the sack inside his coat. "Got me a place I'm thinking of buying."

"Not to live alone, I gather."

Rusty grinned. "Mabel. From the tavern?"

Rein remembered, folding his arms. "Been escorting her about?"

Rusty shifted in the chair. "Hell, man, I've been trying to convince her to *marry* an old boot like me."

Marriage, Rein thought, and Michaela's image immediately burst into his mind. The feel of her in his arms came with it, and Rein closed his eyes, massaging the bridge of his nose with thumb and forefinger. He had not seen nor heard of her since the night at the theater. Though he'd made subtle inquiries, the response was less than flattering, depicting a clumsy bland woman of no consequence. Far from the woman he knew. And he wondered if she was running the streets again like a unbridled runagate.

"See what else you can discover, Sergeant Major."

"Well, when you put it like that."

Rein looked up, and Rusty flashed him a cheeky grin. Clad in street clothing, he looked far different from the sergeant major he'd met in the tavern, and for a man who'd seen more battle and death, he was in good spirits. Rein couldn't help but ask why.

"I'm seeing my ending days lived out in peace and solitude."

Rein gestured to the pocket hiding the coin. "And a place of your own has brought this?" Owning property never gave Rein any comfort.

"Nay, a woman has."

"Companionship for a night or two you could find anywhere for a few pennies." Rein hated the cynicism of his own words, but a few hours of paid female companionship was all he'd experienced in that last ten or so years. And until Michaela, he had forgotten what it was like to experience a simple kiss out of pure, natural want.

"Nay, nay. God, for such a generous man, you're bloody cold sometimes. Anyone ever tell you that?" he said with an irritated look. "A woman wants me, with all the unpleasantness I carry along. Mabel holds no high falutin' thinking about being better than me, or me being better than her. Equals, even if we wasn't already."

Rein folded his arms over his chest and studied him, finding pleasure in the knowledge that Rusty, at his age, had found someone to spend his days with in comfort and companionship. Years before, Rein had been content with such a match, a simple islander's daughter. But it was short-lived, and he regretted not warning his innocent young wife exactly how cruel the world beyond Sanctuary could be. Ugly memories threatened, of blood and torture and a rage in him that endangered his self-control, and Rein squeezed his eyes tightly shut, banishing them back. The blame lay in himself as much as society for her death, its pressures, the strict conduct for the public eye, especially when Rein knew, as well as any other soul in England, that behind the most respectable of doors lay variegated dens of uncivilized pleasures, where one could live out the most primitive fantasy, however unnatural or natural, and debauch one's immortal soul to one's heart's content. Yet one did not dare speak of it in proper circles. The contradiction outraged him, made him long for the freedom of Sanctuary or Madagascar. *But even there, you are alone,* a voice whispered. *And what do you truly desire? Companionship? Nay, a partner, and children to love,* he thought.

"I am happy for you," he finally said when he realized Rusty was staring at him oddly. He pushed off the desk and moved around it.

Rusty stood, taking a few more cheroots from the carved box on his desk and stuffing them in his pockets. "You want to talk about it?"

"Not this time."

Rusty scoffed. "You listen well, but don't give overmuch, do you?"

Rein's gaze shifted, a small smile curving his lips. "Evidently not." He leaned forward and scribbled on a slice of paper, offering it to him. "If you cannot locate me here, check there."

Rusty ground it into his pocket without looking at the address. "You in trouble, Rein? If those runners are bothering you—"

"Nay, they have settled. Though I do not believe I am their first candidate."

Rusty sucked on the cheroot, thoughtful, then sent him a cryptic look. "I'm not one to talk around about a woman, Lady Buckland being gentry an' all. But the woman was not unfamiliar with . . . certain people."

"That is what got me into this trouble."

Rusty chuckled softly. " 'Spect it was rather fun, too. But if a body looked, there are enough suspects to fill up George's court, if you catch my meaning."

Katherine enjoyed the company of men of power, men trusted with their country's secrets.

Men like his father.

"Some things a sergeant major don't want to be privy to. Germain, North, Rathgoode, Kipler," Rusty said as he moved toward the door. "Take your pick. The list is long."

And what, Rein thought, did these men tell her when they were lying in her soft arms? Enough to get her throat cut . . . and implicate him.

Michaela glanced uncertainly at the Lord Whitfield, then to her uncle. Clearly he was not pleased with the invitation to spend a few days with Cassandra.

"Surely you can spare her," Adam said. " 'Tis not as if she is a servant." Michaela's eyes widened, and she immediately looked at the floor. Good show, Adam, she thought. "Not when she owns this house." Oh, cracking good.

"I am her trustee."

"Forgive me, but she is old enough to oversee her own interest, Brigadier." He glanced briefly at Michaela. "I meant no offense."

"None taken, Your Grace."

"And if there is a matter that needs her attention, you are certainly welcome to take care of it now." Adam plucked at the tips of his gloved fingers, sliding the garment free.

"Nay, not as yet, but . . ."

Nay, Michaela thought, the bill collectors haven't arrived yet.

Cassandra, who'd been wisely silent for the past moments, chose then to move around her brother and stand before the Brigadier. "The truth is, Sir Denton, my brothers feel I need a nursemaid." She cast a sour glance over her shoulder at Adam. "I would rather not and though Michaela is a bit of a starched matron . . ." Michaela choked, disguising it with a short fit of coughing. ". . . She is pleasant enough company." Michaela slid a covert look as Cassandra inched closer to her uncle, looping her arm with his and giving him her very best I-am-pretty-and-helpless-and-how-can-you-resist-me look, which Michaela knew to be complete and utter drivel.

"I am counting on Michaela to curtail Cassandra's . . . reckless nature while I am away."

"Please, Sir Denton," Cassandra said.

"Two days."

"We are in need of her for four at least." Adam looked fondly at Michaela, and she felt her heart trip. Too bloody handsome, she thought. "We would enjoy her company for longer."

"Four then." Denton's gaze slid to Michaela. "I shan't remind you to act accordingly."

Michaela tipped her chin, embarrassment tinting her skin. "You just did." You officious toad.

"My thanks, Sir Denton." Cassandra bussed his cheek with a kiss, and Michaela felt a measure of resentment when Uncle Atwell smiled warmly down at Cassandra and patted her hand. He'd never so much as smiled at her.

They departed in all haste, Lord Whitfield insisting he had to be certain the ladies must be well ensconced in Cravenwood Hall before he had to leave.

"He's a pompous fat prig."

"Cassandra!" Adam snapped angrily, jerking on his gloves as the carriage rolled away.

Michaela fought a smile and glanced to the side as Cassandra adjusted her skirts and tossed the fur over their legs.

"He is, Adam, and you are simply too kind to say so."

" 'Tis called manners. You should try them."

"He allowed Michaela to join us, did he not?"

Adam muttered something about feminine wiles and the danger of underestimating their capability. "Aye, my dearest. Commend yourself, if you like, but I am trusting you to behave whilst I'm sojourning across the continent."

"What else can I do? You won't take me along. You baby me, keep me under guard."

"And if you are not careful, I will ask Captain McBride to watch over you."

Her eyes rounded. "You wouldn't."

"Cassandra, you're making yourself a larger hole to fall into, dear," Michaela said, with a nudge.

"Listen to her, sweetheart. If you acted the lady of your station, Jace, Markus, and I would not be forced to constantly change our plans to see who gets to keep an eye on you."

Cassandra was immediately contrite, staring at her lap. "I know I am a trial."

Adam's expression did not alter, yet his eyes softened as he gazed at her sister's bowed head. "And I adore you. But you must learn restraint. Like Michaela."

Michaela scoffed softly. "I am restrained only because I have no freedom, Your Grace."

"Please, Michaela, I have known you for over ten years. Call me Adam. I so rarely hear my name, I often forget I have one." She heard the disappointment in his voice and nodded. "And I will send word to your uncle in a day or two that I am delayed and desperately need you to remain as Cassandra's companion."

A small smile curved her lips. "Do not lie for me, Adam."

Cassandra caught her hand and gave it a light squeeze. "He lies for me."

Michaela pursed her lips and turned her gaze to the window, not seeing the lush scenery passing before her vision. She *was* lying, using them, practically demanding Cassandra to make good her invitation. In two days, she would meet with Nickolas, and she prayed Cassandra would aid her, yet she did not dare drag the innocent girl into her problems. All she needed was a diversion. How she was to manage that when she was along to be Cassandra's keeper was a problem she hadn't solved yet.

Since she left Nickolas in the streets, she was haunted by the vision of Father Joseph dying in her arms. That anyone would kill a priest was horrifying enough, yet she could not dwell on it. Who else but an agent of Liberty knew Father was working with Nickolas, she wondered for the thousandth time. And believed the priest discovered the double agent and was murdered for it. Regardless, the double agent left them open to vulnerability, and since none knew exactly who was delivering false information, their only choice was to set a trap. And she feared, if something did not break, she'd be forced to offer herself as bait.

Beneath the fur lap robe, she wrung her hands, feeling defenseless. She'd spent the past days waiting for the authorities to arrest her, for this killer to name her, or for Rein to betray his promise and reveal her adventures into the East End, which would implicate her. Yet when nothing happened, she had to assume the murderer was waiting for the opportunity to kill her. She leaned her head against the window frame, exhausted and utterly terrified. Venturing to Cravenwood Hall would at least keep her safe a bit longer. No one would dare cross the duke's threshold to get to her, and, unlike her own home, there were too many servants about for a cutthroat to get past.

Cutthroat, she thought ironically and then thought of Lady Buckland, the horrible rumors flitting about, and the mention of Rein's name with every turn. She could not fight the vision of him standing over a bloody body with one of those wicked curved knives in his hand. If he had not been fleeing that night, if he had not disregarded the runaway carriage, she would at least have a thread of trust to grasp. She shaped the blade hidden beneath her cloak. The ugly image warred with the man who'd kissed her so hungrily, so lusciously, in the rain. The man who flirted with her after she'd put a hole in his flesh.

She closed her eyes, leaning her head back against the plush squabs and wished she could believe in his innocence. But Rein Montegomery was not blameless. Not if her uncle had any dealings with him. And she feared she and the mysterious man were on opposites sides of the rebellion.

For days she'd eavesdropped on her uncle's conversations in an attempt to discover who the fifth man was, hoping to hear his name and praying she wouldn't. Yet the men were even more discreet than before, as if the incident at his study door was enough to scare them. She'd been banished to her room whenever anyone arrived, and listening at the brazier served little use except to aid her in identifying some of the group. Winters, which was no surprise, Rathgoode, and Prather. All officers, so far, all with substantial pensions coming to them, homes and families, except her uncle and Major Winters. The last man, tall and slender, always left heavily cloaked and under the cover of night.

Michaela recognized that her usefulness as a spy was running out, and she did not doubt the real possibility that if her identity were compromised, to either side, she would be very quietly . . . eliminated.

Seventeen

Someone watches, I feel it.

Michaela glanced discreetly about, not hearing Cassandra's chatter as they strolled before the line of elegant shops and keeping her attention to their surroundings. Someone other than Adam Whitfield's footman and the armed driver sitting atop the carriage rolling in the street alongside them watched their every move. Though the driver's company was more to curtail Cassandra's reckless wanderings than to protect her person, Michaela did not like the risk. She could have easily slipped out of the house tomorrow evening without Cassandra, and wondered if she could convince the sheltered girl to return to Cravenwood.

"You're awfully quiet."

She looked at Cassandra, smiling gently. " 'Tis not as if you've left me room to interject a single comment."

Cassandra grinned. "I am simply pleased to be on an outing with you."

"Me, too." She sighed heavily and looked at the dresses displayed in the shop's windows. "It has been a long time since I've shopped."

"Then we shall." Before Michaela could stop her, Cassandra slipped inside a dress shop. "Mayhap some French lingerie?" She lifted a gauzy voile camisole trimmed in satin and turned, holding it against her slight frame.

"Why bother?" Michaela scoffed. " 'Tis naught to it." Yet a part of her longed for something so utterly frivolous, so delicate, and the thought of parading about in the privacy of her rooms—she did want to consider wearing the seductive garment for its true intention—made her stomach pitch.

" 'Tis wonderfully sinful," Cassandra whispered with a huge grin and dancing eyes.

"And you will be the talk of the city if you do not put that down." Michaela inclined her head toward the shop window and Captain McBride standing beyond the glass, staring very intently at them. For an instant the girl stilled, and Michaela glanced between the two, arching a brow. The exchange was enough to cut the glass.

Then Cassandra boldly wiggled, dancing the transparent garment before her as if she were modeling it, smiling mischievously. Duncan fused red, and his lips pulled disapprovingly tight as he turned away.

"You are shameless, Randi," Michaela hissed, wisely snatching the thing from her. "And do that just to taunt the poor man."

"He's likely never even seen such a thing." She huffed, turning her back on the window. "Hah. I bet he disrobes in the dark. He's likely never been with a woman or he would not be so unyielding."

"He's a proper gentleman, as you should act the proper miss."

"Not you, too," she groaned, pushing out the door. "I'd hoped to find a compatriot in my mischief."

"Perish the thought. You seek out trouble without help." Already twice this morn she'd shopped, believing Cassandra by her side, only to find her not only gone but leading her a mad search to near the less reputable parts of the city. The girl was a trial to be sure, yet it was Michaela's presence that caused the risk.

They moved down the stone walk toward the milliner's. "See how the men stare at you?"

Michaela slid her a glance. "I am too old for such fantasies." She was well into spinsterhood and did not invite a single fantasy regarding her appearance.

Cassandra made a face. "You need to be kissed. Thoroughly."

She blinked. "I beg your pardon?"

"Kissed. You know, a pressing of lips," she said with a cheeky grin. "Preferably with those of the opposite sex."

She thought of Rein and the dark pleasure he gave with his mouth, and her body tingled with a fresh chill. "Mayhap by him?"

Michaela slid her gaze to Cassandra, then to where she looked. She stopped, people brushing past. *Rein.* Astride his black horse, he gazed across the avenue, traffic shielding, then revealing him. He stood out against the white of the building behind him, an imposing figure as the high-strung mount pranced under his control. She felt his gaze move over her, her garments, the corner of his mouth lifting, as if to say he preferred finding her in the streets in a gown than boys' clothing. A breeze tore loose a strand of her hair, and she brushed it back. He followed the move, and Michaela had never experienced so intense a stare as his. Her heartbeat escalated, her skin warming, and she tried to ignore it, ignore that he might be linked with her uncle, that he was suspected of murder. But in that instant, she could only remember their blood bond and the way he'd kissed her in the rain.

"Mayhap he has already kissed you."

Her gaze snapped to Cassandra's. "He has not," she lied. "Why would he?"

"Obviously you do not recognize desire in a man's eyes. Especially that man's."

Michaela looked back but Rein was gone, yet she eyed Randi with maternal concern. "And who, may I ask, have you kissed that you can discern desire?"

"You may not." She stopped before the shop, peering through the glass.

"Randi, I do not want you to tease a man," she said from her side, staring into the window. " 'Tis very dangerous."

Cassandra slanted her a look. " 'Tis been only one man, a boy really," she confessed shyly. "When I was four and ten. But it was nice." Cassandra leaned forward for a better look into the shop. "I'd think a man's kiss would be even more enjoyable."

Michaela grasped her arm and turned her toward her. "Do not test those waters, swear to it!"

Cassandra frowned at her friend's distress, tossing the edge of her cloak over her shoulder. "What has happened to make you so jaded?"

A shot rang out. Someone screamed. The glass in the shop shattered, raining the women and the ground with glittering fragments. Pedestrians fled as Michaela pulled Cassandra toward the doorway. Cassandra staggered, falling against the frame. Michaela pushed her to the ground and crouched. It was then she saw the blood staining Randi's sleeve.

"Oh, my God!" she gasped, reaching under her skirts and tearing off a strip of her petticoats.

Whistles sounded, constables and soldiers running toward them.

Cassandra blinked up at her, then down at her arm as Michaela wrapped the wound. "Oh, dear," she whispered, the pulse of blood widening the stain. "My brothers will be very angry with me now."

" 'Tis not your fault." Michaela tied it off, glancing about and wishing she hadn't been forced to leave her gun at Cravenwood for the lack of concealment.

Captain McBain suddenly skidded to halt, dropping low and using his body to shield them. "My God. *Cassandra.*"

Cassandra lifted her gaze to the officer's profile and smiled weakly. "Why, Captain McStiff, good of you to join us."

Michaela reached to open the shop door and another shot rang out, plunking into the wood above her head, and she realized she was the intended target. She looked at Duncan, his face mapped with concentration, his sidearm out as he surveyed the buildings, the people gawking as if waiting for more blood to spill. Michaela had to get away from them, away from the people who might be accidentally struck by a bullet. She rose.

Duncan grabbed her, dragging her down. "Are you mad, woman? They will shoot you!"

Nay, she thought, he will shoot *through* you. She gripped his jacket front, shaking him roughly, her gaze hard and unwavering. "Hear me, Duncan. This," she nodded to Randi's wound, "is only a taste of what will happen if I do not flee, *now!*"

"You're distraught," he soothed.

She shook her head. "Hide her, treat her wound and protect her, but do not let them send anyone after me. Swear it on my father's grave."

His gaze searched hers. "What have you gotten into, Michaela?"

"Swear!"

"Aye!"

She bent to Cassandra and whispered, "You wanted excitement, Randi. Happy?"

Cassandra moaned and Duncan paled visibly, looking down at her, and Michaela stole the chance, leaping to her feet and fleeing into the throngs of people crying out deliriously. Duncan called to her, cursing, then flicked a hand toward a handful of troops and they took off in her direction.

"Remind me never to trust your promises," came sluggishly from Cassandra and Duncan did not bother to look at her, his emotions at a dangerously tenuous level.

"Be silent, Lady Whitfield," he snapped angrily. "You are in no position to judge."

The Whitfield carriage rolled to a stop, the driver racing to them, the footman leaping down to open the door. Duncan holstered his weapon and lifted Cassandra in his arms, then stood, moving through the people to the carriage. He ducked, cradling her on his lap as he sat, his gaze scanning the streets as the conveyance rolled away. This, he thought, was a vow he would regret.

"She will survive, you know," Cassandra whispered, and Duncan looked down at her, his hand trembling as he stroked her hair from her face. "She is so much stronger than the rest of us."

Duncan held her warmly against him and prayed Michaela Denton was as smart as she was brave.

She heard the shouts, the heavy trod of boots behind her. *Damn you, Duncan,* she thought with the glance back, and she found several soldiers spreading out to find her. She was too noticeable, her gown and Cassandra's borrowed cloak screaming wealth and marking her for thievery. A man grabbed her and she twisted, kicking him in the shin and tearing away, her steps faster, her hood pulled low. Getting to Nickolas was her only hope and she suspected he was already at the Red Badger, waiting. The thought of traveling on foot, in thin kid boots made her groan, yet she'd no choice. And if a woman alone in the West Side brought notice, one dressed as she was would garner the attention of the worst in the East End.

She dug in her reticule for her knife, concealing her hands and bag beneath her cloak. The temperature was dropping with the setting sun and Michaela knew she would not make the inn before nightfall. The sound of footsteps grew louder and she darted into an alley. A man followed her, but one swipe across his arm sent him back into the street. She pressed tightly against the wall, forcing her thoughts into reasonable order. Her heart still raced, warming her cold feet and hands, and she decided the old stable was her best choice to spend the night. Troops passed the alleyway. And still she waited, her delicate boot heels sinking into the mud.

Rats skittered through the alley, a cat shrieked and gave chase, knocking over crates and driving the mice over her booted toes. She smothered a cry, huddling closer to the wall. The dinner hour would leave the streets fairly empty and she dug in her reticule for her father's pocket watch, then tipped it toward the moon's glow. Two hours, she thought. If she could just stay hidden for two more hours, it would give her a small advantage. The lampys lit the street posts, walking on stilts to reach the globes. The grind of carriages wheels grew less frequent and still she waited. She'd run the streets often enough to know the best times to venture out.

But then she'd been well armed. Her impatience grew, and she dug in her reticule for a hand mirror, peering around the edge, scanning the coveys and doorways. She stepped out, nearly running toward the stable's location. Her only problem now was that on previous occasions, she was dressed to climb the fences.

Duncan paced the length of the library, turning on his heel and completing another pass before the Brigadier. "Mayhap we should send more squads into the East End."

"She would not have ventured there. Too timid a gell, I tell you. She could barely walk the halls without stumbling over her own feet and you think she could last a hour in the bowels of London?"

Duncan stilled and cocked a look at the man. He hovered over a plate of sweets, eyeing the variety, stuffing one, then another into his mouth without so much as looking up. "Then where do you suppose she has hidden herself for two days?" If Denton detected anger in his tone, he made no notice of it.

"A church mayhap, her little charity thing." He waved and slurped tea and any attachment Duncan thought the man had for his niece disintegrated. For they'd already checked the churches, the soup kitchen, retraced her steps over and over, asked questions, and between Cassandra's brothers and himself, a liberal amount of coin was spread about a hundred miles of London in the hopes of unearthing a crumb of information.

But there was none. She'd vanished.

And he accomplished nothing remaining here.

"Continue to search for my dear niece, Captain," the Brigadier said, without a smattering of affection in his tone. "I'll expect a ready report."

"Aye, sir, good day, sir." Duncan saluted and left the library. He walked to the front door, pulling on his gloves and wondering if he was doing the right thing by searching, to bring her back to this.

Nickolas sat on the bed, elbows on his knees. He mashed a hand across his mouth. She was a day late and his contacts throughout the city found no sign of her. He'd gone out himself, for hours, to the stables, to each of their prearranged meeting spots. And when the news of shots fired at Michaela and Lady Whitfield reached him, it confirmed that the priest's killer suspected Michaela had seen him, yet did not solidify that the killer knew she was the Guardian. But he could take no chances.

He raked his fingers through his hair, the long gray locks falling in his face as he pushed off the bed. He paced, plagued with images of her beaten and bloody and helpless.

And he decided he could wait a few more hours before he went completely mad.

Eighteen

"I tell you I've searched all the places where the Guardian would find safe haven."

Rein stared at the fire, his arm braced on the mantel. Nickolas was evading his questions, and he was fast losing his patience. "Do you wish me to find this person or nay?" Since he'd entered the rented room and found Nickolas at his wits' end, Rein experienced an unnatural foreboding, a tightening of his spine that threatened to snap it.

"I appreciate your efforts—"

"You do not have them yet," Rein reminded. "And if you do not cease with your infernal surreptitious manner and describe this Guardian, I will return to the comfort of my ship." Though his voice was soft, his tone hissed with impatient anger.

Nickolas stared at his glass, at the swallow of amber liquid remaining. "Deep red hair, greenish brown eyes." He tossed the draught back. "And my sources tell me that the Guardian was last seen wearing a deep green . . . gown."

Rein cocked a stunned look over his shoulder. "Are you telling me your elite spy is a woman?" Tiny voices, of reason and detail, whispered in his brain.

"Aye."

Rein faced him fully. *"Her name."* His earlier feelings of dread stirred, locking his posture like a sealed door.

"Michaela—" Rein cursed foully, striding across the room before Nickolas added, "Denton." Nickolas wasn't surprised he knew the woman and wondered how well.

"Damn you, man. How could you endanger her like this?" Rein retrieved his tricorn and cloak from the bed, his mind reeling with images of her wounded and lost in the city, each portrayal stabbing at him with the sharpness of a blade.

"She volunteered."

Rein's hands stilled for a fraction in fastening his cloak. A muscle ticked in his jaw.

"She knows her way about, Rein."

Rein methodically checked the load of his pistols. "What else are you not telling me, Nickolas?"

Sweet mother, naught went unnoticed to him, he thought, and confessed, "She has nowhere to turn. Nowhere. She does not trust rebel sympathizers and she'll not trust you. You'll have a time convincing her I've sent you. Even if you tell her you are the merchant."

"I will manage." I will wring her bloody neck for risking it, he thought.

"And . . ."

Rein's gaze flashed to his, his pale-blue eyes glacial.

"Someone took a shot at her. Lady Whitfield was hit, a graze only, I've discovered."

Rein shoved the flintlock into his waistband and faced him. "She could be dead now, you know that." His voice spat with a mix of pain and anger. "How sets that with you?"

Nickolas's stomach responded, churning wildly, and he plowed his fingers through his hair. "Don't you think I have not agonized over this?"

Rein had little sympathy for his plight. "Tell me everywhere she might have gone to wait this out." He would check her residence first, he thought, yet could not make his search known without raising suspicion of her identity or her purpose. Damn and blast, this was a complicated mess.

"I told you, I already—"

"Tell me!" Rein snarled, wanting to thrash something, preferable Nickolas's hide, yet it would do Michaela little good if he lost control.

Nickolas stared at him for a long moment, warring with revealing all their shelters, then his shoulders fell with resolution and he gave over the locations, all but one in the center of East End, one in the west.

"There is one detail."

Rein twisted a look at him. "Sweet mother, Nick!"

"Lady Buckland—" Nickolas swallowed. "She was one of ours."

Rein's features yanked taut, his rage simmering in the tepid air like the aftershock of lightning. "Does Michaela know this?"

"Nay, only you and I."

"And the one who killed her."

" 'Tis possible," Nickolas said, resigned. "But Katherine had many influential . . . associates." He let the thought hang, allowing Rein the freedom to draw his own conclusions.

But no one needed to remind him of Katherine's deeds, for they were going to haunt him for a century, Rein thought, jerking open the door.

He stepped out, the soft, sealing click making Nickolas flinch as he sank into the nearest chair, staring at the fire. He'd known Rein since he was a child, and not once saw him lose his temper, nor become overly emotional. And he wondered if Michaela was in safe hands or if he should worry again.

Rein walked through the common room and out the door without a backward glance. Waving off the livery hand, he headed into the stables and to Naraka, grasping the pommel, prepared to mount, then stopped, gripping the saddle and staring down at the straw strewn floor between his boots.

God of thunder. The Guardian. He should have suspected and felt like a fool.

There was not an authority in the entire of England not searching for the her, not a single soul who'd dismiss the opportunity of money and fame that would accompany her capture. The price on her head had grown to nearly two thousand pounds! She was in more danger from that than this assailant. And Lady Buckland . . . there was a woman who should not have lent herself to covertness. She was a gossipmongering, shallow female, and money would have swayed her to betray the rebellion. Or Michaela. And Nickolas's insistence that none of the spies knew each other would be Michaela's only saving. He prayed Nick knew his people, and Rein grasped the reality that she might have already been taken into custody and was wasting in Newgate or suffering torture now.

Or already dead.

He squeezed his eyes shut and pressed his forehead to the smooth leather saddle. Buckskin creaked. Dust motes skipped around his bowed head like fairy dust carried on the breeze. Rein's fingers flexed on the pommel as he tried to sense her, grasp the thread that would tell him she lived, and when he couldn't, he tried to imagine her warm and safe, holding tight to his anger at Nickolas for using her, at Michaela herself for risking her life. Air passed in and out of his lungs, affording him a shred of composure, and he lifted his head, staring over the saddle at the wide open doors and the pithy night beyond. *Be alive,* he pleaded with any god listening. *Please be alive.* Suddenly, he mounted, wheeling the horse around and ducking to clear the doorframe. He rode, heading to the wharf. He'd call in a few markers this night and would not rest until he found her. Then, he thought, she was not leaving his side until this war was over.

* * *

Rein stared down the length of table, at the men filling the dozen or so chairs. He'd searched until dawn with no success and spent a goodly portion of the morning coming to this decision. Now, he thought, there was no turning back. They'd sworn their loyalty when he'd hired them as crewmen, now they swore to secrecy. None knew the why of it and accepted his word as gospel, and as he met the gaze of each man seated around the wardroom table, he knew they would go to the grave to keep their word.

"Gentlemen, we have a lady to find. Discretion is our initiative, and her survival is tantamount."

"Who is this lass, sir?"

"The woman who shot me."

Half of them scowled, the other half smiled. "Gonna pay 'er back?"

"Nay, Mr. Ashburn, we are going to protect her."

Ashburn sent him a surprised look, then glanced at his comrades. "Ifin you say so, Captain."

"I say so." He turned toward the wall, gazing out the leeward portal. The ship rocked gently against the dock, her coils tugging her back like a wayward child. The sensation soothed, and Rein rolled his shoulders to hasten it along. He'd spent the entire night laying coins in all the right palms, hoping the eyes of London's most disreputable sorts would remain open for him. He would have to pay more for whatever information they garnered, but he also knew the urchins, thieves, and widows would keep their mouths tightly closed against the local constabulary. The benefits of surviving the streets of Ceylon were showing their value.

"Wot we do first, sir?"

Rein cast a look over his shoulder. Their eyes fixed on him, the men waited patiently. Rein turned and described Michaela, keeping her name to himself. "We seek only information, a lead. A location. Do not approach." He did not want anyone hurt. The risks were his own. "Mr. Baynes will remain aboard. You are to report to him or myself alone."

Leelan eyed him, Rein could feel it without looking, and chose to ignore the man's sudden amusement.

"Mr. Popewell, Mr. Bushmara, you start with the taverns." The young black-haired Englishman smiled, casting a look at the bo'sun, who scowled disapprovingly. Fadi Bushmara was a Moor and forbidden to imbibe. "I trust you will not swill ale and tell all?"

"Most assuredly, sir," Bushmara said with a tip of his head, then slid a cutting glance at his partner. Andy Popewell sank in his chair, grousing to himself.

"Mr. Veslic, Basilia, Salven, and Bigby, take the docks. Mr. O'Toole, where the Irish reside." The red-haired man nodded, smiling. Rein eyed him with a warning not to go off drinking till dawn with his countrymen. "Misters Quimby, Needham, and Beswick will cover the streets." They were English, born in the east side and would blend in easily, Rein thought before his gaze shifted to the man at his right. "Mr. Gilbèrt, you have the privilege of seeing to the soiled doves of the city."

The entire table grumbled at the unfairness of that.

Rein glanced and they fell into silence. "Were Mr. Matthews here, he would take this job, but as he is not, Mr. Gilbèrt's silver tongue seems to work on the ladies."

"Oui," he said, wiggling his brows. "Giving them all much pleasure, eh?" The innuendo sent a burst of chuckles around the table. "I appreciate the mademoiselles," he said, his Belgian accent suddenly heavier. "You"—he waved arrogantly at the assorted crewmen—"simply climb on and ride."

"I did not say you were to take a trip, sir."

Gilbèrt looked at his captain, and Rein folded back the urge to smile. He looked as if he'd asked him to cut off his necessary equipment. "But, *Capitaine,* surely a well-loved woman would offer more—"

"Than one aroused beyond thought?"

Gilbèrt smiled, then said, "I make no promise not to fulfill any threats, monsieur."

"One can only hope, Mr. Gilbèrt." Rein surveyed the men, his gaze moving to Cabai. The Arab's subtle nod telling him he understood his appearance provoked a fascination they did not need.

"Mind my askin' what ye're gonna be doin', sir."

His gaze swung to Leelan. "Nay, you may not." His plans to make himself known in the more affluent parts of the city, the clubs and dinning establishment, bullying his way in if he must, were his own, and mentioning he was heading to businesses that would not let these men past the front door was as cruel as the prejudice itself. "You are dismissed." Chairs scraped back as they stood and took their leave.

Yet Leelan hung back. "Why you lookin' for this lass now?"

"She's lost and needs to be found."

Naught was that simple, not with this man, Leelan thought. "And mayhap she don't want to be hauled home."

"That," he said in a tone that snapped like a north wind, "is not her choice."

Leelan eyeballed his back for a moment longer, smiling to himself as he left Rein alone.

The instant the door closed, Rein's shoulders fell. His hands resting lightly on his hips, he stared at the floor, exhaustion seeping into his bones, yet he refused to let it take hold. He'd checked the shelters twice, including the cellar of a hunting lodge on the edge of the city. Night would be the better time to venture out again, he thought, but whatever befell her would not lessen for the light of day. And if she was intentionally hiding somewhere and not stolen away as Nickolas suspected? And if Michaela did not want to be found? And when he did locate her, would she run?

She will not trust you.

Rumor and circumstance painted a murderer for her, and she would likely come with him only with the benefit of a gag and bonds. His lips curled at the thought of tangling with her, and he remembered the last time he'd seen her, resplendent in a velvet cloak, jeweled earbobs, and her wild curls neatly tamed. Properly refined and poised, she was a bright penny against Lady Whitfield's pale complexion and dark hair. And Rein longed to go to her then, to talk with her, to ease the fear and suspicion he recognized in her eyes. It gnawed at his gut that she believed he was capable of killing women. And he wondered who would dare shoot at her in public. Adam must be going mad over Cassandra's mishap, he thought, and considered that Michaela might have taken the heat of the bullet.

Rein made a sound of frustration, his stomach floating loosely at the thought, and he moved to the armoire. He locked and loaded the pistols, put a clean edge to the knives, then strode from the cabin, his boot heels clicking on the polished floor, marking out his anger.

* * *

Adam Whitfield exchanged a look between his brothers and Captain McBain, then returned his gaze to Cassandra's slender back where she sat on the window seat, her head on the pane, gazing forlornly out the window. She'd refused to lay abed and recover, the graze on her arm tended and healing, yet Adam could not help but worry. She had not spoken once since Captain McBain brought her home days ago.

"Cassandra, you really should rest a bit more."

"I agree, Lady Whitfield."

She looked back over her shoulder at Duncan McBain, her gaze icy with contempt. "Stuff it."

The men blinked, censure in their expressions. She dismissed it, turning her attention back to the rain soaked lawn. Her arm throbbed, and though the wound was merely a graze, it had done more than make her bleed. It awakened her, made her see she was rebelling for misplaced reasons, struggling against the wrong people. Her brothers loved her, she knew, they pampered and coddled her, but Cassandra wanted freedom and envied Michaela and her chance to really live her life. Her sigh whispered the sheers and she rubbed her cheek against the delicate fabric. 'Twas a man's world.

"We will find her."

"Nay, you will not."

"Don't lose hope, Randi." This came from Markus.

She twisted, her gaze going immediately to Duncan's. "You should not have sent them after her."

"She was scared. Anyone would be." *Except you,* Duncan thought. Cassandra Whitfield had been anything but calm, and almost remote about the incident.

She stood. "That's a horse crap."

"Cassandra!"

"What?" Her arms out, palms up, she shrugged, looking at her brothers. "Do you not like my language, my attitude? Too bad," she snapped. "This is who I am and I will no longer change to suit you three." She looked at Duncan. "You four." She headed for the door.

"My lady." Duncan reached and she sidestepped him, her gaze biting over his features, and Duncan felt his chest tightened at the loathing he saw there.

She stared into his soft gray eyes, wishing for some peace to her turbulent feelings.

Then she slapped him. Hard.

Her brothers leapt to their feet. "Cassandra, apologize at once."

Duncan continued to stare down at her with frosty eyes.

"You broke your promise to her, Captain."

The imprint of her hand deepened on his cheek.

"You swore an oath and then broke it without a thought. And she knows it. You cannot be trusted."

Duncan's gaze wavered, a hint of regret in his expression. "She was distraught, Lady Whitfield, and blamed herself for your wound."

"She feared for us!"

"I would have protected her."

"You want to protect your honor," she said in an ugly voice. "And sometimes what is right and proper is not the best solution, Captain." Her tone softened and his expression relaxed a fraction. "We are her friends, and now she believes we have betrayed her. That *I* have betrayed her."

"Michaela understands 'twas my duty—"

"Duty?" she cut in. "And where is the Brigadier's duty to her? His brother trusted him to care for his only child and look how he twisted it to suit him."

"What are you saying, Randi?" Jace asked, noticing the sorrow in his sister's eyes.

"Did you think she did not want to be hunted?" she said to Duncan, then shifted her gaze past him to the Whitfield men. "Have you any notion of what she has suffered in that household? How many times she has been beaten for the slightest infraction?"

"Why did you not say something?" Jace asked, horrified.

"Because *I* swore I would not. Yet anyone looking would have seen it, and anyone coming to her aid would seem like defeat to her. She was determined to win over the Brigadier." Cassandra adored her brothers, but too often they were narrow-minded, posturing peers. "She was running for her freedom and the lot of you—" he gestured to the men "—have fifty troops out scouring the city, and she is likely more terrified of the retribution she'll suffer if she is forced into that house."

"The Brigadier commissioned those troops, Cass."

Cassandra scoffed, tossing her hair off her shoulder, her gaze hot with outrage. "And I'm sure the fat ogre is just wasting away with worry. Good Lord, are you all so blind?" She delivered a damning look to each man. "Denton has control over her house, her allowance, and he wants her inheritance. By God, Adam." She moved to her eldest brother, sinking to the floor at his feet in a cloud of sprigged muslin and gazing up at him. Her lovely eyes watered. "Did it occur to you that the Brigadier might have sent someone to kill her so he could have it all?"

" 'Tis preposterous!"

"Is it? He cannot touch her money, her holdings, if she is not under his care. Yet, as her trustee, she could not cast him out. And should she want to wed, he would be left penniless, for her dowry is substantial and the house would become hers. You know that."

"Why did she simply not wed and be away from him?"

"He has done something to prevent it. Though she never confided as to what." Yet Cassandra had her suspicions, and they were ugly.

Adam glanced at his brothers, then the captain. "Is he capable of this, Captain?"

Duncan looked at the toes of his boots. "I'm not certain, Your Grace."

Cassandra shot to her feet. "You lie, Duncan."

His head snapped up, pearl-gray eyes sharp.

"Cassandra!" her brothers shouted at once, but she ignored all but one man, the only man she'd considered honorable and strong, until now.

"When will you cease living in safety and propriety and grow the backbone of the clan chieftain you are!"

Duncan's face showed his anger, his fists clenched white-knuckled tight. "Damn you, Lady Whitfield," he snarled down at her.

"Aye." She moved to stand directly before him. "And damn thee, Laird Duncan McBain. Damn thee for your weak resolve. For succumbing to the simpleton's way and not the warrior's!" She swept past him to the door, pausing on the threshold and looking back at him. His hatred radiated across the separating distance, and Cassandra reveled in the emotion finally coming to the surface. "Follow your orders, Captain. I pray for your sake, she finds safe haven and one of the Brigadier's soldiers does not *accidentally* shoot her. She has tasted true freedom, and she will never turn back." She vanished around the doorframe, and Duncan stood in the center of the elegant room, his heavy breathing the only sound. Then, without a single proper acknowledgment, he quit the room.

Leelan stilled on the threshold of the captain's quarters, a tray in his hand. "You need to eat, son."

"Go away, Leelan." He did not look up, his head cradled in his hands, elbows braced on his knees. Not a word, a single clue. Rein feared the worst. She was dead and the stink of decay would be the only thing to alert them of her whereabouts. His stomach lurched and he swallowed painfully. He'd blanketed the city with his own spies, laced palms with coin, yet naught garnered a scrap of information. He'd visited every inn and tavern, every flophouse and tenement. Bloody hell, he thought, he'd cracked open boarded-up buildings in the slim hope she would be hiding in one.

She had, very quietly, vanished.

"Any report?" Rein asked uselessly.

"I woulda told you first off, lad."

"I know," he said, pushing off the settee and moving about the room. From her spot beneath the aft windows, Rahjin watched him, her head resting on her fat paws, only her eyes following her master's steps.

Leelan closed the door behind him and set the tray on the table, looking on with concern. He'd never seen him like this, haggard and tense, and could feel the energy seething in the room, thick and spiced as Rein moved from his desk to the window, to the rack of books, to the cabinet of charting equipment and liquor, then made the round again. Grease lamps sputtered with his moves. Water shimmered in the bowl on the commode, steaming softly. Leelan poured a cup of tea and cinnamon, watching, waiting, for the room to collapse around them.

"Why have you not done it?"

Rein's head snapped up, red eyes narrowing.

Leelan gestured to the steam, the lamps. "You have the power, Rein, why do you not use it?"

His features tightened. "It is using it for my benefit."

"What about for hers?"

Rein stared at the floor between his feet. It had been so long since he felt it necessary to work the elements. He spent half his time trying to suppress the energy that permeated him like a layer of skin.

"Your mother taught it to you so you could aid others *and* could control your emotions. What would happen if you released it?"

"I do not know. Hell, Leelan, I could kill us all."

"You can control her energy?"

Rein scoffed. "Nay, she controls mine."

Leelan's brows shot up, a surprised smile curving his lips. *Well, I'll be,* he thought. "Ifin I was you, which I ain't, I'd be askin' myself whether or not the lass was worth the risk."

Rahjin rose slowly, sauntering to Rein, and, without conscious thought, he let his fingers sink into her luxurious coat. To uncap it could very well destroy this ship and all aboard. But he'd run out of options. His gaze shifted to Leelan.

"Make certain there are plenty of men prepared for any repercussion." Leelan nodded and Rein moved to the hip bath. Closing his eyes, he passed his hands back and forth over the copper tub, once, twice. The water bubbled.

He blinked down at the foggy liquid. Great thunder, he had to gain better control than that, he thought as he stripped, doused the hot water with a cooling pitcher full, then stepped in.

An hour later, kneeling on the cushion of pillows strewn on the floor, Rein rested his hands on his thighs. Slowly he tipped his head back, his lips moving in a soft chant. The room grew warmer and warmer, sweat breaking over his smooth skin and tickling down his chest. Before him on the floor lay four small earthen jars, their rims etched in silver, ancient markings of Runes and the Celtic knots of his mothers homeland, of places of power. In the jars, a handful of dirt from the Isle of Skye, a twig of blackthorn from a Druid rite, droplets of freshly fallen rain, the last, empty to the untrained eye, yet filled with the wind of the moors. Rahjin curled tighter under the bench, sniffing the air. Fragrances mingled, myrrh and ginger, sandalwood and mint. Rein prayed, to master and conquer, to direct and wield. The furniture rattled in the bolts. Air shifted, skipping over papers littering his desk, toppling candles wisely left unlit. The sheers on his bed swelled as if filled with the fists of a roaring beast, then calmed as Rein took control.

The elements answered him, the rulers taking his energy and sailing it through the city streets, through alleys and windows, over people whose only notice was a sudden warm breeze. In the confines of his mind, color and light rose and splashed, buffeting him. Then he saw her, vague and blurred, and he almost lost command. He banished his emotions, suppressed them as deep as he could and looked harder.

Suddenly, the pot of twigs ignited, the water boiled over, the rich soil spilled, feathering across the floor on a gust of wind.

Rahjin hissed, her black fur spiking her spine as Rein flung his head back, his howl of raw agony tearing from his chest, ripping through the air.

And setting the walls afire.

Nineteen

The cane struck her across the back, sending her reeling forward into the dark hole of a cellar.

"Mademoiselle," the cultured accent said. "Do not attempt such again."

"Then let me the bloody hell out!" Michaela gasped, her eyes shut tight against the pain. She stumbled for balance, glaring at him through a curtain of tangled hair.

He tsked softly, tapping the cane against the side of his boot. "Ladies do not use such language."

Michaela straightened and spat in his face. Slowly, he swiped at the spittle, flicking it aside, then raised his hand to strike. She stared him down, tipping her chin a fraction higher, and he smiled, lowering his arm.

"Do not force me again, *chérie,* you are of no use to me bruised." His handsome smile turned predatory. "Then you are no use to me alive." A knife slid from his sleeve into his palm, and in a flash, he brought his hand up, the silver blade caressing across her cheek.

Michaela retreated, the back of her legs hitting the cot tucked in the corner. Refined and elegantly dressed in dark gray, he stood no more than yard away and radiated evil, toying with her, yanking on his leash.

He smiled and replaced the knife. "You cannot escape."

She had, twice, though getting no further than the upper floor, and each time she received a half-dozen well-placed blows, methodical and precise, damage only a lover could see.

"Do it again and she dies." His dark glance moved to the ragged girl huddled in the corner, and the child whimpered, curling against the wall.

Michaela did not question his threat. He'd made good on each one thus far. And the girl, Diana, no more than ten and three, was waiflike thin, her closely shod blond curls matted to her head. She hadn't spoken since Michaela arrived—she could not remember how many days had passed since she'd been snatched off the street—and her narrow legs and knees were scraped, her body, clad only in a thin chemise, covered in bruises and filth. A single blow would kill her.

Michaela turned her gaze to Jean-Pierre and nodded.

"Excellent. Behave, and you will be allowed abovestairs."

"I am consumed with anticipation."

Jean-Pierre smiled that hideous smile and Michaela swallowed, the crust of bread she'd eaten this morning threatening to reappear. He spun on his heels, brushing imaginary dust from his coat, his cane tapping as he walked toward the staircase. The sound would haunt until she died, she thought, dropping to the cot. The motion sent a cloud of dust in the air with a scattering of bugs. She leapt, then decided it would do little good to stand on her aching legs and settled more slowly onto the straw bedding.

A cracking good fix this time, she thought as disjointed bits of the past days flickered in her mind, of running from the troops and slamming into the arms of a gentleman. She snickered at the notion. For a brief instant, she thought she'd found safety, a carriage to get her far away from the men chasing her for days, yet in her moment of indecision, Jean Pierre DuMere pushed her inside, forcing an almond-scented handkerchief over her mouth. After that, everything was murky and empty.

Until she woke up here.

"Diana, are you all right?"

The girl nodded, biting the edge of her thumb as her gaze darted nervously to the corners of the cellar. The threat to kill Diana was a new avenue of her torture. Michaela could no longer afford her defiance. Yet what he planned for her was still a well-kept secret.

The throbbing in her skull stirred her from a place she wanted to return, a soft buffer where she couldn't feel the pain. The aroma of flowery-sweet perfume assailed her, and she wrinkled her nose, trying to assimilate her thoughts, her last movements. Her mouth was as dry as popped corn, and when she lifted her hand to rub her gritty eyes, her arm jerked back. Both wrists were lashed to the headboard.

She came immediately awake, blinking to focus in the dim light. Cushioning beneath her was the softest down mattress, threatening to draw her back into the painless sleep, and she stared above, at the billowy streamers of silk, bright pink and glittering with gold.

Certainly not the cellar, she thought, and turned her head, her gaze moving over her surroundings. Though she'd never seen the like before, the decor told her without words where she was. A large lady's boudoir, and what caliber of lady shot panic up her spine, her stiffening driving a wave of raw torment over inflamed tissue and muscle. She gasped, struggling to let it pass without moaning, and looked again at the room. Surrounded by a dressing screen, two armoires, a commode, and a grouping of chairs and sofa near the fire, she lay in a massive bed shrouded in seduction, padded for the roll of naked bodies on thick velvet coverlets and satin pillows, privacy and decadence offered in the heavy maroon drapes and transparent sheers.

The reason behind her kidnapping was suddenly terrifyingly real.

And she did not even want to consider what the array of leather straps and collars racked near the bed were for.

She tried to sit up, but the silken cords knotting her arms to the bedpost were snug. She yanked regardless, the bed trembling, sending the sheers to undulate in a seductive wave. *Don't imagine it,* she warned silently. *You'll go mad.* And her head throbbed too hard to deliberate anything beyond the moment, and she carefully inched up on the pillows, trying to give her arms enough slack to ease the strain, yet the motion uncovered a dozen more aches to a taunt her in this pampered prison. And she smelled like a cellar, musty, wet.

Michaela swung her gaze to door as it rattled and a woman dressed in opulent silver taffeta swept into the room. "Well, it's about time you stirred."

"How did I get here?" she croaked.

The woman smirked, her young face contorted with bitterness. "Same as most of us. Snatched off the street. It ain't—it isn't a bad life," she corrected herself. "I sleep on satin and silk and have plenty to eat." As if that justified her kidnapping.

"I know that, I mean *here*. I recall—"

"The pit, aye, black as night, wuddun't—wasn't it?"

"Untie me this instant!" Michaela's voice gained more strength with her words.

The dark-haired woman spared her a thin look. "Making demands will get you beaten, honey. And you are in no position to be making a single one." She cocked her hip, her hand planted there as she eyed her ruined gown, then her face. "What did you do to piss—ah—anger Jean-Pierre anyhow?"

"Insufficiently obedient, I suppose."

The woman met her gaze with haunted eyes. "Do as he says or you'll end up dead." Her tone brooked no dispute as she moved to a commode and poured water into a bowl, drew a towel from the cabinets fashioned into the wall, then faced her. "They're bringing up some hot water for you."

Michaela nearly moaned at the prospect of washing. She could feel things crawling on her and she dared not speculate as to what variety.

"I'm Guinevere."

Michaela arched a bow.

"He changes all our names. So don't bother to tell me yours." She moved to the side of the bed, gazing down at her. "Most call me Gwen anyway." A knock sounded, yet she ignored it, leaning over to loosen the bonds. Michaela immediately sat up, and Gwen shot back, her gaze wary.

Michaela's gaze flew to her, working the kinks from her arms. "I won't hurt you."

"That's what they all say." She inclined her head to the door. "Follow me." She walked toward it.

Michaela did not budge, rubbing her wrists. "Where?"

"To a bath. You might be pretty, but you stink to high heaven."

Michaela smirked, scratching her arm. "What has he got planned?"

Gwen stilled at the door, her expression sympathetic. "Gonna clean you up, *Bridgette,* and feed you. That's as far as I know."

Michaela was not about to turn down the chance for a bath and food. She needed her strength to fight, and swung her legs over the side of the bed and followed Gwen out of the room. Her head swam with dizziness, and she grasped the doorjamb, licking her lips.

"Come on, girlie, there's scones and jam and sweet tea awaiting." Gwen grasped her arm and pulled her none too gently along.

Michaela did not need to be dragged to her fate like a coward, and jerked back, gesturing for her to proceed.

Gwen shrugged. "Suit yourself."

She followed, studying her surroundings, noting the armed men stationed at each end of the long corridor, yet all doors were closed. The guards seemed to understand her thoughts, and shifted to block the only exits, brushing their coats back to show loaded pistols. She would have to wait for the opportunity, yet locating Diana and discovering a way out was uppermost in her mind. She could not leave without the child, nor could she imagine a man bedding one so young and still able to live with himself.

The distinct creak of bed ropes pierced the walls, and Michaela misstepped, a woman's cry and the dark masculine groan of completion blending in the air.

She swallowed, quickening her steps past the doors.

Oh, God, oh, God.

He means to make me a whore.

Wouldn't Uncle Atwell be pleased to know.

She heard voices beyond the curtain and froze in her tracks. She could not do this. She could not. To be put up for auction like horseflesh was unthinkable. The other women thought it an honor, to have a private auction for her alone, insisting that she would be snatched up for some wealthy nobleman's mistress, or mayhap even the courtesan of a prince. Yet all Michaela could think was that there was no escape. She'd been thwarted twice since bathing, the back of her legs still stinging from Madame Goulier's willow whip. If they beat her anymore, she would not be fit for sitting, let alone laying on her back.

"Do not make me drag you," Jean-Pierre whispered in her ear, and she flinched, glaring back over her shoulder.

His pretty smile was thin and haughty, and she could not resist throwing it in his face. "A familiar task, *monsieur,* forcing women?"

His dark gaze took on a feral quality, showing her the man ruthless enough to kill an innocent child to gain her submission. "I would watch your tongue, *chérie.*" He inclined his head to the alcove, and Michaela's gaze shifted.

"Diana!" she gasped. The child stood between two burly men, her hands shackled in their fists, her terror so thick she could taste it, see it in her wide, darting eyes. His threats to snap the child's neck drove her toward the pedestal. He could easily kill her regardless, but Michaela could not chance it. She gathered her skirts and stepped up.

Clasping her hands before her, she sent her shoulders back, the motion pushing the plump curve of her bosom over the obscenely low edge of the black velvet dress.

"Very nice," he said, adjusting the drape of her hem and strolling around her as if he were admiring his own creation. She supposed he was. She looked naught like herself. Aside that her hair was arranged to draw attention to her bare shoulders, her face was painted and powdered, her body stuffed into the gown and leaving no doubt to the flaws and assets of her figure. The stays grated painfully over her abused back.

How she longed for the simple faded dress she'd burned days ago.

"Smile."

"Go to bloody hell," she said through gritted teeth.

He laughed to himself, his gaze flicking to Diana, then back. He was like most men, playing on her fear, counting on her fight to sexually arouse him.

"I will see you pay for this, sir."

He chuckled softly, stepping up on the pedestal beside her. *"Mais non.* You and your pretty body, *ma petite"*—his hand covered her breast, fingers dipping inside to pinch her nipple—"will pay me."

Michaela gritted her teeth, refusing any response, but the bile fuming in her throat threatened to erupt, and she wondered what he'd look like with her last meal all over his pretty coat.

He smirked and stepped down.

Beyond the curtain, a feminine voice grew closer, louder, building the anticipation of her appearance. *Oh, you fools,* she thought. *I will kill you the first chance than let any man touch me.* The curtain swept back. Masculine voices murmured approval, yet Michaela didn't see their faces, staring at the molding on the far wall. The prospect of spending even one instant beneath some lecher depraved enough to lay out coin for a captured woman twisted like a fist in her chest.

Madame Goulier, slim and tall with black hair swept high on her head, and about as French as Michaela was Irish, sauntered close, regarding her carefully before turning toward the men gathered. She squashed down the urge to kick her in the back and run for the door.

"Did I not promise you a wild Irish beauty, gentlemen. Is she not lovely?" Murmurs flitted about the crowd like smoke, accents varied. This house, she'd learned, dealt mostly with foreigners. "The bidding starts at one hundred pounds."

One hundred! Should she be flattered one could waste so much on a mistress?

To her horror, the bidding rose, the men calling out, making ribald remarks about her body, what her breasts alone were worth. Michaela remained stiff and still as Madame lifted her skirts so the buyer could view her stockinged leg, and she tightened her fists, itching to scratch her eyes out. Madame looked up. Her smile tight and too bright, she flicked her hem off her fingers and turned back to the crowd.

The wagers went on and upward. Two hundred pounds, two fifty, three hundred, four. A fortune promised. Then it stopped, no other bids offered, and she heard Madame say, "Ahh, *bonne, bonne,* five hundred pounds, gentlemen, for this Irish beauty. Going once, twice, thrice—"

Michaela tensed for the horrifying word, *sold.*

"You cannot sell what does not belong to you, madame," a deep voice sliced through the auction.

Michaela's fingers worked in the folds of her gown. Thank God. She could not bear to look, praying it was the authorities and then hoping it wasn't. The shame of anyone seeing her like this was almost too much to stand. Growls of disapproval rose swiftly, and she lowered her gaze, scanning the men for the intruder. Then her attention lit on the creature standing at the rear, concealed by the drapes disguising the plain foyer.

Two men stepped inside. Moors, she realized instantly, her gaze flitting over their long, flowing robes, their heads covered in white *kaffiyehs* and banded with heavy-braided black cord. Was she destined to be carried away to a harem?

Then a third man snapped back the drapes and paused briefly to survey the room in regal disdain before striding up the center aisle in smooth, long-legged strides, like a cat on the prowl. Straight white robes whispered against his black-booted calves and leather breeches as he moved closer and she let her gaze climb, to the pistols and huge, jeweled scimitar sheathed at his waist, to his simple black shirt. His head was covered in a drape of dark fabric, gold cording harnessing it in place, a length of it drawn across the lower portion of his face.

She lifted her gaze and met familiar pale-blue eyes.

Her heart slammed to her stomach.

Oh, God. Why him? she agonized, her face flaming with shame. She could not bear to look at him and cast her eyes to the floor.

"This auction is by invitation only, *monsieur,*" Madame said with a sweep of her hand to the attendants demanding he be escorted out and the auction continue.

"Not anymore."

Madame frowned. "Who are you and what do you mean intruding?"

"I am Sheik Kaseem ibn Abduli, son of Rahman." He swept the portion of cloth from his face and tossed it over his shoulder. "And I speak only the truth. You auction one of my women."

Michaela choked at the outrageous claim.

Rein turned to the bidders, his palms out. "Would you take what is already mine?"

"She made no mention." Madame's gaze sliced to Michaela.

" 'Tis because I am—"

Rein tipped his head and warned her with a lethal if-you-know-what-is-good-for-you, shut-up look.

Michaela pressed her lips tight, and she watched her fate unfold.

"She wishes to be first *kadine,* but"—he sighed, sliding Michaela a biting look—"She has not learned her place, as you can see."

Madame agreed, giving the girl and the bidder a speculative look and waging whether she would get more coin from the sheik. "I have already laid out good money for her."

"As have I."

"I expected to make a profit."

Rein tipped a conciliatory bow. "You will be compensated for the trouble."

"Her price is five hundred pounds."

His black brows rose in arrogant speculation as he looked Michaela over as if she were beef for the market and worthy of the sum. Michaela wanted to kick him.

Jean-Pierre stepped forward, whispering to Madame.

"She is no longer for sale," the woman said suddenly.

Rein's gaze slid to the elegantly dressed woman as he folded his arms. "I will have what is mine." His possessive tone shot through Michaela with the heat of a brandy quick drunk.

"Really?" With a subtle gesture from Madame, a half-dozen men stepped from behind the curtain.

"You do not want to do this."

Madame smirked unattractively, motioning for her guards, yet as the men moved forward, the collective click of pistol hammers resonated through the sudden stillness. Madame's gaze jerked around to the shrouded Moors slipping through windows and doors, each armed and pointing the weapons at her. The attendees started to rise, to scatter like frightened rabbits, but the newcomers held them down.

Madame looked nervously at the sheik.

"I will destroy this place, be assured, woman. And bring the public into your privacy."

Her eyes widened with fear. Her customers' identities were sacred. Should one be revealed, she would lose everything. And Rein knew it, counted on it, and withdrew a sack at his waist, held it up, then tossed it to her. She caught it, immediately spilling a fortune in precious gems into her palm as he snapped his fingers and the largest guard shouldered his way through the crowd toward him.

Rein swung his gaze to Michaela, keeping his features impassive, yet noticing the flicker of pain in her hazel eyes. She looked even more beautiful, perfect, prepared. And the thought of what might have happened made his voice harsh. "Come." He offered his gloved hand.

She hesitated, her hand out. "I can't," Michaela blurted, then glanced back to where Diana was hidden in the shadows.

His features darkened. "Impudent female." He grasped her hand and clapped an arm around her legs, tossing her over his shoulder. She cried out at the impact and, inwardly, Rein winced. *But this game must be played out to the end,* he thought, turning on his heels. He strode to the door, his men filing out in backward steps, Cabai guarding his back.

"Let me down."

"Be still, woman," he hissed, and outside, his men converged as he moved quickly to the waiting carriage. He swung her into his arms, refusing to look at her, at the marks of her imprisonment. He would burn the house to ashes if he did. Cabai opened the door and Rein ducked inside, gently lowering her to the seat.

Michaela tried suppressing a whimper, but it escaped, sounding pitifully childlike, and Rein's face mirrored sympathy as he swept his cloak over her shoulders.

"I cannot leave," she gasped, closing her eyes against the pain.

He tapped the roof regardless and the carriage lurched. "You wish to be sold as a whore?"

She flinched at that. "Of course not, but he will kill her now. Diana is just a child."

Rein looked at the house. "Diana? A slight thing. Blond curls?"

She opened one eye. "Aye," came warily.

Rein leaned back in the squabs. "She is kept around for that reason, Michaela. To blackmail women into service." The carriage lurched. "Diana is more of an accomplished courtesan than Madame herself."

She inhaled, appalled, and stared out the window.

Rein jerked her back and slapped the curtain down. "Do you want the world to see you leaving that place?"

She curled from his touch, needles of pain radiating through her shoulder. Lord, she wanted to sleep for a month and heal. "My reputation is in ruins as it is," she said, breathless. "I have been missing for days already—"

" 'Tis been nearly a fortnight," he said softly. Twelve maddening days.

She blinked, casting him a hard look, trying to decipher the truth. She'd been drugged, that she knew, and what went on whilst she was incoherent was—well, too late to consider. "Why doesn't anyone do something about that place? 'Tis a flesh factory."

His tone was lackluster dry as he pulled the *kaffiyeh* from his head and tossed it on the seat. "Because its better customers are the very ones who should close it down."

"You know this from experience?"

His gaze slid to her, yet he did not comment. The white slave market was lucrative and widely dominant, but that she would believe he would purchase a human being, for whatever reason, grated on his last nerve. "Why would you care?"

"I don't." But she did. "Take me home, please."

"You cannot go home, Michaela. Or did you forget that someone tried to kill you?"

"Nay, I did not—" She frowned, staring at him for a long time. "How did you know that? For that matter, how did you know I was there? Why did you stage this"—she waved at his robes— "This—"

"Liberation? Rescue?"

"I did not need to be rescued."

"Of course you didn't," he mocked, and wasn't about to tell her a Prussian prince was bidding on her. "And would you have wanted anyone to know 'twas me who took you?"

"Nay. Branded a harlot is foul enough."

His features tightened, and he looked out the window. His vision had shown him where she was hidden, yet it had taken another day to match the inside of the dark hovel to the elegant house. He thanked Mr. Gilbèrt for that bit of information, yet all Rein had to ponder for the past hours was the image of her being beaten and tied to a bed. And now that she was with him, she was never leaving his side. No matter what she thought of him.

"Nickolas sent me to find you."

"Who?"

He looked at her, and had admire her tenacity when he knew she was in terrible pain. "Ryder. Tall, gray-haired, Carolinian, about three score?"

Her brows knitted thoughtfully. "I don't believe we've met."

She was good, he thought. "I know you are the Guardian."

Her hand stilled in tugging the cloak over her bosom. "Be serious," she scoffed. "Me? An American spy? You have truly taken leave of your sense, Sheik Abduli." She snickered. "Now stop this carriage." She could not endanger anyone else for her purposes and needed to get to Nickolas still. "I wish to leave."

"Nay." He folded his arms, stretching his legs out and aching to take her in his arms.

"You have no right to detain me——"

Ungrateful little wretch, he thought. "I just lost small fortune to regain your freedom, Michaela." He cocked his head a touch. "What do you think I should do?"

She wished he wasn't looking at her with retribution in his eyes. "I will pay you back."

"And if I demand recompense now?"

She was penniless. She was trapped. "So, what will you do with me? Make me your slave, *your* whore?"

A muscle ticked in his jaw. Michaela swallowed, ensnared in the intensity of his pale-blue gaze.

"Nay, my little *rasha*." He leaned forward, his imposing presence smothering the air in the carriage. "My wife."

Twenty

For the space of a turn of the carriage wheels, she let herself believe, let herself want . . . a marriage, a family, a home, and, in the next moment, she knew it was impossible. Her suspicions of him still lurked, growing as the seconds passed.

"Nay," she said softly. "Nay." She shook her head. He was in league with her uncle, he'd killed his wife, mayhap his lover. *But he came for you,* a voice shattered through her thoughts, and she wondered over the look in his eyes just then, brief and gone before she could decipher it.

Her swift rejection stung. He should have expected no less, yet the fear in her eyes wounded him to the core of his soul. He'd given her no honest reason to fear him like this, never once threatened her life, and his resentment manifested in his scornful tone. "Listen well, Michaela. Deny all you wish, I do not care for your spying, your damned rebellion, but I swore an oath to Nickolas to protect you at all costs. And if marriage is the choice, then 'tis exactly what it will be."

"But I know no Ryder—"

"Enough!" he barked as the carriage suddenly slowed, his hurt and temper simmering together. He slapped back the curtain. "Pull up your hood," he said, then turned to her. "Move quickly and keep your head down."

The door opened and, beyond him, Michaela recognized one of his crewmen. Her gaze shot back to Rein. She opened her mouth to speak, to tell him she could find her way home without him when he cut her off.

"Nay, do not explain or deny." His voice bristled with impatience, his body half out the door. "Keep your secrets, woman, but understand that I risked much—my men, my business and contacts in this country, even my ships—to get you free. I am the merchant." Her eyes flared. "And be you traitor or nay, I do not care, but I will *not* break my word to Nickolas, not even for your stubbornness."

"I do not trust you," she said, moving to the edge of the seat and taking his hand.

"You do not need to. Just do as I say and you will be safe."

"Bloody well full of yourself, aren't you?" she muttered under her breath as she stepped out the right side, only to find another carriage parked dangerously close, the door open and a cloaked woman climbing down. A woman with red hair, her build. Michaela frowned, jealousy she'd no right to feel spinning through her as the woman met Rein's gaze, touched his face briefly with a kiss, then slipped into their carriage.

Rein ushered her into the opposite coach, and the carriages immediately divided, one heading east toward the docks, the other west.

"A decoy," she said.

He watched the progress out the window, a pair of Bedouin clad riders following the other carriage. "Aye."

She sat back, saying naught as he rose, and lifted the seat cushion, withdrawing a cloak, tricorn, and waistcoat from the storage hidden beneath. He placed the scimitar inside before closing it, then removed his weapons to don the garments.

"Where are we going?" she asked when he'd taken his seat.

Rein tipped his head back and met her gaze, silent. She would know soon enough, and he did not need her leaping from the carriage just now.

Fine, she thought, continue with this infernal mystery. "You're rather adept at stealing women, Rein." Question colored her tone.

"Adding kidnapping damsels in the dead of night to my many shortcomings?" he taunted.

"Is that to include murder?" she blurted, instantly regretting the slur.

His pale stare turned wild, savagely bright, and Michaela inhaled a sharp breath, pinned by the flicker of raw agony in his eyes.

"I could ask the same of you, manslayer."

Her features yanked tight. "I did not kill you."

The lines bracketing his mouth tightened, yet he did not speak, and Michaela awaited, silently begging him to dispute the worst of the rumors.

He didn't, and the accusation hung like a bleeding corpse between them.

Rein felt his insides chip away like granite falling under a sculptor's chisel. Claiming his innocence would not benefit him. He'd done the like for years and none believed, why should he think otherwise now? The stain of his past had touched her and he cursed at how deeply, turning his gaze out the window.

"Do you deny it?"

His lungs emptied in a slow push. "Would you trust me enough to believe my word?"

A hesitation and then, "Aye."

He scoffed, sinking deeper into the plush squabs and crossing his ankle on his knee. After a moment, he turned his head to look at her, his pale eyes glowing like crystal in the dark interior. "Your life has been naught but secrets and suspicion for the past three years, Michaela. You do not know how to trust."

How did he know all this? Surely Nickolas did not tell him. She looked down at her hands clasped in her lap as the carriage rolled into the more affluent part of the city. But she did not notice, did not care. She could not afford to trust, skepticism was a natural part of her. Why would Nickolas put his faith in such a man? How were they associated? Rein could be, for all the circumstance, the double agent himself, yet he'd offered the code name, something Nickolas did not reveal carelessly. Regardless, one question nagged its way into her confusion.

She lifted her gaze. "Why offer to wed me? To what end?"

"My family's name and this reputation you fear so greatly," came with a flex of acid in his tone, "will protect you now, should anyone find you."

"And you plan that they don't?"

"Not until Nickolas uncovers the renegade."

"And then what?"

He shrugged carelessly. "The choice is yours."

So, he offered marriage for her protection, for a duty sworn to Nickolas and naught else. Though she was honest enough to admit she was not safe until Nickolas uncovered the conspirator, the thread of hope that there was more behind his reasons for marriage still lingered. But what would he want with a clumsy oaf who could not complete a meal without leaving a spot on her gown, nor take a dozen steps without tripping over her own feet? Or a woman so disgraced he would turn away if he knew her truths. Nay, she thought. 'Twas useless and fanciful. She was better suited to spying and spinsterhood.

"I must see Nickolas." She had to tell him about the gold shipment, her uncle and his cohorts.

"You are admitting you know such a man?"

Her chin lifted. It seemed pointless to deny it.

"Out of the question."

"I must!"

"Do not demand, Michaela," he admonished icily. "I can be an insufferably cold bastard when the need arises."

"Really? One would never have thought. You being so open and honest," she said with a tight, sarcastic smile. "I am to be in your company for how long?"

He shrugged.

"I will not marry you."

He arched a brow.

"You cannot force me."

He simply stared.

"I want no man's name for the sake of protection." *I want it for love,* she thought, but he would not offer to make her his wife if he knew she was not far from the whore Madame tried to make her.

"Then you wish to walk the streets whilst there is someone out there waiting to put a bullet in your head?"

"Nay."

"Return to the bosom of your loving family?"

She made a sour face. "Nay." She felt cornered.

"You have run out of options, it appears."

"Marrying you is not one of them!"

The carriage hit a rut, jolting her against the wall, and she cried out. Immediately he reached out, steadying her as the corset stays scraped against her tender skin.

Rein slid his hands inside the cloak.

"What are you doing?" She tried pushing him away, but couldn't budge him. She felt his touch pull on the gown's lacings. "Ow! Oh, cease. Cease! I beg you."

"Shhh," he hushed softly, tugging.

The garment gave, and she moaned at the relief, her eyes watering. "Thank you," she cried softly, sniffling. "How did you know?"

His voice was whiskey rough and unguarded as he said, "Did I not tell you if you needed me, I would be there."

He had, *oh, he had.* "But how?"

A thousand secrets lay behind his expression. It was maddening.

"Someday when you trust me, Michaela Denton, when you can believe my words, I will tell you all you wish."

Her gaze searched his handsome face, skimming his raven black hair, his smooth skin, and she suddenly noticed how exhausted he looked. "You're a strange man, Rein Montegomery."

His hands slid to her waist, warm, so warm. And the turbulence in her calmed.

"So I've been told." He gazed into her eyes, smelling her, hearing her breathe, longing to taste her. His gaze lowered to her wet mouth, ripe and inviting, then back to her eyes. He saw a flash of alarm and distanced himself, sliding back into the seat.

She sniffled and he fished in his pocket, offering his handkerchief. "There are few men who would relinquish their bachelorhood so handily."

His remaining a bachelor was of little consequence to the situation, he thought, watching her blot her eyes, her pink nose. If he wed her, it was for her safety alone. And even before that, she had to know the consequences of the alliance. The thought of revealing his past for her sickened him, and he held no fantasy of having her as a true wife. Yet, for the first time his reputation would aid him. None would challenge him without repercussions. The English wanted his tea as badly as they wanted it and any other goods kept from the Americans.

The carriage slowed, and she looked up as he glanced out the window. His hand immediately moved the pistols lying on the seat beside him.

"What is it?"

The fear rang in her voice and Rein looked at her. "Safety."

The carriage stopped, the door opening. "Quickly, afore the rain breaks." He stepped out and turned to her. Michaela followed, looking up at the house. It was huge and dark but for the glow in the doorway. Holding her elbow, he hurried her up the steps and inside.

Michaela pushed back the hood as three men filed in behind her. Rein turned to introduce them.

"Mr. Bushmara." He bowed, smiling.

"Mr. Popewell." The dark-haired young man grinned, removing the *kaffiyeh*.

"And Cabai."

Her gaze swept upward, and a little smile curved his lips as he bent low. She dipped a curtsy. "A pleasure, gentlemen."

The door closed softly, and her gaze shifted to Rein as he slid the bolts home.

She was a prisoner again and he read it in her gaze. She stood still, her hand hidden in the folds of her cloak as he gave orders to his crewmen, then dismissed them, handing his cloak and tricorn to Cabai. Rein gestured to the staircase, and Michaela proceeded, having little choice in the matter. He mounted the steps behind, watching the seductive sway of her hips, yet feeling her apprehension and seeking a way to alleviate it. Her distrust disturbed him more than it should, and as he gestured to the left hall, moving ahead to open the door, he did not consider letting her simmer in fear. To exert such power of the weak was to destroy their pride and dignity. And his had been torn to ruin too often to not make him keenly aware of it.

He swung wide, and Michaela inhaled, stepping inside.

"It's lovely." A blazing fire lit the room, showering the walls with yellow light, the pale-green coverlet and drapes inviting and feminine.

"A bath is prepared for you." He gestured to a separate room off to the right, a fire glowing in there, too. "I'm certain you are tired. I will have a tray sent up." He crossed to the armoire and opened it, revealing an array of women's garments and when he looked at her, he recognized the question in her eyes. "Nay, Michaela, they are not hers." That she thought him so heartless to give her a dead woman's clothes imbedded her distrust deeper in his soul, angering him. "Aught of hers was burned."

Michaela was trying to understand the look on his face when he showed her the bell pull. She nodded, already crossing to the thickly padded sofa near the fire and warming herself. She slipped the cloak from her shoulders, and the loosened black gown sagged, exposing a goodly portion of her bosom. His gaze lowered to the lush swells, a sudden ache to peel the garment down and taste her clenching his vitals. Having her this close was surely going to test the edges of his will.

"I'm afraid I cannot provide you a maid," he blurted. " 'Tis too dangerous to involve anyone not aware of the risks."

"I've managed well without one," she said, then cocked him a look. "Do they know? Your crew, I mean."

"They know only to help me protect you, Michaela. Naught more. And I wish to keep it that way."

She nodded, feeling like a heavy burden to him. She was not so determined in her need to help the rebellion that she didn't realize he'd hazard much for her. The least she could do was be civil.

"Cabai can assist you in your bath."

Her eyes rounded. "You cannot be serious?"

A small smile touched the corner of his mouth. She was so innocent, he thought, so pure of thought. He hated to destroy it. "He is a eunuch, Michaela."

Her eyes widened, and after a false start she said, "I do not care. I do not need a man helping me with a simple bath."

Rein shrugged. "Fine. Then if you need assistance, I will tend you."

"You will not! 'Tis improper."

"Discard your shyness, Michaela. We will be living in the same house for some time. How proper is that?" He moved to the bathing room door, the leather breeches shooshing softly. "My rooms are through here." He entered the bath, pushing the latch, and was not surprised to find her close at his side. He could feel her as if he wore her against him, and he wanted more than to sense her presence. He wanted to devour it. He never hungered for a woman as he did for her, and as he looked down at her, watching her gaze slip over his rooms, his bed, for a forbidden instant, thought of pulling her inside and laying her upon the soft center, tasting her skin, her secrets.

He wanted this woman, willingly, without fear, without regret. And that, he would never gain. The rubbish covering him was wormed with the stench of decay, and too many rumors had already clouded her judgment.

Abruptly he moved into the rooms, going to a tall oak hutch. Almost angrily, he threw back the doors and withdrew a polished wooden box, carrying it back to her. When she simply stared at it, he folded her hands around the smooth wood, his body pressed to the opposite side.

"You are safe here, Michaela," he said in a low voice "No one knows I own this house, and it's far enough from the city. You are free to do as you please within its confines, and if you need aught, simply ask. The grounds are walled and the house has over a dozen guards about."

All men, she thought. "I am a prisoner."

"If that is how you choose to view it." He looked down at the box. "You fear me and I do not like it. But this—" he lifted the lid, showing her matching pistols and a pair of knives, then meeting her gaze "—should give you some assurances." The corner of his mouth quirked. "You may use it on me, if you feel 'tis necessary."

Michaela stared at the pistols, his initials engraved into the stocks. "I could use these to escape." She closed the box.

"Aye."

"Yet you trust me not to?"

"When you've time to weigh the ramifications, you will see I am right."

Her lips tightened. "I hate that you are always so certain of yourself, Rein Montegomery," she huffed. "Do you know that?"

"I do now." Though he smiled gently, his eyes darkened, a velvety look as his gaze wandered over her hair, her carefully painted face, her bare shoulders, and the plentiful bosom spilling from the loose gown. God of thunder, she was lovely. Even clad for seduction, he could see the purity beneath, and he wanted some of it, wanted to cast the pistols aside and feel her against him, taste her sweetness, the fire she let erupt only twice before.

"If I were so certain of aught, *rasha,*" he said with a slow shake of his head, "I would not put the temptation of you so close." He lifted his hand to her cheek, his touch a breath away, trapping them both in the tiny room.

Michaela stared, hugging the box and aching inside, wanting to feel safe and loved. Wanting what he offered in a single look. And she cursed the men who'd rent apart her dreams so deeply, there was no room left to make more. "Don't invite it, Rein." She looked away, her gaze distant. "You will not like the results."

His brows knitted, his fingers clenching away from her face. He sighed and stepped back, turning into his rooms and closing the door.

Michaela let out a long breath, dropping her head forward, feeling completely drained. He was imposing and strong and captured every sensation running through her body, making her pulse so deeply for his touch she wanted to scream. Regret sluiced through her, and she set the box aside, stripping out of her gown and stepping into the bath.

Such thoughts were tainted and brought only pain, and as she sank deeply into the water, she wondered if she were not suited better to the life of a harlot than that of a spy.

Rein heard her moan, the splash of water, and sagged against the wall, raking his fingers through his hair, then mashing his hand over his face. He resisted the childish urge to bang his head back against the wood. *I am mad to do this,* he thought, pushing away from the wall, and knew if he heard her moan once more, he'd bust his way back inside and soothe her pain. He left his rooms, heading below stairs to have food prepared for her and mayhap get a grip on his desire. He paused at the base of the staircase, glancing up, his imagination brewing the vibrant picture of her body wet and sheened with bubbles. And how much he'd like to lick them all away.

He ground his teeth and headed into the kitchen.

He'd no time to indulge in fantasies.

He had a killer to unmask, a father to find, and a rumor to start.

* * *

Campbell sat astride his horse, well hidden in the shadows. For an hour, he looked through the gates of the house, at the figures moving behind the shaded windows, the lights illuminating the upper floors. She was in there, he knew, though he hadn't gained a decent look at her when she entered the house with Montegomery, but he recognized her walk. She'd gone inside of her own free will. He saw her smile once or twice at the guards the man had crowding the house.

Yet part of him stirred with anger, that she'd run off and put herself in danger again, and that her reputation would be far more ruined than it was already if anyone knew she was here with him. Her uncle had been spouting off at anyone within kicking distance about her behavior enough as it was, as if naught else was expected of Richard's daughter than to run away like a frightened rabbit. *Or with some ne'er-do-well* was the Brigadier's latest summation.

Rein Montegomery was hardly that, he thought. And all Argyle could comprehend was that she was alive and Montegomery had seen her safety hidden away from ridicule. 'Twas a bloody fortress surrounding her, and his relief was so tremendous, his eyes watered. He pinched his nose with thumb and forefinger, his shoulders drooping. At least he could put Agnes's troubled heart at ease, he thought, and decided that he would tell no one about his discovery. That did not mean he couldn't check up on the man's activities, just to be sure.

But he'd seen the way Montegomery looked at her before he'd kissed her that night in the rain, with a need for more than desire, a need for more than the touch of another human being. And Michaela, well, the lass damn near climbed up him to get closer than a kiss. More brewed between the pair than either of them wanted to recognize, Argyle figured. And if he had any smarts left, he'd stay out of Montegomery's way and let it happen.

Michaela needed his strength now. She needed a friend. For with her uncle's dismissal of her plight, she had no one to turn to who could help her.

No one with that much power.

Twenty-one

Rein stood by the bed, staring down at her. She lay on her side, smothered in coverlets, her beautiful face contorted in agony and his mind filled with his vision, of DuMere's cane striking her over and over, of Madame's whip cutting into the unprotected flesh of her thighs. The image had followed him until the moment he'd seen her on the pedestal.

"Are you just going to stare at me?" she hissed softly through her teeth. "Or is entering a lady's chamber to play the voyeur common for you?"

Still frowning, he knelt near the edge of the bed, brushing her hair back off her cheek.

Her lashes swept up, amber-green eyes simmering with pain.

"Must you always be so brave?"

"Aye, my father insisted. 'Twas the curse of not being born a lad."

His lips quirked a bit. "You do not have to suffer."

"Are you claiming to be a healer?" He'd recovered from the shot quickly enough.

"I claim naught but what I know."

"Can you not give me a clear answer?" She tried sitting up, and winced. "Must you be so mysterious?"

"Take off your gown. Is that clear enough?"

"I will not."

He sighed, impatient. "You can hold this on me if you wish." He slid his hand beneath the pillow and withdrew the pistol.

She flushed with embarrassment, yet his expression showed no emotion as he leaned out to light a candle, the glow showering over an array of bottles and a bowl already on the commode.

He stood and turned his back. "Do it, Michaela. I cannot bear to hear you cry out in pain."

"Disturbing your sleep, was I?"

He shook his head ruefully and heard the rustle of sheets, yet kept his mouth shut. She was not prepared to hear aught he had to say and he wondered if she ever would. He stole a covert glance back over his shoulder and, seeing her struggle, he turned to her.

"Kneel on the bed." He helped her sit up, his face close to hers. "You need only lower the gown so I may see the damage."

She gazed into his eyes, warring with modesty and her pain, then did as he instructed, glancing at him with apprehension as she loosened the thin ribbons at her throat. She gave him her back before hesitantly slipping the gown off her shoulders.

His curse fouled the air and she looked at him, her breath catching like a stone in her chest. The rage in his eyes was black and savage, a snarling beast ready to erupt.

His gaze shot to hers. "But God, the bastard was precise." She must have fought him at every turn.

" 'Tis bad?" She held the coverlet at her breast, looking delicate and frail. "Will I be scarred?"

Her woeful tone struck him hard, and his shoulders sagged. "Nay, 'twill heal." He pressed a knee to the bed.

She instantly stiffened.

He reached for the pistol and folded her fingers over it. "I will not harm you, I promise."

She gazed into his pale eyes, seeing the truth more there than in his words. She nodded and stared off at the wall above the headboard. She heard the chink of bottles, water splashing into the bowl, and looked again.

He purposely turned her face away. "Stare at the wall. Think of something pleasant."

"What are you going to do?"

"Heal you."

She made a sound of doubt.

Rein's lips twitched, and he instructed her to scoot farther into the center of the bed, then knelt behind her, and where Michaela expected him to slaver a poultice on the wounds, he did not. It confused her even more. She looked back over her shoulder. His head was bowed, his hands on his thighs.

"What are you doing?"

He did not meet her gaze. "Look at the wall, concentrate on the painting." His voice soothed, coaxed. "Think of naught but the colors, the brush strokes."

To distract her, she thought, and imagined the healing was going to hurt more than the wound.

Rein focused his thoughts, drawing his energy into himself, pulling it from the fire in the hearth, the water in the bowl, the air in the room. His body tingled with the heat of it, and he sent it into his hands, raising them to hover inches from her back. Purple bruises and deep red welts crisscrossed her tender skin, and his hands swept above her flesh, never touching, carefully drawing her energy, her pain, into himself. He felt the burn of it on the tips of his fingers, felt it sear up his palms, and the purple of her skin faded, the welts softened to pale pink. She moaned and he knew she was not conscious of her moves, only the relief of the pain as she rose up and let the gown fall away, revealing the bare curve of her buttocks and thighs—and the whip marks crusted with blood. He fought with his own anger, pushed the need to seek retribution for her pain to the recesses of his mind, to another time and place as his hands roamed a layer above her ruined skin. His palms blistered with the absorption, scalded, heat shooting up his arms into his chest. He flinched, throwing his head back and gritting his teeth.

Raw energy vibrated through his blood.

The fire flared in the hearth.

Night frost melted from the windowpanes.

Michaela sighed with relief, sinking to her haunches, and, after a moment, he slid from the bed, laying her carefully down.

"You did not touch me," she whispered drowsily, staring at him in wonder.

" 'Twas not necessary." He was thankful for small favors, for touching her would result in the complete destruction of his willpower, he thought, and he was hanging on by a slender thread as it was.

He mixed a concoction to take her into a peaceful sleep, tipped the cup to her lips, forcing her to drink it.

"Ick, 'tis vile. What's in it?"

"You do not want to know," he said, pulling the gown up over her shoulders and tying the ribbon. When he looked up, her eyes were closed. A tear slipped from behind the lids, absorbed into the pillow. The sight of it made him groan, and she reached, let her fingers trail across his cheek, his jaw, then his lips. Another tear came.

"Thank you," she gasped. "Thank you."

"Do not cry, please." Her tears made him weak and helpless. He covered her hand with his and leaned forward, no longer resisting his need and brushing his mouth over hers. Her sweet breath spilled into his mouth and she sank into his kiss, moaning, her lips tugging on his.

"Oh, 'tis better than your cures," she whispered unheeded, already tumbling toward her dreams. She sank into the mattress, her hand dangling limply over the side of the bed.

He couldn't move, staring, his body hard from the simple touch of her mouth, his arms howling to hold her long into the night, yet the draught and the loss of her energy would keep her in a healing sleep for a day at least, and by then he prayed he'd have a hold on his desire.

He tucked her hand beneath the coverlet, pulling it up over her shoulders, then stood and gathered his herbs. He left her, moving quickly to his rooms and closing the door without a backward glance. He tossed the herbs aside and rubbed his face. How long did he expect to keep up this charade, he thought, with her—and himself?

The only facet of his life Rein was deadly certain about was that he did not kill Katherine Hawley. The question was, who did, and why. The matter had been the talk of the city, and those who speculated loud enough added Michaela's disappearance to the gossip. Rein seized the opportunity, occasionally adding fuel to the fire and tearing speculation from Michaela. 'Twas simple, he thought, just agree with the rumors. And the comment that Michaela was already dead opened the door.

"You don't suppose he killed her, too."

Only Rein's gaze shifted up from his cards and glanced around the table at Mr. Burgess, Lords Heyward, Sheppard, and Chandler. Christian, he'd come to recognize, was worse than a woman when it came to spreading gossip.

"What makes you so certain 'twas a man who killed Lady Buckland. It very well could have been a vengeful woman." Rein tossed down a card and Sheppard dealt another.

Heyward and Chandler exchanged a glance.

"You can't be serious," Christian said.

"I most definitely am." Rein did not say that Katherine was a spy and whoever cut her throat quite possibly knew it.

Heyward glanced at Chandler, then Sheppard. "Is there something you're not saying, Rein?" When Rein remained silent, he prodded, "Come, man, give over."

Rein scoffed, staring at his hand. "Only that Katherine bedded many a married man. What woman would stand for it?"

"Taking a mistress is naught to get whacked for," Burgess said, and Rein looked up.

"If that is your feeling, sir, then mayhap you should look to your house?"

Burgess stiffened. "That is not what I meant. I'd no association with Katherine."

"I did."

"We know."

Rein smirked and tossed his hand into the pile, folding. "What I mean is, there was no mystery that Katherine wanted to be my mistress." He waved a hand at his gambling partners. "You all knew. Bloody thunder, so did half the city."

"What are you getting at, Rein?" Christian asked, glancing to the side, then leaning forward.

"I am a perfect a suspect for any dastardly deed, considering how my wife died." A flash of something akin to pain flickered in his eyes. "I'd always thought Shaarai took her own life, but what if she did not," he added to the cauldron of speculation. "Lady Buckland's murder is simply a way to point the finger at me again and take it from the real killer."

"You really didn't do it, did you?" Sheppard blurted into the conversation, and Rein swung his gaze to his right.

"Nay, I did not." His lips twitched. "And thank you for gaming with a suspect all these years, my lord. Shows great fortitude." He wished Michaela could be so easily convinced.

Sheppard blustered, "I never thought you did, Rein, 'tis just that . . . well . . . you're always so damned brooding and quiet." He flamed with embarrassment. "And you never did deny it."

"Ahh, but I did. And I spent seven months in Newgate for it.

And the only reason I am not there now is because of Christian's intervention."

Christian looked down at his hand. "I was not the only one who spoke up," he confessed. "Brigadier Denton did."

It was Rein's turn to look surprised as he swung his gaze to the man standing near the buffet. "Interesting," he murmured more to himself. *He still wants the ship,* he thought, *and if he thought the favor would be repaid with one of his prized frigates, he was sadly mistaken.* But just the same, Rein decided he would string him along and nodded. The Brigadier saluted him with a glass of port.

"He seems at no great loss over his niece's disappearance," Rein murmured sadly.

"He claims she is hiding somewhere, too scared or too embarrassed to come out. She's been lost for so long now. Mayhap she fled with a lover?"

Rein looked at Christian. "After being shot at?"

" 'Twas intended for Lady Whitfield."

"You're certain? Well, aye, you are probably correct," he conceded quickly. "She is the weak link to her brothers. And what better way to threaten them."

"Mistress Denton, though," Heyward said in a sotto voice, "possessed the wealth. The Brigadier has only his pension coming. Mayhap Mistress Denton was kidnapped?"

Chandler looked at the others, then Rein, who was scowling at all of them.

"Kidnapped? You think?" Sheppard said, and Rein could see the wheels turning.

Target hit, he thought, hiding a smile.

"Has there been a ransom note?"

"I hadn't heard," Chandler mulled, staring sour-faced at his hand. "Then there is Captain McBain, who has been out searching for her daily with Major Winters."

That immediately grabbed Rein's attention. "The aide-de-camp?"

"Aye," Christian said. "The Brigadier hoped for a match between his niece and his aide, but apparently they had a falling out."

"Why'd she beg off? The woman cannot afford to be choosy. Such a plain, biddable little chit. Except for that hair," Burgess said, eyeing his cards. "A man wants a little fire in a wife."

If they only knew, Rein thought, defensive. "I found her to be most intriguing," he said, and a half-dozen pairs of eyes swung to him. "She's bright and witty. Lovely to look upon." He shrugged. "I saw no faults that would send her into spinsterhood."

"Well, there must be, since she's well past her age of consent."

"Mayhap she prefers remaining unmarried in lieu of the choices." Rein smiled at his partners. "If any of you are the samples," Rein waved at the lot of them, " 'tis no wonder the woman chose to remain unwed."

Chuckles rounded the table.

"And you are supposing she would have taken your favor?" Burgess asked.

Rein tossed a card. "I, sir, am the last person a woman like Michaela Denton would choose for a husband." He looked at Sheppard. "As you reminded, my lord, I am pensive and taciturn, and, of course, there is that dastardly past that would haunt the woman for the remainder of her days and likely keep her up nights. No woman trusts that much." Especially not Michaela. "There simply is no discussion in that course." Rein arranged his cards, aware of the eyes falling upon him.

"You sound regretful, Rein," Chandler said softly, his words meant for the men at the table alone.

"Mayhap." His shoulders moved restlessly. "Often one cannot help the circumstances which lead to a turning point in our lives. If we could, we would all foresee them afore they occurred. And mayhap change destiny."

"You don't really believe life is predestined, do you?"

Rein glanced at Heyward, then tossed a coin into the pile. "I believe that what I do not learn in this life to be a better man, I learn in another. And if my karma is that I am to be alone to ascertain it, then so be it." The ante moved around the table as he said, "But that does not mean I will not do my best to alter it."

"Are you saying there is a woman in your life?"

Rein scoffed as if that were the last thing on his agenda. "I am too busy for women's games, and I meant that I am destined to empty your pockets." He laid down his cards in a fan. "Into mine."

They collectively looked at the spread of aces and groaned, tossing in their cards.

The discussion turned back to Katherine, and the men tried naming her last list of lovers. Rein was at the top, yet he made a point of reminding them that he'd spent but one night with the viper of West End, and that was over nine months ago.

"I'd thought I was her last," Christian said.

"Wanting to be immortalized, Chris?"

Lord Chandler's face flamed. "Nay, but there was another. She left me for him."

"After she sought me out?"

Christian shook his head. "Nay, there was yet another."

"And another, and another," Sheppard joked, but Rein ignored him and focused on Christian.

"Why did you not tell the authorities this?"

They all looked at the earl. "I . . . I . . . well, there is naught to tell." He was decidedly uncomfortable to admit it. "We argued, a small spat really, and, nay, I will not discuss over what." His skin darkened and the men gathered from that. "She rushed off, and that was the last I'd heard of her."

To Nickolas, Rein considered. To deliver information? Was she caught doing it? Or caught in taking some vital piece for the rebel's cause? And who did she get it from? Christian? Rathgoode? Germain? Winters?

"I suspect he was a young one, though."

Rein frowned as he dealt the cards in a swift spin around the table. "Why?" Rein was two years Christian's senior. That meant whoever she sought was under a score and ten.

Christian slunk in his chair a bit. "She claimed that youth had its advantages," he groused. "Stamina was the word she used, I believe."

"Stamina was her forte," Rein commiserated. "Katherine could kill a man with her . . . exuberance."

"By God, you are an interesting set," Heyward said, grinning hugely and looking between the two.

"And she did arrive once with light hair on her clothing."

"Kat was a blond," Rein pointed out unnecessarily.

"Aye, but neither the shade nor those curls were a product of her birth."

Rein frowned, and the party grew silent. He wondered why Christian did not speak of this before, and Rein mentally went down a list of suspects. A list of lovers.

Temple Matthews had curly hair, yet the hue was of some dispute. The age was a concern, too.

Christian, too was fair-haired, though rather dark in complexion. Then there was Major Winters, he thought, staring across the hall at the man and feeling every inch of his hatred. He was pompous and rude, aye, but so was half of England, he thought, dismissing Winters for the moment. His gaze moved around the room.

The impetuous Lieutenant Ridgely was blond, curly-haired and young. And had been known to win the ladies with that boyish face and scarlet coat and was already plying them on Christian's ward, Brandice Coldsworth, from what he'd heard.

Endurance could be mistaken for enthusiasm, and even an elderly man faced with the opportunity to bed a vivacious creature like Katherine would find the stamina to meet her needs. Yet, Rein did not rule out that Christian was merely jealous over being pitched aside for another more creative lover. Katherine had a disease, her need for physical gratification driving her from one bed to another, and Rein wondered what she had been seeking, other than a full purse. At least a half-dozen of the powerful men she'd bedded possessed light hair. Two of the men whispered about were blond—and both men were under suspicion by Rein as being his blood father.

Twenty-two

She heard the sound of hoofbeats, the jingle of a bridle, and dashed to the window, brushing back the curtains in time to see Rein skid to a halt in the courtyard. Her heart did a strange twist in her chest as he swung from the saddle and tossed the leads to a man before taking the stairs two at a time.

Dipping her toes into her slippers, she headed to the door, racing down the hall, and as she met the landing, the front door burst open. His deep, accented voice resonated up to her and she waited, suddenly hesitant, until he appeared.

As if sensing her presence, he tipped his head back.

Eyes locked and held tight.

Michaela's skin warmed, her bedclothes feeling thin and far too transparent under his intense study. His gaze moved hotly over her, licking at her curves, probing beneath the fabric, and while she anticipated familiar feelings of shame and revulsion, she felt only wild heat and greed.

Then she noticed he was bleeding.

Rein froze at the sight of her descending the staircase toward him in a flurry of gauzy white batiste and lawn, skirts breezing a trail, her thick red braid swishing across her hips. In the back of his mind, in the fractured mist of want and hope, he'd dreamed of a moment like this. Someone here, waiting for him, wanting him to return, and he watched her move toward him, without hesitation, without fear.

"You're hurt," she said the instant she was close, reaching for his face.

Her fingers delicately brushed the scrape on his jaw, and he felt the sensation down to his boot heels. How could any man with eyes and blood in his veins think her plain? "And you should be abed." He plucked off his gloves.

"I am fine." Her gaze swept to his. "A matter I would like to discuss with you at length."

"If you wish." Without taking his gaze from her, he removed his tricorn, tossed his gloves in the well, then swept his cloak from his shoulders, handing the lot to Cabai. He gestured to a room off to his right.

She frowned. "You should stay warm till you are well."

He caught her elbow, gently ushering her inside, then whispering to Cabai before closing the door.

He faced her, his hands on his trim hips, his buff-colored shirt clinging only a fraction less than his brown leather breeches. Nothing was left to the imagination, she thought, letting her gaze slide down to his black knee boots, then back up to his face. With his head bowed, his shaggy hair shielded his features and she ached to brush the heavy black locks aside and see every detail of his face. But she didn't need to see his eyes to know he studied her. Her body knew, her breasts suddenly aching in a way they never had before. The air between them charged, and Michaela thought often about how he could evoke sensations in her when no other had. For three nightmarish years she scorned the thought of a man touching her, yet Rein she craved like a starving animal, craved his eyes upon her, the heaviness of his touch. Even when she knew he deserved better than a woman like her.

"Chilled?" he said, startling her.

"I am warm enough, thank you," she said without thinking, and wondered if he knew his effect on her.

He did, his own body jumping to life the instant he saw her. Now it hummed with suppressed desire, thickening through him, and he prayed she didn't notice the evidence. He tore his gaze away and went to the hearth. She didn't move and he glanced back, his gaze roaming her from head to toe, his look daring her to venture closer.

She did.

Her slippers were on the wrong feet, he realized with a private smile, and said, "Come sit." He stoked the fire high, then added another log to the blaze. He sensed more than heard her move up behind him and curl into the corner of the couch. When he faced her, her slippers were on the floor and she was tucking her feet beneath the voluminous folds of her dressing gown. Solicitously, he draped a blanket over her lap.

"Cease. You needn't coddle me." She adjusted the blanket herself. "I have fended for myself for some time now."

It was time she took more care of herself than her bloody cause, he thought, yet said, "Are you hungry?"

"Nay."

"Thirsty?"

She cocked a look up at him, brushing a loose strand from her cheek. "Have any brandy?"

His brows shot up.

"We spies do that sort of thing, you know."

His lips twitched, and he crossed to the lowboy, pouring her a snifter full. She accepted it gratefully, taking a healthy sip. He noticed her hands trembled.

He knelt. "What is it?"

She shrugged, staring at the liquor. It was unnerving, how perceptive he was to her feelings. "When I awoke I realized how fortunate I was to escape a fate worse than death." She sipped. "And when I learned you were gone—" She sipped and sipped again. "I felt, well—" He stopped her from taking another, his hand over the lip of the glass.

"Look at me, Michaela."

She lifted her gaze, sinking into his pale-blue eyes.

"You are safe."

She sighed heavily, her eyes glossing. "I feel foolish. But 'tis been so long that I've been chasing my own shadow or looking over my shoulder . . ." She released a nervous laugh. "I'm afraid feeling protected is a new venue to me."

He smiled, that tender forgiving smile that robbed her of thought. And her gaze lowered to his mouth, entranced by the shape of it forming his words.

"None can hurt you as long as you obey my rules, I swear." A pause and then, "Michaela?"

She lifted her gaze to his, blinking. "Ahh. Aye, I heard," she said with a spark of irritation, although she hadn't.

" 'Tis dangerous, the way you are looking at me, woman."

She lowered her gaze, frowning. "I know," she said softly, the touch of regret noticeable even to her.

A profound sadness swept her. It was complicated, this odd relationship they'd begun weeks past. Yet for years she'd kept a leash on her emotions, but near him, every nuance she'd hidden for so long came to life with a jolt. It was as if he'd crashed through a rusty door in her soul and now it swung wide. The urge to step through was almost painful.

She didn't trust him, didn't love him. Even if his offer was only a temporary arrangement, for she did not dare believe this would last beyond uncovering the double agent, it was no reason to plunge into marriage with him. Despite his nefarious past, her suspicions, and his duty to Nickolas, he merited more in a wife.

She was a traitor.

Tainted goods.

Inflicting such disgrace on him was unconscionable.

Yet she wanted her burned dreams to rise from the ashes.

I feel like a bloody changeling, she mused, trying to duck the glass from beneath his palm. She lifted her gaze to his. He was still so close, staring so deeply. "Rein?"

"Aye." What darkness he'd glimpsed in those eyes, he thought, concerned.

"Get your own drink, this one is mine."

He quirked a smile, and together they looked down.

She inhaled a sharp breath. "Your hand, too. Are you going to tell me what happened?" Immediately, she set the snifter on the table beside her, taking his hand in hers, running her fingers over the scrapes.

He pulled from her grasp and stood, turning to brace his arm on the mantel.

Michaela stretched her neck, peering to see his face. He looked awfully troubled, she thought, recognizing the stiffness in his spine, his fingers flexing and unflexing.

A knock sounded, and Rein barked a command to enter, making her flinch.

"Rein. This is a house, not a ship," she scolded, and he looked up, momentarily amused as Cabai slipped around the edge of the door, a tray bearing a bowl and cloths in his hand. Michaela left the couch to retrieve it, smiling at the big man. He glanced at his employer, then her, bowing out of the room.

Seated on the couch, she patted the space beside her. "Your wounds will get infected if you do not clean them."

She did not know that he rarely fell to taint so easily, yet slid to the couch.

The bowl on her lap, she dipped the cloth. "Good Lord, the water is ice cold," she groused. Rein leaned forward, staring into her eyes and passing his hand over the water. Her gaze snapped to the bowl. Instantly, she felt the warmth through the porcelain. "How did you do that?"

His expression was bland as he said, "Energy."

"Well, that explains a great deal," she mocked, wringing out the rag as if it were his neck. "How stupid of me."

His smile was filled with tender humor. "I control the warmth in me and pass it to the water."

She met his gaze, her expression considering. "Like you did to me?" She washed the dirt and dried blood from his jaw.

"Aye." He found an odd sense of peace, having her tend him, he thought, inhaling her scent, memorizing each feature.

"How did you get these?" Gently, she blotted the wet cloth over his knuckles. They were not even swollen.

Rein stared at her bowed head, battled with concocting a lie to suit, then spoke the truth. "Jean-Pierre paid for what he did to you."

Her head jerked up, warmth surging deeply inside her just then.

No one had avenged her before. No one cared enough, yet she could not help the words tumbling from her lips. "You killed him?"

He thrust from the couch, his back punishingly straight, fists clenched at his side. "You are convinced I could take a life so easily?"

"I do not know what to think, Rein. My God, I was in agony last night and—"

"Two nights ago, Michaela. 'Tis the evening of the third."

At her silence, he cast a quick look over his shoulder and saw confusion and doubt blend in her features.

She'd been missing for more than a fortnight, she finally realized. Her reputation was in shambles. With no way to repair it. And upon her return to Denton House, how was she to explain her disappearance? If Uncle Atwell and his clan were caught, how useful would she be as a spy after that? Who would invite her into affluent circles? And with her dowry nearly gone, if her uncle continued to spend it as he had, that left her with nothing. She could not worry over that now, she decided briskly. Stopping her uncle was her only thought. Except of Rein.

"What can I believe?" she finally said, setting the bowl aside.

"Your heart, your instincts."

"A tender heart will get me caught," she said acidly, jamming her feelings into that familiar pocket that kept her alive since her father died.

He rounded on her. "And distrusting me now will get you slaughtered!"

"I see what I see, Rein Montegomery!" She leaped from the couch, up in his face. "You pop in and out of my life at the most opportune moments, often to stop me from my duty."

"You believe I am a spy?" he barked. "Or mayhap the double agent?"

" 'Tis a thought."

"One I am certain you have pondered overlong, little deceiver."

"You have loyalties on both sides. To Nickolas and to your English business contacts."

He folded his arms, staring down at her, his feet braced apart. "Do go on, I am breathless with anticipation."

She made a rude face. "I heard my uncle bandy your name—"

"He wanted one of my ships," he supplied easily. "Nor did he say why. And nay, I did not give it. Satisfied?"

The gold shipment, she thought, nodding. Uncle needed an armed ship to attack the *Victoria*. God, he was a fool to ask Rein. Yet his quick confession cleared him. For now.

She knew something, Rein thought, his brows knitting.

"You've kept promises to me at the risk of your salvation . . ."

His features softened as he recalled their blood bond.

"Aye, I know you could have told the authorities you were in my company the night Lady Buckland was killed and saved yourself an interrogation."

"Yet you insist I am capable of cutting her throat?"

"You were running that night, too, Rein."

"I have enemies." He refused to drag her into his hunt for his father.

"And if I were to wed you, they would be mine, aye?"

"As I have shouldered yours."

"That counts half of England. You could be arrested for treason."

"I have the wherewithal to fight, Michaela. You do not." There was much more heat in his words than he realized.

"I have done well without anyone's assistance for three years." She did not need anyone, she thought, her chin tipping up.

Instantly he recognized her rebellion and the liability of it. "You don't even realize the danger, do you? Is it a game to you?"

"Of course not!"

"If you were not so careless, Lady Whitfield would not have been shot!" Her features went pale and slack, yet he raged on. "The priest's killer sought you. And you knew it, yet you dragged your friend into the fray without regard."

"I had no choice. Am I supposed to refuse Adam Whitfield without explanation?"

"You underestimate your talents, Michaela. I have seen you hide yourself from the public, acting the dull, obedient doormat," he said, his tone bespeaking his disgust. "You could have claimed illness, a twisted ankle. And you should have remained underground!"

"I had vital information for Nickolas!"

"Give it to me, I will see that he gets it."

"I do not think so." She scoffed. " 'Tis useless now."

She was lying, and the lines around his mouth grew more pronounced. He turned away, crossing to the low boy and sloshing liquor into a glass. He drained a huge gulp before he said, "Whoever murdered the priest may or may not know you are the Guardian. It does not matter. They believe you witnessed the crime and can identify them. Captain McBain is on a personal hunt, and quite possibly your man Campbell. What would the rebels do if he got too close?"

"Kill him," she muttered, trepidation filling her.

He faced her, looking more imposing than ever. "I see you are beginning to understand."

"It appears," she said, sinking to the couch and nearly slipping to the floor.

"And know that your uncle has McBain and a brigade scouring the streets of London and beyond for you." He waited until she lifted her gaze. "And Winters has taken it upon himself to lead it."

Her expression did not alter a fraction, yet, inside, a storm of emotion played havoc on her. The image of the major finding her now, after all this time, left her with one thought. He and her uncle would force her to wed the horrible man. Her tainted reputation would be public knowledge instead of private, and that jeopardy, to her uncle, meant the end of his career and his source of money. And wed to Winters, she could not speak against him. She had to stay hidden. *Till when?* a tired voice shrieked in her head. *Till the rebellion succeeds or someone kills you or one of your friends?*

"And should someone offer your description to Jean-Pierre," he taunted, praying she saw the true peril she was in, though he'd convinced the bastard that to breathe a word of Sheik Abduli's woman to a soul would bring down the wrath of Allah. "This double agent is of little threat to you now, but if it is the same person who stabbed the priest, you are marked."

She hopped up and paced in front of him, her head down.

"If not, he or *she* will continue on, destroying your precious network." His caustic tone offered his distaste for her cause and the risks she took. "God knows what your uncle will do to you, or Winters." He cast her a look and caught the flicker of sheer terror she tried to hide. He wondered what the blackguard held over her, and was loath to make her problems worse. "By the by," he said casually, sipping, "Lady Buckland was one of Nickolas's people."

She froze and flashed him a wide-eyed look.

"She could have been murdered for her spying."

"If her secret was revealed," she said with an objectivity that stunned him. "Mayhap her death was for another reason." She paced some more, her dressing gown molding to her legs, her bare feet soundless. Rein tried to concentrate on what she was saying, yet could feel the energy running through her. "She was not discreet. And I am certain there are *many* a married woman who would love to see her gone and able to find someone to do it."

Those were his sentiments, but he kept that and his plan to himself. She was being far too antagonistic for a woman with a three fingers of brandy in her belly. "Marrying me is your only sanctuary, Michaela."

"I know!"

His brows rose. "Then why are you fighting me?"

"I am discussing, not fighting!"

"Great thunder, you're a dreadfully unmanageable woman!"

She stopped, staring. "Yet you endanger your livelihood, your men's lives, to take me from Jean-Pierre," she said. "Providing clothes and food and protection. And when I was in pain, you healed me." She paused, waiting for him to respond, and when he continued to stare at his empty glass, she very softly confessed, "I am desperately confused. Oftimes I swear there is ice in your veins, then you jeopardize so much on a promise to a traitor. You could easily invite the earl here and compromise me into marriage, yet you don't. And for the love of God, I've never seen nor heard of anyone who could do what you do with your hands." She wished he would look at her. "At times, Rein, I'd swear you are not real a'tall."

His head jerked up, startling her. He set the snifter down with a snap, and in two steps, pulled her into his arms. She fell against him in a soft wave, his body reacting with a clarity that left no doubt to the state of his emotions.

"I am real," he growled in voice thick with sudden desire. "I bleed and I hurt and . . ." His head bowed. "I hunger." His mouth covered hers, softly at first, then harder, and she opened for him, driving her hands up his chest and around his neck, his tongue plunging between her lips, sweeping and stroking the flames lurking inside her.

And she moaned deliciously, her body begging, lying against him like a splash of heat. His embrace tightened, his hands fisting in her gown and driving her harder to him, then spreading, molding her curves. His fingertips dug into her flesh. And still he kissed her, tasting fine brandy and honeyed lips as he swept her up in his arms and bore her to the couch, laying her across his lap.

She whimpered, twisting to feel his chest pressed to hers, and Michaela didn't allow a thought to enter her brain, a single prickle of fear, only that she wanted more. Just a little more of his incredible heat.

She bowed back, purred and tasted him, her fingers sinking into his hair. It was a sensation he'd never forget, her abandon, the crazed grope of her hands through his hair, over his face, his chest, and he laid her back, hovering over her.

He trembled. Her hands swept to his face, cupping his jaw as if he'd leave her. Never, he thought. She was in his arms. A willing feast to the hungry dragon. How many nights had he woken hard and throbbing for her? How many times had he relived their last kiss under the black rain, he thought, licking the line of her lips, her breath tumbling into his mouth.

His broad hand roamed over the layers of fabric hiding her flesh, feeling the indentation of her waist, the swell of her hip. He ached to taste it, feel her skin grow damp with desire, and when she bent her leg, curling closer to him, the fabric fell away, baring her legs.

Rein laid a hand to her bare calf and she flinched. He lifted his head, gazing into her eyes. Her lungs labored. She wet her lips and he watched the slick slide of her tongue, wanting it in his mouth. But he would take nothing she was not willing to give.

And he could see the uncertainty, the fearful confusion in her eyes.

"What are you doing to me?" she gasped, her hands tightening in his hair. "Why you?"

"Kismet?"

"Swill."

Smiling, he bent and kissed her, softly, slowly, then sat up, taking her with him. He set her to her feet and stood. She stared up at him, blinking with disappointment, and his heart jerked in his chest.

"Regardless of what we felt on that couch, Michaela, you do not trust me. And whatever you choose to explore, will not be done without vows. I am the product of such carelessness and will *never,*" he stressed, "allow aught to touch my family, as it touched me."

"You do not know what you are asking, Rein."

"I think I do."

She shook her head, and after a false start, she rushed to say, "If I marry you, you must promise me, never to come to me . . . to our bed . . . in violence. Or hit me."

He scowled, incensed that she'd been abused so often she had to ask. "That's absurd."

"The promise or the act?"

"Have I given you reason to believe I would ever harm you?"

"Look at your hands." She nodded to his tightly clenched fists. "You are angry now. What would they do to me?"

He stared at his fists, letting them unfurl, then lifted his gaze to her. "Hold you, soothe you." He sauntered close, cupping her jaw and tipping her head back. "Protect you. And if you wish, they will never touch you."

Her eyes watered. "You would do that?"

"Our last kiss proved you do not abhor my touch."

"I voiced no complaints."

"If you want more, you must come to me."

The need for his kisses, for the tempting oblivion he created with them, drove her positively mad with desire, and though she'd never known mere kissing could be so arousing, lying beneath him, letting him pound into her, was entirely another matter. She would not force him to remain wed, not for duty and especially when they did not love each other.

"Will you divorce me after this is over?" She was certain he would.

His features yanked tight and he lowered his hand, stepping back.

"As I said afore, the choice will be yours."

He quit the room.

Near dawn, Rein heard sobbing, and immediately left the bed, snatching up a robe and slipping it on as he moved through the bathing room and into her chamber. He walked quickly to the side of the bed. She was in the throes of a nightmare, her body curled into a ball, her hands covering her head as if to block a blow.

Rein's insides twisted, churned. She sobbed in her sleep—pitiful, throat-straining. Wounded. He pressed a knee to the bed, reaching, closing his hands over her shoulders. Instantly she fought him, thrashing wildly, screaming without a sound. He shook her, whispering her name.

" 'Tis a dream, a dream. Naught can hurt you in there. You are stronger than the visions."

She only thrashed harder, kicking out at him, covering her head, refusing to leave it unprotected. He sat, not touching her, willing her to calm, but she didn't, murmuring the same words over and over.

"Papa, help me. Papa, help me."

Rein felt unhinged, his soul stripped and bleeding for her. She was always so strong and resilient, yet her torment found her in the only place she felt safe. He laid his hand to her back, rubbing in gentle, ever-widening circles. It was nearly an hour before she ceased flinching as if struck, ceased murmuring those miserable childlike pleas.

And still he stayed with her, swearing to keep her from any further harm, and hoping someday she would trust him enough to tell him her secrets and let him fight the demons for her. In that, Rein thought, he had more than his share of experience.

He wasted no time. The next morning he pounded on her door, demanding she "hit the deck," and just when she managed the fastenings of her dress, he walked into her room. She whirled about. Dressed in deep green, he devastated her senses.

"The minister awaits." *She looks tired,* Rein thought and when she showed no recollection of last night, he realized she did not recall her nightmares. Nor that he witnessed them.

"Now?"

He arched a brow, tying his neckcloth and jamming in an emerald stickpin.

No sense in putting it off, she thought, and walked to him. He stopped her, turning her back to him.

"You should have called for help," he said close to her ear, sending a chill over her skin as he correctly refastened the hooks. Rein could not help but notice she'd discarded the stays and panniers, and that she wore so little beneath the pearl-gray gown tore through his senses.

She faced him, gazing up into his handsome face.

"Lovely," he said, with a look down her body, and Michaela's cheeks flamed. Compliments were so rare.

"I was thinking . . ."

"Great days, please nay."

She jabbed him in the side. "Last night. After you left so abruptly. I had . . . I mean, I realized that—"

"What are you saying?"

"I'm apologizing."

His features tightened.

"I realized that you could not have killed Katherine. I was unjust. You have given no reason to believe you are capable of such a thing. And I am sorry for holding to rumor."

"And you came by this conclusion how?"

"The way she was killed is too close to your wife's death. It marks you instantly." She pulled the stickpin free and unlaced his neckcloth, retying it. "You were set up to take the blame."

"Ahh, brains, and a notorious spy as well. What a find."

"My, witty this morn, aren't we?" She jerked his neckcloth tight.

He tucked at the edge. "Exoneration from one's fiancée does that to a man."

She blinked as if someone slapped her. Marriage, in moments. That meant they shared a bed tonight. She felt ill.

"Michaela?" God, she was white as a sheet.

"You do not have to do this, Rein." She replaced the pin. "I concede that your protection is warranted. I am grateful. I will do as you wish, but you do not have to sacrifice your bachelorhood for me."

She was terrified, he realized, and her manner, fluffing the folds of his cloth, did not hide the trembling in her hands.

He caught her fingers and she lifted her gaze.

"I am already well and truly compromised." *Tell him,* a voice screamed. *Tell him.*

"Nay, you are not." He smiled, a little coldly. "Society talk killed before, Michaela, I will die before I will allow it to happen again." He took her hand in his and laced it through his arm.

"You aren't going to duel someone, are you? I could not bear it."

He was bolstered by the concern in her tone. "Doubting my aim?"

"Rein!" she hissed, yanking back when he evaded and drawing

the attention of his men assembled in the foyer, an aging country vicar peering up from the center of the crowd. The thin, balding man with tiny spectacles perched on his nose squinted, clutching a Bible.

"Explain this instant, please."

He sighed. "Beyond these walls, the world believes you have been kidnapped."

"Not far from the truth, Sheik Abduli." Her lips quivered.

"Nay, truly kidnapped. And ransomed."

"No one will pay a farthing for me."

The conviction in her voice slayed him where he stood. "I would."

She inhaled, searching his gaze, her mind struggling to see the plan he obviously concocted, when suddenly he paused on the stair case, gathering her in his arms and covering her mouth with his in a deep, soul-stripping kiss. Her response was instantaneous and devastating, greedily taking his mouth, oblivious to the crowd watching, the murmurs and chuckles. He caught her head in his palm and held her there, taking and taking. And she gripped his lapels, her head slanting, sharpening the kiss.

Desperation clawed through him, to have more than a mere ceremony between them, be more than her protector, and Rein forced himself to draw back. "Marry me, rebel."

Her fingers flexed on his coat and she gazed into his pale eyes, felt them skim her face.

"Not for a sentnight, or two or twenty." He swallowed, his voice whiskey rough. "Forever."

Her eyes burned. Forever. She would take it, though she was lying, keeping secrets and her trust from him. She would snatch this fragile thread, entwine it tightly about her dreams and keep it safe.

"Aye. I will."

Ten minutes later they were pronounced man and wife, Rein's crewmen each giving her a polite peck on the cheek and he, a slap on the back. The helmsman, Leelan Baynes, could not stop grinning, and it appeared to irritate her husband.

Rein paid the vicar and kissed her deeply to the roars of his crew. A messenger arrived, a youth clad in a *White Empress* uniform, and after Rein read the missive, he kissed her and with only a vague explanation that he would be back soon, he left.

Hours passed and he did not come home. Cabai brought her a lavish dinner, motioning her away from the window, yet she only nibbled, worried, stealing peeks out into the night. Twilight fell, and Michaela forced herself above stairs, preparing for her wedding night. A night that would destroy Rein's faith in her. The clock chimed, her stomach twisting with each ping and she thought she'd be ill.

Yet he did not return.

The sun rose. And still her husband did not repair himself to his bride.

And Michaela felt that delicate thread snap.

Twenty-three

Brigadier Atwell Denton glanced at the messenger, then opened the note. A lock of red hair lay in the center and he lifted it out, then tossed it on the table.

He read. "Who gave you this?" he demanded.

"A woman."

Denton looked up.

"And she said a man give it to 'er, and other to 'im." The decrepit sailor shrugged, dragging his sleeve beneath his nose and sniffling loudly. He glanced at the room, the table laden with food, then the naval officers staring intently at him. "Near as I guess, it's passed through a few hands." The sentence came out with all the belligerence of a man finding and using the opportunity to snub the gentry.

Winters moved forward and Denton handed him the paper. He read, then looked at the young man. "It's unsigned. Did you know what this said?"

"Nay, Commodore."

"Major," he snapped. "You could be an accessory."

"Seein' as I don't know what it says, 'cause I cain't read and 'twas sealed, 'ow you figure that, Major?"

Denton's posture relaxed and he crossed to the sailor, gave the man a coin and ushered him out the door, barking for Campbell. No response came. The incompetent man was even more scarce than before, he thought, and was forced to escort the messenger out lest he pilfer half the silver on his way out. He stormed back down the hall.

"Kidnapped. Who would kidnap her?"

The three others stared at him, then Winters.

"You believe I perpetrated this?" He was stunned.

"You wanted her for a wife," Atwell said.

"Not after she's been missing for so long. She's publicly compromised."

Denton grumbled to himself, muttering under his breath about the gell being put on this earth to torment him.

"Giving up your search then, old man?"

Winters's gaze shot to Prather. "Nay. We need to find her to discover what she heard."

"Don't be a fool, Tony. That"—Prather jutted his chin toward the note Denton still held—"certainly indicates she didn't hear a damned thing, or she'd have gone to the authorities or told Whitfield first off."

"The talk is already about that she was kidnapped, so this is no real surprise," Rathgoode said, sinking back in his chair. He stroked his pointed beard.

Denton mumbled agreement, waving him off, his concern elsewhere. "This sum is outrageous. Who would pay such a ransom?"

"It appears they are expecting you to do it," Rathgoode said evenly.

Denton glared at him. "A thousand pounds? Impossible! I haven't that kind of money."

"Michaela does." Winters folded his arms and rocked back on his heels. "Mayhap you should let word out of this note and that you cannot pay. Michaela has some influential friends."

Denton scowled, impatient. "Get about it, man."

"Whitfield and McBain are carrying a tremendous amount of guilt over this."

Atwell's gaze narrowed, and he stared at the man for a moment, his gaze swinging to Rathgoode, Prather, then back to Winters.

"The earl would offer the funds charitably."

"Getting one's hands on coin of this magnitude is difficult,"

Prather put in, plucking imaginary lint from his sleeve. A constant habit Denton found terribly annoying.

"Why her?" Denton said into the quiet.

"Her mother's wealth was no secret. Nor how her father hoarded it for her dowry."

"Damn you, Rath, tell me aught I don't know."

"Whoever it is doesn't know you're broke," Rathgoode snickered, fanning his finger beneath his bearded chin, his smile razor-sharp as his features.

Denton furnished him a look meant to snap his bones. "I'm prepared for worthy suggestions, Colonel."

Their gazes swung to the fifth man who sat staring at the fire, his long legs stretched out before him. The wings of a chair obscured his face, and when he spoke, he neither looked at anyone, nor moved. "Leave it be." His tone was strident and strong.

"I—I cannot. I'm already tapped out, man."

"Mayhap you should have been more prudent with your niece's money, then?"

Denton bristled, his thin lips nearly vanishing into his pudgy face to hold back a sharp retort.

"Involving Whitfield is a danger. He will ask questions, be privy at the delivery of the ransom. McBain is so straight-laced, it's revolting. He will insist on a rescue first."

The others exchanged a glance.

"Petition to have her trust released to pay ransom." A pause and they waited, aware he wasn't finished. "If not, leave her to the brigands. In a little more than two months' time, we will all be very wealthy men."

Smiling, Denton stuffed the note in his pocket and settled his bulk into the chair. He poured tea, and the conversation stuck quickly to other affairs.

Argyle Campbell had heard enough and moved away from the door. He did not believe for an instant Rein Montegomery would ransom Michaela to Denton. He already possessed wealth several times senior to most peers and was extremely generous with what he had. Whatever the plan, Argyle decided he'd help it along. If Rein Montegomery wanted everyone to believe she was held hostage, then so be it. He'd watched the house enough to know that the arrival and quick departure of the vicar meant that Michaela was either dead, or married to the man. He believed the latter, for the noise and the smiling clergyman was indication enough.

Argyle passed through the kitchen and around the side of the house toward the stables. Imagine what the Brigadier would do, he thought, if he knew that his niece was wed to so formidable a man, out of his reach, out from beneath his fists. And in the arms of the one man who could truly destroy him. A man who could easily kill him.

"That's the third time you've looked at your watch."

Rein's gaze jerked up and he eyed Christian. "I've appointments later."

"Liar, 'tis a woman."

He arched a brow. "What makes you say that?" Rein asked, though he was entirely too eager to return home to a bride who distrusted him. Spending last night on his ship was a test of strength, and although he'd used the time to write a ransom note and form a human chain to deliver it, one that could not be traced, he also knew Michaela did not want to share his bed. Nay, he thought, she was terrified of it. Leaving her alone and allowing her a night to grow accustomed to the idea of being married, especially to him, was the wisest course. He was having a hard time adjusting himself.

"I'm not sure. But something is different."

Lord Heyward leaned forward, waving with a crust of bread. "Aye, I'm agreed, sir. You are . . ." he shrugged, "relaxed, I think is the word."

"Nay, that is not it," Sheppard said. "He's always too damned relaxed. Aggravates the hell out of everyone. Nay, 'tis contentment."

Rein smiled, pleased he was the subject of tedious speculation when he usually garnered darker subjects.

"See, look at him smile," Sheppard jumped in.

Christian sat back, swiping his lips with a linen cloth and studying his friend. "You showed an interest in Michaela Denton, but I heard this morn that the Brigadier received a ransom note for her, so that couldn't be making you smile . . . Rein?"

"Ransom," Rein said, and hoped his voice sounded devastated. "Oh, God."

Features tightened and men leaned forward. "Were you actually considering offering for the girl?"

Rein mashed his hand over his face, hiding his expression. The entire notion behind the ransom was to throw suspicion off Michaela and speculate who held her hostage. Besides, he needed to at least plant the notion of a personal interest in her, especially when they'd eventually turn up wed. He'd spent the better part of the last night and today laying the ground work. The note and his being seen about, asking after her, was seed enough to take root. He hated using his friends to spirit it along, but he'd no choice. It meant Michaela's life. They needed time to allow the double agent to become comfortable, to dismiss her as a threat and give Nickolas the opportunity to weed him out, and if the priest's killer and the agent were not one and the same, then time for the former to either make an attempt on her life or lose interest and relax his guard. At least until Rein discovered who it was. Katherine's murder was tightly woven into this, he thought, eager to return home and assure himself that none of it touched Michaela.

The chair scraped back as he stood. "If you'll excuse me."

Their gazes followed him as he paid the bill and left the club.

Heyward blinked, then looked at his dinner partners. "I would have never thought he'd get so broken up over the gell."

"Neither would I." Chandler frowned, watching the door long after he was gone.

"He wants her," Sheppard said, nodding as if it made the notion true.

"Even after this mess, after she's been compromised, ruined?" Heyward felt a bit of pity for the gell and could not imagine her with someone so enigmatic as Montegomery.

"His reputation isn't so pristine." Sheppard chomped into his dinner. "Who do you think has her? What were they asking for her return?"

"Thousand pound sterling, I'd heard," Heyward said.

Christian whistled softly. "Think he'll pay it for her?"

They looked at each other and nodded. Heyward sniggered to himself. "Well, if we were doubting whether he had a heart, we ain't now."

Christian's gaze shifted to the window in time to see Rein mount up and ride off. Rein and Mistress Denton. Interesting.

* * *

Sergeant Major Townsend nodded discreetly and Rein's gaze swung to the man sitting in the far corner of the tavern surrounded by several young troops. He'd considered being polite, but he'd little time to spare and was anxious to get home. He strode directly to the table. A soldier or two looked up, then looked him over as they stepped back to allow him into the clutch of men. Rein signaled for a servant, ordering a round for the troops.

"What might I do for you, sir?" the colonel asked.

Rein was thankful he'd the chance to change clothes and looked more the peasant than the gentleman. He slid into a chair. "I am Dahrien, son of Sakari Vasin."

The man's expression did not change.

"You were aboard the *Camden*, anchored in the north coast of India over a score and ten years ago?"

The man was thoughtful for a moment, his wrinkled brow furrowing, and Rein's heart thumped with impatience. "Aye."

The drinks served, Rein cupped the tankard, staring at the warm ale. "Sakari mentioned you."

Colonel Braetwell's features tightened and he waved off the troops. In an instant, they were alone in the secluded corner. "I know no such female."

"Were you not privy to the palace?"

"Aye."

"She was a maid to the eldest princess."

"Ahhh," the colonel said, and with his thumb, smoothed the bushy mustache down over his mouth. Rein thought he looked like a wise old walrus, his blond hair heavily laden with silver, his eyes blue and sharp as he assessed him. "I remember. She was taller than the rest." His gaze swept Rein's long body briefly. "Why do you want to know of her?"

"She is a relative."

Braetwell leaned forward, his arms braced on the table, his hands cradling the mug. " 'Tis not me you seek, son," he said in a low, knowing tone. "I've been wed for thirty-five years and adore my Sally as much now as the day I married her. I never touched one of the little Hindu girls. They aren't my kind, you could say."

Rein's features tightened. "I understand."

The colonel's expression darkened as it swept him. "Nay, you don't. They were royals. The maharajah's women. Would be like trying to take the queen to me bed, man. And to keep the peace, the punishment was harsh." He made a cutting motion across his throat.

"Most evaded punishment, Colonel." Most often, men raped and the superiors cast it off as a right of war.

"I know, I know. But that was the first time I'd been out of England. Didn't like the heat, the bugs, the customs, and could not wait to return here. I took guard duty every chance just to stay aboard ship or in the barracks."

Rein focused on the man's eyes, trying to sense the truth in his words.

"I didn't see much. And I'm not looking forward to Morocco."

It was no secret then, Rein thought, and his earlier suspicions that the high-ranking officers were meeting there for another reason disintegrated into dust.

"We did leave behind two officers and a squad, you know."

Rein did, but needed assurances he was still following the correct course. "Who remained?"

Colonel Braetwell eyed the man, finding something familiar about him, but in the ragged clothing, one could never tell. But he wasn't a lowlife. He carried himself with too much grace for that. Yet, it was not the reason he was leery. There was vengeance in the lad's eyes, a hard rage that permeated his tall body, and he was glad he'd remained faithful to his wife. If not, he could be staring into the eyes of his son.

"Who?"

"You already know who, don't you?"

Rein did not speak, and tipped the stone mug to his lips, drinking deeply.

"I can't tell you for certain, sir, 'cause I was sent on ahead, then detached to the royal guards. But a man has a right to know where he's come from."

Silently Rein cursed and needed to be more vigilant. He wanted to blame the distraction on a certain redhead, but couldn't. This was a part of his life he needed finished and closed. It infuriated him that his father knew who he was and he was forced to hunt the truth.

The colonel pulled out his watch, glanced at the time. Sally would be waiting dinner for him, he thought, then stood, leaving his drink unfinished. "What will you do when you find out?"

Rein stood and finished off the bracing ale, then carefully set the mug on the table. His gaze remained fixed on his fingers as he ran them around the cracked lip.

Braetwell bent close. "Enough killing went on there then, sir. Do not start it up again."

Rein lifted his eyes to the colonel's then, his expression burning with resentment. "I am only trying to finish it."

A figure remained tucked in the shadows, watching him mount his black horse, then ride off. Swinging up onto the back of a common stock mount, the rider wheeled about, away from the street, taking alleys and small roads, following Montegomery, nearly certain he knew where the clumsy little spinster was hiding.

Rein pushed open the front door, immediately discarding his tricorn and cloak to Cabai, then took the stairs two at a time. He moved quickly down the hall, his boot heels clicking on the wood floor until he paused outside her door.

He inhaled a calming breath, and a quick excitement made his blood hum. God, he'd missed her.

He rapped.

She bid him enter and he grasped the latch, pushing open the door as he stepped inside. He didn't get far, the pistol aimed at his chest stopping him in his tracks.

Twenty-four

"You did say I could use this on you."

Not a muscle in his face moved. "Putting a hole in your husband twice is not the way to start a marriage."

"Neither is leaving me on our wedding day without a word."

His eyes softened. "I said I would be back."

"Two days ago."

He stepped forward.

She cocked the hammer. Her hands shook. Tears welled in her eyes.

Rein realized she wouldn't be this upset if she did not care, and his heart did a wild twist in his chest that was almost painful.

"You're angry. I understand."

"Do not patronize me, Rein Montegomery. I am bloody furious! And you do not understand!" How could he? How could he know that for two days she'd been reliving the moment when he'd find out the truth, when he discovered she was tainted and used. Or that he had, and had abandoned her. It beat her confidence into the floorboards, and she'd agonized to the point that she was angry at him for making her wait, making her suffer.

"Then tell me, so I might."

"Nay. First you tell me where you have been. And with whom, husband."

Was that jealousy he heard in her voice? "Will you put that down?" He nodded to the pistol.

She tipped her chin. "If I do not like your excuse, I will simply shoot you."

He stepped forward until the barrel pressed against his chest. He held her gaze, a strangely sweet sensation racing through his blood at the sorrow in her eyes. "You were worried."

"I was not."

"You thought I'd left you forever."

"I thought some bloke managed to put a hole in your crack-brained head!"

He grinned. "Like you are itching to do now?"

That flash of white teeth disturbed her further. "Oh, aye, Rein, aye." She nodded vigorously. "Speak, and do not tempt me."

"I sent a ransom note to your uncle."

She frowned and sniffled. "I beg your pardon?"

"Then I went about town asking after you. I'd already stirred speculation as to your kidnapping. I needed to see how far the gossip had traveled."

"You wanted to drag my name through the mud?"

His expression filled with sympathy. "Nay. I wanted the public and the conspirators to believe I would search for you, that I had a tendre for you." At that she looked entirely too skeptical, and he decided if he wanted this woman's trust, a shipload of patience and absolute candor was all he could offer. "It would not do for anyone to believe that I had naught to do with you when you turn out as my wife."

"Oh." She blinked, a tear rolling down her cheek. "I suppose that's wise enough." She swiped at it, was quiet for a moment, then said, "And what did you discover?"

"Your uncle did not alert the authorities."

She snickered bitterly. "You expected him to? I imagined you much smarter than that."

"You are his only family."

"I am his only source of income, Rein. He does not even pay his own bills. I do."

This was news to Rein. "Why?"

"He lived beyond his means. And used my trust to pay it. Without me to sign the drafts, he is penniless."

"He's a man, a general, for the love of Vishnu, far from a pauper and able to earn his own bloody keep." His tone cracked like fracturing twigs. He'd known she was financially comfortable, but not once did he consider that Denton was dipping into her inheritance. "Why did you not send him on his way?"

"As per my father's will, I am legally his ward." She looked away and mumbled, "I had little choice."

Rein schooled his features. Her words shouted blackmail, and anger seeped through his blood. He filed it away, to a time he could return what was rightfully hers. A marriage would have solved the matter, and he wondered why she hadn't done so before now. Regardless, dealing with the Brigadier was left to him. A task he suddenly itched to attend.

"So. How much am I worth, Rein?" Her voice quivered, pain only hinting in each syllable.

"More than I asked."

She looked at him, a little spark flaring in her breast at his sincere tone.

"A thousand pounds sterling."

She choked, eyes round. "Oh, cracking good notion. Why not

the royal jewels?" Then, just as suddenly she went quiet again, eyeing him warily. "You are tempting him to take me back without paying, aren't you?"

"Such a bright lass I've wed." He grinned. "I want them to focus on me, Michaela, not you. I want everyone who utters your name to believe some horrible despot has you hostage for your fortune."

He knew far too much about her life, she thought, a touch irritated.

"No more notes will come, no more demands. Not until we need it. And anyone's suspicion, including this double agent, that you are a traitor will be overshadowed with the kidnapping."

"I see." Well. He'd certainly attended to every detail. "And if he should gather the funds from elsewhere?" She never believed that would happen. He was too eager to take gold from England's troops, and the shipment would be a king's fortune compared to her trust stipend. "Nay," she said, as if she'd come to a decision. "He will either not bother and leave me to the wolves or find some way to release my trust to pay your ransom."

"There will be no one there to collect it. If you do not reappear, he will be responsible for returning it to you."

"If he manages that, he will simply keep it." Her gaze cooled. "I am not filled with ideas that the man cares a wit of my existence beyond the depth of my purse."

"I am sorry for that." Rein thought of Aurora and Ransom and the love they'd given a boy not of their blood and how lucky he'd been.

She shrugged. "I'm certain my father is not resting comfortably in his grave over the matter." Her tone was remote. "When do I reappear?"

It amazed him how quickly she withdrew, then shelved her emotions. "Only after Nickolas has done his job. He will find the conspirator. For if you show even a toe outside," he warned, "the killer will show his hand. We must wait it out, let the talk die and the killer to believe I am doing the looking for them."

And they will follow him. Why would he take her burdens like this? "And you are certain you were as discreet as possible? 'Tis hard not to be noticed in this city, no matter how you are attired." Her gaze swept over his common homespun trousers and coarse muslin shirt, yet there was naught common about her husband.

"I can only do my best."

She sighed heavily, her mind filtering over his words, trying to find holes in his plan.

"Still want to pull the trigger?"

She cast him a side glance. "I haven't decided."

"But you must decide, Michaela." He held her gaze, bending a fraction closer, over the pistol. "Am I to be your husband or nay? Are we partners or adversaries?" His voice was low and soothing, his pale eyes enslaving her as he wrapped his hand carefully around the weapon. "What will it be, wife? A duel or a bit of faith?"

It sounded profoundly simple. A bit of faith. Oh, to relinquish her secrets, to share them all in the hope that they'd vanish. *Tell him.* He'd withstood her accusations, suffered public ridicule with dignity, surely he would understand . . . Her lips quivered, her troubled gaze flicking to his hands, then his face. Slowly she let go, and he pulled the gun from between them and gathered her quickly in his arms. Her hands flew to his chest.

Behind her back, he carefully lowered the hammer and tossed the gun on the bed. "Thank you," he whispered in her ear.

She gazed up at him, a tiny frown marring her brow. "You would have made an excellent spy, Rein."

His brows shot up.

He could coax water from a stone, she thought. "And just because I have not shot you does not mean you are forgiven." She pushed out of his arms, needing some distance between her and those mesmerizing eyes. "I do not like you manipulating my life without my consent."

"I apologize. I will discuss all manipulations with you in the future."

Her lips curved. The man was positively exasperating sometimes. "You will lay it all out now. Please."

"Over dinner. I am starved."

He moved to the door.

She did not.

"Are you coming along?"

She marched over to him. "Only because I have not eaten lately." He stepped back to allow her passage. "Cabai did not feed you?"

She spared him a sour glance over her shoulder. "I am not a pet, Rein. And, aye, he did. Our wedding dinner was rather good."

He winced. "Michaela, I would have remained if I could."

She made a sound of disbelief. Why was she so upset? She wasn't prepared to share his bed, and that was exactly what would have occurred. Yet she'd felt woefully unattractive and . . . *handled,* popped into the puzzle of a plan he'd concocted so he could finish the game. Marry her, then go on about. It was not her idea of wedded bliss, but then, she never expected to have a marriage a'tall. She should be grateful. *My lord,* she thought, rubbing the spot between her brows. She sounded like a babe too long without sleep.

At the base of the staircase he caught her arm, gently turning her to face him. She looked at the floor and he tucked a finger under her chin and pushed till she met his gaze. "You worried. Admit it."

"We are married, Rein. Of course, I would worry." *And I paced and stewed for hours about this little cabinet of safety coming to a crashing halt,* she thought, then realized how selfish that sounded. Whether she gave him her trust or nay, he was taking her danger on to him. As any husband would. She could ask no more.

Stubborn woman, he thought, smiling. "Is that all, because now we share the same name?"

His voice was sultry, terribly intimate, and she fidgeted, made a sound of distress, yet held his gaze. How could she explain when she did not know herself? He'd made a promise to Nickolas, to protect her at all cost. And he had, and she wondered what would happen to her life afterward, when he divorced her, when he learned that beneath her proper upbringing lay a woman with far more stains than his heritage could ever leave behind. The marriage was in name alone and would have to stay that way so it could be annulled.

He deserved a real wife.

Yet as she gazed into his eyes, all she could think was, *Nay, my feelings are not because we share a name. But because I care deeply for you. Because you've given me a glimpse of a future when I thought I would die of loneliness. I want to be who you believe I am, worthy of your risks, your efforts. But I am not. I am not.*

At her silence, the mystery rippling in her eyes, Rein leaned forward, his gaze linking with her hazel eyes. His mouth lingered warmly over hers. "I worried," he whispered against her lips. "And I missed you."

She came undone, slipping closer, touching him, gliding her hands up his chest and around his neck. Her eyes burned with unshed tears and Michaela kissed him, hungrily, needily, stealing his breath, some pleasure, the affection she'd been so far from touching for so long.

A dark velvety sound rumbled in his chest as he wound his arms around her, gathering her as close as he could, his mouth hot and hard. And she answered, opening for the push of his tongue between her lips, sucking softly, pulling him deeper into her spell until he trembled in her arms. He wanted her now, right now. And he'd make a spectacle of himself, if he didn't stop this. He'd promised her honesty, promised himself that he would not make the same mistakes again.

Rein tore his mouth from hers, trailing soft, wet kisses down the line of her throat. "We must talk. There are a few things about me you must know."

"Now?" she gasped, tipping her head back from him. Oh, she sounded too wanton.

"I cannot have any secrets atween us, Michaela," he murmured near her ear. "I failed afore, I will not jeopardize this marriage with half-truths."

Michaela squeezed her eyes shut, her body singing for more of his touch and her mind snagging on his words. No secrets, no secrets. If he wanted to tell her his past, she would listen, but she could not offer more of her own. He was honest and valiant and a good man. He'd altered his entire world for her, and she knew that when he wanted her in his bed, he would know all her lies.

And she was not ready to be alone again so soon.

He released her slowly and stepped back. She caught the banister and held on, breathless. Her hand flew to her chest, her skin hot and damp, her heartbeat rushing to her ears. The place between her thighs throbbed, clawing her with an ache so hard she felt the urge to squeeze them together. She lifted her gaze to him. He stood a few inches away, his head bowed, his hands on his hips. His queue had come undone and shaggy black locks shielded his features. His chest moved rapidly.

Her gaze roamed his physique, tall and lean with a strength he masked in loose common clothes. Then, unwillingly, her gaze dropped to the bulge in his trousers, the outline of that, long and prominent. Oh, God, she thought, looking away. A suffocating feeling swept her, and she gasped for air, gripping the banister post harder. She slammed her eyes shut, blocking out the memories, the ugliness.

But Rein saw it, saw where her eyes fell, saw the flash of absolute horror. It was a normal reaction from a virgin, he thought, yet it unnerved him, made him believe there was much more to her fear than the unknown of a wedding night. And he found it hard to believe the Colonists' most efficient spy was that totally unaware of men and women.

His shoulders rose and fell in a hard breath. He prayed for patience and held out his hand. She stared at it, wary. "Dinner?"

She blinked. "It is rather late, Rein. Cabai is abed."

"Then we must fend for ourselves."

She accepted his hand, and Rein moved through the house, down the west hall toward the kitchen.

Mr. Bushmara shoved out of the shadows, nodding to her.

"Good evening," she said in Farsi.

Rein arched a brow, watching the exchange.

"I see you did not blow a hole in his rotten carcass," he replied in his native tongue.

"I would only have to take the shot out myself." She cocked her head. "Have you eaten tonight?"

He nodded, then eyed her. "Do you cook?"

"One debates over the results, but aye."

"Well, wife . . ."

She tore her gaze from the Moor and looked at Rein.

"What other secrets will I discover?"

The mark hit too close and she looked away, then in flawless Hindu she said, "There are a few things a woman must keep secret."

There was such emotion in her words, defeat and sorrow, that he frowned, his voice gentling as he said in Hindu, "I will guard them well, my dove. When will you see?"

Her eyes burned, her chest feeling tight. *My dove.* "Shedding light is not a wise move, husband."

He smiled that tender, heart wrenching smile, and it nearly broke her heart. She walked toward the kitchen, and he followed, frowning as she rooted around the large room, putting water on for tea, moving a bowl of fruit to the worktable, reaching for a knife. He could feel her discomfiture, see the tension in her body as if she were prepared to bolt. In the larder, her face tipped up to search the shelves and his gaze followed the slender line of her throat, gracefully sweeping to the plump cushion of her breasts. The deep maroon gown contrasted with her pale, flawless skin, the fabric's shade enhancing her hair loosely braided down her back, the color of her eyes. She looked like a painting, poised there, alone, motionless but for the sweep of her gaze over the shelves. Did she know he watched her? Did she feel the same heat as he did every time their eyes met?

"You were raised in India?"

"For a few years." She loaded her arms with goods.

"Did you like it?"

She brought them to the table and dumped them. "Very much."

"I hated it."

She popped up from searching another cabinet. "Really?"

"Aye," he said, taking a seat on a work stool. She unwrapped a hunk of pork, then looked up. "You eat pork, don't you?"

He smiled. "Aye, beef I do not."

She nodded, picked up a knife and sliced, laying the meat on a platter. Cabai stepped inside, a look of indignation on his face as she destroyed his neat kitchen.

Rein waved him off and he left. "I was born in the maharajah's palace, then stolen from my mother who was a handmaiden to one of the princesses."

She made a sound of sympathy. "That's awful."

He snatched up a crust of bread. "I have been told this, you understand. I do not remember."

"Yet you do not believe it?" She pushed the platter closer, gesturing for him to help himself.

"I have little choice. The first thing I remember is being tossed into a diamond mine, rolling down into the bowels with a half-dozen other motherless boys not yet five." He felt more than saw her horrified expression. "When I escaped there, I lived in the streets picking pockets."

Her heart broke for the little half-breed boy. Dear lord, to live so long without knowing from whence you'd come, if you had a name, a mother searching for you, brothers, sisters. How horrible. "How did you learn this?"

"Not knowing had bothered me for some time until it finally pushed me to search. I found an aunt, and though she was near dying, she recognized my resemblance to her niece and gave me this." He reached inside his shirt and withdrew the medallion, a rounded triangle, filigreed with the *Camden* engraved on the front, his father's rank and the year on the back. No name. "It belonged to my father."

They were given to the officers, not often, but after a large battle or siege, Michaela recalled. She'd always thought her uncle came by his unjustly, yet never voiced it.

"You are half English." He nodded, studying the platter she prepared for them. "That is all you have of him, isn't it?"

His gaze flew to hers. "That and my eyes."

"They are beautiful eyes, Rein."

His lip curved slightly. He tucked the medallion away. "I have been searching for him ever since."

She poured water into a teapot, laid cups on a tray. "Have you succeeded?"

"Some." He left the stool and found a bottle of wine and goblets. "I have narrowed it down. But 'tis not what I wish to tell you." He popped the cork.

"I do not need to hear your tales, Rein."

"Aye, you do." He glanced up from pouring, his expression hard. "My first wife Shaarai did not, and 'tis what killed her."

Michaela had her doubts, yet met his gaze. "If you must."

"She was a chief's daughter, a native from an island my adoptive father owns." He handed her a glass of wine. "I wanted to seek my fortune, to run off with her, but I was wise enough to go alone. Her tribe keeps its women sequestered, for assurances of purity." His lips twisted at that. "I returned, and against everyone's wishes, married her and brought her to England. I was not yet twenty, but thought I was man," he said, a bitter cut to his tone. "I'd a profitable business by then and she was eager to see the sights. She wanted to fit in so badly." He grew quiet for a moment, thinking of the girl barely ten and seven, pelting him with questions, then shook his head. "She learned to read French and Latin, the proper dress and way to set a table. She attended the theater. And she changed."

Michaela slapped a slice of meat and cheese on a chunk of bread, holding it near her mouth. "How so?" She bit.

"She was far more interested in pleasing society matrons than herself. She'd grown up wearing less than a chemise for clothing, and here she was stuffed into stays and shoes, and having her hair curled. She was very careful that shame not touch our doorstep. Within two years, I hardly recognized the island girl."

Michaela swallowed, her voice low. "She did not know you were the son of a maid and Englishman, did she?"

He took a sip of wine, rolling the glass between his palms. "I should have told her, but I did not even consider the ramifications." He made a short, mirthless laugh. "Aurora raised me to believe blood did not matter."

"Aurora?"

He looked up. "The woman who adopted me, became my mother. She warned me not to take Shaarai from her people, that she was unprepared for the world beyond the island. You don't know how many times I wished I'd listened." He finished off the wine, leaving the glass empty. "A woman cornered her at a tea, very harshly revealing the kind of man she'd married. Enough that everyone in the room heard it. She was devastated, denying it. But when she confronted me and learned the truth, I lost her love for deceiving her. No more invitations came, no callers. Her friends turned their back on her when she was on the street." He toyed with a knife, spinning it faster and faster on the tabletop, his eyes on the glittering flashes reflecting with the firelight. "In her eyes, she'd lost everything, social position, respect. She became a recluse, refusing to speak to me, then refusing me in our bed. For months I let her be, hoping she would come around." He shrugged, still gazing at the blade. "She only grew more distant. Then I got angry." He slapped his hand on the blade, making her flinch. His throat worked. "The night she died, we argued—"

"I do not want to hear this." Michaela hopped to her feet. "Say no more."

In an almost predatory motion, Rein left the stool and moved toward her as she turned toward the larder. "You must hear."

"I don't want to." She shook her head. "Nay." She could not bear it, not the slaughter of a woman he loved, not the details that might incriminate him.

He caught her upper arms, holding her there. "Look at me," he said softly. "Look at me." No anger in his tone, only regret, and Michaela tipped her head back. His eyes raked over her face, sadness contorting his features. Their eyes locked. "I held her like this, I shook her, demanding that she dress and prepare herself for a party I needed for my damned business contacts. She refused, and I released her so quickly she fell to the floor. I did not turn back to look as I left her. I did not see her pain, I saw mine." He opened his hands a fraction, rubbing her arms, then drawing her back to the table. They sat on the pair of stools side by side. But he wouldn't let her hand go, his fingers threaded with hers as if she were a rope he needed to stay afloat. "I was standing in the ballroom, prepared to cultivate a new contract or two when I realized I'd been too harsh with her. England had been her first time off the island and she was still so innocent."

He dragged a hand over his face and Michaela didn't think she'd ever witnessed such remorse before. It tore her in half. She squeezed his hand.

"I came home and found her throat cut nearly to her spine."

Michaela inhaled at the gruesome image. "You don't have to . . ."

"Aye, all of it, Michaela." He tightened of his grip. "I cradled my wife in my arms and wailed like a child. I cried more for *my* lies, for *my* need to have so much money none would dare question who or what I was. That it had become a drug. I threw her into that world without warning."

Tears wet her eyes. "You are not at fault for her suicide."

He shook his head. "Don't you see? She was so distraught, she cut through five inches of her own throat. That's not a woman who wanted to die, that's a woman who wanted to punish herself. I pushed her to that."

"Nay!" she said, jerking on his hand and staring deeply into his tortured eyes. "You could not have known her reaction. She is the one who laid so much stock in her social position, *she* chose to put that knife to her throat. You asked her to survive, but she was not strong enough. How were you to know?" Her voice softened. "You cannot keep the burden of her choice, Rein."

Her understanding overwhelmed him and he whispered, "I take my portion of the responsibility for it, Michaela. Spending a few months in prison did not compare to looking her father in the eye and telling him his only daughter was dead, and why." He sagged, deflated, releasing her hand and plowing it through his hair. "The servants fled in fear, but Ransom found one who came forward to clear me before I was hung." He sloshed wine into a goblet. " 'Twas nay enough for the public."

He did not care after that, she thought, watching him drain the red liquid. He'd lost his wife to unwritten rules and proper decorum and he no longer gave a whit to what society thought or said. He'd been branded and he'd kept his distance from respectable women, so they would not be touched by the speculation of his wife's death. To be such an outcast, to keep yourself at bay from the world because you knew the consequences an association would leave on another, was so honorable and gallant. And yet it angered her that he was forced to live so solitary a life, that she, too, had been the public that kept him in hiding.

And tonight, he'd laid his soul open for her scrutiny, for her to butcher it further than he already did himself. "I am sorry," she said softly.

He lifted his head, looking drained and lifeless. "Why?"

"For being like everyone else, for believing you could take her life, take Katherine's."

"And mayhap kill you?"

She looked offended. "Nay, I never feared that."

He quirked an unpleasant smile. "Liar."

"I might have been afraid of you at one time, Rein." Her chin lifted in a way he adored. "And your brooding attitude only enflamed the rumors, I might add, but I've learned other wise."

His look doubted.

"Only a man of tremendous honor would sacrifice so much for a promise to a friend."

"And you think I've married you for my word to Nickolas?"

She looked down, toying with the end of her braid. "I am a score and five years old, Rein, without a single suitor. And then when I wed 'tis for protection, for a reputation that is not worthy." She met his gaze. "I know what I am. I have spent three years blending into the background, garnering no more notice than a servant or a nuisance."

"And acting the bumbling, awkward spinster?"

She scoffed. " 'Twas not an act."

He caught the braid, using it to tug her close, his gaze tightly locked with hers. "Anyone with eyes would see what you hide,

Michaela." Her smile was faint, reluctant. "Did you not notice my crewmen?"

"I noticed their stares, and considering where they found me—" Rein shook his head. "They are envious of me."

She reared back a touch. "You are pouring the swill again."

His gaze swept her, all of her. "I see I have some convincing to do." Instantly his mouth was on hers, liquid quick and heavy as he dragged her off the stool and into his arms. She pressed her palms to his chest, flat and wide, like a barrier. He kept kissing her, and regardless of what kept her from him, her response was instantaneous, her tongue sinking into his mouth, one small hand tunneling in his hair.

She purred for him and he licked it, drank it, rubbing his hand up and down her back. He tore his mouth from hers, dragging his lips over her jaw, the curve of her throat. She clutched him to her, and Rein buried his face to the softness of her breasts.

His teeth scored lightly over her bosom, his hand sliding up to cup the soft mound. He rubbed her nipple through the fabric, the turbulence inside her scratching at her demons, wagging with her need and fear. He coaxed her over the edge, laying delicate, wet kisses over her chest, then staring into her eyes, he dragged her bodice down.

"I want to taste you," he said in a husky voice, then bent his head. He covered the blushing peak with his lips, drawing it deeply into the tender heat of his mouth, and she arched into his warm pressure, a tiny wondrous breath sighing past her lips.

He laved, sampling her sweetly scented flesh, his movements greedy, then languid. He watched her bite her lip, her hands hover over him, and he caught one, pulling it to her breast, letting her shape his face, his lips on her body. A feathery sound hummed though her skin. Sensual, dark, and womanly. He thought he'd climax just from watching her.

He kissed her mouth, lifting her to set her on the table, his hips pushing her legs apart. He cupped her kiss-dampened breasts in his palms, massaging, toying with her nipples as she felt his features like a blind man, touching his throat, her hand inside his shirt. He was strikingly warm, her greed for his skin, driving her hand deeper. So smooth, so hot. She wanted to touch more of him, feel his naked skin, see the lush color of it. Michaela thought she would boil away in an instant, her body screaming for more, yet she flinched when his hand found its way beneath her skirts and covered her thigh. He stilled, waiting for her to grow accustomed, his hand riding slowly upward, hesitating for an instant when he discovered she was bare beneath. He smiled against her lips, and embarrassment flooded her, but he did not give her time to wallow in it, his mouth moving hotly over her bared flesh, his lips plucking softly at her nipples, his teeth scraping gently over the plump cushions before he nuzzled her neck and kissed her again and again. She moaned against his lips, arching harder and harder toward his length, and he cupped her bare buttocks, pressing her to him.

He slid his hand between her thighs.

She flinched, her fingers digging mercilessly to his shoulders. Her lashes swept up, her eyes luminous with uncertainly.

"I will not hurt you, Michaela." He rubbed softly, the heel of his palm firm against her. Her breath rushed past her lips, her skin warming. "I would never hurt you."

He probed and parted, pushing a finger deeply into her. A moan sanded in her throat, her eyes sealing away the light as her body responded, thighs gripping him, feminine flesh drenching him. He withdrew and thrust, her hips undulating with his touch, and Rein held her, kissed her, murmuring against her lips.

"Open for me, *rasha*. Accept it."

She whimpered. "I can't."

His fingers slid smoothly into her heat. "You are too close . . . take it."

"Take what?" she gasped, not understanding, never feeling anything like this before.

"The pleasure," he whispered, fire in his tone, in his touch as he stroked and rubbed, thrust and pushed. Her hips rocked without control, her grip tightened around him, and Rein took her nipple deep into his mouth. She cried out, spreading wider for him, gripping his shoulders. Her nails bit into his flesh. He lifted his head, staring into her eyes. She started to push at him. He rubbed his thumb over the bead of her desire and she inhaled.

"Let go."

"I—I'm scared to."

"Put your hand on mine."

"Nay." She flushed deeper.

"Aye." His husky tone lured.

She did, hesitantly, and he introduced another finger. She gasped and pressed him deeper into her heat.

"Show me how to please you, Michaela."

She caught the back of his head and pulled him down to her breasts. He savaged them, laving, sucking, over and over, rough then soft, his fingers pleasuring her with deeper, longer strokes, making her body sing.

"Come apart for me, *rasha*. Come. Aye, 'tis there. I can feel your pleasure," he whispered into her ear, kissing her throat, then her mouth, pressing his forehead to hers and staring into her eyes as her body wracked with a hard shudder, tensing and taking. His name burst from her lips. A wonderful biting heat spread up her belly, down her thighs, clenching and pumping sensations from her, through her, and she did not want it to end. She bore down, grinding her mouth over his, sobbing and gasping and moaning at once. He held her on the summit, taunting her to the brink of madness, and Michaela thought she would die. Then it shattered, swamping her with liquid heat—extravagant—fresh. Luxurious. Oh, the luxury. She pushed and pushed, trying to keep it within her, yet it faded like a sunset and she sank into him, boneless.

He stroked her to the surface of thought and feeling.

His arousal lay thick against her stomach.

Awareness taunted her. Wonder filled her mind.

"I could spend a lifetime watching that."

She lowered her gaze, blushing and wondering where she found one. He removed his hand, kissing her throat, her breast, as he pulled the gown up a touch.

He searched her features. She returned his stare with uncertain fear, as if she were waiting for something more to happen. As much as he was hurting for her, it would not happen, her fragility permeating like the dew on her skin.

"Tired?"

She closed her eyes, her muscles soft. "I could sleep for a week."

In one motion he swept her in his arms and carried her from the kitchen. Her arms looped around his neck, her head nestled beneath his chin. He mounted the staircase, feeling her tense with each step, her body growing stiff. He pressed his lips to the top of her head, and took comfort that she softened a little as he entered

her chamber, moving to the bed and laying her in the center. He
brushed his mouth over hers and stepped back, the wariness she
tried to hide unmistakable.

"I am a patient man, Michaela Montegomery."

Her eyes widened at that, as if just realizing her status.

"You possess the power. Over me." He made a sound, a half
laugh, his gaze raking her. "When you are ready to tell me what
scares you, keeps you from me, I will listen." He turned, and
Michaela watched in stunned silence as he crossed to the bathing
room, closing the door after him.

Twenty-five

Atwell Denton scowled, his fist clenched. "If he thinks I will
give over my niece in marriage if he should find her, he is mistaken."

"I believe that is his intention."

"I think not," the Brigadier blustered. "I'll not have my name
connected with aught of *that* family!"

"A brood of half-breeds and bastards," Anthony agreed, glad to
see the Brigadier was not influenced by what Montegomery might
provide them.

"Has he any word?"

"He doesn't confide in me, sir."

"Aye, aye." He nodded. "Of course, he wouldn't. You irritate
him."

Anthony stiffened. Denton's constant belittling was too much
like his own father and he wondered when he'd reach his limit and
dress the Brigadier's hide for it.

"I want it made clear, about town, you know, that he is unac-
ceptable, even if he does find the gell."

"He might stop looking."

"Not him. He's like a dammed dog with a bone. Relentless."
Atwell rocked back on his heels, his hands braced at his back as

he gazed out the velvet draped window. "He's not good enough for a proper English gell. Not a Denton."

"Does *she* know that?"

Denton's brow furrowed, deepening the wrinkles in his pudgy face. "After this disgrace, by God, she'll take the husband I give her!"

Behind the Brigadier's back, Anthony smiled.

"Watch him, Anthony. Find out who he talks to, where he goes." The Brigadier glanced back over his shoulder. "We get her first."

Michaela languished in the bath, steaming scented water gliding silkily over her skin, arousing her, bringing memories of last night to the surface with amazing explicitness. A tingling rode up the back of her thighs, tightening between them, yanking the muscles below her belly. Eyes closed, she shifted, her hands covering her breasts, seeing his mouth there, his face whilst he played with her, so wicked and dangerously intimate. She licked her lips, aching for a completion she couldn't reach without him.

He gave her pleasure and took naught in return.

You possess the power. Over me.

Michaela smiled. Having anything over Rein Montegomery was a feat in itself.

She heard a creak and cracked open one eye, then sat up as the door leading to Rein's room opened slowly. Covering her breasts with the washrag, she heard movement coming from inside. She glanced at her dressing gown, wondering if she could reach it without being seen.

She rose up slightly, leaning out for the garment. The door swung fully open, and she froze at the sight of him, stark naked, bent over a basin, shaving. My word. She dropped back into the water, splashing a goodly portion over the sides. At the sound he looked up, catching her reflection in the mirror. Bloody hell, she thought. Trapped.

He stilled, holding her gaze as he finished scraping the whiskers from his chin, then wiped the remaining soap from his jaw with a thick cloth. Michaela couldn't help it—she looked, his buttocks tight and ropey as the rest of him.

"Good morn, wife."

Wife. He said it with such sensuality, evoking abandon and desire in a single word.

"Good morn, Rein." She sank to her neck in bubbles. "Would you mind closing the door?"

He tossed the towel aside, reaching for his breeches, and she watched the muscles of his back and buttocks ripple as he stepped into them. He was her husband, she could look, she thought, then exhaled. Lord, he was beautiful. No other word compared. And her gaze jerked up as he crossed to the door, his steps soundless. He paused on the threshold and she wondered over that little smile.

She looked incredibly fetching, Rein thought, growing hard just thinking about what lay beneath the layer of water and bubbles. "Sleep well?"

Nay. I thought of you touching me, tasting me all through the night until I nearly beat down your door. But he didn't need to hear that. His look said he knew it.

"Well enough." She waved, disinterested, yet her eyes remained fixed on the sleek carved muscles of his chest, bare and richly bronzed. Her fingers curled against the urge to touch him. "The door, if you please."

"My shirt," he said, moving to the hook near the tub.

She inhaled, and he turned.

"Dear Lord, Rein. What happened?" Her gaze was on his calf.

He didn't spare the old wound a glance. "A shark decided I was a tasty meal."

She leaned over the edge of the tub, forgetting her state, her attention on his leg.

His gaze fastened on her as her fingers grazed over the scar tissue.

" 'Tis a miracle you did not lose the leg." It was mangled, faint fine lines of stitches running in a jaggedy pattern through the thick of his calf to his knee.

"When I woke the next morn, I wished I had."

"Oh, Rein." Her throat tightened, and she looked up at him. "The agony you suffered. How did you find yourself swimming with sharks?"

"A man wanting to kill Aurora baited the tidal pool with bloody meat, and a shark managed the reef. Aurora was swimming there. I was her guard." He made a self-deprecating sound. "She warned me not to come after her, that she could handle the shark, but I was scared for her."

"You saw your mother about to be killed, 'tis understandable." Still she touched the wound, shifting closer and offering him a delectable view of her naked breasts pushing against the edge of the tub. "It attacked you instead." She tried to imagine a young lad braving the ungodly predator to help his adoptive mother, to have the sharp teeth rip into his tender skin and try to devour the boy.

"Aurora saved it." She'd fought the ship's physician to keep it and, for that, he was eternally grateful.

"You do not limp. By God, 'tis not even noticeable when you move."

"Gets stiff in the rain . . ." She looked up. And he considered changing the subject, then said, "I've worked hard to keep this from anyone." He thought of the thousands of times he'd climbed mountains to strengthen the torn, weak muscles.

"Why?"

He held her gaze. " 'Tis another mark that paints me different."

"But you *are* different," she said with genuine feeling. "And this, 'tis a badge to be worn." Her hand on the healed wound, her thumb unconsciously rasped over his scarred skin. "You survived a shark, Rein. As a *child,* you mastered this, when another would have lain wasted. You're to be admired. Such fortitude is rare."

He seemed to melt a little before her eyes.

She couldn't know how much her words meant to him, that she was not viewing him with disgust. Even Katherine had insisted he cover it.

He smiled softly, his fingertips brushing lightly over the side of her face, and he bent, laying his mouth gently over hers. And in the tender kiss, she heard his thanks, his pleasure that she was not revolted by the sight.

His kiss deepened, briefly, tauntingly. With his mouth a fraction from hers, his dark lashes swept up. "I slept with your image last night."

Every nerve in her body suddenly danced to the husky sound of his voice. "Oh?"

"Over and over I saw you finding pleasure, riding my hand." She turned her face away. He touched her chin, forcing her to look at him, and searched her features. "You are so unaware of yourself."

She looked confused.

"Making love with me scares you, Michaela. Nay, do not deny it, 'tis folly. You need no man to find your own pleasure, you know."

It was torrid what he was suggesting, and she didn't want to have this discussion. Her expression said it.

He laughed more to himself. "Shall I prove it?"

"That won't be necessary," she said too quickly. "The water grows cold."

"Then you must get out." He reached for her dressing gown, straightening to hold it out for her.

"I can do it myself."

"I am your husband, Michaela, eventually you will hide naught from me."

Eventually, she thought, he would cast her out. He met her gaze in silent challenge, and Michaela turned and rose. He took a long look at her graceful back and round behind before he dropped the dressing gown over her shoulders.

She wrapped it, holding the hem out of the water as she left the bath.

Her back to him, she fumbled with the sash, her hand shaking, her body aware of him, what he looked like from behind, bare and so masculine, sleek. His hand rested on her shoulders and he pressed his lips to the bend of her throat. His body brushed hers, back to chest, thigh to thigh. Heat, so much heat in his skin, she thought, aching for the slide of his arms around her. His lips moved to her lobe, tugging gently, and her nipples tightened, throbbed.

Suddenly, his touch, his warmth, was gone, and she twisted in time to see the door swing closed.

Water pooled on the floor, dripping over her bare feet.

Michaela fell back, banging into the table housing bottles of bathing salts and soaps, rattling jars, her body pulsing on that undefinable edge. He was true to his word, she thought. He would not take her until she came to him.

Dropping to the stool, she clenched her thighs tightly together, but the hard surface beneath her only served to arouse her further. She cradled her head in her hands, struggling for her breath, for calm. Surely this was not rational behavior, to want him so badly, to long for the promises he offered and fear the inevitable outcome in one breath? And when, she thought, would his restraint snap?

On the other side of the door, Rein fought for air, his breeches so tight across his hip, they threatened the buttons. She was his weakness. He didn't have many, and Michaela, wet and aroused, was his worst. His groin flexed, and he rolled around, bracing his palms on the door. His shoulders shook and he lowered his head. She wanted him, would have come with him to his bed with little seduction. But he needed her without ghosts or regrets. During the night he'd considered what might have happened to give her enough fear to make her fight her desire so relentlessly. His conclusions were painfully vulgar and brutal.

Michaela sat at the vanity, dragging a brush through her damp hair, trying to tame her curls. They sprang from the braids like reeds from an old basket, making her itch to take a pair of shears to them. Her unfastened dress drooped off her shoulders. She tossed the brush aside, cradling her head in her hands, her elbows on the vanity surface. Bathed and dressed, her body still hummed for his touch, the sensations he evoked last night and this morn, not far from her memory. Heat stole up her skin, perspiration blooming between her breasts. The place between her thighs tightened.

The door opened and she tensed, not wanting to face Rein. Not yet. She turned her head and found Cabai crossing the room toward her. She yanked her gown up, holding it to her breasts.

"What are you doing in here?"

He did not speak, of course, stopping behind her, grasping the sides of the gown and fastening her up.

She stared at his reflection in the silver glass. "I did not need help."

His look said she did, but was too stubborn to ask. He reached past her for the brush, then took up the coil of hair, running the brush through it, parting it. He was going to dress her hair? He was hardly the lady's maid, dressed much like Rein was last night, in a plain shirt and breeches and knee boots. Except his head was shaved clean of hair.

She tilted hers back to look at him. He repositioned it forward, then braided it. "Is Rein in the house?"

He shook his head and pinned.

"At the ship?"

He shook his head again and her shoulders sagged. In the glass he caught her gaze, his lips curving a bit. He made a motion like riding a horse.

"Ahh, I see." She searched for a topic of conversation. "Did Rein take you from the harem?"

He frowned.

"Escaped?"

He nodded.

"Was it awful, being constantly around women?"

His hands stilled, then he pushed in the last pin and reached around her for a gilt box. He opened it, removing a strand of pearls. Rein had left her a fortune in jewelry, yet she had not worn a single piece. Cabai lowered it around her throat and secured the clasp.

"You did not answer me, Cabai."

He handed her matching earbobs. "His wives talked too much. I was forbidden to touch—" Michaela gasped, spinning on the seat. "And had no desire."

"Why, you little devil!"

His broad lips drew back, revealing straight teeth and gentle humor.

"Does anyone else know?" She fastened the ear clasps.

"Only my master."

She frowned, slowly lowering her hands. "Rein is not your master and neither am I."

"I live to serve." He bowed and salaamed, backing away, and Michaela realized there were some people born and bred to servitude who could not grasp anything else, found comfort in it. She rose and moved toward him. "I will keep your secret, if you wish."

"It is why I revealed it to you, my mistress." He stared down at her with round black eyes, and Michaela knew she had a friend in the giant man. "I am yours to command."

She eyed him, hesitating. "I need to send a note—" He was already shaking his head. "Please. I've people who are worrying." And she needed to get to Nickolas, despite the dangers. He folded his thick arms on his chest, looking far too imposing for her tastes. "Fine." She laid her hand on his thick arm, smiling. "Then feed me, I am famished."

He grinned. "Making love does such things."

Her brow knitted softly, then stretched tight. She looked away.

He'd heard them last night? Surely not. " 'Tis insolent to mention such a thing."

He tipped her face toward him. "You are his wife." He shrugged his broad shoulders. "It is your duty."

"Mayhap in the sultan's house—"

"My master would not harm you. He awaits your summons."

She knew that. After today, she knew.

"I have seen your face with him." He scowled, looking suddenly very dangerous. "You lie to your heart."

She cocked her head. "Am I to get this kind of advice from you with my daily toilette? Warn me now, Cabai, so I am prepared."

He sent her an arched look, then straightened, folding his mammoth arms. "If you need it."

Wonderful. A matchmaking eunuch.

"I will consider it all very carefully."

"Do so quickly, my mistress. He is a man."

With strong desires, and if he did not get satisfaction with his wife, she wondered, looking at the floor, would he seek it elsewhere? The thought drove jealousy through her like a hot spear. He was her husband. And the image of him in the arms of another made her angry, possessive.

"Ahh," Cabai said, and her head jerked up. His smile was far too knowing.

"Oh, you think you are so smart." She brushed past him, ignoring his soft chuckle and heading below stairs at a brisk pace.

Two hours later, she'd been dismissed from the kitchen when she tried to prepare a snack for the men guarding her, ignored in her requests to send a note to Nick, and in a fit of defiance, she grabbed a rag, the need to polish something startling her. She never made it to the dust, Cabai snatching it from her and propelling her toward the study like a punished child with the admonishment that his mistress should obey the master's rules or she risked her life. Master. Rein mastered all right, kept her waiting for him, isolated and bored, she thought, strolling around the study, her deep brown skirts swishing softly. The masculine room was warmly lit, the shades pulled for her safety's sake, and Michaela resisted the temptation to steal a peek. Moving to the bookshelves, she studied his selection, smiling when she found an edition she'd left unfinished at home. Home. This was her home now, she reminded, leafing through the pages and finding her spot. She stood there, reading, turning page after page until the urge to sit took her and she lowered herself to the couch. She missed the edge, plopping to the floor. For the love of Mike, she thought, disgusted. She tried standing, her skirts hampering her climb, and she shifted to her hands and knees, gathering the yards of fabric to the side.

A pair of booted feet appeared in her line of vision. She looked up and found Rein staring down at her, an amused look on his handsome face.

Cracking good, she thought, itching to pinch him.

"Must be a captivating work." He stretched his neck to see the title. *"The Taming of the Shrew?"* He squatted, meeting her gaze and loving her irritation. "A guide book for husbands?"

She furnished him with an artificially bright smile, her skin warm with embarrassment. "Nay, 'tis a paddle for women with slow-witted spouses." She attempted to stand, but the skirts and pannier caging refused to release her. "Rein!"

"Aye."

She thumped his shoulder with the book.

He chuckled. "Need rescuing, wife?"

She hissed at him, and his gaze moved over her shoulders, her bosom, and in an instant she remembered every detail of their last moments together. And so did he.

His expression softened and he clasped her waist, lifting her as he stood. The book thunked to the floor. He held her against him, dangled her above the carpet as if she weighed no more than a feather, and Michaela put her hands on his shoulders. Her slipper plopped off.

Rein fought the rumble of laughter threatening to explode. "You are a danger to yourself, Michaela."

Did all the men in this house wake with an intense need to tease her? "Are you quite through?"

He eased his hold, letting her slide down the length of him till her feet touched the carpet. Her curves yielded, soft breasts pushing gloriously into his chest. "I could not resist. Forgive me."

She had to smile, he looked so rakishly boyish. "I miss my breeches."

His gaze sketched her lovely features, her hair. "You look exquisite as you are."

Her smile caught him like a bolt to the chest.

"And why not simply discard all the underpinning. You are not in public."

"You are far too bold to say such things."

"I would say more, just to see you blush." He leaned down, brushing his mouth over her cheek, loving that she leaned into his touch, tipped her head for more. "I would tell you the scent of your desire haunted me, that I want to taste it."

Her breath hitched, her body suddenly stinging with excitement, need, and she turned her head. Gazes locked, lips a taste apart.

His mouth molded hers and his arm shifted, catching her hair and dragging her head back. Instantly, she twisted in his embrace, frantic and clawing, and he released her, frowning as she stumbled back, gathering her hair to her chest. She stared, her gaze narrow, accusing.

"Michaela?" Fear. He could taste it.

She blinked and he reached. "Nay, nay," she murmured, shaking her head and turning her back to him. She closed her eyes, willing away the sudden burst of memory. "I apologize."

"Talk with me, *rasha.*"

She rubbed the space between her brows. "I need to get a note to Nick."

She was lying, he sensed, and that she could not confide made his voice harsh. "Nay."

"Then bring him to me."

"And risk his life and yours? Never."

"Rein, I need—"

He folded his arms. "You need to cease your attempts to cajole my crew into betraying their orders."

She made a face. "Cabai has a big mouth for a silent man. Cassandra and Argyle will be worried."

He shrugged carelessly. " 'Tis the price of your spying."

Her lips pulled in a flat line. He was right, as usual, and she disliked the reminder, moving around the room. She stopped short at his desk, the scattered papers, ledger, his fluid script across notes.

"Leave it," he said, yet she was already reaching for a square of expensive vellum.

"Oh, God, Rein." She glanced over the words. "What forces are you antagonizing now?" Though he'd made an effort to disguise his handwriting, it was distinct.

And a single line graced the page.

I know you killed Katherine.

A blank sealer lay close, droplets of cooled black wax trailing on the surface.

"I said leave them, Michaela."

Her gaze snapped to his. "Have you sent them already?"

He said nothing, crossing to her.

"What are they?"

"Lures."

She gripped his arms. "Don't do this."

His lips curved. "Worried?"

"Aye, I am worried you have lost all sense!"

"Michaela," he began patiently. "I am still under suspicion, and that means my moves are watched. I cannot protect you with the concern for my freedom at risk."

She understood, at least she was trying. "Your handwriting is recognizable. Do you want this creature to come directly after you?"

"I can defend myself."

"This killer is a coward and will not play fair. Have you considered that? That your plan could lead you into an ambush?"

He caught her waist, drawing her close. "I've taken several precautions." His voice soothed. "Trust me on this."

She made a sour face. "You promised to consult me."

"On affairs concerning you. This does not."

She flung off his touch, glaring at him. "Of course it does. What if this same person is the man who killed the priest? How are we to know?"

He scowled. "You never mentioned seeing anyone else when the priest died?"

"Surely I did."

"I would have remembered."

"I didn't see aught that could help. A glimpse 'tis all."

Without a word, he moved around the room, dousing the lamps, then caught her hand and pulled her to the couch.

"Rein?"

"Lie back and get comfortable."

She eyed him for a moment, then obeyed, adjusting her skirt and settling her head to the pillow.

"What will you do?"

"Close your eyes."

She did, and he adjusted her arms loosely at her sides, removed her shoes and covered her with a blanket. Then he sat on the floor near her head. "Listen to the sound of my voice. Naught else. Take a deep breath and let it out slowly. Narrow your attention to the air moving in and out of your lungs. In your mind form a picture of a clear pool, a pebble dropping into it, the rings fanning out and never ending. Nay, do not talk," he said when she opened her mouth to do just that. "You're going to take a journey to that day, without the distractions, without the risk." Rein counted backward, watching her for signs that she was accepting the dream state, that she'd released herself to the power of her mind.

Her fingers unfurled, her lips parted softly. Like a breeze across her, her body sank deeper into the cushions.

With the sound of his voice, he brought her to the church, the moments before the priest arrived. He took her through the alcoves and halls, letting her grow familiar with the surroundings, see the candles, feel the floor beneath her feet, and when the priest entered the scene, he took her to the figure hovering in the dark.

"A man. Aye, 'tis a man. His hands are large."

"Tell me exactly what you see. He cannot harm you. You are an observer."

"He wears robes and a hood. There is naught to see."

"Remain calm, my sweet. Breathe." She obeyed, her body limp on the sofa. "Look him over carefully." Her eyes moved behind closed lids.

"He wears boots," she whispered. "There is something on the heel."

Priests wore soft-soled leather shoes. "Dirt? Sod? Spurs?"

"Nay." Her brow furrowed. " 'Tis like numbers or letters. I cannot read them. They are tiny."

He heard the frustration in her voice and spoke to her, calming her, letting her see the figure motionless. "Aught else, Michaela?"

She shook her head, her lips tight. Rein decided he would bring her out before the murder occurred and slowly counted forward, telling her she was safe and he was here, she was no longer in danger. One, two, three . . .

She blinked several times to orient herself, then turned her head to look at him. She rolled to her side. Her gaze searched his features. "You are an amazing man, Rein Montegomery."

He grinned, her praise making him blush. "Are you not glad you married me?"

A touch of vulnerability flickered in his eyes, a fracture in his strong veneer, and Michaela realized he was asking more than he was saying. Her fingertips whispered over the side of his face. "Aye, I am."

His face neared, his gaze on her mouth.

"Married? To who?" a voice called.

Rein's head jerked up, his features tightening.

Michaela wiggled upright and peered over the back of the couch. She inhaled. "Uncle Rusty!" she squealed, scrambling off the sofa and dashing across the room. She launched herself into the big man's arms and he swept her off the floor, hugging her tightly.

"God, lass, I thought you were dead."

"Oh, Rusty, 'tis wonderful to see you."

Rein cleared his throat. They ignored him.

Townsend set her to her feet, inspecting her for changes. "You are well?"

"Aye." She hugged him again.

"Michaela," Rein said.

She twisted a look back over her shoulder, her smile lighting her entire face, and Rein wished he could make her do that. "Rusty and my father came from the same village. They grew up together." She glanced at the man. "I haven't seen him since before Father died."

"I was sorry to hear of it, lass." He patted her awkwardly. She accepted his condolences in a warm hug, then stepped out of his arms.

Townsend looked at Rein. " 'Tis true, you've married my Micky?"

Rein's lips twitched. "Micky?"

Michaela blushed, and elbowed Rusty.

" 'Tis true then?" They turned to find Temple Matthews standing the doorway. Michaela's gaze swung to Rein's.

"One of my captains," he said, then looked at Temple. "You're early."

"You're married." His wide eyes darted between him and the woman.

"Aye."

"Sweet Jesus—" He caught himself, and looked down at Michaela. "Forgive me, madame." He tipped a bow. " 'Tis a relatively large shock. Since he swore never to marry again."

Michaela arched a brow in Rein's direction. "Really?"

"I want to know the whole of it." Rusty waved between the couple. "Now."

"I don't believe it's any of your business."

"If her father were here, you'd be answering to him." Rusty unfolded his arms, every inch of his posture screaming with stubbornness. "Well, since he ain't, I'm as close as it gets."

Michaela smiled to herself.

Rein glared at Sergeant Major Townsend.

Temple couldn't decide who to watch.

"Later mayhap." Rein stepped around the couch. "We have imperative news to discuss right now."

Michaela dropped her hands to her hips. "Aye, Rein, what business have you with Rusty?"

Rein recognized the fight brewing in her, and wished he could smother it. "It does not concern you." She knew of his search for his father, she didn't need to be aware of the critical details.

She tapped her foot, her gaze narrowing on him. "Do you always break your promises when it suits you, husband?"

Rein's his features tightened. He had promised to inform her of everything, but . . . "Michaela, sweet, this is different."

His cajoling was pitiful. "It could not be more dangerous than aught I've been through already."

He stepped closer, his voice rough as he brushed the back of his knuckles across her cheek. "I wish to keep you safe from harm."

Her expression softened, and she gravitated toward him. "Then tell me, Rein, so naught comes as a surprise." Her gaze flicked meaningfully to the note on his desk.

Temple snapped his fingers. "Now I know who you are!"

They all turned to look at the man.

Temple grinned at Rein's wife. "You're the one who shot him!"

Rein groaned, raking his fingers through his hair.

Rusty glanced between them, then burst into laughter. "Haven't changed a bit, have you, squirt?"

Looking at her husband, Michaela folded her arms as she said, "How goes that old wound, Rusty? I did apologize for that, didn't I?"

Twenty-six

Biting wind skated through the gaps in the shanty tucked into the wall of a crumbling building. In the ensuing twilight, the odor of unwashed flesh and decaying rubbish filled his nostrils, and Rusty brushed his fist under his nose. He rapped on the door, the wood fracturing a bit, and he glanced at Rein, shrugging as if apologizing.

"Was there no one to look after her?" Rein asked.

"Nay, he wasn't one to save a penny. More likely spent it on gin."

The shuffle of footsteps finally came to them, and Rein glanced around at the squalor, the piles of refuse creating a path to the door. Rats skipped across the mounds and he shivered, turning his attention to the door.

"You're afraid of rats?" Rusty looked shocked.

The shuffling inside was very slow, punctuated with soft groans.

"Nay." Rein's shoulders moved restlessly. "They make my skin crawl."

Townsend grinned. "So you keep the biggest mouser around."

Rein's gaze shifted to him. "Rahjin earns her keep well enough. I lived with rats in the mines. Had to fight them for scraps of food, and swore once I was out, I'd never stand for another within miles of me."

Rusty studied him briefly. "We all have fears."

"Childish, isn't it?" he said, sheepish.

"Nah, I hate snakes."

"Now there is a sleek creature," Rein said, teasing the big man.

The door latch rattled, creaking open a bit, one faded brown eye showing through with a wiry tuft of gray hair.

"Mrs. Eagen?"

"Who wants ta know?"

"I am Sergeant Major Townsend, madame. And this gentleman is Rein Montegomery."

The brown eye widened, shifting rapidly between the two men.

"May we have a word with you?"

"Nay, go on. Git."

"Madame, 'tis of the utmost importance."

"You ain't got nuthin' I want to 'ear. Same as I told the other fellow."

"What other fellow?" Rein asked, his voice gentle and low.

The brown eye shifted to him.

"Young one, light hair."

Christian had mentioned blond hair. "With curls?"

"Nay."

Wind whipped at his cloak and Rein huddled into the folds. "Madame, might we come in. We mean to only speak to you, no harm in that."

The eye stared, then disappeared, replaced with the muzzle of a gun.

Rein and Rusty stepped out of the line of fire, yet the door squeaked open on its leather hinges, sagging pitifully.

She motioned with the pistol and they ducked inside, stooping to accommodate the low ceiling. Rein fought to keep his expression clear, but the odor was horrible, the dirt floor soupy from the last rain. There was a straw pallet on the floor in the far corner, the dingy gray fabric soaking up the dampness from the floor. In the center, near the fire, stood a table with two chairs, a cupboard leaned toward the wall, the shelves bare but for a bowl and cracked cup. Yet on the table was a vase with cut flowers, the stark contrast making the old woman's meager surrounding all the more decrepit. Wind speared between every ill-fitted board, the cracked windows.

She shuffled to the fire, lowering herself slowly into a rocker. As she laid the pistol across her lap, the light shone off her craggy face, and Rein realized that she was not as old as he'd first imagined. She turned her gaze to his, and he saw hopelessness, no reason to continue.

"Clancey wuddn't a bad man, you know," she rasped into the silence. " 'E always did right by me. Kept only a bit of 'is coin for 'is gin."

"What happened, Mrs. Eagen? Surely you and your husband did not live here whilst he served Lady Buckland?"

She laughed, a brittle cackle that turned quickly into a thick, tearing cough. "Nay, we 'ad a spot in the carriage house." Rein moved to her cup, and ladled water from a bucket. "But the creditors took the place. Cast me out without a farthing." He knelt before her, handing her the mug. She drank quickly, greedily. *It must be an effort for her to climb out of bed each morning,* he thought.

"The man who visited you, did he offer his name?"

She shook her head.

He added sticks to the fire, realizing they were broken pieces of furniture. "Can you describe him?"

"Not tall, but bigger than me."

A child would be, Rein thought.

"Real full of himself, 'e was. Might quick to tell me to keep me mouth shut." She shrugged. "But I don't have anyone to open it to, so's I don't see where it matters."

"Keep quiet about what, madame?"

"What I seen and Clancey told me about 'er ladyship."

Rein gestured to Rusty, then to the meager woodpile, and the big man left to gather more. The blast of wind made her shiver violently and Rein removed his gloves, taking the cup and fitting them over her bony fingers. She smiled at him, and he caught a glimpse of the woman she once was.

"I ain't one to gossip—"

Rein smiled at that. He hoped she was.

"But her ladyship was a trollop. 'Ad me Clancey dartin' off all over at night."

"Do you know who she was seeing or visited afore she died?"

"Nay, but a carriage brought whoever it was to the house. She didn't go out for 'im."

Rein frowned. "Did you recognize this person?"

" 'E was cloaked, all scrunched up. Not a big fella, though, near as I could see from the carriage house."

"You didn't see a face?"

"Didn't I just say 'e was wearin' a cloak?" she said, as if he were an idiot. "She was seeing that Chandler boy, too."

It was between that and her death he needed to know. "Can you recall anything about the night your husband was killed?"

She stared, gathering her thoughts. " 'Twas the only time she went to 'er lover, not 'avin' 'im brought round."

"Did Clancey know where they were going?"

Rusty entered, his strong arms laden with thick logs.

Mrs. Eagen waved him in. "Don't be standoffish now," she rasped. "Make yourself useful, young man." She nodded to the fire. Smiling, Rusty laid the stack down and added a log to the small blaze. She inched her feet closer, her toes peeking through the worn leather boots.

"Madame?"

Her pale gaze shifted. "When he come home afore takin' 'er off, 'e said she was being real careful about anyone knowing she wanted to be brought to the road, not to the house. Tol' 'im she wanted to walk up. Ain't that a dilly of a thing to do," she said with a snicker. " 'Er ladyship didn't poop without aid."

Rein choked on a laugh and looked at his bare hands, fingering his knuckles. Behind him, Rusty's shoulders shook suspiciously.

"What house?"

"The gamekeeper's cottage at the Chandler boy's land."

Rein's head snapped up and he frowned. "Are you sure?

Christian had no reason to disguise his affair with Katherine, why would they hide in the woods? But then, the gamekeeper's cottage was deep in the forest, far from the mansion, and anyone could have used it without Christian knowing.

"Sure I'm sure. My Clancey was complaining 'cause she sent him off, made him make stops all about town." She leaned forward, her tone conspiratorial. " 'E didn't do it. Comes home, 'e did. 'e says she ain't paid 'im in a week an' 'e'd go back for her later. 'E was just upset 'cause 'e couldn't do much drinkin' if he 'ad to go about town like that. 'E liked it when 'e'd just sit, waiting for hours. Slept in the carriage, I'd pack 'im a bit of food." Her voice lowered, broke a bit. "When he wents back out to get her . . . 'e never come back."

Her expression fell, and she slumped into the rocker, silent.

So, Katherine had portrayed she was elsewhere that night, likely hoping no one would follow her to the cottage. Who was she seeing, he wondered, that she had to be so clandestine? Perhaps she was meeting with Nickolas? That was one matter he had to discover tonight before going on. Rein fished in his purse and pressed several coins into her palm. She looked down at them without expression, then sniffed and shoved them into her tattered apron pocket.

"My thanks, madame." He stood. "May I send a carriage to collect you to a hotel?"

She shifted in her chair. "Wot for?"

"I will see that you are taken care of."

The woman glared up at him, her pride stung. "I ain't dead yet, you know. Go on with you. Git yer sorry carcasses outta my house." She waved, and Rein bowed deeply and left, closing the door after him. Hunching into his cloak, he braced against the wind, moving to Naraka.

Rusty looked back at the shanty, then walked about the area, gathering more wood and leaving it by the door. He mounted, looking at Rein. "Pride be a nasty thing sometimes" was all he said, and they moved off.

"Nay, I did not meet with Katherine that night. I was here with Michaela." Nick speared a chunk of meat. "And Katherine never worked with me, she was connected to another"—his gaze shifted to Rein's—"more influential Son of Liberty."

"Who?"

"I can't tell you that."

"Damn it, Nick!"

"Nay." He tossed down the fork. "One spy in the ruins will not destroy this labyrinth, Rein. I cannot hand over a list. My God, think of the lives at stake."

"I am thinking of only one." Rein donned his tricorn and moved to the door. "She is out of your ring of traitors," he said with disgust. "I will not allow this to continue."

"Is that why you married her, to stop her?"

Rein stared. Nay, he thought. It was not the reason, and at this moment, he refused to dig into his emotional barrel for the fish Nickolas wanted to hook. He needed his thoughts clear for the night ahead.

"I married her to see her well protected. As I promised."

Nick eyed him. "She won't stand for it. You'll lose her if you force her to cease. 'Tis in her blood to see we hold victory."

Forbidding her to spy, to risk being drawn and quartered, was a matter Rein would never be swayed from. "She won't see your precious freedom if she is dead, will she?"

Nickolas sighed heavily. "I can tell you she did not meet with her contact that night."

It was as he'd suspected. If his tracing Katherine's steps that night was correct, she'd had an affair in the cottage, and, not long after, someone killed her and framed him. Rein knew once he discovered who was in the cottage with her, he would be that much closer to the killer. The notes fanning out over the city now would force the bastard to confront him, and Rein expected to take a bullet in the back.

"I finish this tonight." His gaze fell on Nick like a hammer. *"You* find your double agent. Or I swear, Nickolas, to keep my wife safe, I will bring the entire rebellion down on your head."

She was going mad. Absolutely on the stark raving side of insane. They'd been gone since this morning, after revealing, in her opinion, a rather weak, unsubstantiated plan, then sending Mr. Matthews off on some dire mission. Her husband had left her to the care of Cabai and his loyal men, but not before he'd pulled her into his arms and delivered a kiss so powerful, so heart-wrenching, it left her weak . . . and terrified. It was as if he never expected to see her again.

Her stomach clenched at the thought, and Michaela realized she'd rather die than live like that. Without him. She swallowed, her throat tight, a frustrated scream threatening to erupt and shake the walls.

He could have at least sent word, she groused, pacing in the hall, then moving through the house. Her steps grew more agitated. Cabai served her a light meal, and it remained untouched on the dining table. She carried the tray back to the kitchen, setting it on the table with a thump.

"Give me something to do," she begged the Arab.

He looked at her, glanced around at the spotless kitchen, then shrugged helplessly.

"Laundry?" He gawked as if she were mad. "Dusting?"

He shook his head. His kind smile set her teeth on edge, and Michaela made a gritting sound, then spun about and strode to the study. She felt closer to him there, she reasoned, picking up her cooled tea, sipping. Her hands shook, and she missed her lip, lurching back to catch the drip with her finger. She set the cup down, then plopped into a chair and covered her face with her hands.

There were too many powerful suspects. Men who could wipe a person off the face of the earth and none would dare question them.

And Rein provoked them with the foulest of accusations.

Her eyes burned and she tipped her head up, her fingers sliding over her features.

Be safe, husband, she thought, just as the window exploded behind her.

I know you killed Katherine.
Midnight, the cottage.

Christian crushed the note in his fist, cursing Katherine to perdition for her beauty, for the appetite he could not satisfy. Tossing the parchment into the hearth, he watched the flames consume it like a ravenous wolf to a fresh kill, then strode to the locked cabinet of pistols and muskets. He hadn't paid attention to the stablehand's mention of the light in the forest, yet he'd be damned if he let someone else hunt for a killer on his land.

He loaded and primed, shoving a flintlock into his waistband, then lifting out the long barreled rifle. Leaving the house, Christian didn't wait for the stablehand and saddled his horse himself, sliding the rifle into the scabbard and riding into the forest toward the gamekeeper's cottage. No one had lived there for years, his man having a family too large for the little two-room house, and as the area grew dense, he ducked, holding branches aside, the horse picking his way over logs and bramble. The cottage loomed and his heartbeat jumped when he realized dusky light radiated from the windows, the small, thatched hut bearing the unearthly glow of a skeleton.

The bastard. As he neared, Christian slid the rifle free and checked the prime. With his knees, he urged the horse forward, tree limbs obscuring a look through the windows, yet the door was open. A shadow passed across the floor, and he dismounted, aiming the rifle as he inched closer. Christian held back when he realized more than one person took up residence.

"Keep your mouth shut and all will be fine."

Christian frowned, the voice familiar, and he stepped to the right and saw Lieutenant Ridgely near the hearth, talking to whoever sat in the upholstered chair. This was not the arrogant soldier who'd insulted Rein at White's and at the theater, he thought, noticing the dark smudges beneath his eyes, the gaunt look of his features. His clothes were less than pristine, and a pistol lay on a nearby table with a sputtering candle shoved in the neck of a bottle. To the far left, the only other door lay wide open, the room beyond empty.

"Obviously not. Or these notes wouldn't be blanketing half of London."

So, that's how it was, Christian thought as a prickle of warning climbed up his spine. That voice. He frowned.

"Which means they haven't a clue."

"Don't be a fool. If you had left Montegomery alone and gone on to the barracks . . ."

His gaze sharpened, lethal and mean. "If? You dare speak to me of my behavior, and if you think to betray me now . . ."

"How could I? I, actually, have more to lose than you."

Christian felt his stomach tighten at the sound of that voice, throaty, feminine.

Ridgely's gaze thinned, his smile predatory as he moved toward the chair, flipping open the buttons of his plain coat, then his breeches. "Aye, wouldn't want him to find out, would we?"

"You are cruel."

He scoffed. "And what does that make you?"

"I hate you."

Ridgely stared down at the woman in the chair, then vanished from Christian's sight as he knelt. He heard harsh breaths, the tear of cloth, then the groans and jolts of the bodies banging against the chair back. A slender leg pointed to the ceiling, Ridgely's fingers gripping the tall back of the chair as he slammed into the woman, growling out his climax like a raging beast.

A painfully sharp silence reigned and then, "She was better."

The man thrust back, righting his clothing and looking down with a mix of hatred and regret.

Christian stepped into the doorway. Ridgely paled, his gaze darting to his weapon. The woman rose, turning, and Christian's fingers loosened on the rifle barrel, the nuzzle dropping.

"Brandice."

Dressed in men's clothing, his old castoffs, she held two pistols, each aimed at the other. "I told you coming here was dangerous," she said to Ridgely, and the young man's features tightened.

"They were bound to find out."

"About you, not me!" she shouted, and Ridgely stiffened, his gaze glancing off the pistols on the table.

Christian raised the barrel. "Mine will hit you first," he warned the lieutenant, then to Brandice said, "Put those down, for God's sake!"

Her gaze slipped to him briefly. "I'm quite adept, I assure you."

Shock slammed him in the gullet, and Christian saw the horrifying truth, the ruthlessness in her eyes, the fountain of blond curls doing nothing to soften the sharpness of her features. "Brandice, what have you done, child?"

"I'm not a child," she snapped. "God, you are so blind! You dismissed me to love a whore." Lady Coldsworth snickered meanly. "You treated her better than a queen. You all did." Her gesture encompassed men as a whole. "You trusted her as if she loved you." Her smile was thin and cagey. "She took your letters, you know. Spied on you until you were of no value."

Christian swallowed, horrified. "Brandice, dearling, tell me what's happened?"

"Do not continue to be a complete ass, Your Grace," she hissed. "You adored Kat. She wanted Montegomery."

"But she was her lover," Ridgely said, and Brandice aimed the gun at him, disgrace cloaking her features.

"You bastard!"

Christian thought he'd vomit right there. "Have you no shame, woman?"

"Me?" She arched a blond brow. "You were the slobbering puppy, sniffing after her skirts when she was spreading herself for half of London. It was pathetic."

"I did not love her."

Her face went molten with rage. "I heard you! That's all you could say when you were pounding into her on the library floor!"

His eyes flared. "That was sex talk. I never loved her."

Suddenly, her expression held a wealth of pity. "She had nothing in her heart for anyone, Christian, no one. Not even me. She blackmailed me even before the passion died." The strength of her gaze faltered, her voice lowering. "She threatened to tell you, to tell everyone. I could not bear that. And when I discovered we'd been followed here, that I had a witness—" Her gaze fell on the soldier. "I had a way to repair the damage."

"Brandy," Ridgely warned. "We'll have to kill him."

Both ignored him. "She was killed in her carriage." Christian shook his head, refusing to believe her guilt. "You could not have outdistanced her to the coach from here."

She smiled, thin and brittle, her gaze darting to Ridgely. "She was in skirts. I was like this, on horseback. Of course, I could."

"But your leg?"

She scoffed as if she were conversing with an imbecile. "I twisted it jumping from the carriage."

And Ridgely had brought her home that night, Christian thought. A riding accident. But the blood on Brandice was Katherine's. Christian turned his gaze on the soldier. "You covered for her, started the rumors about Rein? All because he dismissed your accusations!"

Ridgely shrugged, stepping away from her aim and toward his pistols. "I loved her."

She inhaled, rounding on him, her eyes wide. "You lie! You only wanted to see him pay for humiliating you! But you weren't man enough to meet him on the field, were you, Dougy?" She inched back toward the hearth, a brightness gleaming in her eyes. "So you tried to take Katherine from him." She laughed, the sound hedging on hysterical. "But she rejected you, you sniveling coward, and if you couldn't take Montegomery's lover for the insult, you wanted his freedom!"

Christian's scowl deepened miserably. "Tell me you didn't kill her, Brandice."

Her troubled gaze shifted feverishly between Christian and Ridgely. "The driver was drunk. It wasn't hard to distract him . . ."

Christian's expression crumbled. "Oh, God."

"Jesus, woman, shut the hell up!"

Rein stepped from the back room. "She didn't kill her." He met Ridgely's terrified gaze. "He did."

Ridgely darted for the door, but before anyone could give chase, he stumbled back into the cottage, a pistol poised at his forehead.

"Get the hands up, Lieutenant." Rusty nodded to Rein. "You were right, I'm thinking. She didn't have the strength to cut her throat like that."

Rein didn't take his gaze off Brandice. She wasn't lucid, and still held two loaded weapons. "You rode together and you distracted the driver until he was inside the coach?"

Brandice nodded, childlike.

"Don't say another damn word, Brandy!" Douglas shouted.

Rusty jabbed the barrel into his neck.

Her gaze snapped to him. "It's over."

"Brandy, sweetheart," Christian said. "Give me the guns."

She looked at him, her gaze softening, the guns lowering a fraction.

"Do not press her," Rein hissed.

Ridgely tightened his fists.

"Brandice, the guns, dearling. Put them down." She started to bend, to obey.

Ridgely lurched forward. In a smooth motion, Brandice swerved and fired. He dropped to his knees, his dying expression stunned. Her grip loosened, her features mirroring his as she watched him fall face first into the dirt floor. Slowly, her head tipped back, her gaze darting between the men.

"You all know now."

Rein recognized the resignation, the shame-filled defeat in her eyes. He darted forward for the second gun, but she lifted it, pulling the trigger and sending the shot into her temple. Her head jerked. Blood, chips of skull, and brains splattered the wall behind her before she dropped like a broken puppet to the floor.

Christian moaned and turned away.

Steam swirled from the gaping wound.

Rein stared down at the girl, then closed his eyes. "Gentlemen."

The magistrate and Lord Henry stepped inside, Temple Matthews behind them.

Lord Henry kept his gaze from the girl, swallowing repeatedly.

"My deepest apologies, Mr. Montegomery," he said. "I can assure you, full restitution will be—"

He snapped a glacial look at him so harsh, it sent Henry back a step. "I need naught from you or England," he snarled. "Just leave me be." He turned to Chandler, giving his shoulder a supportive squeeze.

Christian lifted his gaze to Rein's, his stare bleak and confused. "My God. She was so shy and amiable."

"She was duped by them both, Christian." Rein cast a glance back as Rusty covered her with a moth-eaten blanket, his gaze unwillingly lowering to her feet, then to Ridgely's. A chill drove up his spine, tightening his scalp. His heavy boots bore the markings of initials, but the letters were too worn to decipher. He turned back and bent, rubbing his finger over the tooled leather.

"Who's are these?"

Chandler blinked, dragging his gaze from his ward to Rein. "Uh, mine."

His gaze flew to Christian's.

"I threw them out." He shrugged. "Gave them to the stable hands."

"When?"

"Month ago, mayhap longer." His brow furrowed. "She probably gave them to him?"

"Probably." Rein straightened and continued on to his horse. He swung into the saddle, and, without waiting for Rusty and Temple, he rode toward home, toward his wife.

Twenty-seven

Orange-red glowed on the horizon, billows of white smoke lashing the black sky like a great fist trying to punish the night. Rein's heart dropped to his stomach. Flames devoured his house, licking up the walls like talons clawing at tender flesh. He flung from the saddle before Naraka came to a halt, the animal racing away from the smoke and flames as he ran to the stairs. The door was still closed.

There was no one outside.

He slammed his shoulder against the door, squinting against the smoke curling from beneath the wood. Rusty was behind, and together they barreled into the thick English oak and the door smacked against the wall.

A blast of fire shot up with the blistering gust of air and Rein called out for her.

"You go that way!" Rein pointed down the hall. And Rusty moved through the house, his head bowed, his arm across his nose and mouth against the smoke. Rein found Fadi at the base of the staircase, a bullet in his side. Temple raced in behind and started toward the hall.

"Nay, get him out. Go back around and see if you can enter from the kitchen!" Temple hefted Fadi onto his back and ducked out the flaming door.

Rein moved to the study, praying she wasn't in there. It was nearly engulfed. His heart squeezed down in his chest as he called for her, his lungs searing with each breath. The bookshelves collapsed, knocking over tables and glassware. Sparks and ash shot into the air. He crouched, searching the floor, violently overturning burning chairs and carts and knowing the next would reveal her blackened body.

Wood crashed, the pop of shattering glass like gunfire.

"Michaela!" he screamed till his throat was raw. He touched softness, skin, and scrambled to move debris. He found her huddled under the desk. And she wasn't moving. Blinking against the stinging smoke, Rein pulled her from beneath and into his arms. He darted over the rubble through the flames, fire scorching his back as he burst through the wreckage and stumbled to the ground. He rolled, clutching her, protecting her.

Choking and coughing, he laid her on her back, brushing her hair from her face. She wasn't breathing, and in an instant Rein's entire world focused down to one second filled with denial and panic and ungodly fear.

"Michaela! God of thunder, Michaela, please don't. Please, love, *please."* He shook her, and her head lolled. "Michaela. Damn you, woman. 'Twould be just like you to defy me now!"

Bent over her, his hands hovered helplessly, his heart slowly shattering in his chest. Suddenly, he caught her face in his hands and fastened his mouth over hers, forcing air and his energy into her.

Come back, my rasha, *come back to me,* he chanted. *Breathe.*

She arched, her lungs expanding, then, jolted with a fit of coughing, rolled to her side. He caught her in his arms, crushing her to his chest, rocking her, stroking the back of her head, her hair.

"Goddess of light, I thought you were dead."

"I shall be headed in that direction," she gasped, "if you continue to smother me."

He tipped her head back and she breathed deeply, her eyes closed. The serenity of her expression reminded him of how lifeless she was moments ago, and his hand trembled as he cradled her jaw. "You scared the bloody hell out of me." His tone held a turbulence of unspent emotion.

Her eyes drifted open, and Michaela experienced a sudden painful clenching in her chest, like bruise or a cut. His face was black with soot, white ash fluttered on the edges of his hair. But his eyes, his eyes were red-rimmed from the smoke, yet clear and penetrating, as if searching for an unforeseen change in her.

She touched his cheek, the trail marked clean with smoke tears. He turned his face into her palm and closed his eyes.

Wood fell and they looked up as the west side collapsed into itself.

"Cabai? Where's Cabai?" She sat up, looking at the yard. "And Andy." She gripped Rein's arm, blinking back dizziness. "Andy's missing."

There were eight of the twelve out on the lawn. "I don't see them."

"He's still inside." She tried to get up, but he held her fast.

"Are you mad?" Flames billowed like streamers out of the upper floor, lapping at the sky.

"Cabai went upstairs to get the pistols before the fire. Rein, he's in there!"

Rein lurched toward the house, nearing the front steps when the house imploded, beams snapping, and Michaela rose and staggered to him. The dining-room window fractured like a bull butting a fence, and Rein pulled her back, shielding her as debris sprayed the ground, a figure stumbling through the fresh opening, hitting the dirt and rolling into a ball.

Rein shot forward, grabbing a seared arm and pulling him clear. Michaela fell to her knees beside them as Rein rolled the man over.

"Cabai!" Michaela scrambled around, cradling his head in her lap. "Oh, Cabai, why didn't you get out?"

He pushed the wood box clutched to his chest toward her. "I live to serve, my mistress."

"We are going to have to discuss the lengths you go to please me." She leaned down in his face, using her skirt hem to blot at the sweat and ash on his forehead. "I really am a rather accommodating person, you know."

Rein scoffed and slumped to his back in the dirt. "Since when?"

Michaela lifted her gaze to her husband's. "So nice of you to come home in one piece." Her look said a full accounting would come soon.

"Least you could have done was have it in one piece when I arrived."

She frowned, looking at the burning house. "All those beautiful things."

Rein shifted to his elbow, wincing a bit. "They can be replaced. You cannot." He touched her face, rubbed his thumb over her lips, then rose up to kiss them.

Cabai cleared his throat. They looked down. With the back of his hands, he brushed them apart, then climbed to his feet. He faced them, motioning that they could resume.

She studied him. His breeches were burned away across his thigh, his shirt was black and torn. "You're not wounded?"

He didn't give his blistering arm a glance. "I will be fine," he said in a hushed voice, then left them.

"I must account for the others." Rein opened the box, checking the load of pistols. He handed one to her. "The culprits could still be here."

Michaela nodded and stood, leaning into him as they moved into the trees.

Rusty came to her, hugging her. "Ahh, thank God, squirt."

Rein coughed up more smoke and looked at the men, relieved to see Leelan virtually untouched by the flames or gunfire as Rusty moved up beside him.

"Your Mr. Bushmara is dead. A bullet."

Michaela choked and ran to the Moor, falling to her knees. Tears filled her eyes as she stroked his choppy black hair from his dark, still face. "Oh, nay," she sobbed, then looked up at Rein. Her tear-stained face ripped him in pieces. "Is anyone else . . . hurt?"

Rusty looked at the ground, and Rein came to her, pulling her to her feet.

She braced her palms on his arms. "Tell me."

"Andy lives, but Renée Gilbèrt is dead." She howled before the words were out, her legs crumbling.

"Nay. Oh, nay, this is my fault. Mine."

"Aw, Michaela." He caught her, carrying her to privacy.

She sobbed into his shirtfront, her fingers digging into his arms. "Damn them. Damn them!"

He gripped her shoulders. "None could have predicted this, do you understand?" She nodded resolutely, yet the tears still came, each one like a blade slicing at his composure.

"No one knew I was here . . . that we were. Who could have done this?"

Temple cleared his throat, standing off to the side, scanning the area, his gun out. They turned to look at him, Michaela swiping her face with the back of her hand.

"I'm afraid it's my fault." He hunched his shoulders. "I didn't know you were hiding her." He nodded to Michaela. "Anyone could have followed me from the ship."

" 'Twas bound to happen." Rein looked at his wife and smiled weakly. "I could not keep you to myself for that long."

Warmth filled her at that, comforting her. "This was not a rescue, Rein. If anyone thought you'd kidnapped me, then burning the house down around us was not a way to return me to my family." The last came out with a pinch of anger.

"You think 'twas you they were after?"

She glanced to the side. "They fired several shots at the window." She looked back at him. "At me."

His gaze swept her for wounds, and she twisted her head, showing him the scrape from broken glass. Rein examined it, plucking a splinter from the cut. He tore his sleeve and pressed it to the blood-caked spot.

"I am fine, for pity's sake." She pushed his hands away. "The fire started at the window, a soaked rag around rocks, I think. It happened so fast. They kept shooting, even after the fire started. I couldn't get out."

Rein settled to the ground, calling for someone to round up as many horses as they could. At least the stables were intact.

She picked at the threads of her gown. The pannier caging was crushed and misshapen. "I've been compromised."

"I am trying," he said with a wiggle of his brows. Even under the soot and dirt, he could see her blush.

"I think the Sons of Liberty believe I have divulged their secrets."

His brows shot up. "Are you saying people you have aided for three years are trying to kill you!"

Her look was belligerent. "I was aware of the dangers when I began this life, Rein. And made aware of the consequences should I be caught. I am a viable threat."

A missive to Nickolas would clarify the possibility, and his decision to not allow her back in this game just solidified to stone. He had to get her out of the country. Tonight. And he could think of no safer place than Sanctuary.

Michaela stepped into the cabin, glancing at the blackened imprint of flames on the walls near the floor. She looked at him, arching a brow.

He cleared his throat. "A little too much . . . uncontrolled energy."

"I am in danger of being burned?"

"Only if you want to be," he growled in her ear, ushering her inside.

Michaela took three steps, then stopped short, staring wide-eyed at the panther crawling from beneath the window bench. "Rein." She back stepped into him. "Rein!"

The panther growled softly, sniffing her burned skirts.

"Be still," he whispered.

"This is a pet!" she said in a loud hiss. How else could the creature be in here?

"Aye. Rahjin, this is my wife."

Rahjin looked up and settled back on her haunches.

Michaela lifted her fingers to the animal's beautiful face. Rahjin sniffed, catching Rein's scent on her, she assumed, then the panther pushed her head into her palm. Michaela smiled, rubbing her behind the ears. Rahjin purred softly, and Michaela knelt.

"We are going to be allies. We girls," she whispered and, above her, Rein smiled. She stood, still scratching the cat, and glanced around the room. The last time she was here, she scarcely noticed anything but Rein and the hole she put in him. But now she studied her surroundings, where she would live for the next few days. On her left lay a long table surrounded by chairs, along the wall beyond were cabinets, some with shelves housing books, some with locked doors. To her right was an alcove fashioned by an carved armoire, a commode and basin, a small table and a decently sized tub. Near the aft windows and starboard wall was Rein's desk, a broad leather chair behind it, a worn, overstuffed sofa before it with a pair of equally worn chairs. A working cabin.

Her gaze swung to the only other encompassing piece of furniture, the bed, its headboard carved with the White Empress emblem, the canopy and posts uncovered and draped simply with sheers and mosquito netting. It reminded her of India, exotic and mysterious. Thick velvety coverlets heightened the bed, making it appear to loom and taunt her. She swallowed, the past days vanishing under the realization that they would share it. In hours.

"A bath is ready for you." She flinched at the sound of his voice, turning as he crossed to the tub.

Rein was agonizingly aware of her turmoil, sensing it with a poignancy that made his skin hurt. And he wondered when she would find the courage and trust to confess her secrets.

Michaela watched him pass his hands over the water, steam quickly rising. She tipped her head to the side, studying the man she'd married. He was fascinating to look at, even filthy and weary, his tall, slender body holding much more power than one would assume. She realized he cared deeply for people, a kindness he spared from himself. She admired him, the way nothing seemed to daunt his resolve. He wasted no time in idle speculation and simply did what was necessary, though one step ahead of everyone, especially her. And as he laid out a towel and soaps for her, she realized how fortunate she was to call him husband.

And when will you be his wife, give him the honesty he has given you? a voice pestered. Immediately she looked away, stroking Rahjin's fur. The cat nudged her and she glanced at Rein, waiting patiently. She crossed to him, giving him her back.

Without a sound, he gathered her hair to the side and unfastened her gown.

"I'm afraid I've naught but a robe for you."

She nodded, holding the garment to her breasts, then turned, lifting her gaze. He didn't smile, his eyes rapidly shifting over her.

Rein thought of the moment when her soul had left her body, when she lay in the dirt, lifeless, and his chest tightened miserably. He swallowed, wanting to smother her with kisses, crush her against him, but she was trembling. She needed to rest, he reminded, to sleep, but the need to hold her overwhelmed him, and slowly he slid his arms around her, drawing her gently against him. She laid her head to his chest and Rein smoothed his hand up her bare back, feeling her heavy sigh, her arms winding loosely about his waist.

And Rein knew the sweetest contentment.

He pressed a kiss to the top of her head. "Get into the bath, then to bed."

"Is that an order, Captain?" She tipped her head back to look at him.

"Aye." He released her, and felt a disappointment he couldn't touch. "Rahjin, guard her." The cat sauntered lazily toward the bed. "Ah-uh, you know better." Rein slid a glance to Michaela, winking. The cat sniffed the air, then moved to the door, plopping to the deck. He looked back at his wife, then brushed his mouth over hers, a gentle whispering. Michaela tasted him just as softly, lips tugging, her tongue sliding. It was the most intimate of kisses, their bodies a breath away, the banked fire stirring. Slowly, he stepped back and exhaled.

"I must see to the ship."

She nodded, delicately breathless. Rein forced himself to turn and leave her, sealing the door softly behind him. It was pitiful how easily the woman could stir him to a frenzy, he thought, and, crossing the passageway to the hatch, he stepped onto the deck, ordering the stores checked, the lines keeled.

He hoped Nickolas did his job.

He wasn't bringing Michaela anywhere near England until he did. He glanced back, wondering how she'd feel when he left her with his family to go search for his blood father. Rein's features creased with uncertainly as he climbed the quarterdeck ladder. He had to finish this, for the last candidate was going to be in Morocco in a fortnight.

An hour later, Rein met Cabai in the passageway, just stepping out of his cabin, his arms filled with Michaela's burned clothing. The man's frown gave him concern, and Rein looked past him into the room. He couldn't see her, then heard the splash of water.

"Still in the bath?" Surely the water was cold by now.

Cabai shrugged helplessly, and Rein shifted past him into the cabin and shut the door. Rahjin mewed softly, looking at him, then her new mistress. Rein walked quietly closer, staring down at her. Though her hair was obviously washed and pinned out of the water, she scrubbed furiously at her arms, her throat, her fingers. He called her, she paused only for a second, then continued to scrub and lather and scrub. Beside the tub, Rein warmed the water for her, then knelt, catching her hands.

"I am still dirty," she whispered, not looking at him.

"Nay, you are—"

"I am!" She jerked free and scrubbed her throat, her shoulders, her breasts hidden beneath a mound of suds.

"Michaela, you are going to rub the hide off, if you do not cease."

She froze, her gaze flashing to his, her expression bleeding with shame and remorse. " 'Twill not come off," she said in a dead voice.

"What? What won't?"

"The stain."

"I see no mark."

Her chin tipped up, her gaze locked tight with his. " 'Tis there."

Rein stared, hurting for her and finding himself at a complete loss. "If this stain were gone, then what?"

Her eyes softened, her shoulders drooped. She looked weary and defeated. "Then I could be your real wife."

His features yanked taut, her meaning sinking with the force of a cutlass into his chest. "You already are, Michaela. Naught will change that."

"You deserve someone else, Rein."

"I deserve you," he said, and stood, pulling her to her feet. Water and suds slid down her body, yet Rein kept his gaze locked with hers as he wrapped her in a soft cloth and lifted her from the tub. She went without protest and he carried her to the window bench, settling comfortably in the corner. She shivered, and he rubbed her arms and shoulders, waiting for her to stop trembling, waiting for her to speak.

"Whatever burdens you, Michaela, we can solve it together."

Michaela fingered his damp shirt, then looked at him, finding comfort in his steady gaze. " 'Twas silly, wasn't it, trying to scrub off the past. We can't. None of us can. 'Tis done."

"Facing our mistakes is the trial of an earthly soul."

Her brows knitted.

"Learn in this life, and the next one will be free of burdens."

"Karma. Reincarnation." She smiled slightly at his surprise. "I learned a bit in India, too."

He leaned and brushed his mouth over hers. "Unburden yourself, Michaela. It tears at you. I can see it."

She inhaled a deep breath and wiggled out of his arms, holding the cloth at her breasts, and he gestured to the robe left for her. Quickly she slipped into the heavy velvet, swallowed in its warmth, his scent, then sat down, facing him, gathering her courage as she drew her knees up and wrapped her arms around her legs. She stared out the windows, into the night and England fading in the distance.

The ache that started the instant she stepped into this cabin swelled to agonizing proportions, threatening her composure. From the moment she wed him, she recognized all she could lose in these next moments, but she could not go on, not and be fair to him. He'd lain his past out for her, his life for her, and she could do no less than risk her future on him. She glanced at him, her heart breaking for the concern she saw there, her throat tight and dry, and after a false start, the words tumbled out.

"Major Winters and I were to be married."

"I know."

She looked at him.

" 'Tis been the rumor since you disappeared."

She shrugged as if it didn't matter, returning her gaze to the sea. "There was a time I thought myself madly in love with him. He was handsome and gallant in his uniform. We'd shared a few kisses in the garden." *Nothing compared to yours, Rein,* she thought. "Banns had not yet been posted when he came to me, to my rooms. I was shocked and, even more so, when he expected to share my bed without benefit of vows."

Rein's fingers curled into a fist gone to a bloodless white.

"I refused, but he cajoled and teased, insisting that my kisses said I wanted him." She turned her head and looked him dead in the eye, and from across the short expanse, Rein felt her pain, her humiliation. "I didn't, you see. I felt so alone and wanted to be loved, have a home, some children." She hugged herself. "But not before I had the right." She let out a shuddering breath. "When I asked him to leave my rooms, he hit me. I was so stunned, for a moment I did not react. He thought he had my compliance and when I fought, he held me down . . ." She swallowed, smothering the flood of tears, the sound strained and pitiful. ". . . then took a husband's rights."

Rein schooled his features, masking the rage boiling inside him. He'd suspected this, but a dark part of him refused to imagine her helpless, fighting off a man who wanted nothing but to satisfy a moment of lust, without thought to the price.

"What did your uncle do?" he asked.

She rubbed the space between her brows, her fingers shaking. "Major Winters spoke to my uncle first, claiming I'd seduced him to my rooms, then dismissed him when he was too enamored to stop." She tipped her head, her voice surprisingly innocent when she said, "Nay means nay. What was so hard to understand with that?" Tears spilled, rolling heedlessly down her cheeks.

"Any fool would, Michaela." His words fell on deaf ears, for she continued on as if he hadn't spoken.

"The final cut was that my uncle actually believed him. He said I'd always been a wild girl, and now I was forward and promiscuous and I would be a whore if not for his rules. Not even the bruises would convince him. God, I hated him for that," she spat. *"I* was his family. But he took his aide's word over mine." She rubbed her arms, sniffling. "Be grateful Winters still wanted me, he said, insisted I marry the man. I refused and he threatened to reveal that I'd seduced Winters and turn me out into the street." She looked down at her toes, covering them with the robe. "I was scared. No

one had ever treated me so horribly. I didn't know what to do."
Her voice fractured, bleak and lonely. "I could not marry him. And
if I left without a husband, I would lose every penny of my inheritance to my uncle. I agreed to care for him and the house, in exchange for a roof over my head."

She shifted on the seat, drawing her legs to the side and resting
her head on the thick pane. "He kept his word never to tell a soul,
but constantly reminded me that I was a less than acceptable woman
and that I'd made a choice, to live under his rule for the remainder
of my days or try my newfound knowledge out in the streets." Her
face contorted with disgust. "Winters never ceased trying to lure
me. Until I stabbed him."

"Then he is lucky you did not have a pistol."

She smiled weakly, swiping at her cheeks, still gazing out at the
window. "I stared at my greatest shame in the face nearly every
day." She drew circles on the glass. "I met Nickolas at the soup
kitchen, and I suppose he overheard my position on the rebellion."
She shrugged, feeling cold and very alone. "I started spying on
Uncle Atwell a week later."

Neither spoke, Michaela staring out the window, Rein staring at
her.

Her shuddering breath and her red-rimmed eyes delivered him
into a hell so hot with rage, he wanted to smash something. "He
deserves to die."

She looked up. His pale eyes glittered with a possessive threat,
his need for retribution warming her and scaring her. "He deserves
to pay, aye. But I am not dead, I do not bleed." She covered his
hand with hers and his posture softened.

"You have bled for three years, Michaela, 'tis his turn."

"My virtue is not yours to avenge." Her voice lowered as she
bowed her head. "It was yours to take."

His heart crumbled, her shame thickening her words. Rein drew
her into his arms, pressing his lips to the top of her head. "Do you
think I want you less for the lack?" After a moment, she nodded.
His arms tightened. "I will tell you a secret," he said close to her
ear. "I am not a virgin."

Her shoulders shook with a quick laugh.

"You are not at fault," he continued.

"Mayhap, I did lead him. I wanted him to kiss me, to hold me."

Her shame over wanting simple human contact slayed him. " 'Tis desire, Michaela, only your desire. You have a right to it, just as any man."

"Uncle said I was no better than a whore—"

He hushed her, wanting to kill the Brigadier for massacring her feelings. "He was wrong, Michaela. *Wrong*. And I find it preposterous that he could say such a thing when you are not even aware of how seductive you truly are."

She made a sound of disbelief, and he tipped her face up, holding her gaze. "I am weak for you, my *rasha*. You possess a power over my very soul that I cannot fight. You are in control, haven't you known that?"

She had. He could have demanded and taken, yet he bowed to her reservations, leaving her alone. Even when she wanted to be with him. She brushed her fingers down the side of his face, through his hair, touching the loop in his ear and marveling at how easily he accepted. "Thank you."

He laid his mouth to her trembling lips, his kiss tender and slow, and she pushed deeper into his arms, clinging. He rubbed her back, ending the kiss and simply holding her. The ship heeled with the buffet of waves, rocking them, and still he held her, feeling her grow lax and boneless against him. Rein tipped his head back against the frame, his face illuminated by the moon's reflection off the sea as he wondered if she'd feel content in his arms when he forbade her to spy again.

Twenty-eight

Rein startled awake, blinking into the darkness, then he looked down as she shifted fitfully against him. He tightened his arms around her, about to whisper in her ear, into her dreams, when she wrenched away, smacking at his hands, shoving.

"Don't touch me!" she snarled, curling against the pane.

"Michaela, 'tis me, Rein." She didn't see him, staring just to the right of him and Rein realized a nightmare held her prisoner. He reached for her and she scrambled off the bench, backstepping, her stare venomous.

His chest clenched. "Ah, my dove, 'tis me."

She darted across the room, banging into the cold brazier, knocking a cup to the floor, and Rein followed, grabbing her elbow and a hank of her hair.

"Nay!" she cried on a long moan and stumbled toward the commode, reaching out like a child grasping for its mother. She slapped her hand over the edge of the commode, over the razor lying there. She twisted, her arm raised to slash at the auburn locks trapped beneath his hand when Rein snatched her wrist. She hissed at him, her eyes blistering with hatred. He squeezed, and with an angry cry, her hand opened. The blade clattered to the floor. He released her hair and she backed away, gathering the curls as if gathering a blanket, holding them to her chest. Innocent, frightened.

" 'Tis me, Rein," he repeated over and over. She was motionless, wide eyed.

Her vision cleared, and she looked at the hair in her hands, then to him.

Moments passed, her breathing swift, her body trembling. Her throat worked as the pieces of her dreams chipped away, her posture softening. Her lip quivered, and with a moan seeping with despair, she covered her face with her hands, sinking to the floor. He went to her, offering her the shelter of his strong arms.

She cried, folded over, his body curved to hers as she emptied her pain, spilling her agony in tight, wretched sobs. His gut twisted, her anguish cinching his breathing as he rocked her gently, pressing his lips to her temple, telling her she was safe now, protected and no one would touch her unless she chose.

"Oh, God," she muttered. "I'm sorry."

"Nay, nay, ah, *rasha*. 'Tis not your fault."

"I'm so ashamed."

Rein swallowed, lost, then whispered in her ear, "He held you down by your hair, didn't he?"

She nodded. He stroked his hand back over her head, pushing the mass from her face. " 'Tis beautiful hair, Michaela."

She lifted her gaze, sniffling, and Rein sank back on his rear, pulling her between his thighs. "And I am not him."

"I know, I know, but . . ." Ugly sensations shivered through her. "I want this to go away."

" 'Twill leave in time, I swear." He nestled her head under his chin, pressing his lips to the top.

"Bloody sure of it, aren't you?" she said on a hiccup, her gaze on his mouth.

His lips curved slightly. "Irritating, isn't it?"

"Kiss me."

His brows rose.

Her gaze flew to his. "Kiss me," she repeated. "Make it go away."

"Michaela," he cautioned. "I don't think that is the solution."

"Hold on to my hair."

He frowned.

"I want to shear it off, Rein, I do." Her lips trembled. "I want it gone like these dreams. Make them go." Her voice broke like cracking glass. "Kiss me. Take me past them."

Her pleas drained him, took the last of his common sense, and he ducked, his mouth nearing, gazes locked. Tentatively he touched his lips to hers, and her breath shuddered against his mouth. His palms hovered near her jaw as she returned the kiss, covering his hands, pushing his fingers into her hair.

She moaned and he jerked back, searching her face, but she only leaned into his mouth again, her wet, soft lips torturing him, fighting her demons for a moment in his arms. Michaela felt as if she were sinking deep under a rushing current, struggling to reach the surface. And still she kissed him, aching for him and hating that another man took what should be his, hating that she'd had, for those horrible moments, lost absolute control over her life. She wanted it back, demanded its return, needed it to be worthy of this man, to discard the weakness brought from that one night.

Rein would not hurt her. Never. Never.

And in his arms she found herself, stepping past her own barriers, letting freedom sweep her, accepting his energy, and when his fingers tightened in her hair, she experienced only the power he held in restraint, the lure of the exotic pleasure only he could give her. A sweet blistering sang through her blood, a captured bubble breaking the surface as he nurtured her lips, holding his body away from her, and she took command, her hands sweeping up his shoulders, cradling his face, imprisoning him. She plundered his mouth.

And he groaned, a dark rumble familiar to her now, a sound that made her body burn lush and hot, her heart expand, and she let him in, hungering to hear the music of his pleasure.

She unleashed, and Rein's entire body clenched with hot desire. She stole his energy, sucked it from him with her ravenous kiss, and when she crawled onto his lap, he felt the mooring on his restraint slip free. He cupped her buttocks, pressing the heat of her sex to his aching groin, sending a rush of blood pulsating through him. He trembled, and tried not to crush her to him, tried not to push her to her back and satisfy the hunger raging between them. She was fragile and seeking an end to her torment, and if she wanted control, he would gladly give it to her. For with it came her trust, yet when she drew back, he saw her heart laid bare in her clear hazel eyes.

He searched her features, felt her breath rush against his lips. He smoothed her hair from her face and she closed her eyes, serene under his touch. He wanted to shout for the sheer joy of seeing it.

"Husband" was all she whispered, clinging, spent, as she buried her face in the crook of his neck.

"I am here, *rasha,* always."

She snuggled in his embrace. "I know," she said on a sigh, soft and pliant in his arms. Rein held her, stroking her back, then cocked his head to look at her face. He found her sound asleep, smiling. And his heart sang.

Michaela curled into the warmth of the coverlets, nuzzling her face into the pillow. A distinct weight stretched across her hip, Rein's hand settled familiarly between her breasts. She felt no fear, no reservation at his touch, and with it came a cocoon of tranquility she never thought to feel. She kept her eyes closed, enjoying the sensations, the clean, freshly washed scent of him and she wondered when he'd carried her to his bed.

Their bed. He'd accepted her, without hesitation or revulsion. Her lips curled in a sleepy smile. Somehow she'd always known he was not like other men, he'd proven it enough, and she despised the her lack of courage. But then, she'd never thought to fall so deeply in love with him. Her eyes flashed open, and she slipped to her back to look at him.

He was naked. Completely. Gloriously. Facedown, his arm across her middle, one leg drawn up, he looked more like Rahjin than a man. Powerfully sleek and long, his skin was deep bronze, his body flawlessly smooth and tight with muscles. She swore they rippled whilst he breathed. Her gaze rolled downward from his inky black hair draping to his shoulders and fastened on his buttocks. Tight, a little indentation on the sides. Her fingers itched to touch him, feel male skin beneath her palms. She swallowed, her body humming with fresh desire, and she dragged her gaze back to his face. He slept soundly, the natural warmth of his skin radiating through the sheets and into her. A tiny knot thickened in her throat and her vision blurred.

I love this man, she thought. *I love him.*

" 'Tis impolite to stare." His hand splayed over her ribs, he dragged her against him.

"Oh. You're awake," she said stupidly, the sudden rush of heat spinning down to her heels.

His lips curved, his eyes still closed. " 'Tis difficult to sleep with you so near."

She was silent, gazing at his handsome face, then pushed a lock of hair from his cheek. " 'Tis badly singed."

He grinned sleepily, his face half buried in the pillow. "My wife will trim it for me."

This seemed to be a highly irregular conversation for two people lying abed, one of them startlingly naked. "Do you always sleep without a stitch?"

"Aye." His fingers brushed the underside of her breasts, and Michaela's entire body tingled and tightened. "Aught else you wish to know about my daily habits?" His fingers made slow, soft circles over her robed skin and her breathing quickened. "I shave without a stitch on. I swim without a stitch on, and"—he opened one pale blue eye—"I make love without a stitch on."

She swallowed, an act that stole her strength. "Do you really?" Her gaze flicked to his body, and she was suddenly nervous and excited and filled with a longing she wanted desperately to explore with him, to be touched by him, more than that night in the kitchen, more than kisses, and he seemed to sense it, and when she brought her gaze back to his, his pale eyes smoldered with capped passion.

"Really."

Rein wanted show her right then, but her innocent stares reminded him the last man she'd been with had brutalized her, humiliated her enough that she'd fought her own desires, discarded her needs as vulgar, because she felt they made her less than acceptable, less of a lady. He wanted to kill the bastards for shaming her passion into the recesses of her mind.

And he would draw them out, languidly, opening the sensuality he knew was locked inside her. The freedom she but sampled last night.

Curling his arm deeper around her waist, he pulled her flush against him, the jumble of coverlets and sheets a fresh barrier between. Her hand settled easily on his bare shoulder. And he ducked his head, his intent on her mouth.

"You have that look about you."

His sooty lashes swept up, and Michaela was transfixed at the heat in his pale blue gaze.

"And what look is that?"

"That I-will-consume-her-till-there-is-naught-left look."

"Nay," he murmured against her mouth. "You, *rasha*, are the fire that consumes me." He laid his mouth over hers, gently, insistently, and Michaela drank in his flavor, sliding her arm around his neck and pressing him harder. A dark groan worked in his throat, his body ablaze for her, and he parted her robe, slipping his hands inside and touching sleep-warm skin. She surged against him, full of eagerness and desire, and Rein quaked, throbbing, driving his hand up her back, her smooth skin inviting his stroking.

The rub of his calloused palms created a delicious friction that sent her into a place of scents and taste. Her kiss grew feverish, her tongue pushing between his lips. She cupped his jaw, her head rolling ravenously back and forth.

He fell to his back, taking her with him, and she flattened her hands to his chest, rising up to look at him. He smiled devilishly, curling his fingers behind her knees and working her legs around his hips as he sat up. She gasped at the mold of masculine flesh to her softness, skin to skin, and the place between her thighs grew moist and tight with yearning. The urge to climb higher than his thighs nearly overwhelmed her.

Rein spread the robe, pushing it off her shoulders, his gaze raking her body, her full, plump breasts. He brushed the back of his hands across her nipples, lightly, teasingly, and her breath shuddered like the fall of warm rain. His hand rode down her arm to her wrist and he threaded his fingers with hers, drawing them to his mouth, kissing her delicate knuckles.

She watched his lips, fascinated with the sight of them on her skin. He rubbed her fingers against his cheek, suckled the tips, brushed them over his throat. She'd never experienced anything so arousing as his mouth on her palm, the scrape of his teeth to the heel. Then he pressed her palm to his bare chest.

"Feel me," he whispered. "Know there is no part of me that will harm you."

Her expression darkened briefly, and he brushed his mouth across hers, keeping his body back. He waited, gazing into her eyes, his smile small. Her fingers flexed, slowly exploring the shape of his flat coin nipple, the hairless curves of his chest. Her hand stilled at his waist.

Rein thought he'd lose control, enjoying her touch, the sound of her breathing. Yet she refused to look anywhere but his face.

"Look at me, Michaela."

She licked her lips and still stared.

"Look where you touch."

She did, her gaze lowering over his flat stomach, the dense black hair nestled between powerful thighs. She inhaled. He was erect and growing wider, longer.

He captured her hands, rubbing his thumbs soothingly over the back. " 'Tis a part of me, Michaela, like a hand or an arm, not a weapon." He led her closer.

"I know." Her fingers immediately closed over him. Her breath rasped out in a breathy moan. Velvet steel, she thought.

Rein growled, her fingers delicate and light. Curious. "I want you, not this. *I do.* This is part of me as these"—he enfolded her breasts—"are to you." She thrust into his touch, her fingers sliding over the smooth, slick tip of him.

" 'Tis wet."

His hand slipped between her thighs, fingers dipping, and she gasped and shuddered and squeezed him. "So are you," he rasped, and closed his lips over her nipple, drawing it deeply into the burn of his mouth. She offered herself, holding his head there, her own thrown back in abandon. Rein tasted her, smoothing his hands over her chest, mapping the contours of her ribs, her hips, her thighs. He pushed her gently to her back, nipping at her belly, laving the sweep of her hip, the bend of thigh, pushing her legs apart. She looked down at him, her brow furrowing a touch, utterly entranced by the sight of him dragging his tongue over her flesh.

He circled the bead of her sex and all restraint left her. "Oh. Oh, God." She arched, her hips lifting, offering herself. He scooped his hand beneath her buttocks, holding her gaze as he covered her softness with his mouth. She shrieked softly, digging her elbows into the bed, her heels pressing. She turned her face away, thrilling at the intimate feel of his mouth and she sank her fingers into his hair.

He growled with pleasure, laving and sucking. She twisted and he tasted. She bucked and pleaded, and he chuckled, torturing her.

Rein watched, watched her writhe and bow, her skin grow damp and glistening. He felt her body trembling on the sweet explosion, and he pushed two fingers inside her. She bore down, clawing at the sheets, driving her fingers through his hair as feminine muscles clamped and flexed. And still he tasted her sweetness.

She looked down at his dark head between her thighs, his bronze hands playing over her skin. It heightened her senses, made every touch shoot to her bones, scrape her raw, pull on every nerve and draw it into an ever tightening knot. She thrust against him, and he made that sound of dark pleasure and mystery and then—the string broke. She stiffened, and his motions grew heavier, deeper, and Michaela pulsed and pushed, cried out his name and melted into a bath of rapture and luxury and gloriously searing heat.

She sank into the bed.

He rose up, sitting back on his haunches, smoothing her legs. "Michaela, look at me."

She panted. "Must I?" A deep blush crept up her body.

He loomed over her. She could feel his heat. Slowly she opened her eyes, gazing into his. He smiled. She blushed deeper.

"I could spend a lifetime watching you take your pleasure."

Her expression softened, and she brushed a black lock from his forehead, thinking of how much she loved him, how much she needed him. "How could I resist?"

He grinned. " 'Tis the very idea."

"And when can I give it to you?"

His pale eyes smoldered at the thought.

She reached between them, closing her hand around him, and, with a growl, he sank onto her, taking her to her side. She felt every inch of him, smoothing her fingers over the slick, velvety tip, and her womanhood flared and clamped. But it was his reaction that enflamed her, the sharpening of his features, his ragged breathing, his weakness to her touch. He was pliant and boneless.

"Ahh, my *rasha,* you torture me." His hands charged wildly over her body.

"No more than you have me." She traced the deep muscle in his buttocks. "I've wanted to do that since I woke," she confessed, then suddenly bowed her head.

He tipped it back. "What else do you want to do?"

She sketched his sultry features. "Explore you."

A rap sounded, and Rein cursed and fell into the mattress. She kept touching him, and he caught her hands.

"What is it?" he called.

"A brig, sir. Starboard bow." The voice came from the other side of the door.

"In a moment then."

He looked at her, apology and disappointment in his smile, then rolled away and left the bed.

Shifting upright, Michaela wrapped the sheet about her, watching him as he washed, pouring cold water over his arousal and sending her a blaming look. Michaela flushed at his frankness, his comfort in his nakedness.

"Does it hurt?"

He met her gaze as he tried to stuff himself into his breeches. "It hurts to be pleasuring you."

She inhaled. "Oh!" She cocked her head. *"Oh."* The single word and her smile turned instantly seductive. "And you are so certain I will find pleasure?"

He shrugged into his shirt as he crossed to her, and she enjoyed his long-legged approach. "Find it, achieve it, and scream with it," he said with every step, and on her knees on the bed, she gazed up at him, the sheet clutched to her breast. He wrapped an arm around her waist. "Have you heard of *Kama Sutra?*" he asked.

Her eyes widened. "Aye." It was an explicit book of the pleasures of the flesh. Sensual. Forbidden. "Aye," she said, a little breathless.

"I have learned much of it."

She leaned back. "And practiced it?"

He loved the jealousy glinting her eyes. "That will begin tonight."

She huffed, though every cell in her screamed for him to begin now. "Your conviction is irritating," she said even as her hand slid to his stomach, dangerously close to his arousal. He clapped her fingers, a warning look in his eyes.

She grinned, and Rein recognized that she understood the strength of her femininity. "I have unleashed a temptress," he groused when he had to go up on deck and leave her looking like a siren, rumpled and freshly loved in his bed. Sweet mothers, he was in trouble. Exquisite trouble.

He bent and kissed her, a wet slide of lips and tongue, and she slipped off the bed, pressing her body to his hard length, tunneling her fingers in his hair. His knees softened, and when the rap on the door came again, he snapped, "In a minute," then kissed her some more.

She pushed him toward the door, and he looked back, her draped sheet revealing the plush curves of her breasts, the delicate line of her spine. His expression darkened, his gaze raking her. "You are a most delicious creature, my *rasha.*"

Her skin flushed, her nipples peaking against the thin sheet, and his lips quirked as he grabbed up his waistcoat and reached for the door.

"And what do you taste like, Rein?" carried softly to him, just as he stepped through the hatch. He froze, squeezing his eyes shut, then continued on, closing the door behind him.

Rein leaned back against the wood, swearing this was what he desired most, her trust, her need of him, and he strode to the passageway, ready to blast the brig out of the water so he could get back to his bride.

Nickolas stared down at the missive, his heart skipping as he read Rein's revelation of Katherine's killer, the sketchy account of the fire and shots. Regret for the lives lost sluiced through him, and he sagged into the chair. That the Sons of Liberty would send an assassin for one their own left a sour taste in his mouth. Even if they'd done it to protect his life, Michaela would never have betrayed him.

Crushing the parchment in his fist, he tossed it into the blaze before turning to the scarred little desk. With Michaela safe, he could press his colleagues for stronger action, since she'd been taken out of the network for some time now, proving she was not the risk they sought. Nickolas dipped the quill and wrote, prepared to garner every favor owed him and force the hand of a traitor to raise.

She was dead in the water, Rein thought, peering through the glass and calling out orders to come about the leeward side of the vessel, then to raise signal flags. The brig was unrecognizable. And at this distance he could not make out her colors, not that he'd any intention of engaging the ship. The *White Empress* was a cargo ship, and though gunned for her defense against marauders, she was not stacked for battle. What he wouldn't give to have the *Red Lion* beneath his feet, he mulled, suddenly hungry for a fight.

He frowned at the thought, lowering the glass.

Lust was maddening. Anticipation was killing him.

And after leaving her hours ago, looking so ripe for ravishing, Rein knew if he did not gain control, he'd hurt her. Her last words vibrated through his mind. Did the woman know how easily she could bring him to his knees?

"Rein."

He slid Leelan a glance. The helmsman nodded, and Rein followed the direction, lowering the spy glass. "Sweet thunder." It was Michaela, in dark buckskin breeches and a threadbare muslin shirt, that mane of hair catching on the wind as she climbed the quarterdeck ladder!

"Well, 'tis a right fetching sight."

Rein cast him a censoring side glance, then moved to the ladder, his gaze sweeping the crewman who paused in their work to fasten their attention on her figure. Rein clenched his fists. She was his wife! Those curves were for him alone to see, to explore, and his glacial look warned them back to work.

"Permission to come above?" she said, and his gaze flew to hers. He folded his arms over his chest. "Where did you get those?"

She frowned. "Cabai altered them to fit." She tipped her head. "Did you not ask him to?"

"He was to repair your gown until he could fashion another."

His words snapped, and Michaela felt her throat tighten. "And you expected me to remain in the cabin, alone, until you presented yourself?" she gritted under a sweet smile. "I think not." She overtook the rungs, forcing him to backstep or let her fall.

He made no effort to help her, to touch her, his posture uninviting and remote. "I expected you to be properly clothed afore my crew."

"I am adequately covered."

"That shirt is bloody damned transparent!" he hissed. By the gods, he could see the pear-shaped curves of her breast, the darkness of her nipples. And so could every man about. The damned buckskins looked more like skin than softened hide, and Rein immediately stripped off his leather waistcoat and held it out to her. "Put it on and braid your hair back afore you are spotted."

Michaela looked at the garment, then him, an uncomfortable coldness settling between them. Obviously he didn't want her up here, and she spun about, quickly descending the ladder and striding back to the passageway.

Rein blinked, stunned motionless as she left, his gaze falling to the shift of her bottom in those breeches. She'd worn them before, and it never bothered him, why now?

"Well, now . . . that had all the tact of a bull sniffin' at a cow."

He snapped a look at Leelan. His features went taut, then he groaned, rubbing the back of his neck.

Michaela resisted the childish urge to slam the door and shut it softly. Rahjin looked up as she moved to the window bench, sliding into the corner. She folded and unfolded her arms, shifted her legs twice, glaring out the foggy windows. Damn him, she thought, and a second later, lurched off the cushions and paced.

How dare he talk to her like that! She'd been in here for hours, trapped, bored, and when Cabai had brought the clothing, she thought Rein wanted her with him. Hah. Apparently she was quite the uneducated lass when it came to ships and proper protocol. The borrowed boots thumped on the rich carpet, her hair falling in her face. She tossed it back over her shoulder, refusing to braid it.

Amy J. Fetzer

She tensed when the door opened and gave him her back, watching the brig in the distance. She felt him move up behind her.

"You are not allowed above decks without permission."

She stiffened. "I see."

"Nay, you do not. A woman aboard offers reason enough to incite riot and attack, Michaela. Your hair can be seen for miles—let alone your figure."

"Forgive my ignorance, Captain." That did not excuse the way he spoke to her. "I did not know that I could only share your bed and not your life."

His shoulders fell, and he wished she would look at him. "That is not true."

"Oh?" she scoffed. "Apparently I must be issued an invitation to come to you."

"Michaela."

She snapped a venomous look over her shoulder. "You embarrassed me, Rein. Treated me like a half-witted child who did not know her place." Her voice cracked. "Like my uncle did."

He groaned miserably. "I did not think . . . I was concerned that . . . that every man on this ship was ogling you, when you are mine!"

She faced him. "Then you should have told me what is expected of me, and not in front of your crew!" Rahjin slithered from beneath the bench, sinking down under the desk. "I will not be addressed in such a manner." She poked at his chest, forcing him to backstep. " 'Twas rude and disrespectful and do not think to *handle* me! Do we have an understanding on this?"

Rein only nodded, the blaze in her eyes, the flush to her skin, so intense and primitive it ignited a heat in his belly that spread rapidly. His groin thickened. God of fire, she was magnificent in her anger!

"I will not be remanded below decks because you are feeling a bit possessive. And if you do not like what I am wearing, then I suggest you either stay here with me or find me some proper clothes! I am tired of being on the outside." His gaze swept her breasts, her tight nipples thrusting against her shirt, her breathing rapid. "I have been ignored for three years, and now that I do not have to hide, I will not tolerate being sequestered like a mistress."

She inhaled hard. "And if I must, I will come above your bloody decks *naked!*"

He leaned down in her face. "You want to make love with me." His gaze slicked over her. "Now. Right now. You are so aroused you cannot stand it."

She blinked, taken aback for only a moment. "Do not think to ply me with passion, Rein Montegomery." She shoved at his chest with both hands. "I am in no mood for it."

He grabbed her to him, his mouth crashing down on hers. He kissed her and kissed her, his strong hands grinding her to his body, letting her feel every tight, aching inch.

Her legs buckled and he drew back, nose to nose, gazing into her eyes. His lungs labored as he breathed, "Tell me now you are in no mood."

She gasped for air, her gaze searching his, then a wicked smile curved her lips and she grabbed handfuls of his hair, dragging him to her mouth, savagely taking his with a force that rendered him helpless. She surged against him, groping at his chest, his hips, cupping his buttocks and squeezing. Aye, she wanted him, a fierce clamoring inside her ready to explode, and she yanked at the buttons of his breeches, shoving her hand inside, and he groaned, rocking against her fist.

"Make love to me, now."

"I would have you at my leisure."

She stroked him mercilessly. "I would have you now."

He covered her mouth with his, flipping shirt buttons, shoving it and her chemise to her waist, then bent her over his arm, his lips closing hotly over her nipple.

She clutched his shoulders.

He drew the tender tip deeply into his mouth.

"Oh, Rein, aye."

He jerked on the fastening of her breeches, driving his hand inside. He found her, slick and tight, and he played and probed, whispering how much he ached to be inside her, that he'd waited a lifetime for this moment and just thinking of her made him hard and ready to pleasure her, and Michaela's insides shifted and burned.

"Oh, Rein, aye, pleasure me," she rasped.

He bathed her breasts with his tongue, suckled and scraped his teeth over the soft cushiony underside, and she squirmed against him. Panting. Impatient. He straightened, toeing off his boots, backing her toward the bed as she laved at his lips, his throat, and plucked the buttons of his shirt, then shoved it off his shoulders.

"You are mine," she breathed, tugging on the garment, her kiss hot and firm and never-ending, and Rein did not know if his legs would hold him. "Let me show you how much."

She took control, demanded it, needed it, and God above, he let her have it, couldn't wait to feel it, and he yanked off his shirt, yet when she lowered his breeches, bending, Rein wondered at his wisdom when her lips grazed his erection.

He grabbed her up against him, pushing his knee between her legs.

"But I want to taste you."

Just hearing her say the words made him shiver with heat.

He shook his head and murmured against her lips, "I will come apart and I want to do it inside you."

Her eyes swept closed, a heavy shudder ripping through her.

"I want to feel you wrap me with your softness . . ."

She moaned, undulating against him.

". . . so wet."

He pushed her garments down over her hips.

"Grabbing me . . ." he said, smoothing his hands over her bare buttocks.

He ducked and suckled each nipple, stripping her bare to his gaze as he fell back onto the bed, taking her with him, rolling over the wrinkled sheets. She squirmed out of his embrace taking his breeches with her as she slipped off the bed. Her gaze slid over him, her smile wicked and bright as she kicked off her clothes, her eyes never leaving his, her seductive smile so hungry he could taste it.

"You are a witch," he growled, scooting back on the pillows.

"I thought that's what you were." She caught his ankles, pushing them apart, kneeling between them, and Rein did not think he'd seen anything so magnificent as Michaela reveling in her womanhood. She was exquisite, a water spirit, untouchable, her hair a wild mass of curls, shadowing her lush body to her hips, her pale skin flushed with excitement. Her eyes glittered, moss green and velvet heat. The place between her thighs glistened with moisture.

His manhood flexed at the sight, his gaze raking her as she bent and kissed his scarred calf, dragging her tongue mercilessly over his skin. He reached for her, yet she brushed his hands aside.

Rein arched a brow. She smiled that powerful smile and snaked her tongue across his flesh, her hand molding him to the memory of her palm. Rein groaned and briefly closed his eyes, flashing them open when he felt her breast against his thighs.

"You are mine," she murmured as her fingers wrapped his arousal, and she adored the way he flinched, adored the smoldering look in his eyes and that she put it there.

"Michaela? You are not thinking to—"

She ducked and took him into her mouth, deeply, using her tongue as he'd used his on her.

"Ahh, sweet thunder," he growled, twisting restlessly, his moans low and thick in his throat. Michaela discovered a desire she never knew existed. Pleasuring him enflamed her, watching him accept it aroused her to maddening heights. This, she thought, was the power.

"Michaela, oh sweet goddess, woman, come here, come to me, love."

She refused, torturing him, staying out of his reach, and he twisted and thrust, and her gaze flew to his, to watch it, to see the tension spiraling through him.

He clenched fistfuls of bed clothes, groaning, sweat beading on his chest. And when he cursed and called her name, he grabbed her under the arms, dragging her up his length.

"You, madame," he said in seductive threat, "are utter madness," then drove his tongue into her mouth, his hands wild and strong over her body as he rolled her to her back, then taking her nipple into his mouth, licking her belly, dipping his tongue between her thighs. She spread wider for him, holding him there, but he turned her onto her stomach, licking a path down her spine, nipping her soft buttocks. He ravished her, grasped her hips and brought her upward, teasing her with his mouth, his fingers.

She squirmed on the bed, biting the pillow.

"Nay, scream out, let me hear you."

She did, telling him how good his touch felt, that, aye, that spot drove her insane. He probed and stroked, and she shrieked, cursing him and begging him, and when he pushed her to her back, his mouth found hers again, found her nipples, the ticklish spot at the side of her breast.

She clawed at him, touched him everywhere, discovered how sensitive he was behind the ear, and suddenly he rolled to his back, shifting her to straddle him. She rose up and smiled, flinging her hair back.

She looked like a pagan goddess demanding succor from her consort.

And Rein reveled in her expression, empty of demons and brimming with sensuality. Then she enfolded him and his eyes flared. Yet he didn't move, taking in every detail, his look telling her he would bend to her will.

"God, you are beautiful."

She felt it, felt wild and free, empowered and adored.

Her gaze slid over him, his dark beauty, his pale-blue eyes shimmering with a fire so deep she felt it grip the core of her. She taunted it, sliding back and forth against his arousal, slickening him, adoring that his fingers dug into her hips, that he chanted her name and begged for more. And she gave it, rising, guiding him into her silken depths.

With a shuddering breath, she sank fully onto his thickness.

He sat up, loving the hot flare of her eyes, the rock of her hips, the delicate little pants brushing his lips. Her fingers dug into his shoulders and he filled his palms with her breasts, unable to tear his gaze from her face as she left him and returned with an ever increasing vengeance.

"Rein, oh, Rein." She ravaged his mouth, whimpering with each frantic push. She gripped handfuls of his hair and stared deep into his eyes, absorbing the energy he gave her, let her take. Michaela never knew loving a man could be so pleasurable, never that this hunger existed. His features tightened and she smoothed them. His skin grew hotter, his masculine strength throbbing with every damp stroke, and she whispered that she wanted all he had, that she wanted to see him ignite and burn and come apart and know she brought him there.

"God woman, you undo me," he growled, strong hands and arms holding her tight to him as he laid her to her back. Braced above, he withdrew and sank deeply. Over and over. And she watched him fill her, bowing beautifully to greet his thrusts.

Bewitching.

Raw.

Exotic copper skin gliding against refined porcelain.

Primal hunger and heat.

She quickened, reaching for the treasure, her hands and legs driving him harder into her, her blood singing with his energy. Seeking, seeking.

Then she found it.

Feminine muscles clenched, her body stretching in a long smooth arch beneath him. Womanly ripe and abandoned. She threw her head back, exposed her throat and Rein felt her rapture unfold like a hot summer storm and take him with her. Liquid pleasure drenched him, squeezing and squeezing, and she cried out his name, the savage burn of her climax snapping his will.

With a dark growl, he drew back and plunged, driving deep and touching her womb. For a breath he held her, suspended on the edge of pure, untamed desire, bodies fused, straining, gazing into her eyes as it wracked him with long, bone-quaking tremors, swelling through his groin, his blood. She held him, the tiniest smile of completion curving her beautiful mouth, her ragged breathy shudder spilling against his lips.

He absorbed it, drinking in the fresh taste of her freedom, the sweet sound touching his heart and branding his immortal soul.

Twenty-nine

Rein sank onto his side with her, raining kisses over her face, her throat. She laughed deep in her throat, arching, flinging her leg over his thigh and holding him close. She caught the silver loop piercing his ear with her teeth, tugging gently, and he moaned, dark and satisfied. It made her smile widen.

"You are incredible . . . sweet thunder," he said, still catching his breath, still buried inside her. Her passion was unequaled, leaving him drained of energy and indecently replete.

"Aye," she said, her throat tight. "Sweet thunder."

He heard the catch in her voice and met her gaze. "Did I hurt you?" He searched her face.

Michaela shook her head, her lips curving tenderly. He looked as if she'd suddenly break, and after the spectacle she made of herself all over him, she wondered how he could ever believe such a thing. But it was endearing just the same. It was wild this love she had for him, and she prayed deep in her soul that someday he'd love her back, that he truly wished a future, and mayhap children, with her. He'd wed her for her protection, and though their passion was a sweet reckoning, Michaela had had so many precious things stolen from her when she was least aware, she could not dwell hard on the distant future. She refused to consider anything that could destroy this incredible contentment.

I love you, Rein Montegomery, she thought, staring into his eyes. *I love you as I have never loved.* Not in her wildest dreams did she think a man possessed enough patience and understanding whilst she rediscovered the woman her uncle and Winters had tried hard to destroy. It was sheer joy to touch him without ghosts lingering in her heart.

She mapped his features with her fingertips, her eyes intense, and Rein felt a sliver of uncertainty slide through him.

A single tear brimmed her eyes and rolled down her cheek.

"Talk with me."

"I . . . I didn't know . . . I could . . . that . . . there was so much to feel, so much in me." She blushed, and when she was wont to look away, he caught her chin and held her gaze.

"Do not be embarrassed, my *rasha.* Never with me. 'Twas a beautiful thing to see and feel your freedom." His smile was slow and roguish. "You are a most passionate creature."

"Apparently," she said, pressing closer to him, wrapping her arms around his neck as the sound of footsteps penetrated the walls. "They will miss you above decks?"

"Ahh, so that is it." He tsked softly. "Take your pleasure and cast me off."

Her eyes flared, and she jerked on his neck.

He smiled. "Ready to be rid of me?"

"Not since I have found this use for you." She choked at her own impertinence, yet Rein merely grinned. "Mayhap you should go above." At his curious frown, she shrugged. "If you remain, they will know what we've been doing."

"After all your wild screaming, I believe there is little doubt." Michaela buried her face in the crook of his neck as Rein's chest rumbled with quiet laughter. It would take some time for her to grow accustomed to her own passion, he thought, but her lusty outbursts and candid blushes held a pleasure he was quick to enjoy. He adored her, craved her, felt marked with her loving, and Rein didn't think he had any desire remaining until her hand slithered under the bed sheets.

"I love touching you," she whispered. "The color of your skin invites it." Her hand meandered down his chest, fingers teasing his nipple. She felt him flex inside her and her eyes flashed up. "Oh, my."

His lips quirked. "You are an addiction, I fear."

She thrust her hips softly against him. "Show me more."

"With pleasure." He rolled her beneath him.

"Oh, I hope so."

He retreated and thrust into her, and she moaned, throwing her legs around him, and Rein sensed her sudden urgency and pushed her legs higher, giving her long, torturous strokes, watching her desire tear at her composure. He was near bursting after the first moments, yet hungered to hear her little whimpers, her feathery gasps, and he touched the bead of her sex, circling it delicately. She tensed, her body clenching him, her hips slamming frantically against his.

He rubbed.

She cupped his buttocks and drove him harder into her.

"Give to me, Rein," she panted, twisting, and he plunged deeply, his own release stunning him, and she laughed and shrieked and kissed him as they rode the waves of heat together.

"My God, woman, you are insatiable."

"Nay, right now I am quite sated, thank you, sir," she said primly.

"Your humble servant," he groaned, leaving her and falling onto his back.

Outside the door, someone cleared his throat loudly, then rapped. Rein scowled at the closed hatch. "Aye?"

"The brig is approaching, sir."

"Her gun ports?"

"Closed, sir, but she is heavily armed."

"Load and stand ready, Mr. Basilia."

"Aye aye, Capt'n" came before footsteps retreated and Rein's expression did not clear as he rolled from the bed, moving to the commode. He washed, then walked about the room, gathering his clothing, his boots, donning what he found.

Michaela curled against the pillows, shrugging without a trace of remorse when he held up the shirt sans its buttons. He sat at the foot of the bed, pulling on his second boot.

"I suppose you want me to remain here."

He looked back over his shoulder. "I do not know if this brig is friend or foe. She's sat in the water for hours and now comes to us." He shrugged, yet deep concern marked his features. "We are not gunned for a battle."

"Battle? Surely not?"

"One must expect the unexpected." He gave her a long velvety look that spoke volumes. "My plan was to get you to Sanctuary as quickly as possible."

She frowned at that.

"My fath—Ransom's island."

"He possesses an entire island?"

"Aye."

"Alone?"

He laughed. "Nay, my sweet, 'tis heavily populated. He even paved a few roads this last year, I heard."

"When last you saw your family?"

He looked thoughtful as he stood to button a fresh shirt. "Four years mayhap." He jammed the shirttail into his breeches, then took a step and stilled. "Nay, once atween there somewhere." He circled the bed and unlocked a cabinet, removing pistols and a beautiful sword, the hilt studded with gems.

"That is magnificent," she said, leaving the bed and dragging the sheet with her. She ran her fingers over rubies, sapphires, and golden topaz, and he turned the thick hilt into her dainty palm. "Good balance," she said, hefting it like an expert.

He watched, captivated by the way she stood there with a sheet clutched to her bosom, testing the sword.

"You have a strange fascination with weapons. Should I be worried?"

Her gaze flew to his and she smiled, letting the blade tip sweep under his chin. "My father insisted I learn to shoot, but he would only allow me to raise a foil. Naught like this." She handed it back, and Rein sheathed it in the scabbard, then buckled it on.

" 'Twas Ransom's. And his grandfather's afore him." He sighed heavily, the weight of his misdeeds to the man who'd given him a home, a future, hitting him with a clarity that stung. "And who knows how many Montegomerys afore that." He went silent, fisting the jeweled hilt, and Michaela experienced a tugging in her chest at his somber expression.

"Talk with me," she said, sending his own words back at him.

"Aurora and Ran do not know I have been searching for my real father."

She inhaled.

"And when last I saw them, we . . . had unkind words."

She could only imagine what that meant, and since he did not offer more, she let it rest. "You must tell him. You owe him that."

"I know," he said a touch sadly. "But do you think . . . I mean, will . . ." He rubbed the back of his neck. "Will you stand with me when I do?"

She never suspected him to have a fear in the world, and Michaela suddenly ached for him, the shared vulnerability offering a crack in his indestructible veneer. "Aye," she said, stepping close and laying her hand to his chest. "Of course I will." His shoulders drooped with relief. "From what you tell me of Aurora, she will understand."

He covered her hand with his, looking skeptical. " 'Tis not her I worry about."

"Think you that Ransom will be angry?"

"Ran has his opinion about those who sire bastards, for he is one himself."

She frowned. Though the exploits of Granville Montegomery and his offspring were whispered about enough for her to know the details, she said, "A child cannot be accountable for the actions of a parent. Surely he has realized that."

He adored her just for saying it. " 'Tis a stone in his boot, but I will tell you of it later." He pressed his lips to her forehead, then suddenly gathered her close and smothered her mouth with his, kissing her until his knees buckled, until he felt anything but his guilt over deceiving Ransom. He drew back, gazing down at her and loving that it took a moment for her eyes to open.

A flicker of worry darkened his eyes. "If the worst happen—" Her eyes widened. "Submit."

"Nay! Oh, God, do not ask that of me!" She tried pushing out of his arms.

"Aye!" He shook her, his eyes wild with fear for her. "Submit and live. You have no chance against men like this and you know it. If I am alive, I will find you.

"Swear to me, Michaela. I will kill you myself before I let them have you. Swear!"

"Aye!"

He kissed her hard, stealing what he could of the moment, then released her quickly and then moved to the door. "Lock this behind me, Michaela." His gaze roamed from her tousled hair to the tiny toes peeking out beneath the sheet before he inclined his head to the cabinet he'd left opened. "Your pistols are in there."

'Twill never happen, she thought. None would dare touch him or his ship.

"Rein?" He paused, his hand on the latch as he looked at her. "You have a right to know your real father. Ransom will understand."

Would *she,* he wondered, if she knew he sought his blood sire only to kill him?

Nickolas flattened his shoulders against the wall, under the easement, his body shadowed with heavy rain and darkness. Water dripped from a crack in the porch roof, missing the protective oil cloth and spilling down the back of his coat. *I've grown too old for this,* he griped, shivering, watching the sparse traffic move along the East End. Ragged children scampered from doorway to doorway, seeking shelter and stealing what food they could from the vendors closing up their carts for the night.

Please let this be the night. He was bloody well tried of hiding in the stink of London to apprehend this traitor, and he prayed the information, the false tales he'd allowed to leak, would bring this mess to an end. There were already several of the network held in secret until this matter was solved, and Michaela was fortunate that Rein cared for her so deeply and interrupted the Sons' pursuit or she would be in the cellar of a decaying house right now. Convincing his superiors that she was not the source of it had taken hours of endless pleading, and even her stellar acts over the past three years had not weighed too heavily in their minds. They'd given him one week to uncover the traitor. Nickolas had allowed the speculation that a cache of weapons, muskets the Americans could use yet were hard pressed to fashion in the Colonies, would be loaded at the dock tonight. To add to the convincing tale, Nickolas had a ship to load the empty crates on, its captain hiding opposite the street from him. 'Twas damned charitable of Rein to lend him the vessel, though Montegomery had ulterior motives behind the act, Nick thought, his gaze following the tall figure moving suspiciously within the shadows. Nickolas straightened away from the wall, looking across the street to Rein's man, Temple Matthews, hidden against the tool shack of a cabinetmaker's shop. Captain Matthews nodded that he'd seen, stepping out to follow. Rein had assured him he could be trusted, yet his lack of sympathy for the cause made Nick wary. Rein was a decently good judge of character, and he owed Michaela this, nor could he fault her husband in his arguments. Keeping his wife out of this dangerous game was the only way to keep her alive. For now. Her identity as the Guardian had been compromised with only a handful of people, and all but one were stout Sons of Liberty. The other, he hoped, took the bait and walked the streets this night, ready to betray the English and the Americans with only a few choice words.

The clop of hooves came to him above the roll of carts, the muffled voices of citizens heading for safety and warmth, and he swung his gaze to the rider astride an unforgettable piece of horseflesh and moving farther toward the wharf, disguising his intent. Common clothes or nay, Nick recognized gentry when he saw it. He motioned to two other men hiding in doorways and alcoves, then stepped out into the rain, walking briskly, his folded arms tucked under the oilcloth protecting his weapons. Tonight, he would compromise himself and gain a traitor.

And a murderer.

The *White Empress* skipped along the water, a sleek, delicate lady dancing ahead of the brig. Rein would take no risks, not with his wife aboard, and through the spyglass watched the approaching vessel. Few of its crew scrambled on her decks, yet her sails unfurled to give chase. And her waterline was dangerously low. Rein lowered the glass, tapping it against his lips.

"Orders, sir?"

"Open ports. If she pursues for a half league, then send a volley across her prow." That should hold her back, he thought, not wanting to engage the brig without sufficient ballast for maneuvering.

Basilia's thin black mustache outlined his pleased smile, and the Grecian spun about to do as bade, calling orders as he went. The *Empress*'s speed was her advantage.

The brig continued, her gun ports lifting like lids to a cauldron. And Rein spied, trying to make out her figurehead. Immediately, he snapped the glass closed and strode to the rail.

"Fire when ready. She's the *Galley Raider!*" Rein shouted, then ordered a warning shot fired. Excitement teamed the air, and beneath his feet the cannon rolled into position, yet before the ball expelled, the *Raider* opened fire, slamming grapeshot and langrage into the *Empress,* yet out of range to do sizable damage. "Starboard fire!" The *Empress* repaid, spitting fiery smoke and metal from her sleek hull. Water fountained, awash over the foredeck of the brig.

Rein stood on the quarterdeck rail in plain sight and an easy target. He'd no time to deal with the pirates who obviously had a hull full of booty to protect and sought the swiftest end.

"Come about Mr. Baynes. We take this head on."

Leelan grinned, watching the water as he spun the wheel. The *Empress* listed dangerously, and briefly Rein thought of his wife, who was likely tumbling across the cabin, and prayed a few bruises were her only injuries.

Still the *Raider* did not return fire, and Rein decided they were either low on ammunition and were waiting for an unquestionable range or they wanted little destruction and sought to board and take the ship.

Leelan glanced at Rein, then the brig. "We ram her?"

"Nay. Keep going."

"Captain."

"Keep going."

"We'll hit."

"Keep going, Leelan."

Baynes pressed his lips tight and did as ordered. "Full sail, halyard out."

Men scrambled up rigging like monkeys to a nut tree. Ropes uncoiled, track and pulley ground and spun as pristine white sails snapped, curling the wind in her palm. The *Empress* lurched on the cup of breeze as Leelan steadied her approach.

"Just to port, Leelan," Rein said. "A knot before you—"

"Before we crash into her?"

Rein's lips quirked, and briefly he slid his gaze to the helmsman. "Aye."

Leelan grinned and the *Empress* sailed effortlessly alongside the brig, armed men lining the rail, cannon ports open.

"Fire, gentlemen," Rein called softly into the breathless silence, and guns roared, spitting sixteen pounders into the center of the brig. The mainmast cracked and topped like a felled tree, crushing men on her deck as the *Empress*'s cannons rolled back to reload. Rein's features tightened at the screams and blood spilling over the decks of the brig.

He did not take killing lightly, and as the *Empress* swept past and shifted windward, Rein knew it would take a moment to come about.

"Cannons a'ready!" the boson shouted.

Rein only nodded, his stomach clenching.

Below decks Michaela watched out the window, the room behind her already in shambles. She gripped the wall hooks as they swept past the brig, and she wondered what Rein was doing. Grapeshot hit the hull, the metal spires piercing the wood before her face, and she jerked back on a gasp. Gripping the table ledge, she prayed for their survival. The *Empress* shook with the force of cannon fire, and when Rein said he wasn't equipped for battle, Michaela wondered who he'd expected, for his vessel was surely getting off a few good launches.

Suddenly, there was silence. Frowning, Michaela plucked the fallen books from the floor, replacing the items lost in the maneuvers. She heard shouting. Rein's voice, thick with fury and outrage. The *Empress* shot across the water so hard, Michaela lost her balance and fell to her rump. Struggling to her feet, she moved to the aft windows. The brig was afire, her mainmast bent like a splintered bone, a gaping hole in her side above the water line. Whilst crewmen scrambled to douse the blaze she saw a man climb the capstan amidst a curl of smoke. He was tall, thick sun-bronzed arms folded across his black-shirted chest. His hair was exceptionally long, catching on the wind, and about his waist was a wide belt, a dozen weapons tucked into the leather. Like Rein.

The door burst open, and Rein stormed inside, tearing off his scabbard and flinging the priceless sword aside. It hit the desk and fell to the floor as he removed his pistols, tossing them on the table and cursing foully.

His gaze on the floor, his arms at his side, he clenched and unclenched his fists, over and over. The water in the basin steamed. Michaela's gaze shot around the room, the air growing stifling hot, the sheets on the bed limp with the heat. A bottle exploded, brandy spilling to the carpet. Rahjin shifted out from under the desk and Michaela waved her back. The panther retreated, her gold-green eyes wary.

"Rein?"

His head jerked up, and her breath caught at the fury in his pale gaze. It snapped and sparked, pinning her, scraping her like a dull blade. She backstepped, bumping into the bench and reaching for the brace of the windows.

"My God, Rein?" He looked ready to eat her alive.

Rein blinked, his tight shoulders loosening, then he dropped his hands to his hips, tipping his head back. He breathed deeply, then raked both hands through his hair.

"What happened?" She took a step.

"Stay there!"

She froze, blinking, looking at the brig, then to him.

God, Rein thought, he would kill her with this energy if he did not stop right now. "Damn and blast, why did he not show his colors!" he muttered more to himself.

"Who was that?"

"The *Galley Raider.*"

"Oh, dear." She sank numbly into the seat. Pirates. The *Raider*'s captain still stood on the capstan, still watching. And if she didn't know better, smiling. "I don't understand. I'm not saying you are not a great captain, outmaneuvering him like you did, and I am certainly not looking forward to any more of the like I've just experienced, which was magnificent by the by, but the brig is massive, with more guns. . . . why don't they pursue?"

"Because that marauding fool, unfortunately"—Rein lashed a hand toward the window and the burning ship—"was my little brother!"

Thirty

He was retreating from her, she could feel it. His disappointment in his brother, a fact she found utterly fascinating, had sent him into a pensive silence. After a short rebuke that he was not fit company, she bent to his wishes. Yet hours had passed, the sun crashing into the sea, and still he did no more than order a meal and bath. Huddled in the corner of the settee, a blanket about her shoulders, she studied him as he stripped out of his smoke-soiled clothes and into a bath.

She supposed this wasn't the best time to tell him about the gold shipment, and tried pushing the deception to the back of her mind. She'd decided midway during the battle that she'd tell him as soon as he returned. But now, she wished he would talk to her, yet the energy of rage was slipping from his control. He loathed the lack, she knew, and now understood why he'd learned to command his anger. The shock of seeing it was enough to scare her. He'd almost killed his own brother this day, and although she wanted to know why Colin had chosen to become an outlaw, when it was plain that he did not have to turn to crime, she kept comments to herself. Yet when he sank into the bath and draped his arms over the edge, Michaela considered he'd found some of that exhausting domination.

Leaving the settee, she moved to him. He didn't look up, his features still tight with anger, yet his arms hung loosely over the copper lip.

"Do not come near me, woman. I warned you."

Uncontrollable tears filled her eyes. Despite his anger, she could see how much Colin's act wounded him. His brother had to have known it was the *Empress* he'd attacked. There was no excuse for the despicable act. And at this moment, Michaela wasn't above bashing Colin a good one for hurting Rein like this. Pirating, Leelan was kind enough to enlighten her, apparently ran in the family.

"Rein, please, at least look at me."

His lashes swept up, and she stepped back as his frighteningly pale eyes scored her with unmistakable lust. Carnal, primitive. His eyes fastened on her breasts, the thin shirt hiding nothing from him. Her breasts tightened, and she folded her arms over her middle, shielding herself. His gaze snapped to hers.

And in his eyes she saw nothing, no emotion, almost lacking in recognition, his smirk repugnant to her—turbulent with a vile twist.

Michaela backed away, and Rein cast her one last look, thin and brittle before he closed his eyes and sank into the water. She hurried to the bed, sliding between the sheets and wondering if she even knew her husband. Hurt swelled in her throat.

At least he had warned her.

Temple Matthews ducked behind the barrels, his stomach churning at the odor of spoiled fish and bile radiating outside the warehouse. He waited impatiently for something to happen and turned sharply when he heard movement behind him.

" 'Tis me. Grandfather."

Temple smirked, finding the codes and clandestine rubbish rather amusing. The shock of discovering Rein's wife was the elusive Guardian had worn off, leaving him a little envious of his employer's luck at finding such an exciting woman. Damned soft on the eyes, too. No wonder Rein kept her to himself.

Grandfather nudged him, and Temple looked.

"Go left," Nick whispered. "There are three men on the right. Ours." He nodded to the figure standing outside the wide warehouse doors, the ships in the distance knocking rhythmically against the pier. "He will meet with our man when the cart arrives."

"And if he does not?"

"Then I've trusted the wrong person, and my man is keeping the rifles for himself."

The information leaked was that the rifles were supposed to be on a ship with fresh troops headed to the Colonies in just over a fortnight and that the rebels sought to take the weapons. Nick smiled to himself. He'd had them in his possession for two days already, and though the theft would delay the English vessel's departure, Nickolas needed the guns as bait. The double agent would attempt to bargain or simply take them back for England, since none knew Nick had lifted them already. And the agent had not been assigned the mission.

Whoever stood out there, prepared to do business with his man, Nick thought, was marking himself. For, save Temple, not even the men with him knew what this was about. The figure moved beneath the lamps glowing blearily through salt-stained panes. Nickolas lifted the spy glass, peering at the man's boots.

"Are they there?"

"Not that I can make out."

"How's your eyesight, old man?"

"As good as my damned fists, you impudent whelp."

Temple tapped the spectacles poking out of Nick's coat pockets. "Want to risk it?"

Nickolas glanced at him, then handed over the glass.

"Not there."

Nick grunted.

"But that means little."

"It would be good evidence," Nick said.

"And who would testify, and to whom? Rein won't allow her to get back into this foray, I saw it in his eyes. And you know how unbendable he can be."

Nick agreed. "Which means we must catch the bastard with his hands in our coffers."

The traitor withdrew a cheroot, discreetly lighting the tip, and Nickolas thought it damned arrogant of him to do such a thing when he ought to be hiding. It told him he did not consider he was under suspicion. And as Nick consulted his watch, the cart rolled into sight.

The traitor pushed away from the wall and moved into the darkened edge of the street, his face still covered against the heavy breeze spearing off the water. He flipped back the tarp as the driver jumped from the cart, putting a bar to the crate. The crack of wood resonated through the hollow street, muffled conversation floating on the air. Nick nudged Temple and they moved, crouching low as Nick's men rose, bent, darting between rubbish piles and barrels, and he prayed the Bow Street Runners didn't spot them. They could offer no explanation and would share a cell in Newgate. Behind him, Temple moved, the South African as silent on his feet as Rein. They slipped to the entrance, and when the shrouded man hefted the rifle, Nick made to step forward. Temple stopped him.

Nick scowled.

"He'll recognize you." Temple pulled his tricorn low, then, like their traitor, gathered a strip of wool about his face. He stepped forward.

Their suspect turned sharply, a pistol sliding out.

"Nervous?" Temple said, feeling Nick's eyes boring into his back.

The man didn't speak.

"I am the captain." He nodded to the ship and hoped none recognized the *Sentinel* in the dark.

The man nodded, then spoke softly. "Forty pounds each box."

"Done." Temple took the rifle from him, slid it carefully into the box and adjusted the lid into place.

"You do not quibble?"

"We don't have the time." Temple threw the tarp over the crates, casting a tight glance at the weapon trained at his stomach. "The ship sails tonight."

"Nay." The man frowned at the vessel, then the captain. " 'Tis to sail in seven days' time."

At that, Nickolas stepped forward. "Only one person knew that."

The figure stilled, his cold gaze lowering to the pistol, then to Nick's face. "Grandfather."

Nick's features tightened with shock and disappointment. *"God damn you."*

"I think he will."

Nick took a step forward to unveil him, but the cloaked man swung the pistol around. Temple shoved Nick as the weapon discharged in a spike of fire and smoke, clipping him in the side. An instant later, the cart driver brought the bar down on the man's head and he crumbled to the ground.

People came from taverns and homes, a few sailors running toward the noise. Nickolas climbed to his feet, his gaze on the man lying on the ground. Temple, clutching his side, bent and twisted the man's boot around. "God, he has nerve!" He looked up at Nick. "They are the same ones."

Nick squatted and knocked off the tricorn, then yanked the scarf from his face.

Temple's features tightened. "This is the man who's been trying to kill her?"

"Aye," Nick said sadly, mashing his hand over his face.

"He's not going to like this." Temple stared down at the face of a murderer.

The face of the Earl of Stanhope, Christian Chandler.

For three days he didn't speak, remaining above decks and seeing to repairs. From Cabai she'd gained what little information she could about the battle, but other than that, Michaela had even less clue as to what was going on inside his head. Meals were silent, her bed was empty, Rein sleeping above deck. He might as well not join her at all, she thought, for his company was that of a ghost. She tried to console herself that he was doing this for her, but she was getting damned tired of his cutting looks every time she spoke, the way he snapped at everyone.

She plucked at the folds of her velvet gown, Cabai's repairs incredible. The burned funnel sleeves were cut away to her elbows, and without the pannier caging, the extra length was sheared away to a fresh hem trimmed in a gold cord. *At least I am presentable,* she thought. Restless, she rose from the bench and moved to the shelves, looking for an edition she'd not read already in the past days. Her hand rose to take another volume, then fell to her side. She looked at Rahjin, then motioned. The great cat sauntered over to her, her spine slung low as if she feared a scolding.

"Oh, lovey," she soothed in a whisper, sinking to her knees to scratch and pet her friend. "It has been a bit of a trial, eh?" The cat flopped at her feet, and Michaela nuzzled the silken fur with her cheek. Together, Rahjin and she sighed.

The door opened, and Michaela glanced at Cabai.

The tall Arab smiled tenderly, and with one hand shut the door, the other holding a tray for her.

"I am not hungry."

"My mistress needs to eat."

"Your mistress doesn't feel like it." The thought of food was as unappealing as eating it alone.

"Mistress," he warned softly.

"Is Rein joining me?"

He shook his head.

Michaela looked down at Rahjin, nose to nose. "This ends now," she whispered. "You'd best run for cover."

Michaela rose and walked to the door, ignoring Cabai's insistent pleas that whatever she planned was unwise. She stepped over the raised threshold, catching the fresh scent of sea air and the warmth of the tropical breezes and realized Rein had not even bothered to tell her whether they were near the island or nay.

For the love of Mary, he'd not even said good morn.

She walked out into the sun, tipping her face to the sky and breathing deeply.

Warm air whipped at the sails. The activity aboard was quick and precise, the chatter subdued, and as she looked to the quarterdeck, she saw her husband, his booted foot braced on the rail, his gaze on the horizon. He waits for Colin, she thought. Smiling at the crewmen who stepped out of her way or helped her over coils of rope, she moved to the ladder, thinking that if she suffered Rein's silence, they'd suffered the brunt of his temper. She gathered her skirts and climbed.

One would think stairs would better suit, she thought, hoisting herself up the rungs. She peered over the edge, her gaze swinging to Rein's back, then to Leelan. The helmsman sent her a warning look, glancing at the captain. Michaela tipped her chin and continued. Immediately two mates came to her, helping her negotiate the edge.

"Good morn, Mr. Basilia, Mr. Quimby."

Whilst the Englishman blushed, the Grecian smiled, his mustache bowing. "Good morn, my lady."

"How far are we from the island?" Basilia and Quimby looked at Rein's rigid spine, then back at the helmsman.

Leelan simply nodded ahead. She turned, her eyes flaring with wonder, then narrowing with sudden anger. Less than a hour's sail away lay Sanctuary. She clenched her fists, hurt and anger swimming through her. She was about to meet his family, his mother and father, his childhood friends, and he'd done naught to prepare her, to warn er. Michaela stomach tightened and she felt like an outsider again. he next few days would be spent under the study of his family and he would not shame him by giving them a less than perfect picture f bliss. But he apparently was ready to disregard her.

She spun about and strode to his side. "I want to speak with ou."

"Not now." He did not bother to look at her, his forearm braced n his knee, his boot on the rail.

"Aye, now."

"Michaela."

She leaned close, staring at his profile. "He is gone. He is not coming back. He had his reasons for attack and you can do naught about it till you meet again."

"This does not concern you."

His dismissing tone slapped, and her spine stiffened. "If you warn me off again, so help me, Rein Montegomery," she hissed, "I will run you through with your grandfather's sword!"

He stiffened measurably. "He is not my grandfather."

"He is. And Ransom is your father. Aurora is your mother. And this brooding . . . your family will surely hear about it as soon as we embark. And what will you say when you must tell them Colin is marauding the seas?"

"I won't."

"Then you and I will continue with the uncomfortable silence?" He didn't respond, and Michaela felt her sympathy for him wane to absolute outrage. "I want to speak with my husband, not this damned wall. I want to hold him in my arms at night and soothe him, even if he"—her voice broke and she swallowed—"does not want me."

He didn't spare her a glance, his gaze on the water foaming behind the *Empress,* yet his fingers flexed in a fist, and for a moment she thought he would look at her, touch her. But he didn't, and she damned him for being so unfeeling, damned him for making her love another man when this one was locked inside.

"Come to the cabin and talk with me in private."

"We have naught to discuss."

"I see. Apparently our marriage, or anyone else, means little to you when you are in a *mood.*"

He turned on her, his eyes wild, his voice cutting. "I do not want your sympathy nor your incessant prodding, woman. It does not

concern you, nor will it ever. Go back to the cabin and leave me
be!"

Around them, crewmen gaped, yet she stood up to him, her glare
broken with hurt. "I can see why he fired on you," she snapped.
"You have filled the shoes of the bastard you did not want to be!"

Rein's eyes flared and he blinked, watching her move to the
ladder. She did not turn to descend, but jumped. Rein raced to the
side to find her in Cabai's arms. She hugged the giant man about
the neck as he carried her quickly from view. Rein started after
her, then turned and moved back to his spot at the aft deck. He
raked his fingers through his hair and watched the sea, waiting for
Colin to return so he could thrash his insolent hide for taunting
him into battle, for turning his education away and into piracy.

Michaela stood at the prow, composed after a well-deserved bout
of tears. She didn't think she could be this angry at him, this hurt,
but he'd severed her from his heart in one slice. How could he be
so gallant and open, so kind and generous, all these weeks, then turn
her away with such heartlessness? And in the next breath she recognized how he'd gained such a ruthless reputation, yet never imagined he would inflict it on her. She looked down at the sea, the sharp
hull splitting through the water. Her heart throbbed with hurt, and
Michaela tried to see his side, to see why Colin's attack wounded
him into this horrible silence. Mayhap if she left him be, he would
come back to her, she thought, and decided she could give him the
peace he desired when he had given so much to her. She did not
have any choice. He might be a few yards away, yet he was already
gone.

The *Empress* drew closer to land, skirting submerged reef and
passing alongside slate-gray cliffs sparsely dotted with brush and
vines and between a hook-shaped tip of land jutting out to the sea.
The channel was not navigable by a ship larger or with more weight
in her hull than the *Empress,* and because of the high tide, Leelan
had taken the time to explain, it would be like pushing a child's
sail toy into a tub.

She gasped when the *Empress* came about, listing low to port
side and around a break in the reef line. She gazed skeptically at the
jagged reef she could see beneath the dark water, then to the serrated

jetty on her right, then to the cliff so close on the left she could reach out and touch its slick, slate surface. Her heart skipped several beats, and she was certain they'd hit something when the *Empress* slid effortlessly through the narrow channel and into the basin. Sails snapped as crewmen rushed to lash them to the masts and halt the ship as the ship moved deeper into the cove. She looked aft, the entrance invisible by the overlap of the jetty and cliffs, and Michaela realized this was why Rein's father had chosen the island. None would know it was inhabited if they could not negotiate the channel, and should anyone try, they would run aground or crash on the jetty.

Her gaze swept the ship of eager men ready to step onto land, then to her husband. He issued orders with high-volume impatience, and across the distance, met her gaze. He stilled for an instant, a fracture in his steely composure, then moved on with casting lines. Rahjin nudged her palm, and her fingers sang through her luxurious coat.

"You are still my friend?" she asked with a glance down. The beast purred, sagging against her, and she caught herself before the cat knocked her into the rail. She looked at the island.

It was a city. Vibrant green vegetation coated the land, lush cloud capped mountains clashing against the blue sky. Water foamed as it hit the jetty, then rippled into the cove like the wind dancing over silk. Pink sand hemmed the shoreline, rising to a profusion of flowers and plants. Color splashed the land. People moved through streets and the houses—they were everywhere—burned white by the sun and portioned off with wide yards. The avenues forked off in ten directions, the main street turning to wrap farther down the shore and around the island where she could see a lookout post and beneath it, on the sweeping mountainside, coffee groves and sugar fields. From her high position, she viewed shopfronts, children racing about, heard laughter and smelled the mouth-watering scent of roasting pigs and baking bread. Paradise, she thought. Valhalla. Shielding her eyes, she lifted her gaze to the largest house, perched in the center of the mountain above the village, as if the land had grown around it. Two floors, it was wide and bleached white from the sun, fashioned into the mountain with brown wood archways shaping the doors and windows, railed porches and balconies stilted on posts to accommodate the uneven terrain beneath. A stone road led from the village street up toward the house, its path intermittently hidden by a jungle of vines, bushes, and flowery trees. The fragrance of the blooms, exotic and sweet, filled the air, and Michaela inhaled deeply, the scent and sounds soothing her, calming her. Oh, to have grown up here, she thought. How lucky he was.

The sound of footfalls and the clop of hooves drew her attention to the village, and she watched with trepidation as a man rode toward the quay, a woman sidesaddle on his lap. Several people followed, waving excitedly to the men aboard, and she cast a quick look at Rein. He did not watch them and still studied the sea.

Men flung over the side, not waiting for the gangplank to greet friends and family. Michaela's heart clenched at the sight of a squealing child running into his father's arms. She glanced at Leelan waiting on the pier, wondering if he had family, then realized the bulk of the brood running down the quay were headed toward him.

Her gaze returned to the man and woman, and she knew a sense of foreboding when she recognized the resemblance between Colin and this man.

Ransom. *Amar Asad.* The Red Lion.

Oh, she thought, to meet a legend.

Her gaze dropped to the woman, Aurora. A petite thing, her black hair fell over her shoulder to graze below the belly of the horse, streamers of silver sparkling around her face. Her figure was voluptuous, clad in a simple blue dress, without stays or pannier, Michaela thought with brush of relief. Apparently, the heavy accoutrement beneath one's clothing was passed by for comfort in this heat.

She moved from the prow, Rahjin close at her side, and went to the rail. The gangplank was in place, the portion of the rail swung back for descent. She looked at Rein and cleared her throat. He glanced over his shoulder, his features tight.

A shriek came from the crowd, and Michaela looked as Ransom and Aurora dismounted. Ransom led the way, yet stopped at the foot of the plank, his arms folded over his chest. Michaela felt his intimidation across the distance.

Aurora batted him aside with the back of her hand. He blinked down at her, his lips curving and his gaze fastening on her behind as she marched up the gangway. With little effort, she stepped on the deck and faced Michaela.

"You must be Aurora."

"That I am. And who might you be?"

Michaela glanced at Rein's back, then to his mother. "I am Rein's wife, Michaela."

"Och, lady be praised," she said, taking Michaela's hands in her own. She looked at Ransom and called out, "I was right."

Ransom's arms unfolded slowly and he scowled, a fiendish look as his gaze fell on Rein. "You tell that son of yours that he best get his arse off that ship and make a proper greeting."

Aurora laughed, a deep, throaty sound as she looked at Rein, then at Michaela. She tipped her head to the side. "Being a wee bit of beastie, is he now?"

Michaela's throat tightened. She was mortified that this was her first greeting to his family. "A wee bit."

Aurora turned, and in a voice with more volume than she expected, shouted, "Dahrein Vasin Montegomery!"

Rein's shoulders tightened, and he turned, moving to the ladder.

"Dahrein?" Michaela said, looking at her husband as he crossed to them.

Aurora spared her a glance. "Och, so 'tis lying to you he's been doing too, neh?"

Thirty-one

Rein stared down at Aurora, an uncomfortable silence flickering between them. Then she reached, brushing a lock of hair from his forehead as she'd done a thousand times before, and he remembered growing up around her, learning from her, and then he recalled the last words he'd said to her were hard and brutal and meant to wound. And before this visit was done, he would hurt her again.

Rein swallowed, capturing her hand and bringing it to his lips for a kiss. "Forgive me, Mother."

Michaela watched the pair, envying the unmistakable connection between them, that they seemed to speak without words. Then she saw Aurora's eyes tear.

"I forgave you the day you left us, my son," she said, patting his jaw. He smiled tenderly, for the first time in days, then gathered her in a warm embrace, lifting her off the deck. She hugged back, her expression peaceful.

Rein set her down, gazing at her lovely face, and something broke inside him. She laid a hand to his shoulder, to the spot where he'd taken Michaela's bullet.

" 'Tis well healed," she said, and he heard Michaela's indrawn breath.

His lips curved. "You know it is."

"I've met your wife." Her tone rebuked that he'd not introduced them himself, and over her head, he met Michaela's gaze. She stared at him blankly, her lips tight in a benign smile, yet her eyes were unusually bright. She looked so forlorn, standing by the rail, and he felt like a scoundrel of the first order. He'd embarrassed her, yelled at her, and she was alone if not for him. His expression softened a bit, and he came to her, sweeping his arm around her waist. She went stiff against him, and he pressed a kiss to the top of her head. She ducked from his touch, yet he kept his features impassive, recognizing the damage his runaway anger had wrought.

Aurora's gaze shifted between the two, then she eyed Rein, clearly laying any blame at his feet. "Come. Ransom grows impatient."

Rein looked toward the pier, to Ransom's fierce expression, and with his mother and wife, he crossed the gangway. He stopped in front of his father, and they stared, Rein's chest tightening. He was a little grayer, with a little more flesh to his big bones, but the same. Ransom smiled and enveloped him in a slow, warm hug.

"We have missed you." Briefly, his arms squeezed harder. "And if you keep your mother waiting, staring out at the sea like that again," he whispered into his ear, "I will thrash the friggin' hide off your insolent arse."

Rein smiled. "Aye, sir." He stepped back and drew Michaela forward. She stared at Ransom with something akin to awe. "My wife, Michaela Denton."

She offered her hand. "Montegomery," she whispered softly, dipping a quick curtsy. "A tremendous pleasure, milord."

Ransom brought her hand to his lips for a kiss, holding her gaze with his smile. "Do not look at me with such fear, lass. I do not bite."

"Aye, you do, love, oftimes." Ran blinked at his wife's words. "And in all the right places."

"Cheeky wench," he muttered with a grinning glance as he released his son's bride.

"Aye. 'Tis just so," she popped back, then looked at Michaela. "Come, to the house. You must be hungry and tired."

"Hungry, aye, tired, nay. I've done naught, but rest in the cabin since we sailed."

Aurora looked at Rein, her gaze chastising in one long sweep. "Not being the proper husband, either, I see," she said with mild admonishment, then swept her arm around Michaela and parted her from him.

The two women walked side by side, talking softly, Rahjin at Michaela's heels, and Rein and Ransom followed, Ransom pulling the leads of the horse along.

"She is lovely," Ransom said. "Right General Richard Denton's daughter?"

Rein wasn't surprised Ran knew. "Aye."

"What is amiss atween you?"

Rein stared ahead. "Naught."

"Do not lie to me, Dahrein." Ran tipped his head close, his voice for Rein's ears alone. "I can see it as well as any. You fix whatever muck you've made and be about it quickly."

Rein eyed his father. "You blame me?" His tone lacked defense.

"I blame no one, for I do not know what keeps you from being at least civil to your bride, but I know you, my son."

Inwardly, Rein flinched.

"Your damned temper grew as you did, and need I remind, the last time we heard your voice," his voice took on a sharper edge. " 'twas to wound your mother."

Rein stiffened, ashamed of the memory of shouting at Aurora to cease smothering him, that he'd married Shaarai and look what happened, that he was fine alone and chose to remain so, regardless of what her *keek stane* showed her. And then he told her to stay out of his life. Ran had nearly beat the stuffing out of him then.

"I have done as she wished. I have wed."

Ransom looked at him with a jaundiced eye. "She wanted to see you happy 'tis all," he said tiredly, following the crowd. He inclined his head toward his own wife. "Such feelings are rare, and to ignore them is the cost of your soul."

Rein looked at him, skeptical.

"One does not live under the same roof with your mother and not learn a few things," he said with a wry quirk of his lips.

A sudden delighted scream, several of them, rent the air, and Rein looked up as a brood of children raced toward him. Ransom stepped back, smiling, and Michaela watched as the children collided into Rein, smothering him with hugs, hopping up to catch his cheek with a kiss until he bent to accommodate. Grinning, he swept a ten-year-old boy onto his back, hefted a younger girl in his arms whilst another brown-haired boy clung to his leg. He moved stiff-legged, the child attached to his ankle, to Michaela.

"These monkeys are my brothers and sisters," he said, tickling them each as he introduced them, yet before she could comment, his gaze caught on something behind her, and Michaela turned to see a young woman not more than seven and ten walking toward them. She was breathtaking, the image of her mother, bloodred streaks against coal-black hair. It was unadorned, swept to one side and falling to beyond her hips.

Rein winked at her.

Her hands on her trim hips, she stuck her tongue out, and the clinging children dropped like squirrels from a tree before Rein dashed after her. She turned and ran, and in a heartbeat he caught her, tossing her over his shoulder for a pace or two, then swinging her down in his arms.

After a few steps, he set her to her feet. "Michaela, this is my baby sister, Viva."

"And if I'm looking the wee babe, then you are so old you need spectacles," she said with a petulant tip of her head and a cocky glance.

"Mouthy brat."

"Barnacle bum." She brushed a kiss to his cheek and whispered, "Welcome home, brother," then looked at Michaela. "Geneviève," she said with a pointy elbow into his side.

"A pleasure," Michaela replied, her gaze swinging up to Rein's. He was smiling, hugely, and she wished it was bestowed on her.

"Geneviève. How grown up," he mocked, ruffling her hair.

She shrieked and smoothed it back down, her gaze dancing between husband and wife. "Apparently, brother, acting it more than you." With that, she swung the toddler into her arms and herded the children ahead with her parents.

"She's lovely." Michaela's gaze followed the handsome brood up to the house.

"And wild."

She met his gaze, his smile fading at the hurt in her eyes. "A large, loving family, what a surprise," she said acidly, and Rein realized he hadn't prepared her for any of this.

She looked at the ground, then lifted her gaze to his. "What's happening to us, Rein?"

His expression immediately closed, and inside he warred with his bitter disappointment in Colin, his part in pushing the man to piracy and the position he left him in. "Naught. We are the same."

"I am, yet you are showing what a cold-hearted beast you can be—and why only to me?" She turned away and walked woodenly behind the crowd.

Scowling, Rein watched her go, hating the dejected droop of her shoulders and shouldering the blame. Seeing Colin as he was affected him harder than he ever dreamed possible and he needed time to command his anger and, yet, as he followed behind her, watching the enticing sway of her hips, he considered that when he did find the peace he'd lived with for years, she might not deem to speak to him. But he could not touch her. He'd promised her that he never would, not in anger, not with any residue of it. And he prayed she'd understand.

Ahead of him, the children scattered, and Aurora waited at the doorway, then immediately escorted his wife through the house to the second floor and into a room. Rahjin entered behind her, finding a spot and plopping to the floor. Rein stood in the doorway, watching his mother move about his old bedroom, insisting on an herb tea to restore his wife's health, whether it was failing or not, and although Aurora did her best to make her feel at home, Michaela, he thought, was uncomfortable with the attention.

"When your trunks are brought—"

"I have no trunks."

Aurora looked at Rein, a scolding on her lips.

He put up his hand to stop the tirade he was due. "We left London in haste. There was no time."

Aurora inspected Michaela's figure. "I have several garments you can wear. And Viva will, too."

"Viva's a child. Her clothes will be too tight," Rein said, then swept a glance at his wife. "In the bosom."

Michaela blushed, and Aurora's lips quirked. "You are familiar enough with her bosom to know, are you now?"

"Sweet thunder!" he groused.

"Och, dinna be going all starch and puddin' on me now, Son." She moved to throw open the curtains, white light spilling across the deep blue carpet and over the rich wood furnishings.

Cabai entered, bowing deeply before Aurora, salaaming.

She returned it, then looked at Michaela. "Cabai is familiar." She waved to the room. "I will leave you to his care." She paused at the door, looking back. "Take your privacy, as there is little of it," she said on a light laugh, "in this house. I will call you for supper."

"Rein?" Michaela stretched her neck to see him behind Aurora, but she put her arm up, blocking him.

"I will keep him busy."

"Nay, you will not." Rein stepped through the door.

Aurora swung around and slapped both hands to her son's chest, pushing him out. "I've a word for you, Dahrein. Come."

Michaela smiled at his helpless expression as his tiny mother shoved him back, then sealed the door behind her. She heard her voice, soft and brisk and rolling with a Scot's burr, but Michaela doubted her mother-in-law could do much to end Rein's mood.

She plopped on the bed, and when Cabai knelt to remove her shoes and pushed her onto the down, she insisted she was not tired, yet within moments she was asleep.

Aurora marched through the hall and down the curved staircase not bothering to see if Rein was behind her. She knew, just as she knew he was being a complete and utter lout with his wife. She'd seen it in her *keek stane,* the dark red curls, and much more, but since the last time she'd mentioned such to him he'd left for years, she kept the knowledge to herself.

Walking into Ransom's study she let Rein pass, then closed the door after him.

Ransom stood near the window, his hands braced behind his

back. He gave her a side glance, his brow knitting a fraction. "Shall I take the china down?"

She smirked, then looked at Rein. He'd grown into such a fine man, so powerful and handsome, and pride swelled in her. "You've crossed paths with your brother."

Rein's features stretched taut. She should not be so shocked that she was aware of it.

"I dreamt last night, but dinna ken the why of it till just now."

"He has himself a forty-gun brig." Ransom's brows rose sharply, half in surprise, half in admiration. "And he fired on the *Empress.*"

Ransom's curses blued the air, and Aurora pinched him. "You canna help what he does."

"He's pirating!"

Ransom looked ready to explode. "Grievin' mothers!"

"Aye. I damn near sunk his brig, the ruddy little brat. And he laughed. God, 'tis as if he wants to be killed." Rein rubbed the back of his neck. "He resents me." Rein just didn't know how much until now.

"He's been gone a wee bit, and 'tis nay your fault you were in our lives afore him."

"He thinks I've stolen you from him. He's your firstborn."

"You are," she said with absolute certainty, coming to him, gripping his arms, and Rein felt the cut of the deception he led around them. "We gave naught to him that we did not give to you."

All three of them knew Colin had more, for he'd had Ran and Aurora for his lifetime. Damn the man, Rein thought, for not seeing the fortune he had right here. "I would have let the *Empress* go under before hurting him, and he knows it. He's used my loyalty and, damn him, I want to bash the stuffing out of him for his cavalier manner!"

The air in the room simmered with sudden heat, and Aurora stared into his eyes, warning him to dominate his rage, and when he'd managed a wee bit of calm, she squeezed his arms, then stepped back.

" 'Tis nay your doing. And who's to know what's in Colin's heart but Colin. He wants to *be* you. He envies the life you had, sailing with Ransom, to challenge the world as you did. But 'tis his own choice to pirate." She shrugged. "You canna be the wiser older brother to him any longer. He is a mon, full grown and learned."

How like her to put it into perspective, he thought. "Why would he toss his education aside to ride the sea like his father?"

From the corner, Ransom chuckled low in his chest. "If he's thieving his way across the Mahgreb, then he isn't."

Rein rubbed the back of his neck. "He knew 'twas my ship and he knew I would not sink him, just as he was aware that he'd leave the task of telling you to me."

"Colin has some growing to do, Rein," his father said regretfully. "We have to let him be to do it."

"And if he gains a rope around his throat?"

Aurora cringed. "I will watch after him."

"And if you are too far, if we all are too far to help him?"

"Your mother is right."

She eyed her husband. "Don' be plying me with compliments, Ransom Montegomery, they will get you naught."

"They got me over a half-dozen children so far, love," he said, grinning and dropping a kiss to her nose. "And all the practice atween." He looked at Rein, his manner relaxed as he nestled his wife in his arms, her sweet bottom pushing into his groin. "If Colin is man enough to captain a ship, he's man enough to pay the price."

Rein looked doubtfully between the two.

"Trust your mother's ways, Rein."

Rein's lips curled softly. "Oh, I do."

Aurora did not look convinced.

"What have I done now?" Rein looked between his parents.

"Control your anger, Rein, dinna be pointing it at those who aren't deserving of it." His features tightened at the censure. "Or you will lose much more than you realize," she said. "There are more ways to soothe your upset than I've taught you, Rein. Go to her, let her help you."

"I cannot. I'm afraid I will hurt her. I promised not to come to her in anger. I cannot break the vow. Not after . . ." He stopped himself, looking away. "I simply cannot."

She studied him, then nodded approvingly, stepping out of Ransom's arms, catching his hand and pulling him along. "Come, my love. I've a meal to see to, and you've some children to find."

Ransom jerked on her hand, pulling her back, smoothing the wisps of hair from her face. "Nay," he growled. "I've a wife to love. Rein, leave us."

Rein did, quickly, pulling the door closed as Ran kissed Aurora. He looked up the curving staircase, then rubbed his hands over his face. A moment later, he took the stairs two at a time. He found the room empty, the depression in the pillow the only sign she'd been about. Cabai was placing borrowed garments in the drawers and armoire, and when he inquired, the big man shrugged, his irritation felt from across the room.

Rein dismissed it to find his wife, and headed belowstairs, through the kitchen, yet found only servants scurrying about. He greeted them, not recalling a single name, then headed outside. He searched for an hour and grew worried until he heard laughter.

Brushing back a viney branch, Rein peered into the garden near the left of the house. Viva and Michaela sat side by side, their skirts hiked, bare feet swishing in a stone fountain. Rein let the branch fall behind him, then braced against the trunk, watching. The contrast between them was startling. Viva was a beautiful, wild creature, but still a child, her slim body not yet reaching womanhood, whereas Michaela was round and lush and . . . ripe. Like Viva, her hair was unbound, dark-red curls rising in the breeze, spilling down her back. He listened, and though he could not understand the conversation, Viva's tone was high and soft, Michaela's deeper, like rustling satin to his ears. His body tightened, yet he knew she would not speak with him, just as he knew Aurora would watch over Colin in her damned *keek stane*. Fleetingly, Rein wondered if he simply resented that he did not have the power to see into the black seer's glass when she did.

He heard his name, Viva bent close and whispering to his wife. If Michaela's reaction was any indication, it was scandalous. So like Viva. Suddenly, his sister stood, grabbing her sandals and urging Michaela to join her. Michaela bent to scoop up her leather boots, availing him an enticing view of her plush bosom. And he remembered the last time he'd held her against him, her mouth moving beneath his, and tasted the sweetness of her flesh.

Felt her take him inside her.

His body thickening with need of her, he rolled around the tree and started for the mountain.

* * *

"He is there." Viva pointed, and Michaela's gaze followed to the mountain.

"Oh, my," she breathed. Shirtless, bootless, his hair unbound, he overtook the land like a creature born to the jungle, primitive, untamed. Ropey muscles flexed his back and his long arms as he climbed, and she stretched her neck when he disappeared beneath the vegetation, then inhaled when he reappeared near rocky cliff.

" 'Tis too dangerous!" she whispered to herself just as he leapt and caught a ledge of rock. Her heart clamored as he hoisted himself up and continued up the sheer rockface with only the strength of his fingers and bare toes to carry him.

" 'Tis like taking stairs for him," Viva replied matter-of-factly, grabbing her hand and pulling her along. Michaela backstepped, entranced by the sight of his lithe, muscular body scaling the rocks like a cat. It was a side of him so far removed from the gentleman who gamed at White's, who held himself with such stoic dignity. This man was exotic, primal—in his element.

And she wanted to be with him.

But Viva had other ideas, and when she tugged her hand, Michaela stumbled, righted herself, then followed, glancing back to catch a glimpse of him. But he was gone. Following Viva, they headed first to a little house filled with herbs and fermenting tinctures, then onto a shop for spices. Aurora met up with them, toting a dark-haired baby, and by the time they reached the house, all she wanted was to see her husband.

She found him, fresh off the mountain, covered in grime and sweat and looking rather fetching for a terribly dirty man.

His boots in one hand, his shirt caught with two fingers and slung over his right shoulder, Rein paused in the foyer, ignored his mother's and siblings' chatter to stare at his wife.

Eyes locked and held.

He was winded and wild looking.

She was flushed and barefoot.

"Michaela, I—"

He took a step. She retreated, a touch of fear sparking her hazel eyes. It killed him to see it. His father called, then appeared in the foyer, his gaze darting between them, then to his wife across the foyer.

Neither Rein nor Michaela noticed the exchange.

"Wash up and ride the fields with me, Dahrein. Mayhap you should see what you're selling."

"Michaela? Lend me an extra pair of hands with these two," Aurora called anxiously and the toddler plowed into Michaela's legs. She lost her balance. Rein shot across the room and caught her elbow, keeping her upright.

"I need to speak with you."

Her eyes clouded. "I think you have said enough this day."

He groaned softly. "Michaela . . ."

Her chin tipped, rebellion in every cell of her small body as she pulled from his grasp.

Rein didn't know whether to smile or nay. Ransom called again, and the children tugged her toward the kitchen. Sighing, Rein turned away.

"A bit of contrition to suffer still?"

Rein's gaze jerked. "I beg you," he groused, "do not mock my misery." Rein's expression turned imperial. "For I recall when you upset my mother's karma, too."

Ransom's look said he was sadly mistaken, yet as they moved through the house, Rein recounted the facts. And, of course, his father disagreed with all of them.

He'd tried twice more to see her, talk with her, but no one in the damned house would give him the opportunity. If his mother wasn't off showing her how to make tinctures, or Viva was chatting about Leelan Baynes's oldest boy and how handsome he'd grown, then Michaela was avoiding him, one step away from his touch. After the way he'd treated her, he deserved it, but a moment was all he needed. The rift between them was deep and he'd no intention of allowing his asinine behavior to make it wider. When he found her, she was in the smallest room, his youngest brother Max in her arms, asleep. The sight struck him like a blow, and he leaned against the doorframe and watched her stroke the babe's cheek, kiss the top of his downy head. As her lips worked, Rein frowned as she curled tighter into the rocker, snuggling the babe deeply to her breast as if he were the only person she'd left to cling to. Then he heard her sniffle.

Rein stepped away, sagging back against the wall beyond the door, rubbing his knuckles across his forehead. He admitted he was terrified of losing her and wracked his brain for a way to approach her. He lowered his hand, glancing at the open door.

His mother bustled past him, her arms full of freshly laundered sheets and blankets. "You've a look about you, son," she whispered.

Rein grinned, hearing Michaela say the like to him often enough. "I know," he said with a lecherous wiggle of his brows.

She hurrumphed by, her steps brisk, her smile hidden in the folds of sun-dried bedding.

Thirty-two

He came to her like smoke through a keyhole.

Without sound.

Only scent and the heat of his skin.

Hovering over her.

"Forgive me, love," he whispered into the darkness. "Forgive me."

"Where did you go?" Her voice fractured.

"Away, love, away, so I would not hurt you. I promised not to touch you in anger. I promised."

The sheets dragged across her warm body, unveiling the lovely sculpture of womanly softness.

Her lashes lifted and she saw him, a shadow clashing against the silver light spilling into the chamber.

"Forgive me," he whispered in a dusky voice. "I did not mean to be so cruel."

She brushed his hair back, cradling his face. "Colin hurt you, I know. But if you'd only talked to me, Rein. We could have—"

He silenced her with a finger to her lips. "I was afraid if I touched you, I'd want you so deeply, want to bury my pain in you, that I'd wound you with more than my words."

"Oh, Rein!" she cried, her heart breaking for him, and she pulled him down to her mouth, to her body, moaning at the warmth of his nakedness to her own. His long body slid smoothly over hers, essing into the mattress, against his heart, as he kissed her and issed her. She tunneled her fingers into his hair, eliciting a dark rowl, and he rolled to his back, taking her with him.

His hands toured her body in slow, deliberate caresses, his mouth eeking the softness of her throat, loving that she arched and offered im more, and he took, drawing her high on his chest. His mouth ound her nipple, his teeth, the curves of her breasts, and she let im have his fill of her, let his touch master her, legs entwined, odies undulating softly on the lake of wrinkled sheets.

Rein sampled her treasures, his tongue sliding, lips sucking, and e shifted her to her stomach, drawing her up against the bend of is body. She pressed back into his groin, his hands memorizing he fluid shape of her, and his fingers found her wet center, stroked nd probed, and he whispered how much he adored her body, how eductive and ripe it was, how he burned to be moving inside. He old her that her gasps enflamed him, and drove one from her lips, nd then he encouraged her to find her pleasure, to know herself s he enfolded her hands over her breasts. Her head fell back gainst his shoulder, and he watched her movements, discovered a ender, arousing spot as she discovered herself. His whispered vords spoke of making love to her until the sun rose, that she was he second beat of his heart, and then he laid her on the bed again nd drank of her as if she were a cool spring. And when she lutched him, his mouth rolling hotly over her softness, Michaela nuffled her cries in the down of a pillow. And he gave her more, efusing to let her touch him, telling her he would find his end nside her wet depths and only there. Only with her.

Michaela felt cherished and wicked, seductive and alluring under is watchful eyes as he yanked her off the sheets and into his arms, ending her back, her hair spilling over the white sheets like rasp-erry wine as he suckled the fruit of her breasts. She wrapped her fingers around his arousal, but he would not have it, could not take he seduction of her touch, and cupped her back against his chest and stroked her curves, bending her to lay wet succulent kisses over her spine. His fingers dipped and teased, drawing her body like a well strung bow, letting her hover on the edge of extravagant ecstasy again and again until she was squirming, begging him to fill her, threatening to scream and alert the entire house. His chuckle was rough, diabolical, as he drew her hands to the carved board, whispering that this was a night of carnal pleasures and she was his most voluptuous feast.

"No more, please, Rein. Come to me," she panted, looking back over her shoulder, her gaze devouring him from his broad shoulders twisting with muscles down to his arousal, rampant and thick for her. She leaned into him, spreading her thighs over his, reaching pressing his hardened flesh between her plush heat. He threw his head back and growled, rocking with her.

His hands splayed over her buttocks, his thumbs parted her dipped, and she shuddered, a breathy sound of anticipation. He entered her, slowly, the pressure exquisite, her need to slam back into him, to take him all, quaking through her. He pushed, and the moist glove of her drew him deeper as he swept her hair aside to taste her throat, the bend of her shoulder. And she pulled away, smiling at his lavish moan, the air hissing through his teeth.

The breeze fluttered the sheers draping the bed as he grasped her hips and plunged, retreating, savoring his roughness to the slick of her silken folds, feminine muscles seizing him home. He palmed her contours, his fingertips glazing over the tender core of her and she bucked, rocked, demanding his passion, and with it, went his heart.

Bodies clashed.

Sweat sheened her spine, his chest.

The only sound that of eager breaths and the hush of love.

Skin to skin. Exotic spice and elegant cream.

And Rein loved his wife in the seclusion of a childhood chamber, clinging to her, calling her name in a phantom's whisper, claiming her beauty, that only she made him feel the strength of his hunger. And she accepted, mastered, reclaiming his soul with every breath, every subtle touch, and as she cried out, her rapture floating on the midnight air, Rein joined her, pulsing his life into her, finding his end, and knew, as he had from the first moment he'd seen her, that it began with her.

Rein stirred, a tingling running up from his feet. He opened his eyes and focused in the darkness, rolling to his back. A dark specter lay near his feet, tasting the arch of his foot, working higher, over his scarred calf, his knee. He smiled, enjoying the attention.

"Your mouth is an amazing thing."

"Thank you, my love. Let me show you how much."

She closed her lips over him, the sheer touch of her catapulting him into fierce pleasure and near pain. He reached for her, but that only intensified her assault. Rein simply stared, his body under her command.

"Oh, sweet thunder!" He clenched fistfuls of sheets. "Michaela!" he hissed. "Oh Swee— Oh, God."

"Want me to stop?"

"Nay! Aye!"

She laughed softly, possessive and smug, then came to him again. He trembled, her hands on his thighs driving him wild, and he felt the hot roll of the coming explosion, his muscles taut, thrusting. He grabbed her, rolling her to her back, kneeing her thighs apart and driving into her, pounding her across the bed, and she clung, laughing at his eagerness, at her power to make him so mindless but for the satisfaction he could find in her. He thrust and thickened, and she shuddered with release, pushing and grinding to him. They held each other, on the edge of it, to the hard crash to the center of the earth and through the soft float to heaven.

"Michaela, my *rasha*." He took her mouth, hot and heavy with the remnants of his passion. "I— forgive me. I didn't mean to be so harsh."

He never expected her to laugh.

"I thought it was rather fun."

His head jerked up and he stared.

"I've shocked you, haven't I?" Her expression wasn't the least bit contrite.

After a false start he said, "Well, aye."

A slow grin spread across her face and she brushed his hair back to see him clearly in the dark. "Seemed fitting to torture you a bit." Her smiled broadened. "My Hindu is pitiful at best, but I did manage a few interesting passages."

The *Kama Sutra,* he thought, grinning. "You crafty little tiger."

Her expression bore a bit of pride, a touch of smugness, and she leaned into him, a delicious mash of her breasts to his naked chest as she whispered, "There was this passage I did not quite understand . . ." She paused, lowering her voice. "Mouth pressing." She tipped her lips to his ear. "At the same time."

A dark, lustrous groan rolled from deep in his chest as he fell to his back with her. He showed her, introducing her to another passage, and long into the night he reaped the carnal delights of a woman in the throes of her own power.

And Rein was defenseless, unprotected from the desires of Michaela.

Michaela walked softly down the hall toward the stairs, a light shining from a half-open door catching her attention. Aurora sat with the baby in her arms, her head drooping, then jerking upright in her battle with exhaustion. Max sat on her lap, playing with a wooden horse, kicking his chubby feet and gnawing on the animal's head. Envy slipped through her, and Michaela stepped into the room and could not name the tiny thrill of having Maxwell recognize her and bounce on his mother's lap.

Aurora stirred. "Goddess of light, go to sleep, child," she said softly, kissing his head. She looked up, drowsy and disheveled, and offered a saucy smile. "Just like a man, waking a lass in the middle of the night to have his pleasures." She flicked a wry glance at her open robe, her breast half exposed from nursing him.

Michaela grinned at her bold talk and moved closer, reaching for the babe. "Go on to bed, Aurora, I will care for him."

Aurora closed her robe. "I should tell you to go be with Rein, but from all the racket coming through the wall . . ." Michaela inhaled. "You should let him rest up a bit, thinks I."

"Oh, nay," she said, blinking and blushing. "I am sorry."

Aurora waved her off. "Dinna be ashamed of loving," she said, smiling as she rose from the rocker. "Laird kens I've enough proof of it." She cupped the back of Max's head, kissing the top. Her eyes flashed up, her smile mischievous. "And how much fun 'twas getting them all."

Michaela smiled. She loved this woman's frankness.

"Rein adores you, you ken."

"I love him, Aurora." But she was afraid to say the words to him, afraid he might turn away again.

Her expression was soft with pleasure. "I ken you do," she said, pushing back the younger woman's curls, wild from her son's exploring hands. "He needs you so much."

"Oftimes I do not think he needs anyone."

"We all crave another, lovey." She gazed into Michaela's eyes, commanding her attention. "I know my Dahrein, yet oftimes, not the man you wed. After all my talking and teaching, he still holds far too much in his blackened lineage." She shook her head sadly. " 'Twill be a great pain, I fear, to learn otherwise."

Michaela thought of her husband, the task of telling his parents he hunted his real father, and her sympathy went out to this family. It could tear them apart.

"He will learn, though."

Michaela's brows rose. "Good Lord, you sound so confident in that, just like he does."

She laughed lightly, smiling. "Of men we can ne'er be certain, can we now?" She leaned close. "Especially a Montegomery."

"So I have learned. Colin is a test to that."

Her expression turned a bit sour. "Colin has yet to find the man inside the body of his father. But he will."

There it was again. That certainty.

Aurora yawned, and Michaela hefted the baby. "Go back to bed." She urged her toward the door. "Max and I will be fine. He's going to help me make a light repast." She looked at the boy. "Aren't you, my lad?"

Max gave her a toothy smile, bouncing in her arms, and Aurora smiled tenderly. "He's got himself a fresh nappy and light repast himself," she said with a cheeky grin. Together they walked the hall, and with her hand on the latch of her chamber, she turned to Michaela. "My son is a hard man, Michaela. Hard on himself. He'd prefer the world to bend to his ways."

"He's rather successful at that."

"Aye, but do not ignore your own convictions for him. He's commanding, aye, like Ransom, but loving means acceptin', too. Sacrificing your beliefs will hurt you in years to come."

Michaela's brow knitted. Did she know she was a spy, that she had to get information of the gold shipment to Nickolas, whether Rein liked it or not?

"Your happiness is important too, neh?"

"Aye," she said, and Aurora nodded, satisfied, then slipped into her room. Still frowning, Michaela moved quietly down the hall to the stairs. She lit a taper at the base, though the house, with all its windows, was filled with moonlight. She headed to the kitchen, and with Max on her hip and talking softly to the dark-haired, green-eyed boy, she rummaged for a snack.

An hour later, Rein peered into the kitchen and sighed relief. It had scared him, to wake and reach and find his bed empty. They'd been locked in a cocoon, in each other's arms all night, and he didn't want the morning to come, didn't want anything to break the fragile moments he had with her. He remained in the shadows, sensing everything about her, her warm skin beneath the dressing gown, the scent of her mixed with his. Every moment in the last hours came painfully clear, bludgeoning him with their sensuality, and as he watched her with Max, he wondered if his child took seed and grew inside her. And in that instant, Rein wanted it to be true, wanted to see her round with his babe, help her bring it into the world, to shower their child with love and have it given back unconditionally.

He wanted her bound to him through flesh and blood as he was bound to her.

For a decade, he'd put the thought from him, especially when Shaarai did not conceive and Rein considered the failure lay with him. It was a possibility he hadn't discussed with Michaela, and he didn't want to cloud her dreams just yet, for seeing her with Max, watching her nurturing spirit unfold as it had with the ducklings on that country road, he knew she wanted children.

His lips curved softly as she talked to Maxwell, who was perched in the center of the table, jamming a heel of bread in his mouth. Michaela was slicing bread, a wedge of cheese, and cold meats onto a platter.

"Did I thank you for the promenade about the house, sir?"

Maxwell smiled, soggy crumbs on his cheeks. He garbled in response.

"Aye, 'tis a lovely night. Is it always so warm and breezy here?"

Max's head jerked in response. Michaela blinked, then shook her head and went back to slicing. "You really should get acquainted with your big brother, you know. He's a fine man." She leveled the baby a look. "As I'm certain you will be someday."

His chin seemed to tip a bit, and Michaela would swear, if she didn't know better he understood her every word. "So, Maxwell

Montegomery . . ." She arranged meat on the platter. "What will you become when you grow into those big hands of yours, lad?"

Max simply stared at her, unblinking.

"Aye, 'tis a bit soon to consider your future, I agree. But speculation is always fun. A barrister, mayhap?" He gave a little shriek, enjoying the sound of his own voice. "A ship builder, then? Ahh, nay, nay, lad," she said, lurching to keep him from grasping the crock of butter. She set it out of his reach, then gathered him off the table, setting him on the edge. "Let's see." She eyed him. "A merchant like Rein?" She shook her head. He mimicked her, and her voice lowered. "A pirate like Colin?" He squealed. She blinked. "I think not," she said in a strident whisper. Max offered her his crust of soggy bread. She pretended to nibble and he frowned, looking from the crust to her and back. He shoved it at her again.

She took a tiny bite to satisfy him, cringing over the mushy feel of it in her mouth.

"Utterly delicious."

"I'm hungry, too."

She jolted, her gaze flying to the door. He was simply too handsome, she thought, wearing only his breeches, his hair mussed, his eyes sleepy lidded. " 'Tis impolite to eavesdrop. This is private." She looked at Max. "Tell him." She inclined her head toward Rein.

Max turned his head to look at him, and Rein was struck down to his bare heels by the look in the child's green eyes. An old soul is locked in there, he thought before Max launched into a stream of unintelligible sounds.

Michaela blinked at the boy. "You bright little lad!" she said, scooping him off the table and nuzzling his belly. He laughed uproariously, his chunky legs punching the air, and Rein didn't think he'd ever seen his wife smile quite like that before. *From the depths of her it comes,* he thought, walking close. She propped Max on her hip, gazing up at him.

"Should I be jealous?" He rubbed the back of Max's head.

"Aye, most definitely. I'm in love with him."

Something slammed through his chest just then. "Really?"

"Happened just now." She kissed the boy's cheek. Max leaned out, reaching for the crock of butter.

"I would duel for you, but I'm afraid 'twould be most unfair." As he spoke, he slid his hand around her waist, drawing her up against him. He brought his mouth down on hers, outlining her lips with his tongue, drawing a breathy shudder from her, the reward of it, her body pressing tighter to his. Max made a disappointed noise.

Rein's senses came alert with more than his wife's lush curves yielding to him, and he opened one eye, then snatched the crock from the air. He brushed his mouth over her face, her throat, then looked at the child, a warning in his eyes as he carefully slid the pot back on to the table. God of fire, his mother was going to have a time with this one, as if Viva wasn't trouble enough, and Rein decided to keep the discovery to himself as he took the boy from her and rubbed his lips down to the neck of her gown.

"I missed you in our bed."

"Hah. You were snoring away, you did not miss me a'tall."

He jerked back, affronted. "I do not snore."

"All right then, there were bees buzzing in our room." She smoothed his bare chest, her nails teasing his nipple, and he clutched her tighter.

His breath hissed out through clenched teeth. "Bring the tray when we have finished with it . . ." He licked her moist lips. "I will dine on you."

Moaning, she sank deeper into his kiss. "I am your willing feast, my love," she murmured.

He stepped back, and with the tray, she moved through the house, Rein cradling his sleepy brother against his chest. In their chamber he laid the boy to the center of the bed and they crawled in after him. Facing the other crosslegged, they sampled the fare, exchanging kisses and warm glances. Max shifted to his side and drifted off to sleep.

Michaela smiled down at him, brushing the dark curls from his forehead. "He's so beautiful," she said, a catch in her voice. She marveled at his tiny hands and fingers, his nose scrunching up as he dreamed.

"You are very good with him."

She shrugged, still staring at the sleeping infant. "He is such a pleasant babe. Smart, too. 'Tis hard not to love someone so helpless and innocent."

Rein's features tightened. That's what he'd thought when he'd first seen Colin, but the way his father discarded him like worn boots was proof that there were people who could turn their backs on a child and live with themselves.

He took a deep breath and said softly, "You could be increasing right now."

She smiled, then glanced at him. "I know. Does that upset you?"

"If it did, Michaela, I could have prevented it."

She blinked.

"My mother is adept at tinctures, though they are not absolutely foolproof."

"Obviously," she said with a light laugh and a gesture to the house full of children.

He wasn't going to mention that the Montegomery men were notoriously potent, since he was not a blood heir. "You want one."

"Nay," she said, and he frowned. "I want many."

He brushed her hair back, noticing the glassy look in her eyes as she stroked Max's fingers, his unblemished arms. "Why do you hunt your blood father, Rein when you have all this?"

"Michaela," he warned softly.

"Your real father is naught but a selfish fool and he doesn't deserve your attention." She shoved her hair back and looked at him. "Discard the quest."

"I cannot. I need it done, so I can begin again."

Her expression crumbled. "I thought we already had."

He tipped her face, gazing to her eyes. "Can you say the same, with your revolution?"

The spark that he'd seen a thousand times when he mentioned her cause lit her eyes bright. "That is not the same and you know it. 'Tis the will of many, not one, that makes this rebellion move toward victory. And when it happens, many win."

"You would still spy?"

"I would see it to the end. I must."

His hand fell away. "As I would with my blood sire."

She opened her mouth, then snapped it shut, unwilling to ruin this night with arguing. The matter could wait. She wiped the crumbs from Max's face, then scooped him into her arms and edged off the bed. Rein followed, coming to her.

"Let me put him down." She gave him up, and Max stirred, then snuggled with a contented sigh into his brother's arms. "We've a private chat to have."

"Ahh," she said with a knowing smile. "Man things."

Rein pushed the boy up onto his shoulder, patting his diapered behind as he padded across the moonlit chamber and out the door. Max looked like a speck against such a big man, she thought, and could hear him through the walls, murmuring to the child as Michaela set the tray aside, stripped off her dressing gown, then slid into the bed. Rein returned, stopping at the side of the bed, hesitant. She held out her hand, the sheet clutched at her breast. He shucked his breeches and slid in beside her, into her arms.

He made love to her body, made love to her soul, mindlessly, desperately, clutching her tight and praying she would forgive him for breaking her heart.

Thirty-three

Rein stirred awake, his gaze searching the room for his wife. He found her sitting near the window, bathed and dressed, Cabai standing behind her, brushing her hair into a neat coif. He leaned up on one elbow, watching her, her brow knitting for a moment, then smoothing to a blissful smile.

"Thinking of me?"

She turned her head and smiled, her gaze touching over him with the warmth of fading embers. "I was," she admitted as Cabai inserted the last pin and whispered in her ear. She rose, moving to him in a swish of green-sprigged muslin as Cabai departed. "I was thinking that your family will believe I have you lashed to the bed if you do not make an appearance belowstairs sometime today."

He smiled, reaching, grasping her hand and pulling her down on the bed. " 'Tis an interesting prospect," he murmured, catching the back of her neck and drawing her down for his kiss.

Michaela sank into his mouth, her body jumping to life. How she loved this man, she thought and longed to tell him, yet she did not want him to think she was saying so because of the intimacy they shared last night. She was by no means a dreamy-eyed maid, and the feelings running through her were real and strong and they filled her with a happiness she never thought to feel. She'd been loved all night, the damage Winters had done washing further away every time he touched her and releasing a part of her she was having a tremendous amount of fun exploring.

Her tongue outlined his lips, and Rein groaned, the warm feel of her igniting his blood. By the gods, once tasted, he could not get enough of her. And that she was more than willing to give it to him so adventurously delighted him beyond all measure. She drew back and he chased her mouth, stealing another kiss before letting her have her way.

His gaze swept the cut of her gown. "I could have you out of that in seconds."

"And your mother would find us. She awaits me now."

His brows furrowed.

"I asked about her cures and she agreed to teach me some."

"Then you'll be with her all day," he groused.

"Can you not find something to amuse yourself with until later?"

"I'd planned to be amused with you," he said, his eyes intense as he toyed with a curl laying enticingly over her breast.

She inhaled softly, her expression tender as she leaned closer to outline his lips with her tongue. He was motionless, breathing heavily, and it fired the desire racing through her blood. "So, I am not but a plaything, eh?"

His eyes grew fierce with possession. "I do not play." He gripped her arms, pulling her atop him and kissed her, thoroughly, deeply, his hands finding their way beneath her skirts and smoothing up the back of her thighs. She moaned, taking his mouth with a fervor that left him panting and hard.

Someone called her name from the recesses of the house and she rose up, pushing off to stand beside the bed. Rein blinked, then threw off the covers, revealing his state of readiness. "You do not think to leave me like this?"

She smiled. He sounded like a child denied a treat. "Aye, I do." She darted out of his reach. " 'Twill make the coming together later all the more sweet."

"How much later?"

She stared for a moment, then said simply, "Later," before moving briskly across the room to the door. She paused, her hand on the latch, and twisted a look back over her shoulder.

Rein frowned. There was a strange look in her eyes, a sadness so faint he almost did not catch it. "They will tease you this morn you know."

"I am not ashamed of what we've done, not that the business of it belongs to anyone but us, husband."

He smiled. "You've grown accustomed to my mother's blun way of speaking, I see."

"One does not have an alternative," she replied, and when the call came again, she sent him a promising look and closed the door. Rein jammed his fingers in his hair and looked around the room, then immediately left the bed and stepped to the hot bath Later, he thought, would come sooner than she imagined.

Rein descended the staircase, his gaze on his wife as he rolled back his shirtsleeves. She was in the dining room, seated between his mother and Maxwell, feeding the babe, chatting with him. After she'd left, he'd found his clothing brushed and laid out in an orderly fashion, his boots cleaned of mud and shined. He'd thanked Cabai only to discover it was his wife who'd seen to it. The thoughtful gesture endeared her to him more, and he realized that he'd been living alone for so long, he'd forgotten what it was like to have someone take the time to look after his needs.

He stood in the doorway, watching her, then snatched up a scone, biting into it as he moved around the edge of the table, greeting his family, yet his eyes only on her. She looked up, a tiny spoon poised for Maxwell, and he leaned down for a kiss.

She gave it willingly, and when he straightened, he slid quickly into a seat beside Max to hide her effect. "Is it later yet?" he whispered, and she blushed.

"Not yet," she said, leaning to feed Max, who stole the spoon and scooped it himself.

"About time you roused yourself," Ransom said from the far end of the table.

"Ransom," Aurora scolded. "Leave them be." She looked at her son. "Sleep well?"

"He didn't sleep at all, I'll wager," Ransom said good-naturedly.

Michaela flushed, her gaze on Rein. "As a matter of fact. . . ."

His kiss silenced her, and the tableful of people erupted in soft laughter.

"If you can pull yourself from your wife's pockets"—Rein glanced at him, a warning that he'd had enough of his teasing—"I've a need of your help, Son."

Rein's expression immediately clouded, and he took a huge gulp of coffee before he said, "I must see to the repair on the *Empress* first."

Frowning softly, Michaela reached across, covering his hand. He gripped her fingers briefly, then stood, the chair scraping back. "Excuse me."

Michaela watched him go, then rose, tossing her napkin aside as she looked imploringly at his parents, then followed Rein's steps. She reached the porch in time to see him ride off on Naraka.

Ransom moved up beside her, and she looked at him, his face marked with concern. "What troubles him?"

"He will tell you in his own time, Ransom. That is all I can say."

Ransom nodded, glancing back at his wife before moving off, his shoulders hunched. She pulled her gaze from the older man to her husband, admiring the magnificent picture he was astride the back beast as he rode the streets, and cursing him for this infernal need to clear his conscience. She understood the war he waged in himself, for one battled in her as well. She turned back into the house, feeling as if she awaited the blast of cannon fire to rip her contentment apart. She'd planned to tell him this morn of the gold shipment, but after seeing how deeply troubled he was about revealing his quest to Ran and Aurora, Michaela decided to postpone her confession. He did not need another burden right now, and he needed her support. But she couldn't wait long. Her uncle would have found a ship by now and could possibly be sailing in a fortnight or less to attack the *Victoria*.

And she had to get to Nickolas, which meant that when Rein was ready to undertake his search for his blood sire, she would be with him. Nothing would separate her from the man she loved, she thought, now that she'd found him. She had to believe that, for when she confessed of the gold shipment, she knew he wasn't going to be pleased.

* * *

"Michaela, you are not concentrating."

Michaela offered an apologetic smile and wiped up the spille tincture. "It's just that I am worried, he's been gone so long."

Aurora eyed her. "He was at the ship until an hour or so ago."

Michaela's features tightened. Why didn't he come to her? Sud denly, she knew, and pulled at her apron strings. He was shutting her out, closing them off, as he had before with his anger ove Colin. She could not risk the separation that was too hard to breach She excused herself, walking briskly toward the stables, ducking inside the darkness.

Over the back of a chestnut mare, a young man looked her over with skepticism.

"I need a mount."

He didn't respond, looking defiant before his gaze shifted be yond her, his expression questioning. She turned and found Ran som walking toward her.

"I have to go to him."

He gestured to the lad to saddle a mount for her. "What can I do to help?"

Michaela smiled sadly, touching Ransom's arm. "Love him."

"God knows I do. He might be well grown, but my heart does not know the difference." Ransom's features creased with worry, and he pointed to a clearing. "There is a cave up there. 'Tis where he might be." At her look, he said, "He thought 'twas his secret place. But we all knew."

He smiled was tender and she leaned close, brushing a kiss to his cheek. "My husband is fortunate to have a father such as you, Ransom."

He grasped her arm gently. "Your own sire was a fine man, Michaela."

She inhaled, her eyes wide.

"I went to school with him. I have some letters of his, if you'd care to read them." She nodded, her throat working. "I am sorry for your loss and hope that one day, you'll accept us all as your family."

"I do, Ransom," she said, her eyes tearing.

He groaned at the sight, feeling useless, and drew her into his arms, patting her back. "Go, lass." The hand brought the mount orward, and he threaded his fingers for a step up. She mounted, itting astride, adjusting her skirts.

Ransom eyed her dubiously. Her chin lifted. "I learned to ride n elephants," she said.

"Your father hated the damned things."

She smiled with the memory. "Camels, too, but much to his isappointment, I mastered the ugly beasts." She shrugged. "I think e was trying to discourage me all whilst wishing he had a boy."

Ran's lips quirked. "I think he got exactly what he wanted."

He gave her instructions and watched her ride toward the old road eading to Shokai's cave, feeling a little jealous that this woman had is son's confidence, when he'd possessed it all these years.

She found the cave, its entrance overgrown with vines, but the ole in the earth was wide enough for her to duck through. It was mpty but for an old cracked pot and the remnants of a dead fire, he ground undisturbed, and Michaela left, walking the path to her orse. Then she heard Naraka's blustering whinny and followed the ound through the brush. The area grew dark with heavy vegetation, yet she could see the path the horse had mashed through the underbrush. Gradually, the density of the jungle thinned, and she stopped at the edge of a small clearing. She could hear the rush and spill of water and realized there was a valley beyond the little copse.

She scanned the area and found him to the far right of it, standing beneath a spreading tree, flowers blooming in the vines overtaking the branches. She sighed with relief, and though he appeared relaxed, she sensed his anxiety. Like a beast coiled to strike, his spine was punishingly straight, his hands clenched behind his back. She tried to understand his feelings, why he felt compelled to seek out a man who had destroyed his childhood, yet knew he needed to be honest with Ransom and Aurora.

"Rein!" she called for the third time, and he threw her a haunted look. "Oh, my love," she cried, and she came to him, but his cool response made her stop just short of a yard from him. He stared down at her, not speaking, simply memorizing her features.

Rein made no more to touch her. He couldn't, his self-disgust so great he thought he might hurt her.

"Share with me, please. I cannot bear this silence. Let me help you." She reached, her fingers trembling as she brushed a lock of hair off his forehead and he melted beneath her touch, catching her hand.

He placed a soft kiss to her palm and murmured, "Ah, my *rasha*. Forgive me, but I have made my own mess of this."

"What kind of wife would I be if I did not share your pain, try to ease it?" she whispered.

"I could hurt you."

"If you keep this inside, aye." She moved closer, her skirts brushing his legs.

He could not tell her the truth, could not withstand seeing disgust in her eyes when she discovered his true intent, and he released her, turning away.

Michaela felt the barrier rise as if he'd closed a door. "Are you certain you are not doing this simply to unburden yourself? For I see no good in coming with the telling."

"I've never lied to them, Michaela. I cannot hide this another moment." He flung a curse at the lush valley below. "Part of me wishes I'd never begun this search."

"Then why do you continue?"

"I—I need the questions answered. And why this man wants me dead."

She inhaled a sharp breath and he looked at her through pain-filled eyes. "Aye, the night Katherine was killed, he sent men to take the medallion, the evidence. Even to kill me for it."

"So you seek to unveil him, shame him?"

His shoulders moved restlessly and he paced, mashing fragile pink flowers beneath his boots and sending their sweet fragrance into the air.

"Rein!"

He looked at her, his beautiful eyes fouled with anger.

"Nay," she gasped with understanding. "You seek to kill him!" She backstepped, the moist ground shifting beneath her feet.

Alarm sharpened his features as he lunged, reaching for her and missing. The ground crumbled. She flailed, her expression filled with helpless horror, and he dove, catching her about the waist and dragging her away from the dangerous ledge.

He clutched her tightly to him, looking down at the hundred-foot

op onto boulders, quaking, squeezing her. His lungs labored as
e buried his face in her hair, and with a curse, he bore her further
vay, his heart thundering against her ear as she pressed her head
his chest.

He sank to his knees, his entire body trembling. "Oh, Michaela,
y sweet. Oh, God," he moaned, running his hands over her back,
er shoulders, over and over, his mind replaying the moment, im-
edding in him how close he came to losing her, how empty he'd
e without her, and how much his anger had pushed him to this.

His breathing slowed and he eased his hold, enfolding her deli-
ate face in his palms and kissing her like a ravenous beast.

And she accepted, took his anger, his fear, and turned it into
assion, urging him to let it go in wet kisses and heavy strokes.
he gave him no choice, her kiss devouring, her hands molding
vildly over him, shaping him, letting the passion escalate and burn
way his rage for a faceless man.

"I could have lost you," he whispered near her ear, his mouth
coring over the flesh of her throat, the swells of her breast, before
e captured her lips.

"You didn't. You caught me and I am still here, Rein," she
rooned on a breathless gasp, covering his hands and forcing him
o look at her. "I will always be here."

Something shifted in his eyes just then. "Forgive me."

"There is naught to forgive, my love, yet if you must do this, if
ou must find your father—"

His gaze flickered, pale eyes intense. "I must."

"Then I will be here for you."

His features slackened.

"You know what you need to do to be happy and if finding him
s the end you desire, then I am . . . I will stand by your decision."

Incredulous, his gaze searched her gaze. "And if I choose to kill
he man?"

Her lower lip trembled. "You are strong and honorable, Rein.
You say now that you have the desire to end his life, but I know
you, you cannot take a life for such a reason. Confront him, aye.
Have your say, aye, but to murder . . ." she shook her head. "You
von't."

He clutched her hands to his chest. "You are so certain, for I
am not."

"I believe in you." His features yanked taut. "I believe in the man who flirted with me whilst I dug in his flesh, the one who refused to show the public we knew each other for my reputation's sake. I believe in the gentleman who kept his promise to a friend, jeopardizing his livelihood. And the man who masqueraded to rescue me from being sold to the highest bidder." Her voice softened with her gaze. "I accept the man who hid his anger for fear of hurting me, and I adore the tender soul who took me gently past my pain and showed me how to easy it is to love."

His throat worked. "Michaela," he said, his voice breaking.

She cradled his handsome face in her palms, gazing deeply into his eyes. "Even your hatred did not change that. You bend to no one, my love. You will not let them change you for it."

His eyes burned.

"I love you, Rein Montegomery. I love the man you are. I want to share everything with you, grow with you, give you sons and daughters and peace. Not for the fatherless child you were, for the man I held in my arms last night."

Her face neared, her mouth a breath from his.

"I am in love with you, Rein." The words shaped his lips and he groaned, sinking into her kiss, dragging her against him. He kissed and kissed her, his heart aching with his love for her, and he buried his face in the mass of deep red hair, inhaling the fragrance that was hers alone.

For a long time, he simply held her, reveling in her love, holding it close.

Michaela closed her eyes, telling herself she didn't need to hear that he loved her back, that it was enough to know he cared deeply and that someday he would say the words.

Then very slowly he tipped his head, his lips pressed to her ear. "I love you, my *rasha*."

Her grip tightened and she squeezed her eyes shut.

"You captured my heart the day you foolishly risked your life for some silly ducklings."

She reared back, her eyes filled with tears. "I wasn't foolish. They were babes. And you wait till now to tell me?"

"I was afraid you could not love someone like me."

With a disgusted sound, she shoved him back and climbed to her feet, moving swiftly toward the horse.

"Michaela." What had he done now?

"I would have never shared your bed if I did not love you, Rein. Surely you knew that of me at least."

"I knew no such thing."

"Calling me a tart, are you?"

He groaned and stood, overtaking the distance in three strides, catching her arm before she could mount, and spinning her around to face him.

She was smiling. Hugely.

"Michaela," he said, frustrated and confused.

" 'Tis later, Rein."

Towing the mare and astride Naraka, Rein pointed out spots in the city, showing her where he'd been attacked by the shark, taking her through the fields and introducing her to the families along the way. Her manner was easy and generous, her smile blinding, and when she grasped the stump of a man who'd lost his hand without a flicker of aversion and shook it gently, Rein felt no small measure of pride. And in that breath he loved her more and he finally understood what Ransom had been telling him, that to find the perfect mate, one you respected and adored, was a treasure that made a man rich in his soul.

Rein tightened his grip around her waist, burying his face in the cloud of curls unrestrained and blowing against his shoulder.

"Astride does not hurt you?"

She laughed lightly, and tipped her head to look him in the eye. "Fine time to ask. Or are you asking me if I've had enough of you?"

His grin was slow. "Nay, but now that you speak of it . . ." His hand slipped lower on her waist, feeling her curves wrapped in the sprigged gown.

She leaned into him, cupping his nape and bringing his mouth to hers. "Never, my love," she said against his lips and kissed him.

She loved him. Rein was still marveling at the concept when they rode up to the house. Then he saw Aurora and all pleasure fled. He dismounted and helped Michaela down, holding her in his arms for a moment and drawing on her strength.

"Get it done, Rein."

Lashing the horse to a post, he held her hand as they moved up the steps. They found Ran and Aurora standing together.

"I need to speak with you both, in private," Rein said, and the words nearly killed him. Aurora eyed the pair and nodded to Ran's study, pushing open the door and letting them pass. She exchanged a glance with Ransom as she plucked a sliver of grass from Michaela's hair. And Ran quirked his lips, shrugging.

Rein turned to his parents, his father moving behind his desk, his mother perched on the edge near him.

They waited.

Michaela gripped Rein's hand, then released him.

"A little over three years ago I found a woman, my aunt, a blood relative . . ."

Aurora inhaled, then looked at Ransom, but his expression was unreadable, his gaze moving over his son as Rein stood motionless and told his story, of his search and elimination of each man.

"I will not ask why you do this, for I can see why," Aurora said.

"Well, I do not," came from Ransom, soft and filled with hurt.

Rein's expression crumbled.

Aurora went to her husband, touching his shoulder, rubbing it gently. "This is the anger that has built in you since you were a boy, Rein, and if you must find this man to end it, then do it."

Rein lifted his gaze, meeting Ransom's across the room. "I do not do this to hurt you both. Can you understand that I must face him?"

Ransom left his chair, coming around the edge of the desk and staring his son down. "This scoundrel who cast you aside is more the bastard than you and I combined."

"I know that."

"Then why go to him?"

"Ran," Aurora pleaded.

"He does not deserve your consideration, Dahrein. And were I to meet him, by the gods, I would run him through for the child he left to die in the streets."

They stared, and Aurora stepped between the two. "You seek to kill him." His gaze flicked to her, and she moaned, "Oh, nay, Dahrein. Naught will come of it but loss."

Rein looked at his wife, saw her straight posture, her encourag-

ing smile. "A day ago I would have thought I would kill him on
the spot, but now . . ."

Michaela came to him, sliding her arms around his waist and
simply holding him.

Aurora pulled Ransom toward the door. "You go to this man,
Dahrein. Be done with it and remember all you risk." His mother's
words hung in the air.

Rein's arms tightened around his wife, and he turned his head
to look at the people who'd raised him.

Very softly, Aurora said, "Who you seek is the man you already
are, Rein Montegomery. And this faceless sire will not give you
that freedom." Ransom stared at him, the hurt mirrored in his
craggy features and, for a moment, he looked older. His big shoulders slumped, he turned away, wrapping his arm around Aurora
and leaning into her.

Rein swallowed, suddenly ashamed of his need and praying they
would someday forgive him.

"I love you," Michaela whispered, and he closed his eyes, pressing his lips to the top of her head, and in the darkness brought by
twilight, a tear rolled down his cheek.

Thirty-four

The roar of double cannon fire startled Michaela awake. Rein
was already moving across the room to the balcony, a spyglass in
his hand. He paused at the rail, scanning the horizon. His shoulders
fell with relief and he closed the glass, turning back into the room.

"What is it?" She clutched a sheet to her bare breasts.

"An approaching ship."

"Shouldn't we be about? Battles a'ready, that sort." She waved
to the walls beyond, the commotion she could hear beyond.

"Nay." He removed his breeches and slid back into the bed beside her.

"Nay?"

He smiled and tugged the sheet lower, exposing her breasts. " 'Tis the *Sentinel.*"

"Temple?"

"Aye." His mouth opened over her nipple.

"Rein! That means the double agent has been found."

"I know." His lips closed and she gasped.

"You are not the least bit curious?" came in a powdery rush.

"Nay. For when I know," he switched his attention to her other nipple, loving her sketchy breath, "I will only want to put a bullet in his head for trying to hurt you."

She pushed him back to look him in the eye. "Are you always so vengeful?"

"Only since I fell in love with you."

Her expression softened and she sank down into the bed. "This charging-knight side of you is something we must put into place."

"Put me in my place," he said cheekily, moving over her, spreading her thighs.

"How can I speak with you when you've naught on your mind but having a bit of pleasure."

"I was hoping for more than a bit."

She tsked softly. "Such high expectations."

"Uh huh." He slipped his hand between them, finding her softness, his fingers sliding wetly in her silken depths. She thrust into his touch, then hurriedly shoved sheets aside to find him, guiding him. He entered her in one stroke, grinning down at her.

"He can't make the cove, and we have time before he rows ashore."

"How much time?"

"Two hours at least."

"Oh, then we're in for more than a *bit* of pleasure."

He smiled, withdrawing, then thrusting into her and watching desire bloom across her face. He could live a hundred years and never get tired of seeing it. "There is naught small about loving you, Michaela."

"Oh, Rein!" she cried, her eyes tearing as she wrapped her arms around his neck. "I do love you."

"I hope so," he said against her lips, loving the little shudder when he left her, then plunged home. "For I cannot live without you."

"Or neither can I. Shhh," she hushed, clutching his buttocks, pulling him deeper, and he groaned darkly, quickening his pace, the slick glove of her gripping him.

He braced himself on locked arms, pushing and pushing, stroking the bead of her sex, ignoring the world beyond, the man he'd hurt last night, and losing himself in his woman, in her pleasure, in loving her body and giving her his soul. And when she cried out, tensing beneath him, he drove into her, throwing his head back and calling her name.

Rein watched as she stepped from the bath, draping the Turkish cloth around her. "You are wonderful," he whispered, dropping kisses down the line of her throat.

"Why, thank you, my love." He was a far cry from the somber man she'd held last night, so filled with regret, and his roguish smile made her heart clench.

She'd just slipped into her dressing gown when Ransom shouldered his way through the door.

"What is this I hear about someone trying to kill your wife?"

"Ransom!" Aurora chased in behind him, grabbing his arm. "You should learn to knock. They could have been abed."

Rein smiled. "We were." He wiggled his brows.

Ransom folded his arms, eyeing them both, unconcerned over the interruption. "Well?"

Michaela didn't wait for Rein to speak. "I am an American rebel spy, sir. The Guardian."

Ransom's features yanked taut, and he looked to Aurora, then her. "Nickolas's Guardian?"

"The very one."

Ran plowed his fingers through his hair and Aurora went to him, sliding her arm around his waist.

Whether it was his intention or not, Ransom Montegomery could intimidate with a look. Michaela swallowed and offered, "I was hunted, kidnapped, and your son rescued me from certain shame and married me to protect my person and my reputation."

Rein looked at her then, his eyes soft. "I married you because I could not live with you and not touch you."

She smiled, reading his desire even then.

"Och," Aurora said. "And here I was hopin' you were with child."

Rein grinned. "Not yet."

Michaela eyed him for a moment, a frown briefly tightening her brow, then focused on Ransom. "How did you know?"

"Temple. He negotiated the cove without a scrape this time."

Michaela looked at Rein. "I will be ready in a moment. Wait for me. Ransom, out," she shooed, and Aurora pushed him toward the door.

"Are you going to give me some answers?" he said over his wife's head.

"Aye, Ransom, when she's properly dressed."

"I am her father-in-law. She is dressed enough!"

Michaela giggled, then slipped out of her robe, parading across the room to her gown.

Rein whistled softly, watching her sweet behind rock with each step.

She donned her garments, pushing Rein's hands away when he made to help her, for she knew she would not finish her toilette if he continued to tease.

A few minutes later, they descended the staircase together, following the sound of heavy footsteps. They found Ran pacing, Aurora watching it, and Temple sitting aside Viva, talking softly.

Rein halted immediately. "Get away from my sister."

Temple looked up, frowning.

"Rein?" Michaela tugged, but he tore from her side and strode over to Temple. "Matthews, I swear if you so much as look at her crosswise."

"Rein!" Aurora scolded.

He threw them a look. "I trust him with my life, not my little sister."

"She was just checking his bandage."

Rein scowled, just noticing the blood seeping through his side.

"Hardly in the way to do damage, mate."

Rein did not concede the point.

Michaela came to him, pulling him aside. "Look at me," she said when he continued to glare at Temple.

"That man goes through women like a shark to fresh fish."

"I know. I saw him at the theater. Warn him off later, and tell your father if you must." She smiled encouragingly. "I'm certain he will put the fear in him enough. But he's hurt, Rein, let her tend him."

Rein nodded, his stiff posture going lax. He pressed a kiss to the top of her head, then turned to Temple.

"How?" He gestured to the wound.

Temple turned his gaze to Michaela. "Your double spy." He struggled to sit up. "I'm sorry, Rein. 'Twas Christian."

"Lord Stanhope!" Michaela sank into a nearby chair, covering her face. Her eyes teared. Her neighbor, her father's friend, she thought, trading information to both sides. It was one thing to fight for a cause, quite another to play them against each other, and drag this war on.

She lifted her gaze to Rein's. He stared at the floor, his hands on his hips, and her heart ached for him. She left her chair, moving to his side. He gathered her in his arms, hanging on to her, breathing in her scent.

Rein felt the heat of betrayal sear through him. That he was a double agent, playing both sides, he should have seen. But Christian had tried to kill her, hurt her. And for that, he was unforgiving.

"Nickolas's trap—"

"Did he admit to killing the priest?" Rein interrupted sharply.

"After a fashion," he said with some discretion.

Michaela's eyes widened a bit. "Does he know it was me in the church?"

He searched his memory. "He admitted to little, Michaela. But he actually had the arrogance to wear the same boots."

Her gaze swung to Rein's. It was confirmation enough. She could read it in his eyes. "I'm sorry, Rein."

"Ridgely wore the boots the night we caught them. Christian admitted to me that he'd given them to a stablehand." He shook his head. "And I believed him."

"His mission was not to be found out, Rein. Even if it was to play two sides of the coin."

"Nickolas gave me this for you, Michaela." He fished in his pocket, and Michaela accepted the folded parchment.

"You need to rest," Viva said, furnishing her brother with a chastising look. Ransom rushed forward as Temple struggled to his feet. Ignoring their assistance, he stood on his own power, his gaze on Rein as he took a few steps, stopping in front of him.

"I would never hurt her, Rein." He glanced at Viva. "Never." He turned his gaze to Michaela. "I am glad you are happy with him." He leaned close and whispered loud enough for Rein to hear, "Though it surprises the bloody hell out of me what you see in him."

Michaela swung her gaze up to Rein. "You'd have to be a woman to know that."

Temple snickered and shuffled off, Aurora on one side, Ran on the other.

Viva looked at her brother. "If I can fend off the rogues in this town, Brother, I can take care of a randy harlot in breeches."

Rein's brows shot up and he smiled. He should have known, he thought.

Alone, Michaela looked at the folded parchment, the red wax seal like a rippling ribbon over the seam to ensure it had never been opened. Woodenly, she walked to a chair, sinking into the cushions. She brushed uselessly at the curls draping her shoulder, her hand trembling slightly. Turning the letter in her hand, she was suddenly afraid of what it might say, yet knew her happiness would be interrupted when Rein discovered her deception.

Rein eyed her, then the note. "Are you not going to open it?"

She nodded. Yet she did not, a part of her eager to return to the fray, another aching to remain where she was, to be with her husband, to love him and feel his love surround her, to be needed for more than serving tea and scones. She was married now, what good would she be to Nickolas? Rein didn't live in England, he only visited. She would no longer have access to anything of value. Yet her part was unfinished, and she could not ignore it. If she wanted peace, she had to complete her last mission. Allowing her uncle to succeed would be like losing the revolt, for he was her truest enemy.

She slipped her thumb under the wax.

Trepidation danced up Rein's spine as he watched her pry the seal and unfold the letter. She scanned it, a shuddering breath passing through parted lips.

"I have to go to England. I must speak with Nickolas."

"For what reason?"

She looked away, then met his gaze, her chin lifting, and he knew whatever she had to say, he was not going to like it.

"There is a gold shipment leaving on the *Victoria*. Salaries for British troops, and fresh armaments. Nickolas is unaware of it."

He cursed, raking his hair. She'd tried to send Nick notes, insisted when he'd taken her from Madame's that she had to consort with the man. "You say you trust, Michaela, yet you still do not know how. You've kept this secret for how long?"

"The night after the theater."

His eyes narrowed on her bowed head. "You did not think this piece of information could have helped us find who was trying to kill you!" He ended in a harsh snarl that made her flinch.

Her head jerked up. "It had naught to do with the double spy. And with this kind of information, I could not trust anyone but Nickolas."

"Not even me?"

He started to walk away, push her away, and she left the chair, reaching for him, grabbing his arm. "Nay, not even you. Listen to me." She shook him. "The men involved, they have more power than any of us, Rein. Five high-ranking British officers prepared to attack the *Victoria* and take the gold for themselves. They will kill everyone aboard to cover their tracks." She drew a breath. "My uncle is one of them. 'Tis why he asked you for the use of your ship."

His features sharpened with anger and disappointment.

"I could not trust you, not when there was a suspicion that you might be involved."

"You knew I cared naught for this revolt."

She eyed him thoroughly. "You had connections on both sides, Rein, and have the uncanny ability to hide your emotions." Until now, she thought, seeing the wound she'd opened and watching it bleed. "When I wanted to tell you, it was too late. We'd sailed."

"Who are the others?"

"Prather, Rathgoode, Winters." Her gaze pinned him then. "And another who I could not identify. But he's very tall."

"And what do you propose to do?" he asked coolly.

"Stop them."

"Why? Let them take the gold, bankrupt England, and you are closer to ending the war."

"Because that coin is for the troops. For their families and their children. I will not take the food from babes. Nor see families in the poorhouse because my uncle wants more than my money."

He stared out the window, refusing to look at her. "I will tell Nick for you."

"Nay, they embark in less than a fortnight and 'tis my job."

"Not anymore."

Her spine stiffened. "I am a soldier, Rein, part of the Army. I will not shirk my duty. So, I suggest you either rethink your disposition or . . . or . . ."

Now he spared her a brief, thin glance. "Or?"

"Or I will be on the next ship home."

"You are home."

"Nay. I am not."

"Then I recommend you grow accustomed. You will not return to England, Michaela." He turned his head, his eyes as glacial as the winter sea. "Ever."

She sketched his features. "What are you saying?"

"Your days as the Guardian are finished. I am your husband, and you and I will live on my plantation on Madagascar. The revolution will have to make due without you from now on."

Her hands clenched. "You came to this decision without so much as a by-your-leave to me?"

" 'Tis for your own good."

"Horse crap," she snapped. " 'Tis for yours!"

He straightened, glaring down at her.

"When my uncle was kicking me like a bothersome dog, I had the revolution to grasp, the taste of helping the Americans win their freedom whetting my appetite. And when I wed you, I did not give it up. When I said I loved you, I did not say with it that I will not be who I am. I cannot ignore my duty. I must finish this. I am—we are too close."

"You are of no benefit."

"You know that is untrue."

"I will see that it is."

She inhaled and backstepped. He would reveal her? "I could be drawn and quartered!"

"Then stay where I tell you."

She fumed. "Do not blackmail me, Rein Montegomery," she said in a voice edged with anger.

"You give me little choice, woman. You are wanted! Did you not think that you could be carrying my child into the center of a war!"

Her brows shot up, a look of absolute horror on her face as she recalled the conversations this morning and the nights before. "Is that what these past nights have been? Your quest to get me pregnant, to stop me?"

He simply stared.

"Is it?" When he didn't answer, hurt simmered in her, brightening her eyes. "I would have thought we'd make a child out of love, not as a weapon."

His features did not alter a fraction, yet his eyes flickered with something akin to regret. "I do love you. And any child we make is of it."

She gripped his arms, gazing up at him. Her voice faltered with tears as she said, "I love you so much it hurts to think of a moment without you." Her expression fell into despair. "But I stood by you, Rein. When you confessed to Ran and Aurora, I was there for you. I understood your need to find this cretin you call sire, and even if you chose to kill him, I would still love you."

His expression crumbled. "Michaela, 'tis dangerous, more so now that Christian has been uncovered. Do you not think he has more than one person working with him?"

Her fingers flexed on his arms. "Chandler is not a threat to me."

"How can you be certain?" he growled down at her. "You could be shot the instant you set foot on English soil."

"Then you take me there."

"Nay. I'm going to Morocco."

Her features tightened. "When?"

"The morning tide."

She thrust away from him. "So even if Temple hadn't arrived, you were going off without me?"

"Aye, 'twas not necessary for you to accompany me."

"I am your wife! Where else do I belong?"

"Here. Safe!"

"You do not see it still, do you? Just as you need to go to find your blood sire, I must finish this." She shook the paper. " 'Tis my duty!"

"Your duty is to me!"

"And who is yours to, Rein? Yours, alone? Your needs, your purpose?" The truth of her words bit into him with the sting of a blade, inciting his rage.

"You will not leave this island," he said, measured, precise.

"I must."

"There is not a soul on Sanctuary who'd defy me, if I forbid it."

She scoffed, her hurt turning mean. "I think you put high value on your reputation, Rein."

Her tipping chin told him she would find a way. "You leave here, then you do so at the cost of our marriage."

She inhaled. He would dismiss all they had so easily?

"The choice is yours."

"You or the rebellion? That is unfair, Rein. What say you if I put the same to you. Your blood sire or me?"

He stared down at her, his features sharp. "Your revolt will survive without you."

Anger and hurt and disappointment swam through her, and in a fractured voice, she whispered, "And will you survive without me?"

His features yanked taut. She turned away and then looked back, her voice thick with hurt. Tears spilled. "Pray you did not give me your child, Rein, for it may bear your name, but you have by no means this day earned the right to be his father!"

He took a step, regret in his eyes. She darted out of his reach and fled the room. She felt betrayed, almost violated, that her husband would love her and adore her body with every intention of keeping her from the revolution. She would not be swayed. They were so close, and though the news was sparse, her conviction to see the Colonies separated from England kept her from bending to Rein's will now. Covering her mouth, she gathered her skirts and raced up the stairs, her heart shattering with every step. She'd been living a fantasy. Rein could not love her, not if he was so willing to dismiss all they'd shared, using it as an ultimatum to have his way. If she folded to his command, she would be betraying her deepest convictions, and as much as she loved him, her chest clenched at the thought, she could not live with herself. Nor him.

She would end this. She would get back to tell Nickolas.

If she had to bloody well swim the distance.

Rein dropped into a chair, his elbows braced on his knees, his face in his hands. Goddess of light, what have I done? He dug the heels of his palms into his eyes. The hurt on her beautiful face, the horrible destructive words he'd said. Would she ever forgive him? His breath skipped, and he raked his fingers through his hair, holding his skull.

He loved her beyond reason, beyond anything. She was his wife, damn it! It was his duty to protect her, even if it was from herself. The thought of her going back into the fray, of running the streets, mayhap encountering her uncle or Winters, made his entire body slam with fear. She would die if she returned to England. He was certain of it, for if there was shred of suspicion that Chandler knew it was Michaela in that church and he played the other side for bargaining, she would be shot on sight. He couldn't risk it. And he could not take her. He had to confront his sire and end this so he could start his new life with her.

If he had one when he returned.

His muscles squeezed down on his heart, threatening his breathing, and he mashed his hands over his face, the image of her pain imbedded in his mind. She might be hurt and angry now, but at least she would remain alive. He could not win her back if she was dead.

He looked down at the note lying on the floor.

It read:

Freedom calls. Come home.
Grandfather.

Thirty-five

Clad in breeches, a dark shirt, and pulling on gloves, she trotted down the staircase and past him without a glance. Rein didn't think anything could hurt as much as Michaela hiding her wounds.

He crossed and reached for her. Her head snapped around, an for the briefest instant he saw her love trickle through her steel gaze.

"Where are you going?"

She jerked free. " 'Tis no longer your concern, Rein." She walke away, walked out of his father's house and out of his life. He starte after her, freezing in his tracks when she whistled and Narak pranced up to her. The betraying animal even went down on hi forelocks so she could mount. When Rein managed to gather hi senses, she dug her heels in and lurched from the yard, hooves tearin the lawn black. His throat tightened, his eyes burned. And he praye it was not the last time he saw her. He started for the stable.

Someone caught his arm, and Rein found Aurora close at his side

"Leave her."

"I can't." He took a step.

She gripped him tighter. "You have beaten her heart, Rein why?"

His expression fell into complete misery. "She would go to wa Mother. She would willingly risk her life for this revolt, without care to herself, to me, to the child she may carry."

"So, you hide her to keep yourself from worry." Aurora scoffed "You are such a fool." She thumped his forehead with the heel o her hand. "I raised you better than this. You think women dinna have purpose, have strong enough feelings? Did you forget I spen nine years searching for my father? That a woman ruled England." She narrowed her china-blue gaze. "The goddesses of wind, earth and fire and water, Rein. Have you forgotten?"

His lips flattened. "Of course not."

"Then why can you not see you are smothering her beliefs a they tried to smother mine in Scotland. You're oppressing her a well as England does to the Colonies. How can you not expect he to follow her heart?"

His expression tightened at the mere mention of the revolutio that tore his wife from him.

Aurora softened, lightly touching his strong face, her heart aching for his pain. "Michaela loves you as Shaarai never could. She loves your soul." She patted his broad chest. "But marriage does not give you the right over her convictions, and you know it. And now, you have made her choose." She stepped back, glancing toward the street then back to her son. "You have asked her to give up what has kept her alive for three years. Before you, she had naught." Her expression was infinitely sad. "And now 'tis all she has left."

"She has me! Our life, our future."

"Not from what I heard."

Rein clenched his fists, wanting to shake the women in this house, and he left, heading to the stable. In minutes, he had a horse saddled, yet he did not go after his wife and instead headed down to his ship. The sooner he was gone, the sooner he could get back and repair the damage.

Michaela slid from the saddle and fell to her knees, choking on her sobs. She hugged herself, folded over, letting her cries echo into the valley. Here she released her torment, alone, in private, and cried till she had no more tears. She ached until she was numb with pain. She loved him. No matter what he'd said, she still loved him. The afternoon sun sank lower and still she did not move, her hand fluttering over the spot where he'd loved her, where he'd claimed she possessed his soul and he hers. It felt like months, instead of sweet precious hours.

In the whole of the past years she counted those moments as the happiest in her life. And now they were crushed, beaten, and as she brought her trembling hand to her lips, she knew she would never feel his touch again, never feel his eyes upon her, his kiss. She lay down in the pungent grasses, smoothing the depression their bodies made in the earth.

She was reborn with his love.

And now, her heart was dying.

Hours later, Rein entered their bedroom and stilled. She was nowhere about. His bags were on the floor near the door. His weapons lay across the top, cleaned and loaded, and, despite his anguish, a tiny smile quirked his lips. Until he saw the medallion laying beneath. He reached for it, hesitating, then grasping the chain, slipping it on.

His gaze moved over the dimly lit room, to her clothing discarded over a chair, the bed a lake of wrinkles where he'd loved her only this morn. It was gone, destroyed with a few choice words, a mountain of pride and conviction, and Rein hated this feeling, hated that he was pushed into giving her an ultimatum to keep her alive. He wanted to shoot every Colonial and end this rebellion now. Take away the risk, take away the pain.

He swallowed, his Adam's apple grating like broken glass in his throat. His eyes burned. He bent to his bags, then straightened, moving to the bed when he glimpsed a bit of color. Lifting a ribbon caught in the tangle of sheets, he brought it to his nose, inhaling her scent, then tied it around his wrist. With quick strides, he hefted the bags and left. In the foyer, his father stepped from his study, his expression grave.

"Did she return?" Rein asked.

Ran's gaze swung to the right and Rein followed it. His heart slammed to his stomach. She stood motionless, her hair unbound, her eyes a touch swollen. Rein lowered the bags to the floor.

"I sail at dawn."

"Good journey, then."

He took a step.

She put up her hand, her lips trembling.

"Michaela . . ." he whispered, agony in his voice.

Her eyes turned venomous, her words a soft hiss. "Go! Go find your blood sire and kill him, Rein. For all the grief he has given me, I want him dead!"

She darted toward the stairs, but he caught her arms. She struggled wildly, her hair covering her face. Her whimper drove a spike deep into his heart. He swallowed her in his arms, and still she fought, cursed him. He tightened his embrace, fisted her hair, and tipped her head back. She glared at him, rage and hurt and love in a single look.

"I want you to *live*."

"I need to finish—" Yet before she finished, he shook his head.

"I love you, my *rasha*."

She choked, her knees buckling.

"I love you," he rasped again, fiercely. "And I will be back."

Then he brought his mouth down on hers, holding her when she was wont to be free, kissing her with all the desperation running through him, all the love he held dear for her. And she responded like a tempest. She devoured and ravished, clawed and took. Then she tore her mouth free and shoved him away.

For the space of a heart, they stared, breathing heavily, then she turned and raced up the stairs, past his mother ascending, her run sending Viva into the walls.

Rein stared up at the empty hall long after the door had slammed, long after her cries softened. He dropped his head forward and lifted the bags. Without a backward glance, he left. And he was terrified that there would be nothing here when he returned.

At dawn, Michaela stood on the balcony, watching the *Empress* sail through the channel. She could see him on the quarterdeck, his black clothing stark against the white of the ship. She felt as if she were watching her life sail away. She'd considered stowing aboard, but he could sense her presence or have expected as much from her, and searched the ship.

It made her more determined to get off this island.

She turned away from the sight and went about the room, collecting her borrowed clothing and stuffing it into a worn leather bag. She blinked, her eyes stinging. She had naught left but her fight for freedom.

Then so be it.

The man shook his head and turned away, ignoring her pleading. Michaela sighed, sitting on the thick-roped post of the pier. Rein was true to his word. He'd forbidden every captain to take her off the island.

Ransom approached, and Michaela refused to fall to guilt and met his gaze as he walked down the dock.

"What the bloody hell do you think you are doing?"

"Trying to get off this bloody island."

"Rein wants you to stay."

She leapt to her feet, in his face. "Rein can go to hell!"

His brows shot up as he folded his arms, staring down at her. "He does it for your own good."

"Nay, Ransom. He does it for his. His mind is comforted that he knows I am marooned. With naught to do but stew, he thinks I will forgive, be pleased to see him when he returns."

"Are you saying you won't?"

She looked away, at the sea, at the *Empress,* a white speck on the horizon. "I won't conform to his wishes simply because he wants to entrap me."

"He loves you."

Something clamped a vise down on her heart just then. She knew that, no matter what, she knew. "He has a terribly peculiar way of showing it," she murmured, her voice cracking. She stepped closer, laying her hand on his thick arm. "Take me off the island, Ransom. Take me to England so I can be done with this and salvage something of my marriage."

Ransom held her gaze, warring with the requests of his son and the pleading in her soulful eyes. Loyalty won. "Nay."

She threw her hand off. "Won't anyone take me to England?"

"I will."

She spun about.

Temple moved toward her, his gait slow, his smile bright.

Ransom unfolded his arms. "I don't think Rein would like his wife in the company of the likes of you, Matthews."

"No worries, Ransom. She is off limits. A married woman." He tipped his head, winking at her. "Besides, she is too good with a pistol and," his gaze swung to Ransom's, "Rein did not forbid me. In fact, he's expecting the *Sentinel* to carry your sugar back to London." He consulted his pocket watch, then looked at Michaela. "We leave at high tide."

She glanced uneasily at Ransom, waiting for him to deny passage.

"I am not king here, lass. If 'tis freedom you seek, remember the risks." He waved her off and turned away.

She looked at Temple, not feeling as excited about this as she'd thought. "My thanks."

He scoffed. "Tell me that when Rein beats the stuffing out of me for it."

"I can't take the captain's cabin."

Temple stood on the docks, staring down at Rein's wife. "It isn't much of a sacrifice, Michaela, it's not like the *Empress.*"

"Just the same—"

He put up a hand, the gesture brooking no argument.

"You do as I say, not that a soul on this ship would dare approach you. And you go nowhere without him." He nodded to Cabai. She agreed. "Nay, do not smile at me, woman, for I fear I will be run through for this. And he will enjoy it."

Her expression fell. "He does not care."

"Oh, aye, he does. Mayhap too much." Temple tipped his head back. What he wouldn't give to love someone so deeply he would die for her, he thought. "You've got about ten minutes afore we must sail to make the tide. You should get aboard."

She took a step, then turned when she heard her name on the air.

Aurora, the white of her gown glaring against the later sun, Viva in tow, was coming down the pier, and she braced herself for a scolding, yet Aurora's expression was filled with sympathy.

"I willna be nipping off your head, Michaela."

She smiled. "Your husband wanted to, I think."

Aurora sighed. "Ransom feels as if he must defend Rein to you."

"And you don't?"

"I know what a horse's behind he's been."

Michaela's lips quirked, but at the mere mention of his name, her eyes teared.

"Oh, lovey," Aurora said, wrapping her arms around her and simply holding the girl.

"I love him so much, Aurora," she whispered. "How could he do this to me?"

"He's a mon. And they canna show their fears in any other way, oftimes, than smothering us."

Michaela nodded, trying to understand, then stepped back, wiping at her cheeks. She was so wise, she thought.

"Take these." She pressed a heavy leather sack into her arms. "There is a black vial inside. If you dinna want a child, you must drink the whole of it soon."

Michaela stared. Rein had mentioned such a potion. "Nay, I cannot."

Aurora nodded, neither in argument nor approval. "Pleasure should not have so high a price. Nor a child used to bind a man and woman." Now her irritation with her son showed, and Michaela realized the entire house must have heard their fight. Or was she just incredible perceptive?

"If you want to know if you carry, I can tell you," Viva piped in.

"I beg your pardon?"

Aurora laughed at her stunned expression. "Viva can sense a new life, Michaela. She did with each one of her brothers and sisters after her."

Michaela's gaze shot between the two, her hand unconsciously covering her stomach. "I would rather not know."

Viva shrugged, unconcerned, then said, "This is my wedding gift to you." She added a cloth-wrapped bundle to the pile. "They are some new dresses, altered now."

Michaela's gaze shifted between the two. "Thank you," she whispered, touched.

"And you canna forget your companion." Viva twisted, her hand lightly sweeping the air, and Rahjin loped down the hillside, sending people scattering out of her way.

Michaela smiled.

"She will protect you." Viva bent, rubbing her ears. "Won't you, my lady?" The big cat slicked her tongue across her cheek, then went to stand beside Michaela.

They stared.

Temple called to her.

"There's a bit of coin in there, too." When Michaela made to return it, Aurora shook her head, staying her hand. "Nay. You will need it, hiring coaches and such. And it isna much."

Temple called again, and Viva hugged her, whispering that everything would be fine if she had the strength to withstand the trials ahead. Aurora brushed curls from her forehead.

"We are glad you are a part of this family, Michaela, no matter what occurs."

Michaela's eyes teared, and she embraced her quickly, then turned and walked up the gangplank, Rahjin at her heels. Men secured the rail, and she remained on the deck as the ship lumbered away from the dock.

Aurora waved to the parting ship. "Is she?"

Viva smiled. "Aye."

Thirty-six

He sought control like the bare-backed child running the streets searching for his mother. He tugged at the coats of strangers, lifted a purse or two along the way, yet he kept reaching, reaching—and touched nothing, his energy leaving him. He struggled to grasp it, needed to grasp it, but it slid through his fingers like sand, the haze of pain sinking him deeper into a darkness he no longer resisted.

Numbing freedom. Yet he moved and experienced quick hot slashes of sheer agony racing over his skin. He arched, howling, unaware the sound came from his own lips. And the pull took him farther away from the pain, farther away from her.

His only peace was that she was safe, away from this, away from seeing him brought so low. He would give up his life for one last touch, one smile from her. He would lose his pride if he could have the chance to rebuild what he'd burned with harsh words and demands. What a wretched creature he'd become, he thought, letting the void take him. For too late he realized, without her, he was nothing.

Michaela warred between anger, hurt, and resolution. Yet when she tried to focus on a plan to get back into England and to Nickolas unnoticed, her thoughts always returned to Rein. And his image brought love and heartache, and then the cycle of regret and hurt would start again. She was a pitiful mess, she thought, wrapping her arms around her bent knees and resting her chin there.

A knock sounded and Michaela swiped at her wet cheeks, calling out from her spot in the bunk. Expecting Cabai, she was surprised to find Temple crossing the threshold, dragging his tricorn from his dark head. She hadn't seen him in a few days, not wanting to inflict her foul mood on anyone.

"We're near Morocco."

She inhaled, leaving the bunk to look out the aft windows. Rein was there, searching. She kept her back to him as she said, "You need not be waylaid, Temple. Not for me. If my husband wanted my company, he would have asked for it."

Temple caught the hurt in her tone and hated to deliver more. "The *Empress* is in the harbor. Under guard."

She sank to the bench, her complexion pale. "What could have happened?"

His look said he hadn't any idea. "The crew are lazing on the deck and there are troops on the pier."

"They are refusing them shore leave, then. Did you see Rein?"

"Nay, and I've been in the crow twice." Rahjin curled around his legs, purring, and he stroked her head.

She stood. "If we were to dock, how long before we reach shore?"

"Mayhap four hours."

She cocked her head. "You intended to make port all along." They wouldn't be this close if he hadn't.

"I thought that mayhap you—if you two met up—" He rocked back on his heels and looked elsewhere.

"Why, Temple, the heart of a romantic beats in that chest."

He slid her a rascally smile. "Breathe a word and I'll deny it. I've a reputation to maintain."

"Not one you should be so proud of, from what I've heard."

He blushed a bit and said, "What do you think we should do?"

She blinked. "You're asking me?"

"You lived here once."

"As a child, but—"

He folded his arms over his chest. "Or is the Guardian fresh out of ideas?"

The challenge in his words struck her backbone. She lifted her chin. "Make port at the east end, away from the *Empress*. We don't want anyone to recognize the sister ship." She moved to Viva's bundle, pausing in untying it. "Have we any Moroccans aboard?"

"Two, I think."

"Good. Tell them what we know, then bid them go ashore and ask about."

Temple smiled. She was moving about the room, collecting

items, laying out her pistols. And he could almost see her forming a plan.

Michaela dug in the sack Aurora had given her. Days ago, she'd discarded the black vial out the portal, made use of the comb, brush, and toiletries, yet dismissed the bags of herbs, and the coin. Until now. Mayhap there was enough . . . She inhaled, spilling gold sovereigns and glittering gems into her palm. "Oh, it isna much," she mimicked to herself. Lord, she hated to think what the woman thought was a fortune. "Give your Moroccans this." She tossed him one of the coins. He snatched it from the air, examining it, then eyeing her. "Rent a carriage, a fine one," she said, as she shook out the gown. Oh, Viva, she thought. She'd never seen anything so costly. Black moiré silk embroidered with silver threads and beads.

"What are you planning?"

She stilled, quiet for a moment, then looked at him. "The British guards are not to be taken lightly. They do as they are told. It is by whom, we must discover. That they are keeping the exit off the ship guarded means they hope to catch Rein when he tries to board, or they have him already and don't want anyone to get to him."

"Why was he here?"

It was no secret now, certain Temple had heard them argue. She told him.

"Think his blood father could have done this?"

"I would say 'tis assured." The man had already tried to hurt Rein before, which is one reason she wanted to see the cretin revealed and punished.

"So, after we find out what's going on?"

"Then I plan to throw my weight around a bit."

His gaze swept her and he watched her blush. "There isn't much of it to throw."

Her smile was sly. "There is in the guise of Right General and Brigadier General Denton's only living relative."

He grinned and turned to leave.

"Oh, Temple."

He glanced her way. She was bent over the bunk smoothing wrinkles from the black gown. "Ma'am?"

"How are you at forgeries?"

"Forging what?"

She met his gaze and grinned. "The Earl of Stanhope's seal?"

* * *

The sleek black carriage rolled down the quay. Fortunately, the street ran along the edge of the pier, the ships docked close. She would not have to parade down the pier. She tapped the roof, glancing at Temple and Cabai, then, when the carriage stopped, she waited impatiently for the footman to open the door.

"Be careful." Temple shifted position, prepared to take aim out the window.

Michaela nodded, then alighted from the conveyance, turning and motioning. Rahjin slid from the carriage like spilling black oil, tucking close to her side. She was chained about the throat and went to leash well, she thought, stooping to whisper, "Behave and I might give you a bit of English ankle to nibble upon."

A snicker came from inside the coach. She straightened and moved toward the short gangway. Two guards immediately crossed rifles to keep her from boarding.

"What meaning is this?"

"No one goes."

"I see that. Why?"

"Colonel Kipler's orders."

Kipler, she thought. She knew him, met him a few times when she was a girl. Was he Rein's blood father?

"I would speak with her captain."

"Nay, miss."

Rahjin growled at her side. The guards' eyes widened and they stepped back. "Shall I call upon your superiors? Where is your sergeant major? Your lieutenant?"

The young men stiffened. Rahjin's hackles rose, and the darling creature bared her fangs. They backstepped. One guard nudged the other, then inclined his head to the ship. She waited, endlessly it felt, for someone familiar to appear. When Leelan did, she nearly lost her balance and fell into the brink.

He trotted down the gang, stopping before her.

"Madame."

She motioned for him to move off with her. "Where is he?"

"Dunno."

He wasn't being congenial a'tall, and Michaela frowned, then her features tightened.

"I am here to help."

"You done enough. Ain't you supposed to be in Sanctuary?"

She grabbed his arm, her words hissing in the dark. "He is my husband and whatever is between us is our business, it that clear? He is trapped in this brittle city and I mean to get him out. You will sail the *Empress* to England."

His brow shot up. "I beg your pardon?"

"Try to leave. I would have one of his ships survive."

He folded his arms. "I won't leave him."

"Neither will I!" Rahjin paced around her, intermittently snarling at the guards, then Leelan. "And you best be prepared to take some fire. For getting him out of wherever he is will take more than picking him up like a new gown."

She spun away and strode between the guards, batting their weapons aside. Rahjin followed her as she stepped into the carriage and shut the door. The guard motioned him back into the ship, but Leelan kept watching the elaborate carriage's retreat. She looked so different, he thought, the black tricorn draped in sheer fabric, her gown refined, and he recognized Viva's embroidered Celt symbols edging the neck and sleeves. His lips quirked. She was a termagant, he thought, and she was right. What went on between Rein and her was none of his business.

He would prepare to sail.

There wasn't much the dozen guards could do until they got to open water. And with no word of Rein, where he was or what happened, Leelan was as good as stuck here until something occurred. They'd stripped the vessel of weapons, except for the cannons, but without fuses, they were useless.

The guard pricked him in the back with the barrel, and Leelan spun, snatching the tip. "Leave off, puppy." He released it and stepped onto the deck.

It was up to her.

The carriage halted, yet Michaela continued to peer out the window. " 'Tis your men. Open the door." Temple did, motioning, and the two dark-skinned crewmen slipped inside. They eyed the panther with trepidation, but Michaela's tone garnered their attention.

"We've little time, gentlemen. Did my coin buy us?"

"You understand that it is most unreliable. They are scared, the servants. But one who feeds the soldiers said he was ordered to bring a pauper's meal to the headquarters, in the belly of it."

"Not the cells near the barracks?"

The man shook his head, his look apologizing. Michaela chewed her lip. Damn, she could have lied her way past the men at the barracks, even managed a look into the cells, but headquarters? The commander's house. Kipler, she recalled the young captain she'd met when she was a girl, was a rather officious man, by the book and all that rot. She prayed the years had softened him. And why was Rein in the headquarters and not the cells?

She looked up, staring at nothing. Unless they did not want anyone to know they had a prisoner.

Her gaze sharpened on the Moroccan. "Did you discover why they have a captive in the house?"

One man shook his head, dragging the black cap from his head. "Madame. One cannot get into the commander's house. It is heavily fortified."

She looked at all four. "Take position on the boot. You are armed?" They nodded. "Excellent. We head to the commander's."

"Michaela," Temple protested.

"Nay, do not gainsay me in this, Temple. British officers are as familiar to me as the sea and soiled doves are to you."

His lips quirked at that, yet she did not mistake the hint of a blush.

"I can get inside, 'tis the getting out that has me puzzled right now."

"Sweet mother, you can't think to go in without an escape?"

"He would not dare touch me, Temple. Trust me. He's a boot licker," she lied. She had to get to Rein, for she could not lose the feeling time was critical.

"What are you going to say about even knowing he's there?"

She waved him off. "I'll think of something. If he is not imprisoned, then we have naught to worry about. A simple inquiry will do no harm." She shrugged. "No one knows we are wed." For if Kipler was Rein's blood father, this was an uncharitable way to show his affection for a newfound heir.

She motioned, and the two Moroccans departed, the carriage rocking as they climbed to the rear of the conveyance. She nodded to Temple, and after a considering look at her, he rapped on the roof.

Rahjin sensed her agitation, growling, and Michaela patted the space beside her. The cat leapt, dropping like stone and burying her muzzle under Michaela's arm before she scratched her ears.

Temple leaned forward, eye to eye with the panther. "I am jealous, my sweet. I thought you loved me best." He offered his cheek.

Rahjin rolled over like a dog and her mistress rubbed her belly.

"Fickle females," Temple muttered.

But Michaela wasn't listening. Gazing out into the night, she considered her plan.

"Kipler is a bastard of the first order, Michaela," Temple said into the silence. "He's been known to take a whip to his own men for discipline." He let the thought hang, and Michaela's stomach clenched.

But she would be no good to Rein in a fit of hysterics. "We find him first, his condition comes later."

The carriage jolted to a stop. She peered at the commander's house, a walled villa with guards everywhere.

"Take one of your crewmen and search the grounds, see if you can find an entrance to the rear. There should be a carriage gate somewhere," she said to Temple, while checking the load of her pistol, then hiding it in her pocket. She removed a blade from her reticule and slipped it down her bodice between her breasts. Temple smiled, wiggling his brows, and she sent him a chastising glance, then handed the second pistol to Cabai. He shoved it into his waistband with his scimitar.

Michaela adjusted her bosom in the gown, ignoring Temple's snickering, then swept the veil over her face and alighted, Rahjin and Cabai following.

She prayed her ability to act the lackluster female for three years would work in the reverse.

A slim turbaned young man rushed into the room.

"I told you I did not want to be disturbed, Halim," Kipler snapped, hovering over his meal.

"You have a visitor, sir."

Kipler looked up, frowning when the boy kept glancing behind himself. Nervous little twit. "Well, who is it?"

"A woman. She is English, sir."

Kipler's brows rose. Katherine, he thought, leaving his chair and reaching for his coat. "Give me a moment, then show her in."

He adjusted his jacket edges, smoothed his graying hair back, then gave his long mustache a twist. The door rattled, and he turned as Halim entered, pushing open the double doors wide, then stepped back to allow her entrance.

Francis Kipler was stunned to say the least as the woman in black silk sailed elegantly into the room. He took a step back at the sight of the black leopard sauntering at her heels and his eyes widened at the huge Arab guard positioning himself behind her.

She dipped a curtsy, her face concealed behind the sheer lace draped over the black tricorn, the ends tucked under her chin and thrown back over her bare shoulders to reveal a generous bosom. Pale as cream, and lush. Definitely not Katherine, he thought with a stirring in his blood. She did not speak, yet inclined her head toward Halim. He dismissed the child, and not until the doors were closed did she face him, lifting her hand.

"Madame," he said, pressing forward, grasping her gloved fingers, then dropping a kiss to the back. Her silence was intriguing, and couldn't wait to hear her voice. "Light Regiment Commander, Francis Kipler, your humble servant."

"I would like to think so," she said, and the husky breath of her voice skipped down his body. "I apologize for interrupting your evening repast." Deftly, she pulled free and waved at the unfinished meal.

"Think naught of it. Would you care to join me?" She shook her head and he caught the scent of her perfume. Spicy, exotic. By God, he had never been so entranced by a woman. "How may I be of service, madame?"

" 'Tis miss, sir, and I won't trouble you long, Commander. I've come for the sake of my uncle," she said, as she slowly pulled the lengths of cloth free. Kipler was so interested in watching the cloth slide over her skin, he scarcely noticed the black panther come between them. He looked down and jolted back. Her head tipped to the beast, and she whispered in Hindi. The animal settled to the floor near her feet, its green-gold gaze fastened on him. The creature made him nervous.

"Your uncle?"

"Aye and my father." She carefully folded the veil back, and Kipler's brows drew down.

"Have we met?"

"Years before," she said in a voice so dusky soft, he leaned closer. Her lashes swept up and he inhaled, startling hazel eyes giving an innocence of a child.

But naught about her was childlike.

"I am Brigadier Atwell Denton's niece, and Right General Denton's daughter. And only heir, sir."

He straightened, duly impressed.

"And I wish to see your prisoner."

His features tightened. "I have no prisoner."

She moved around the animal at her feet and stepped closer to him, her head tipped back, exposing her slender throat, the expanse of her bosom. "I have been dispatched to bring him to England for trial. He is suspected of crimes against the Crown, you know."

"Nay, I did not."

She laid her hand on his arm, her skirts brushing his boots, and he felt his groin clench. "Something with the Guardian creature, I understand," she said in a covert whisper, smoothing her hand back and forth over his arm.

"Why would they send you?"

"Discretion. He is a powerful man, you know. Many friends in very high places."

"Aye, I do. The half-breed deserves to lay waste down there."

"What has the foul creature done, not that it's of any consequence?"

He cleared his throat and looked away, briefly. " 'Tis a private matter."

"Forgive the intrusion, my lord."

"Brigadier Denton sent you, eh?"

"Well, not exactly."

He scowled.

"My party wishes to remain nameless," she continued, "but if you doubt me—" She reached into her reticule and came out with a fold piece of parchment, the Stanhope seal crimping the edge.

His eyes flared at that.

"All haste has been charged to bring me to you this quickly Commander. I have the authority to take him out of here. I've been given a ship to sail immediately for London. His Majesty needs to have justice done swiftly in this chaotic time, sir. What with those Americans thinking they can have a country of their own." She scoffed bitterly, and he agreed. "They mean to hang him, I think but then," her voice lowered and she leaned a bit closer her breast pressing against his arm—"even the king must show a fair hand these days and have a trial."

"I truly can not allow this."

"Francis . . . may I address you so?" she said in that voice that was driving him insane.

He nodded.

"Mayhap he is no condition to travel. Let me at least look at the cargo and then we can decide together. Would that be preferable?"

He was undecided, his gaze sweeping her face.

"Mayhap all this is for naught. Should he be near death, then I do not have to reroute my plans further. I could remain here, let you show me about the city."

A smile emerged from beneath his mustache.

She offered the sealed document. "One does not want to anger the monarchy, sir, trust me, that Georgie, ah, His Majesty is in a bit of a fracas with the Guardian running about, and undue distress will be the worst for all of England."

He looked at the seal, then her. It was one thing he could not ignore, he thought, taking it, then tossing it on the table. "This way, Mistress Denton."

"Michaela, please." Covering her face with the veil, she followed him out of the room and down several corridors, the guards snapping to attention as he passed. He paused on a short, narrow landing, a staircase leading down, beyond.

"The bastard's in there." He pointed to the door.

"You do not accompany me?"

He looked at the locked door in disgust. "Nay . . . Protect the general's daughter," he ordered his men, then addressed her. "After you've . . ." He waved. "Do join me for luncheon on the morrow."

Her smile was slow, seductive. "I'd been waiting for the invitation, Francis."

He blushed like a schoolboy, then turned away.

Michaela watched him go, then she dared a step forward. She stopped outside the door, then motioned for the guard to unlock it.

"He's a wild one, missy, best you stay back."

"I assure you, Corporal. I can take care of myself." She stroked Rahjin's head and the fellow's eyes widened.

He opened the door.

The odor hit her first. Rotten food and blood and urine. Michaela swallowed, then forced herself to move into the stone storeroom.

Oh, dear God in heaven.

He was chained like an animal. Tears burned her eyes. Her knees wobbled. Blood stained his clothing, old blood, and his face was unrecognizable. Michaela took a step and realized she couldn't hear him breathing.

"Remove these at once!" The guards darted forward to do her bidding, and she thanked God no one could see her face as she motioned to Cabai. He came forward, bending. "Please be careful," she whispered, her voice cracking. Cabai hefted him in his arms like a child. His head lolled over his arm. Michaela whimpered, resisting the urge to stroke his hair, his swollen face. Cabai carefully adjusted him higher and Michaela staggered. His back was bleeding.

Rahjin hissed, circling their legs, circling around to the soldiers. "Quickly." They had to get out of here before Kipler broke the seal. She led the way, Rahjin in the rear, snarling and snapping at the men. They backed up, then aimed their weapons.

"Nay!" she said. "Rahjin." The cat came to her, the growl low in her throat raising the hackles even on her arms. "Open the door."

The men stared her down.

"Open the door." In a swift move, she withdrew her pistol and pressed the point to the soldier's head. "I am a general's daughter. Think I do not know how to use this?"

"Do it, Benny. Kipler said to."

The soldier darted to the door, flipping a ring of keys, then unlocking it. The blast of clean, dry air hit her and Rein moaned. She brushed past them, her steps measured and brisk but not hurried.

She could not alert anyone until she cleared the grounds. She passed two more guards at the gate and smothered the urge to bark at them when they were too slow to swing it open. She stepped into the dusty street, turning when she heard shouts. The seal.

She whistled sharply, moving faster, Cabai trying hard not to jostle Rein. *Please be alive,* she prayed. *Please, oh please.*

She lifted her skirts and ran, the carriage rolling around the west side and jingling to a halt. The door burst open and Temple leapt into the street, covering their backs.

"Hurry. He's read the note by now."

Temple got a look at Rein. "Oh, sweet Jesus!"

Cabai ducked inside with Rein just as the troops opened fire. She returned fire with Temple, and together they climbed inside. The coach lurched, the four bays speeding down the avenue toward the sea.

"My God, why would they do this?"

"I don't know . . . oh, God," she said, her hand hovering over his bruised face, then clenching into a fist. "I will kill the coward myself, I swear." Gunfire hollowed through the night, a ball hitting the coach door.

Rein stirred, his lids sluggish, his eyes glazed as he stared at her.

"You are safe, my love. You are safe."

She pulled the veil free, pushing off the tricorn.

Recognition flickered in his eyes. "Mic—"

"Aye, Rein. I am here. Don't worry," she sobbed. "Shhh," she said when he struggled to talk. "Nay, don't. Shhh, save your strength."

The carriage jolted and he howled in agony, and Michaela thought she would die from the tortured sound. "Make them hurry, Temple. Hurry!"

"They are, Michaela." He loaded his weapons again, and she forced herself to arm the other pistols. Temple fired into the darkness. "The *Empress* has sailed."

"Thank God." They would have taken them prisoner and burned the ship, she knew.

They traveled farther into the city, the carriage nearly tipping in the wild ride, and when Michaela didn't think the horses could take another step, they were at the east docks.

The *Sentinel* was anchored offshore. They scrambled from the carriage, Cabai taking measured steps. His muscles flexed as he put Rein to his shoulder, and Michaela nearly fainted at the sight of his back. His shirt was in tatters, his back blazed with red, oozing stripes. She reached for Temple.

He gripped her arm, supporting her as Cabai stepped into the longboat. "He will make it. He survived your gunshot."

" 'Twas a scratch compared to that!" How was she going to help him? "Quickly. Quickly."

She was in the boat and helping to row, digging the oar into the rocking water. Tears streamed down her cheeks. She could not look back, not at her husband, her strong, beautiful husband beaten like an animal. Rahjin moved between the men, lowering in front of Michaela, her head on the woman's lap. Still she rowed. Temple called out to the ship, the rope ladder rolling down over the side, and Michaela nearly fell into the water trying to reach the leadlines. Gathering her skirts, she climbed, the men behind her. Temple shouted orders to open sails. Cabai, thank God for Cabai and his strength, for he overtook the hull and stepped onto the deck in moments. She headed immediately to the cabin, snatching the blankets off the bed, and Cabai laid his master down like a child to its nap. She stripped off her gloves, rushing to fill the basin with water, then tore a sheet into rags. Her hands shook, and Cabai positioned a chair beside the bunk and she dipped and wrung, tenderly blotting Rein's face. He moaned, trying to push her away and she called his name.

"Cabai. The bag, Aurora's bag. Hurry." She emptied it on the bedside, checking tag after tag, closing her eyes as she tried to remember Aurora's teachings. "A cup of water." He produced one and used her teeth to uncork the bottle and pour a few drops into the water. She cradled his head and forced him to drink. Water trickled into his mouth and she rubbed his throat. "Rein, my love, drink, please."

His lips formed around the rim of the cup and he drank. At least he will not be in so much pain, she sighed, laying his head on the sheets.

"Cabai, I need hot water, more rags. Bring a small table here. Aye, that one," she said, pointing. She pulled the knife hidden in her bodice and slashed angrily at the sheet, nearly cutting her gown. She stilled, tipping her head back, breathing deeply.

"Micha—"

Dropping the knife, she sank down on her knees beside the bed, her hand trembling as she brushed a filthy lock from his forehead. "Aye, my love, I am here."

"You dis-disobeyed me."

"Are you not more fortunate for that?" she said, trying to show him a smile.

His lips quirked the faintest bit. "Forgive . . . me?"

Her tears came harder, her lip trembling to hold back great wrenching sobs. "Of course, my love."

But he was already unconscious. She touched his pulse, then bent her head to the straw mattress and, clasping his bloody hand, she cried.

Thirty-seven

Rein walked the empty street alone, his footsteps echoing. Fog rolled around his legs and he looked back, at the open door, the light shining.

Fight for me, my love, fight.

He turned and moved toward the darkness. A dirty, half-naked child raced before him, stopping to stare. He reached out, so familiar, the face, the eyes. Before his fingers touched, the child vanished like smoke.

A light shone at the end of the street, a woman, a tall man, a youth not yet grown to a man, tightly holding each other. The boy looked at him and waved, then the threesome turned, fading into the darkness. He took another step and found his path blocked.

Shaarai, her face only contours in mist.

He tried to touch her. "Forgive me," he whispered.

She touched his face, an icy stroke on his skin, her expression sad. *"Forgive yourself,"* she said, and pressed her hands to his chest, pushing him back. *"You do not belong here."*

Cold clenched his heart.

"Then where do I belong?"

She pushed and nodded.

Rein turned his head, the doorway filled with the shape of a woman.

"Come to me, Rein, I love you."

Her energy pulled him, growing stronger and stronger.

"I love you."

Michaela. He ran toward the door, toward her. Just short of it, he stopped, looking back.

Aurora, Ransom behind her, smiling. *You search for who you already are.*

Rein nodded, then stepped through.

Rein stirred, his body numb, and he forced himself to remain still. He knew if he moved, the pain might take him away from her again. A fierce sense of determination rushed through him, and he absorbed his surroundings without looking, the scents sweet and fresh, the cool air brushing over his skin. He lay on his side, pillows stuffed around him, a thin sheet covering him, and felt the pulse of the ship, its glide over the water. Then he remembered.

Michaela in black. Michaela crying over him, calling to him, forgiving him.

He breathed deeply, his lids fluttering, his eyes gritty and dry.

He blinked, sunlight glaring through the portal.

He scanned the cabin, recognizing the *Sentinel*'s interior, the table with bottles and rags, the clothing discarded, then he looked down slightly and saw her, sitting on the floor, her head on the mattress. She looked damned peaceful, he thought, yet needed to touch her, to wipe the salty trail left by her tears.

He lifted his hand, his fingers fluttering over her hair.

She jerked awake, meeting his gaze. "Thank God."

"Nay, my love, thank you," he rasped.

Her tears came, unmanning him, wounding him for the pain he caused her.

"Ahh, love, do not weep."

"I can if I want."

His lips curved.

"Rein, I thought I'd lost you."

"Never" came fiercely.

"How do you feel?"

"Alive."

She eyed him, love in her gaze. "You do look better."

He frowned. "Than what?"

"Than dead." Her eyes watered again.

"I am sorry—"

"Shhh, don't speak of it. Please." She brushed his hair from his face, then offered him water. He sipped slowly. "Can you tell me what happened?"

His forehead knitted as he tried to focus. "I made a single inquiry and was clapped in irons."

"Kipler?"

"Aye, yet I don't recall aught after being shackled and tossed into a room."

"Why did they beat you like that, Rein?"

He touched her forehead, his fingers moving over her features, feeling her cheek, her lips. "He wants me dead, Michaela, but could not kill me himself."

That hurts him, she thought, so deeply.

"Kipler? Is he the one?"

"Kipler was following orders, I think. He didn't know what I was talking about when I mentioned Sakari."

Michaela nodded, loving the feel of his touch, the fingers moving slowly down her throat.

"I need to hold you, my *rasha*."

"You cannot, your wounds."

"My need of you is greater than any pain."

Her look doubted, yet she rose and carefully lay down beside him. He buried his face in her hair, reveling in her scent, her warmth, sliding his hand over her stomach, and curling her toward him. Pain stung through his back, but he focused on her.

"I am going to sleep very deeply for a while. Do not be frightened by it."

She tipped her head, her lashes sweeping up. She searched his face, the blackened bruise along his jaw, the cut over his brow. "Heal yourself, my husband." He opened his mouth to talk and she hushed him. "I will not leave your side."

His smile was rich and adoring. "Never, my love. If I have to lash you to me and join your cause . . ." She inhaled, her eyes flaring, "We will never be parted again."

"Rein?"

He squeezed her, ignoring the pain the effort caused and snuggled her closer, whispering, "You win, Michaela. I cannot fight your rebel heart." He kissed the spot near her ear. "My freedom lies inside it."

Michaela felt silly tears burn her eyes, and she closed them, sinking into the mattress, into the feel of her husband wrapped close to her, and for the first time in four days she slept.

Propped on a mound of pillows, Rein put a finger to his lips when Cabai entered the cabin. Michaela slept on, her beautiful face serene in her slumber. She'd been close for the past days, he'd sensed it, drew on it to help heal himself as she'd bathed his wounds in Solomon's seal.

The scent of food made his stomach clamp in protest, and, carefully, he eased up off the bunk. Cabai handed him a pair of breeches. He slipped them on, still watching her sleep. She had defied him to return to England, but then, in his heart he knew she would find a way.

But that she came to Morocco, risked reaching England in time to warn Nick, to help him out of that foul place, made Rein realize the gap he'd made between them had never destroyed their love. So damned brave, he thought, moving to a chair, sitting carefully, his back tender. He inspected the marks on his wrists and ankles, red but not infected, then cocked a look in the mirror. What had she seen when she found him, if he still looked this bad? he thought. The skin over his eye and along his jaw was bruised a hideous yellow, and he recalled delivering at least a few punches before he'd been blindsided with a pair of musket stocks to the back of his head.

Cabai nudged him, and when he looked, he pointed to the soup and biscuits. Rein ate slowly, unable to drag his gaze from her.

"We are in open water?" he said to Cabai. "Near London?"

He nodded. "You have been unconscious for nearly a week." Rein could see the toll it had taken on his wife. She looked thinner, her cheekbones more prominent. Rein finished off the soup, then munched on a biscuit, staring at his feet.

She stirred, and his gaze jerked up. He smiled, watching her stretch, her body bowing and showing him her curves. She wore a simple homespun skirt and blouse, and naught else from what he could see.

"What are you doing out of bed?" she said, sitting up and nearly banking her head on the bunk casing.

"Watching you."

"You should be resting."

"You should eat something. You are thin, Michaela."

The thought of food made her stomach roll as she swung her legs over the side of the bed. "Then I won't have to wear my stays, will I?"

"You can prance naked for all I care."

"I do not prance."

He leaned out, taking her hand in his. "Yet you step around a subject we must discuss."

"There is naught—"

"Michaela."

"Nay, Rein." Her throat tightened. "I cannot." *I almost lost him,* she thought, and would not risk it again.

"We are at London's coast."

Her shoulders sagged. "I see."

"I meant what I said afore, Michaela."

She faced him, her eyes suddenly blazing. "Which time? The time you forbid me to spy, the time you admitted to trying to get me with child? Or making me choose you over the rebellion?"

"I forbade you to spy to keep you from being riddled with shot the instant you set foot in England. And you did choose your rebellion over me."

" 'Twas all I had!" she said, coming to stand before him. "You left me."

"I would have returned."

"And how long would that have been had I not found you? And you could have come home to me in a coffin, so do not speak of risk and safety, Rein."

Guilt skipped over his features. "You are right."

She was gracious about the victory, and said, "And what of attempting to get me with child? Why would you be so under-handed?"

" 'Twas was not underhanded! I made no secret of wanting children with you. And you did not protest a single time we made love, Michaela."

Her lips quirked.

"The outcome is inevitable. And I admit, I did think motherhood would smother some of your infernal drive to spy for the Americans, but . . ."

"But what?"

"I was scared," came barely above a whisper.

She blinked, sinking to her knees before him.

He leaned closer, taking her hands in his. "I was terrified of losing you to your duty. Of losing you over mine. I wanted to bind you to me, wanted a chance to begin again with you. But the instant I sailed away, I knew that I already had what I desired most, a woman to love, who accepted me and would stand by me. But I'd failed you." He pressed his lips to her forehead, briefly closing his eyes. "I wanted to kill my sire for the pain of my life, for making me hurt you." He met her gaze. "When 'twas me who kept it, brewed it. And then inflicted it on others. On you."

"And now?"

"I have no more energy to waste on him." He touched her hair, her cheek, feathery touches she missed so much. He bent, his face near. "I want to spend it on loving you." Eyes locked, and he whispered, "I love you, my *rasha.*"

"I love you," she murmured against his lips.

"Am I forgiven?" He caught her lower lip between his teeth briefly.

"Do you forgive me for being—"

"Stubborn? Argumentative?"

Her gaze flicked to his, her smile against his mouth. "Aye." Her hands moved to his thighs. "Kiss me, Rein, before I die from wanting."

"We cannot have that." He laid his mouth over hers, kissed her deeply, slowly, cradling her face in his hands.

"Touch me, please, my love, I have missed it so."

He thumbed open her shirt, pushing it off her shoulders and

enfolding her breast. She moaned and arched into the tender pressure, her hands moving up his thighs.

"I want you, now."

"But your back?" Still she kissed him, still her hands roamed higher. "Oh! I see the injuries are not here."

He chuckled and eased her onto his lap, her thighs straddling his. He drove his hands under her skirt, cupping her buttocks, smoothing her thighs, then, leaning out, his lips hovering over her nipple. His gaze flicked up and he loved the look of anticipation on her face. He took her nipple deep into the hot suck of his mouth. She gasped and offered him more, frantically opening his breeches as he suckled one, then the other, laving languidly. Her nimble fingers closed over him and he nearly came out of the chair.

She stroked the slick tip of him against her softness, her breathing increasing with every lush touch. "This is decadent."

"You are decadent," he said rocking her, her dewy folds sliding over his arousal. "Oh, God, I never thought to feel you again. I missed you, I love you. Oh, Michaela," he groaned as she guided him inside her.

Smiling down at him, her hands braced on the back of the chair, she rose and sank, her eyes fluttering closed. His hands were everywhere, playing and arousing, his mouth tasting her sweet flesh as she lifted and plunged.

But they could not be contained, passion renewed and erupting like a galestorm, and he grasped her hips, feeling their motion, the heat of her grasping him, flexing and pulling, and he greeted her with abandon, uncaring of the sting in his back, and thrust deeply. Eyes clashed and locked as she pushed into him, her scent and skin enveloping him, and he saw her pleasure, felt it grip him, and when she begged for his heat, his energy, he gave it, jamming her down, rocking and fusing. He thought he would cease breathing, cease living, then it came, the hot rush of her feminine muscles, rippling, taking him over the edge of delicious pain and into rapture. He would follow her, always. She possessed his soul, would take it from this life into the next and he would love her, he knew, for centuries past. Without her, he was lost. With her, he was alive, and when she chanted her love, kissed his mouth with unleashed hunger, Rein knew he had come home again.

And he would never be parted from her again.

* * *

From the chair, Rein watched her bathe, finding the toilette utterly fascinating. "You are out of time, aren't you? The *Victoria* may have sailed already."

"Mayhap. If Uncle has not found a ship, then the rebels will have naught to worry over."

"He found one, I would wager a diamond on it." What was it about wet skin that drove him mad, he wondered as she dragged the soapy rag over her breasts.

"I am not certain Nickolas will have time to stop him anyway."

"Then *we* must stop *him.*"

Her gaze snapped to his. "I beg your pardon?"

"I have two ships here, Michaela. That's as much gun power as the *Victoria* would have."

"Are you serious?"

"I would not offer if I was not."

Her smile lit her entire face, and she reached out, grasping his shirtfront and pulling him down to meet her mouth. "Thank you, my love."

"I will expect a reward for such daring." His fingertips slicked over her nipple, and he heard her indrawn breath.

"Oh, aye. Many rewards." She kissed him. "Many." Then she released him and tended to her bath.

"You wish to see Nickolas, do you not?"

She shook her head. "Nay. I'd planned to send a missive, then return to Sanctuary."

"And do what?"

She looked at him. "Wait for you."

"You would give up, when you are so close?" He waved toward the windows, toward the sea.

"Of course not. But after the lies I'd spun in Morocco, when I reach England I will be sought for more than treason." Her gaze softened on him. "And I would not risk losing you, Rein, never again."

The muscles in his chest clamped a vise on his heart just then. "Then I think 'tis time we appeared as husband and wife."

She blinked. "Now I know you are not serious."

He arched a brow, his lips twitching. "Cabai should return with

my clothes any moment, and the carriage arrives in an hour. So
unless you want to parade on my arm naked for the whole of Lon
don . . ."

He laughed as she splashed him, then scrambled from the tub
his gaze roaming over her plush, wet figure. London could wait
he thought, leaving his chair and moving toward her.

Thirty-eight

Rumors flew about the city.

Michaela Denton had been freed from her kidnappers and she
was seen in the constant company of Rein Montegomery. Had he
hunted for her? Paid her ransom and won her heart? Were they
wed? Lovers? Who took her and why? Why didn't her uncle do
anything for the pitiful girl? Wasn't it shameless how they were
seen at the most elegant restaurants, in shops and racing to his
brownstone like little heathen children. People were aghast at their
open displays of affection, the way he touched her with such sensuality and how she had eyes only for him. He spared no expense,
in carriages and footmen, nor in the ring he designed himself for
her. And nay, he did not commission it from the finest jewelers in
London, but some Jewish man, paying an exorbitant price to have
the piece completed by nightfall. It was reputed to be breathtaking,
and, aye, she did cry when he slipped it on her finger. Lady Heyward would swear to it.

He never left her side, not for an instant, refusing even the slightest encroachment on their privacy. And wasn't he a sport to take
her shopping, carry all those parcels. And didn't she look lovely
last night?

Rein knew of the talk, had more than his share of nosy questions,
and as he relaxed in the chair, watching seamstresses flit around
his wife as if she were a queen, he knew she was receiving only
a portion of the attention Denton had denied her these past three
years. He intended to give her back all that the bastards had stolen,

and was eager for a confrontation. Soon the word of their marriage would reach the Brigadier. And Winters.

The burden of the gold shipment was now on Nickolas, yet the look on his face when Michaela offered his ships was priceless. Rein's brows drew down. They still had no notion if Denton had found a ship yet. And the *Victoria* had been mysteriously delayed.

"Rein," she pleaded, and he focused, smiling. They were hovering over her, pinning and pinching fabric and more than their share of her skin.

"Enough."

The women froze, looking wide eyed at him.

Michaela bit the inside of her mouth to keep from smiling. They all looked like frightened deer before a hungry wolf. He left the chair, and she watched him come to her, her heart picking up pace with every long-legged step.

She cocked her head. "I rather like it up here. First time I do not have to crane my neck to look at you."

He brought her hand to his lips, kissing her palm. "I will stoop from now on, my love."

The maids sighed dreamily.

She shoved his shoulder. "You will do no such thing."

"Whatever you say, my love."

Out of anyone's vision but his, she crossed her eyes.

Rein grinned. "Ample gowns?"

"I should say so." Around them lay four completed, a dozen more commissioned, along with matching undergarments and slippers for each. "There are not enough days to wear them."

He pulled her down off the pedestal and into his arms. "There will be centuries, my *rasha*," he said, then kissed her, lightly, softly. And Michaela touched her fingertips to his healed jaw, the slide of her tongue over his lips a promise of more. The young girls gathering fabric and tapes giggled and left them alone.

He exhaled through clenched teeth, muttering a curse and putting her from him. "Go change, please, I am starved." He ordered the parcels delivered to the brownstone and was pacing the shop when she finally appeared. "Damn me, I thought I would have to search for you in there." He waved to the fitting room and all the frippery men were kept in secret about.

" 'Twas your suggestion to have me pinned in gowns all morning, Rein."

He draped her cloak over her shoulders and whispered in her ear, "I want to get you unpinned and out of that one. Now."

"Well, then." Her smile was devilish. "We best be about it, eh?" She grabbed his hand, pulling him from the shop. "Before Madame talks you into buying the building, instead of shopping in it," she muttered, and they stepped into the waiting carriage. Instantly, he pulled her into his arm, kissing her warmly, then snuggling her against him as the carriage rolled toward the house. For a mile or two, he enjoyed the silence, holding her, unaware of the stares and pointing fingers directed at them.

"I feel bad for Cassandra, being sent away like that." She yawned hugely, patting her mouth.

"I'd heard Captain McBain agreed to escort her."

She tipped her head, smiling. "That should be interesting for her. She loathes the man." Burrowing into his side, she was asleep in seconds, and he carried her from the carriage into the house, going directly to their bedroom. She stirred awake, insisting she was fine, but Rein stripped her out of the gown and tucked her in bed. She fell back to sleep within minutes. Frowning, he touched her forehead, felt her pulse, then decided it was simply the excitement.

Hours later, Michaela woke with a jolt, dashing from the bed and retching into the chamber pot. Instantly she knew the reason behind her fatigue, her tender breasts. She had been with Agnes through her last child enough to know. She splashed water on her face, rinsed her mouth, then summoned Cabai to help her dress. This would be a special night, she thought. And she would have fun teasing him about getting his wish.

The lobby of the Royal Theater on Drury Lane went suddenly quiet.

Heads turned.

"Oh, dear," Michaela said. "This is rather peculiar."

"Not to me."

She looked up at him, sympathy in her smile. "It must have
been difficult having everyone whisper and point."

He shrugged. "One becomes accustomed."

"Well, I stared because you are so bloody handsome."

He actually blushed, and she laughed.

"And you looked at me with that I-wish-she-were-not-wearing-
-stitch look."

He leaned close and pressed his lips to her temple. "That's exactly what it was." He met her gaze, his eyes velvety warm.

"There it is again."

He tried hard not to grin, but couldn't stop it. She was undoubt-
edly the most beautiful woman in the room, and though he noticed
the men staring at her, she didn't. And across the room, Rein saw
Sheppard nudge Heyward, who nudged Burgess, who nudged whoever was beside him. For that, he received a slap with a fan from
his wife.

"Prepare yourself. Lord Heyward is coming with half of Parliament."

"I like him. He's sweet. Pudgy. Reminds me of dough rising."
Rein was laughing foolishly as Michaela greeted Lord Heyward
with a smile. She elbowed him, and he focused.

"So you did go after her."

"Of course."

"I did not doubt it," Sheppard said.

"Really, m'lord?" Michaela glanced between her husband and
his lordship.

"Aye, he was frantic to find you. Where did you say you found
her, by the by?"

"I didn't."

Sheppard reddened, and his wife pinched him. "Ah, I understand. Tell us, though, did the Brigadier—"

"Did not meet to deliver the ransom," Rein said, his words
clipped. "I did, followed them, and took her back." He looked
down at his wife. "I would have given everything to see her safe."

Ladies Heyward and Sheppard sighed. "May we see it? The
ring. I hear it's positively splendid."

Michaela smiled and lifted her hand. The women sighed and
ahhed, and Michaela resisted the urge to tuck her hand away. The
ring was private, Rein's love in the two entwined gold bands, one

studded with rare pale-blue diamonds, the other emeralds. She me
his gaze. It was the inscription that stole her breath: *My freedon
is loving you.*

"Gad, you two. Don't even know we are here, do you?"

Rein grinned, not removing his gaze from her. "Nay, and I d
not care."

"Rein." She jerked on his arm, flushing. They laughed as th
bells rang, and they started moving with the crowd into the theater

"You aren't going to fall asleep on me again," Rein said wher
they were seated in the private box.

"Nay, I'm well rested. Still a bit hungry I'm afraid."

"After that horrendous meal?"

The orchestra began.

"Well, aye, that's true, but then . . ." She leaned close, holding
his face. The music climbed to a high crescendo, then lowering
just as Rein shouted, "What!"

Heads turned as he swept her into his arms and kissed her with
all the love spinning through his heart. He didn't care of the scan-
dal. Didn't care who saw them. He wanted to shout, then wanted
to keep the news secret. Theirs alone. His eyes burned as he kissed
her again and again.

Adam Whitfield sat in the next box, applauding slowly. "Good
show, Rein. Damn, I need a wife."

They didn't accept the invitations for a midnight meal, and nearly
ran to the carriage.

"I suppose it was cruel to tell you in public."

"Never," he said, smiling that sappy grin he'd worn all night.
"God of thunder, I love you," he rasped hoarsely, and she paused
on the carriage step to kiss him.

"I know." She ducked, and he followed.

"How do you feel?" His gaze swept her as he sat.

"Do not start coddling me."

She sounded like Aurora, he thought. "Humor me."

He tapped the roof, then shifted to sit beside her. She leaned
into his warmth and he covered her with a lap robe.

"Do you think he knows by now?"

"After luring Argyle away?" He scoffed. "We've shamed him

letting it be known he didn't try to pay your"—his lips
uirked—"ransom. And he did petition for your inheritance. No
ne I spoke with had heard about it, but the money, I'm sorry, love,
gone."

"It was my mother's anyway. But do I think whoever helped him
ke it is more powerful than either of us thought."

Sergeant Major Edward Townsend slid from his mount and
ushed up the theater steps. Winded and harried, he paused to
earch the crowd, then tapped Lord Sheppard and tipped a careless
ow. "The Montegomerys, have you seen them?"

Lady Sheppard frowned. "They left as soon as the curtain went
own. In each other's pockets. 'Twas terribly darling to see—"

"How long?" he interrupted.

Lady Sheppard blinked, then glanced at her husband. "A half
our at least, wouldn't you say, dear?"

Sheppard nodded, his expression concerned, and he stepped
loser to the sergeant major. "Something amiss?"

"I fear, m'lord. Did the guards attend?"

"Nay, they followed only moments ago."

Rusty bowed and left, mounting his horse and riding off. Had
ue not been outside Mabel's tavern to see the armed coach, he
vould never have suspected. And now, with such a head start, he
eared he would not reach them in time.

The gunshots came out of a serene silence. "Down on the floor!"
Rein ordered, withdrawing his pistols, grabbing for the two others.
Michaela slid. He looked out the window just as another dozen
shots fired, lighting the tree line with smoke and flashes of light.
The driver fell with the footman. The coach heaved forward, throw-
ing him against the squabs, tipping the rear wheels off the ground.

"They've shot the horses," he said. Where were the riders, his
guards? They should have heard this. Rein felt trapped, outnum-
bered and damned angry. "Stay there." He kicked open the door
and fired, taking down a soldier, and instantly Rein knew who had
perpetrated this. Michaela handed him another pistol. She sat huddled on the floor reloading another when the opposite door opened.

Rein stilled, his hands up. "Don't shoot!" He could not ris'
them firing into the coach, not with his wife there. Smoke drifte¢
around the conveyance, and he stepped out, turning to Michaela
He admired the lack of fear in her eyes, only rage as she looke¢
past him. Rein followed her gaze and saw the Brigadier and Win
ters, surrounded by several troops, move from the tree line. In a¤
instant, Rein realized his guards were either dead or detained.

Michaela stepped down from the coach. "You cannot possibly
think to get away with this?"

His smile was thin for such a large man. "I have."

"You have no reason!"

"You know I do, Michaela, don't you?" He strolled forward an¢
she stared him down, refusing to give him anything. "You fooled
us all well, you know. I see naught of the clumsy gell who served
in my house."

"It was *my* house!" she hissed. "Do these men know you stole
from me? That you are penniless."

"Not anymore," he said in a voice so cruel and ugly, Michaela
didn't recognize him. "But you are aware of that, too, eh?"

He motioned with his pistol, and guards surrounded them.
Michaela whipped around and found four muskets aimed at Rein's
head. His expression didn't alter a fraction, yet his eyes held a
savage rage so potent, Michaela thought he would spend it on the
troops and get himself killed.

Denton grabbed her arm, yanking her from Rein's side.

"Unhand her now, Denton."

"You are not legally wed, no banns were posted. I am her guardian, I say who she will marry, and it will not be a half-breed bastard!" He pointed the gun, his aim falling off to the side as Michaela
struggled.

Rein took a step, his fists clenched. "Release my wife *now!*"
he roared.

"She is where she belongs, under my roof."

"You mean under your bloody fists!"

Denton's eyes flared. "How dare you!"

"I would dare much more than a few insults where my wife is
concerned. You have done naught but beat and steal from her for
three years."

"Those are harsh words, Montegomery." Winters stepped between them, pressing the blade of his sword to Rein's chest.

He stared at him, his eyes glacial with hatred. "You deserve to die for what you've done."

He spared a glance at Michaela. "Telling tales, darling."

"Rein, don't." She could feel the seething energy around him, almost see it darkening his skin, flutter his clothes.

Rein grabbed the sword, and Michaela gasped as he yanked it from Winters. For an instant the man stared wide-eyed at Rein's bloodless fist. Pistol hammers clicked like a resonating song around them.

"Don't shoot," Winters said with a feral grin.

Rein flipped the sword into fighting position. "Give him one." He nodded to another soldier.

"Do not do this for me, Rein. He has no hold over us."

"He pays tonight, my love."

Michaela's gaze shifted to Winters, then back to Rein, her love in her eyes, and understood he could not be swayed. If anything else happened tonight, he would deal the first blow.

Winters held out his hand, wiggling his fingers impatiently for a sword, and a soldier darted forward with one. He hefted it, then immediately struck. Rein caught it, his sword sliding down hilt to hilt, bringing him face to face with the man who had stolen his wife's dignity.

"I am going to enjoy this," he hissed.

"As much as I enjoyed your wife?"

Rein's eyes flared.

"She was a sweet virgin, Montegomery, tight and hot. I think she found it rather pleasing."

Rein did not respond to the taunt, letting his anger build, his energy sweep through him and into the hilt of the sword. He shoved. Winters went flying backward, stumbling. With a growl, Winters charged, and Rein lashed across his chest, severing open his coat and drawing first blood. Winters was an accomplished swordsman, but Rein was driven, the ring of metal to metal blistering the air. Sparks rained over them as Rein jabbed and struck, parèd, then struck again and again.

Vicious, unrelenting.

Avenging.

His blows vibrated down Winters's arm, causing him to falter his grip, and Rein struck blow after blow, fury unleashed. The major was winded. Rein looked composed except for the hatred on his face and he caught the major's sword against the hilt, swung his arm around, sending Winters's sword to the side, out of strike distance, then drove the blade into his heart.

Winters looked down at the sword, then to Rein. He fell to his knees, then onto his face.

Denton looked down at Winters, the blade protruding from his back. "Arrogant fool," he muttered, then looked at Montegomery. "Seize him."

Guards rushed forward, and Rein fought, his feet connecting with a jaw, a nose, a tender gullet. Strong hand gripped his arms, three more fought to hold him, grabbing his shirt, and in his fight, it tore, the medallion gleaming in the moonlight. From the shadows, Lord Germain strolled forward, stopping in front of Rein. He grabbed the medallion, then met his gaze.

Rein frowned, his gaze searching, and recognition dawned.

"Hello, Father."

Germain's features tightened with anger. He jerked the chain, breaking it, then pocketed the medallion. "Take him away," he ordered.

"Nay! Rein!"

Denton dragged her toward his coach.

"Michaela!" he howled, fighting the restraining hands.

She broke free, running, but before she could touch him, soldiers yanked her back.

They struggled to reach each other, gazes locked, his fear for her life in his eyes. "I love you. I will find you."

An instant later, someone struck him on the back of the head. He slumped, supported in the grip of soldiers, and she clawed to be free, to go to him.

"Rein. Wake up!" But she knew he wouldn't.

Denton nodded, and guards bound and gagged her, stuffing her in the coach. Denton and his niece rode off as Germain looked down at Montegomery, grabbing a fistful of black hair and yanking his head back. His gaze raked his features and he let him go with disgust.

"Take him to Newgate."

Thirty-nine

Rein threw back his head and howled, the anguished sound echoing throughout the empty cells surrounding him. He shook the bars, his eyes burning. Mortar sanded his hair. He didn't expect a response. No one knew he was here, the gaoler ignoring his calls for two days. Breathing heavy, he squeezed his eyes shut, praying to anyone who'd listen to keep his wife safe.

Thrusting away, he paced the tiny dank cell, his boots sloshing through the water coating the floor. Torment clawed up and down his spine, his heart refusing to cease its hard, thundering pound. Where was she? What had he done with her? Was she hurt? Had he killed her and dumped her body in the Thames? He drove his fingers through his hair, wincing at the fresh scrape and crusted blood. *Please be alive,* he chanted, his throat tight with sorrow.

He stilled, tipping his head toward the dripping ceiling and closed his eyes.

Michaela.

He concentrated, trying to sense her, sense anything beyond his surroundings, but nothing worked. This was a dead place and his fear stole his control.

And Rein knew what it was like to go very slowly insane.

Brigadier Atwell Denton stood on the deck, his stomach rolling, perspiration beading at his temples. He tugged his collar, the restraint of it magnifying his need to vomit, and he was glad it was night so none would see the shade of green of his skin. He'd hoped the years had relieved him of this aliment, and it grated on his pride. Richard, on the other hand, was far better at sailing. Then, Richard had always shown him up. Even as children.

He smiled to himself, taking a seat in the bench behind th
wheel. Cool air skated over his face, ruffling the tufts of hair. Ricl

ard, my dear brother, he thought with a smile, what would he think if he knew his precious daughter had betrayed the Crown. Or that he was financing this entire mission?

Richard's daughter had been a surprise, her backbone, that she had fooled them all for so long. Clumsy chit, he thought. It was damned convenient of her to get herself kidnapped, though. Saved him from worrying how he'd get those drafts signed. She was not worth such a price, inadequate servant, but the ransom note was enough to get his hands on the accounts. But then, to find her wed to that heathen bastard was beyond consideration. Damn the gell for refusing Winters and then bedding down with Montegomery. Proved she was mad.

And stupid, he decided, then glanced at Germain. Damn but the man had a stiff posture, and he wondered what he'd done with Montegomery. He wouldn't say, wouldn't discuss the matter. All the better, he thought. He didn't want to meet up with Montegomery, especially not at sea.

Rein looked up at the sound of footsteps. His back braced against the wall, he waited for them to draw closer, though in the past hours, past days, they never had. He cursed and listened, then looked up as a shadow moved against the opposite wall. He stiffened as Lord Germain moved before the cell door.

Rein stared into the eyes of his father, disgusted that he was a part of this man, that he'd taken his comments at the Denton party as truth.

"Hello, Father."

Germain stiffened. "Don't call me that."

" 'Tis true, is it not?" Rein pushed away from the wall, moving closer. "If it is not, then free me."

"And have you spout to the world you are my son?" He shook his head. "You are no more than a mistake, Montegomery. The result of a moment of careless lust with a Hindu slut that has haunted me for years. Why couldn't you have simply died in that mine?"

Rein clenched his fists, his features impassive as he stared into eyes the same shade as his own. It was the only resemblance, thank the gods. And he realized Germain's words did not strike the pain he desired. "I learned to survive there. I suppose I should thank you." Rein inched a bit closer to the bars, enjoying the man's flinch. "I am here, and that scares you."

Germain made a disgusted face.

"You couldn't kill me with your own hand."

Germain braced his hands behind his back, his posture straight. "What do you want from me?"

Rein's eyes narrowed with a sinister gleam. "To kill you."

Germain scoffed. "You can't touch me. No one can."

Rein shrugged. Arrogant fool, he thought. "You are not worth the bother."

Rein knew what he'd always known, what he realized as he'd sailed from Sanctuary, from the people who loved him. Blood was not thicker than water. Family came from love and caring and not from the seed that made you.

"Where is my wife?"

Germain smiled thinly. "You will die here, Montegomery." He turned away, yet stilled at Rein's words.

"Do not be so certain, my lord. You thought the same over three decades ago."

Germain looked back over his shoulder.

"And if my wife is harmed, it is you who will die."

Germain let his gaze cover him from head to toe, then clashed with his bastard son's. "She is dead. The Guardian is dead, hung this morn for treason."

Rein clenched the bars. It was not true. He would know.

He would.

Ahh, Goddess, he begged, pressing his forehead to the bars. *Help me.*

Ransom Montegomery handed over the sack of coins, then withdrew his pistol. The turnkey's eyes swelled wide, and Ran's gaze shifted between the gaoler and turnkey. He gestured with the barrel. He followed them down corridor after corridor, deeper into the belly of the prison. Hands grabbed at him through the bars, and he shrugged them off, the common room full of prisoners enjoying smuggled gin barely sparing him a glance. He looked around with disgust, thinking of a time when Rein had been a boy, trapped in the sultan's palace, and once freed, defended his back better than any of his seasoned crewmen. He was a brave child then, a survivor. And Ransom had long ago known this need to find his blood father brewed in him. He hadn't wanted Rein to find him, afraid he'd take him from him. 'Twas selfish, he knew, but Rein was special to him.

The turnkey stopped before a narrow cell. He peered inside. Rein sat against the wall, his knees bent, elbows braced there, his head in his hands. Ransom's heart shifted in his chest. He understood his torment of not knowing where his wife was, if she was hurt or dying. Or even dead.

"Rein!" he called, and his son's head jerked up. Ahh, God above, he thought, so tormented. "Having a bit of trouble, I see."

Rein offered a weak smile as he stood. "A bit."

Ransom waved to the turnkey, and the obese man lumbered to unlock the door. Stone to stone grated as it swung open. They stared, and Ran's gaze swept his face, the dark circles under his eyes, then the blood staining his shirt.

"Did you find what you needed?"

"Nay."

Ransom frowned.

"I'd had it all along."

Ransom's eyes glassed, and Rein stepped forward.

"Can you forgive me, Father?"

Ransom wrapped his arms around him, patting his back as he had when he had nightmares as a child. "Aye, my son, aye." Ran leaned back, gripping his shoulders. "Come, let us find your wife."

"Is she all right?" he said, and heard the desperation in his own voice. "Germain said she was dead. They . . . hung her."

Ran's features tightened, thinking of the torture he'd suffered believing that. "No one has been hung in a week, Rein. Nickolas would have known." His son looked as if he'd pass out with relief, he thought. "Germain might have power, but he wouldn't hurt her. Blood on his hands he can't wipe away is far different than an attack on a payroll ship." He squeezed his shoulders. "We will find her, Son."

Rein found comfort in his father's words and they headed quickly back up the corridor. "How did you know?" He waved to the prison walls.

"With your mother, you can still ask that?"

For the first time in days, a faint smile curved his lips.

"Your back healed, by the by?"

Rein shook his head and quickened his pace, nearly running to the gates, to freedom, his father paving the way with sacks of gold and bottles of gin.

With a forged set of orders, Sergeant Major Townsend performed his last official act for the Crown and with his wife-to-be safely with the Montgomerys, he stepped onto the pier and ordered half the troops guarding the vessels back to the barracks, double time. The other half he sent to a few select members of Parliament with missives implicating Germain, Denton, Winters, the bloody rotter, Prather, and Rathgoode in the attack on the *Victoria*. By the time they understood, they would all be at sea.

He followed the squad of troops as far as the second block past the pier, then turned back. He rode hard, hooves clattering on the wooden docks. The ship already underway, he slid from the mount and raced up the gangplank.

Rusty sagged to a crate, trying to catch his breath. "Gad, I'm too old for this."

"Do not tell your fiancée that," Rein said as he passed, inclining his head behind him. Rusty turned to see Mabel moving toward him, fresh clothes in her arms. He stood and stripped off the uniform coat, throwing it over the side of the ship, then taking her in his arms and kissing her.

Rein climbed to the quarterdeck. He opened the spyglass, watching his father climb from the longboat and board the *Islander*. They were at full sail, and it was going to be hard to get out of the harbor without scraping a few hulls. Nickolas was aboard the *Sentinel*, with Temple, but that was only fourteen cannons. The *Islander* was built for comfort and pleasure, yet gunned with only eight cannons. The *Empress* had twenty. Forty-two to the *Cavalier*'s twenty-four seemed decent enough odds. But then, he had to question whether the *Victoria*'s captain would band with Denton and follow Germain's orders. They would be facing fifteen more guns then. He was counting on skill to aid them.

Except the *Victoria* had an escort with unknown cannon power. And he suspected Michaela was aboard the *Cavalier*.

At least that's what they had to assume. She had, again, vanished.

Rein closed the spy glass, his fist so tight around it that he nearly fractured the lens. His throat worked, his Adam's apple shifting like sand.

I will find you, my love. Hold on.

Forty

Rein ceased barking orders three hours ago. He could not make the ship move any faster, beg for more wind. And his torment was private. His imagination was running mad, believing Denton had left her to the lust of his men, then believing her dead for two days had destroyed his resolve and it was difficult regaining it. He'd cried like a child, wept for the woman he loved, for all the bright smiles he would miss, her teasing and candid talk. And for the child she would bear.

He had to recognize the risks her captivity involved, that she could lose their unborn child, that if Denton suspected, he would beat it out of her, for the sake of its father. If she lacked food, water, anything—God, he didn't want to consider it, and Rein focused on Michaela, her survival, her life.

Never in his life did he think he could love someone so much. She was his breath, his release from his past. He felt whole and fulfilled with her. Every time he looked at her, he saw something new, a different expression, a glitter in her eyes. He adored the way she cocked her head and considered before she spoke. Most times. And her passion was unceasing, vibrant. Captivating him, snaring him in body and soul. He remembered every detail, her scent and taste, the silky feel of her hair through his fingers, the devilish look in her eyes when she told him she carried his child.

Rein breathed deeply, closing his eyes and desperately reaching for the domination of his emotions that had ruled him for years. For if he had needed it before, now her life depended on it. Suddenly, he left the quarterdeck, making his way to his cabin. He could not take this uncertainty. He had to know where she was before he fired his first shot.

"Ship ahoy!" the crow shouted, and Germain spared a glance at the officers. "Go below if you are going to be of little use, Denton."

"I am fine."

"You look positively ashen."

"I know. Damn it, man, have a little sympathy."

Germain's pale eyes turned feral, biting, and Denton frowned, seeing something familiar in the stare, yet unable to grasp it. "Not in war."

Denton's brows tightened. Rathgoode stroked his mustache. Prather rubbed his sleeves. Yet all three stared at Germain. "This is not war, your lordship. We run blockade, give her chance for quarter, and board."

Germain spared a look over his shoulder. "I intend to remain Secretary of the State of War, General."

Denton looked at the others, then Germain's back. He swallowed.

He was going to kill everyone, and Denton felt a chill up over his spine. Did that include them?

"Rein?" Leelan whispered, not wanting to disturb him, but forced. He sat on the floor, cross-legged, pots before him, a candle burning. Rahjin lay under the aft bench. The heat in the room was stifling, and Leelan feared he would catch the walls again. The pots spilled, water boiled, warm air spun through the room, mixing, blending.

Rein lifted his arms, letting the cultivated energy take him, control him, spend him.

Goddess of fire, earth, wind, water, help me, let me see her.

For several moments, he was motionless, sweat dripping down his bare back, his head tipped. Still—in a room full of movement.

Then he lowered his arms, his smile slow, and when the air died, he turned his head and looked at Leelan.

"She's alive. And she's on the *Cavalier*."

Leelan grinned, his eyes suspiciously bright. "Ahh, God, Rein, that's grand. Grand. 'Cause there be a ship or two off starboard bow."

Rein hopped to his feet, snatching up his shirt and scabbard as he moved. Above decks, Rein sighted the *Cavalier,* and beyond her, the *Victoria.* Rein swung around, looking behind. The *Sentinel* and the *Islander* were a mere league behind them. He smiled when he saw his father on the deck, grinning. *Damn me, he is eager for this.*

Rein swung back around, adjusting the glass. If he could see them, then they could see him.

Germain spied the ships, cursing under his breath, then calling for battle stations. "Denton, get your niece," he ordered.

"What!"

"Montegomery is coming for her."

Denton whirled around. "God save us. I thought you took care of him."

"Obviously not well enough."

"What do you want of her?"

"He wouldn't dare fire on us with her in harm's way."

"Don't count on it, sir."

"He loves her, he wouldn't dare—"

Prather cleared his throat. "Then you don't know Montegomery, sir. He won't have to fire much. He's like his father."

Germain whipped around, his gaze pinning all three. "What do you know?"

Prather shifted his feet. "He's spent his life at sea. Sailed with the Red Lion."

"That means little."

"Alone, mayhap, but the stories I've heard . . ." Germain's irritation showed what he thought of such tales.

"Mayhap we should get the *Victoria*'s captain to defend."

"We will." Germain turned back. Three to three. This, he thought, should be interesting. "Ensign Lackland, signal the *Victoria* and her escort, tell them who is aboard this vessel and that we are about to be attacked. We need assistance." His voice lowered, and he glanced down and to his side. "In the fracas, we will seize the *Victoria*. We trade ships." He scanned the decks. "Get her."

Denton stood, his gullet threatening to cough up the biscuits he'd managed to consume earlier. He lumbered to the stairs and headed for the forward hatch.

Michaela bolted upright when she heard the hatch rattle and smacked her head against the ceiling. Wincing, she dropped her head forward until the pain subsided. Her wrist throbbed against the ropes, her stomach growling for food. She hadn't seen a soul since she'd been dumped her days ago, food and water left behind, forcing her to grub like an animal or starve. The hatch sprung, sunlight blaring down at her, and she turned her face away, blinking. Instantly, she recognized her uncle maneuvering down into the hole.

"Get up."

"Go to bloody hell."

He snickered, his booted feet landing near her. He grabbed her arm, dragging her forward, then hoisting her to her feet. Her head spun from lack of food, her mouth unbearably dry. He turned her around, cutting her bonds. Michaela rubbed her wrists, watching his face.

Her voice was soft when she asked, "Why did you do this?"

"A fortune, woman, now get moving."

"Why did you treat me so horribly, Uncle? What did I ever do to you?"

"Don't go all melancholy." He moved toward the hatch.

She grabbed his arm, jerking him back. "You owe me!"

He pulled free, meeting her gaze. "You were born."

"What!"

His gaze roamed over her face, and Michaela never thought to see such a look from him, tender, almost loving.

"Damn, but you look just like her."

"Mother?" Her father had said as much when she was younger, that the resemblance kept his wife alive.

"Elizabeth was a beautiful, graceful woman." His expression said she did not compare. "She was far too good for Richard."

Michaela searched his face, the uncharacteristic tenderness in his eyes. "You loved her!"

Denton's expression clouded. "I—I—did not." He turned away, but she latched on to his coat and forced him to remain.

"This is why you have been so hateful, taking my money?"

"It was mine!" he shouted, all semblance of gentleness gone. "She should have married me. She was going to marry me until Richard returned from school, the bastard. He stole her, wooed her right out from under my nose whilst I was at duty."

"If she truly loved you, he never could have won her away."

"What do you know! You killed her!"

Realization dawned. "Mother did not die birthing me, Uncle. She died of malaria when I was seven."

His eyes flared with his shock.

"You have misplaced your rage."

"It no longer matters," he scoffed, pulling her along.

"What would Mother think if she knew how you have treated me, that you let Winters rape me in my own bedroom!" He looked as if he might be ill, Michaela thought, but three years of anger boiled to the surface. "She knows." He paled. "She looks down upon us, Uncle, and she knows you did naught to stop him, that you chose not to believe my account because you were still hurting over being jilted years before. Over something you could never change!" She looked at him with utter disgust. "So petty, such a pitiful, desolate man you are."

His gaze thinned as he studied her. "What would she say if she knew you wed a half-breed bastard?"

"She would not judge for the color of his skin or the lineage of his parents. She would be pleased, Atwell. Thrilled beyond repair that I have loved in my life as she loved my father."

Denton's arm jerked up to strike her, and Michaela stared him without flinching. His hand never met the mark, his arm lowering slowly.

"My husband will come for me."

"He already has."

Relief and excitement lit her features.

"He will not win, gell." His expression twisted, a reckless instability in his eyes.

Minutes later, Michaela understood his intent, and from the mainmast, watched the *Empress*'s rapid approach. The three ships positioned for battle, and she wondered if she had gotten this close only to see her husband die.

* * *

The *Sentinel, Islander,* and the *Empress* formed a line of defense. Lighter, with empty holds and less cannon weight, they maneuvered more easily than the heavily loaded *Victoria* and *Cavalier.* Yet the escort ship was armed solely for protection. And Rein decided that would be the first ship to disable. Then the *Cavalier.* Ran, he, and Nick had agreed earlier that they would spare the *Victoria* and her complement, but for the revolution, the arms would be taken.

The *Victoria* and her escort were out of firing range, and Rein signaled the *Sentinel.* Nickolas, he knew, was eager to give chase to the cache of rifles and cannons that would eventually kill his countrymen. The *Sentinel* headed for the weapons.

Rein focused on the *Cavalier,* bringing the glass to his eye and scanning the decks. There were few men, a half complement to what a ship that size would normally retain. He swept the deck, then jerked the glass back, to the center.

His heart jumped in his chest, then dropped to his knees.

Michaela was lashed to the mainmast. In clear view, a taunt, assurance that they would not be fired upon. *They will pay for this dearly,* he thought, trying to see if she was injured. He focused on Germain, his smile smug, his hands braced behind his back as he stared back at him as if he were naught but a few feet in front of him.

Rein looked over at the *Islander,* and could tell his father had realized the same. Ransom went after the escort, to delay her, for the *Islander* was vastly undergunned.

Rein tapped the glass against his lips.

"Fire on the quarterdeck," he said to the bos'un. "Do not let a single shot hit the main deck. Below the water line we aim. No grapeshot or langrage, 'tis too inaccurate."

Popewell departed, calling orders, and the word filtered down to the gun decks below.

"Mr. Veslic, signal the *Islander* the same." Rein handed the glass to Leelan.

The older man sighted, and cursed under his breath. "Sweet Jesu! He's a friggin' coward."

"He's crafty. And he's assuming I won't attack." Leelan swung around to look at him. "Accuracy, man. Bring her close enough for it." He would not waste ammunition on the sea.

Leelan spun the wheel, calling for adjustment of jib and halyard

"Fire at will!" Rein commanded, and the *Empress* listed with the jolt, smoke and ball erupting from the hull like dragon fire. Cannons rumbled beneath the decks. He watched through the glass, trying not to look at Michaela's frightened expression when the shots rocked the *Cavalier,* shattering wood and bodies. Men scrambled, and Rein realized that the British crewmen did not deserve to perish for greed they were not aware of as he ordered Leelan to sail the *Empress* alongside.

"You cannot be serious!" Leelan shouted. "They will have range!"

"Full sail. They are heavy, Leelan. Come on, show a bit of spirit. Look."

He did. The *Victoria* did not remain behind to aid the *Cavalier.* It was sailing out to sea. The escort was under the *Sentinel's* attack as the *Empress* turned, sliding smoothly closer and closer to the *Cavalier.*

Rein could see the gunners rolling out cannons. "Fire at the cannoniers." The blasts ripped above the water line of the *Cavalier,* shaking her masts, tipping her leeward with a tremendous shudder and spilling cannons into the sea. Yet the *Empress* kept coming. The *Cavalier* fired, ten guns at once. Four shots met their mark, cracking the bowsprit of the *Empress* and sending it into the sea. Yet the *Empress* advanced, hull to ram, then turned sharply, listing, and Rein left the quarterdeck, climbing over debris and men to the mainmast.

"Closer, Leelan!"

"Damn fool-hearted man," he muttered and spun the wheel. Rein climbed the rigging, grasping a pair of ropes. Across the distance, Rein met Germain's gaze over the smoking decks. The man had not flinched, standing back and shouting orders. Rein ordered the quarterdeck hailed with gunfire. Germain did not move as the area sprayed with shot. He grinned at Rein, tipping a bow as Prather and Rathgoode died at his feet.

Rein did not care, his attention shifting to Michaela.

She smiled weakly at him through her fear and the smoke.

Then he saw Denton moving toward her, a sword in his hand.

* * *

Ransom and Nickolas joined guns to attack the escort ship, the *Victoria* sailing swiftly out of range to avoid being boarded. Nickolas ordered constant shots fired, then maneuvered the *Sentinel* himself around the escort's bow and along the far side to draw range from the *Empress*. He looked back at the *Victoria* and cursed her evasion.

The escort fired, destroying the *Islander*'s mizzen. Men screamed, a few diving into the sea to avoid being burned to death. Yet the smaller *Islander* expelled her iron, smoke and fire spitting balls into the decks of the escort and, on the opposite side, Nickolas followed suit. In minutes, the escort dipped and took on water. Nickolas immediately turned the *Sentinel* into the wind to chase the *Victoria*.

Ransom stood on the prow and met the gaze of the captain of the escort. "Do you beg quarter?"

The captain's lips tightened, and he lashed the air with his sword. Able cannons roared like the growl of tigers, hitting the *Islander* broad side and nearly ripping her in half.

"Board, board, board!" The word filtered down on the *Empress* as the *Cavalier* fired, tearing a hole in the deck of the *Empress* that made her foremast sink into her belly. Rein grasped the ropes and swung out, sailing across the open sea, losing his pistols into the water, unaware as he landed near the mizzen. Sword in hand, he headed to quarterdeck, to Germain.

Michaela screamed a warning.

Through the thick smoke Rein saw Germain lift a pistol and take careful aim.

He reached for his own and found his supply gone. Germain smiled thinly, yet before the man could fire, he jerked to the side, cloth and flesh exploding from his ribs. Germain flinched, and Rein ducked as his shot went wide, scanning the area for his savior.

A hundred yards away, the *Galley Raider* advanced starboard, his brother Colin on the sprit, his feet braced for balance and a long rifle at his shoulder.

He saluted him, then shouted, pointing, and Rein turned just

as a man's sword sliced the air near his face. Rein caught it with
his own, throwing him off, then drove his blade deep into his
chest, shook him off and advanced, hacking his way toward the
mainmast, toward his wife.

But Denton was closer.

Ransom shouted for longboats to lower, the *Islander* taking on
water and sinking fast. Someone called out, and Ransom turned,
scowling at the ship heading toward them. Then he recognized
his son in the rigging and grinned. Damn the pirating puppy.

Michaela coughed against the smoke, turning her face away
from the stench of burning flesh. She begged men to free her,
but they ignored her demands, and when she saw her uncle moving closer, stumbling over debris, stepping on the backs of his
dead comrades, she knew he'd come to kill her.

Then she saw Rein behind him.

Her heart slammed.

He looked like a black dragon swooping down for the kill,
fighting with a vengeance, dispatching man after man and climbing over rubble, his expression harsh with rage and determination.
The sight of him made her renew her struggle against her bonds.
Hurry. He would not reach her before her uncle. She stretched
her leg, trying to reach a fallen man's sword as the crew of the
Empress lowered boarding planks across the sea and rolled onto
the deck of the *Cavalier* like ants to a picnic. Gunfire pinged in
the wood around her. She hunched. Her uncle neared, and she
stared in horror as he raised the sword above her head.

"Uncle, I beg you—!"

"Michaela!" Rein screamed, his terror ripping through the
smoke filled air as Denton brought the sword down, slicing the
ropes. Her freedom sudden, Michaela fell forward, catching herself on the capstan.

Denton turned sharply to Rein, weapon raised in defense.

"Take her."

Michaela was already scrambling to her husband.

"Take her off here," he gasped, clutching his stomach, blood seeping through his fingers. "I would have something of Elizabeth . . . survive. Forgive me," he rasped, then fell to his knees, his eyes glazed with death.

Michaela turned her face into Rein's shoulder as Denton slumped to the bloody decks, then lifted her gaze to his. Oh, God, it was good to be this close to him again, to feel his heart beat.

"Hullo, husband," she said numbly, smoke tears dripping, her lip trembling. "Capital of you to arrive in time."

Smiling, he sketched her features, her dirty face, her wild hair and never thought he'd seen anything so beautiful in his life. "God of thunder, I thought I'd lost you," he choked, blinking back the burn in his eyes.

She touched his face, his emotion unveiled there. "Never," she whispered, and he kissed her quickly, then ushered her toward the mizzen rigging, urging her to climb.

"Are you all right? Did he hurt you?"

"I am fit enough, though hungry as all bloody hell." He grinned down at her, helping her up to the crossjack. "What are you doing?"

Balancing on the crossjack, he looped a rope around her ankle and beneath her foot. "We have to get to the *Empress,* this one is sinking."

"Oh, nay." She shook her head, looking across the sea. "Can't we take the planks?" Just as she spoke, the ships divided, the slats falling to the water.

He grasped the ropes, then wrapped his arm around her. "Trust me?"

"Of course."

He lurched off, her scream muffled against his shoulder, her fists in his shirt as they swung across. Steady hands caught them as they twisted over the quarterdeck, helping them free. Rusty smiled at her, yet Rein didn't spare a second, pulling her into his arms and covering her mouth with his own. His hands drove up her back, grinding her to his body, and she pressed into him, plowing her fingers through his hair, holding him for more.

"I love you, I love you," she chanted against his lips.

"Oh, Michaela, I thought I never . . . oh great thunder . . ."

His voice fractured, and he cradled her head to his shoulder, squeezing her, his body wracked with hard shudders.

But the sound of cannon fire drew them around.

Immediately, Rein ordered the *Empress* to approach, the *Victoria* and the *Sentinel,* still in heated battle, the *Galley Raider* gathering up the *Islander*'s men from the water, while offering cover fire from the still attacking escort brig. Rein kept her at his side. Behind them the *Cavalier* was sinking, the longboats dropping into the water. He offered quarter to the survivors.

The ship neared, and Michaela could see Nickolas's arm raised to give order to fire all guns again.

Michaela tore from Rein's arms and rushed to the rail, climbing to the ledge. "Nickolas, nay! The gold stays!"

Across the distance, Nickolas looked at her, scowling. "Are you mad!" he roared. "This gold will buy arms and clothing and food. We will win then!"

She grabbed a pistol from Leelan and leveled it at him. "The arms and naught more." She waved the barrel at the destroyed ships. "They did only as ordered. They may not make it, but we give them the chance." The surrounding noise lessened, attention riveted to her. "Prove we are more tolerant, that we strive for better with our fight, not more of the same. Taking food and clothing from wives and children is not in our cause. There is no liberation in cruelty, in stealing the dignity of the innocent. 'Tis England's way. Germain's way. We will win, for our cause is justice. We fight to be beholden to no one, for the choice, not more tyranny and *not* to make them all Americans!"

Nickolas faced her, still winded, and lowered his arm. He nodded.

Michaela sighed, the gun lax at her side.

And in that moment, Rein finally understood her drive for liberty, and he was infinitely proud of her, her compassion and valor, her courage when she, above all, had reason to seek vengeance.

"Here, here!" someone said into the silence, and then another joined, and Michaela looked around, blushing, sheepish, as the sailors and soldiers smiled at her.

"Cracking good," she muttered, hopping down from the rail. "I shall never live this down."

Chuckling softly at her embarrassment, Rein came to her, gripping her shoulders and pressing a gentle kiss to her forehead. "Wonderful oration, my love. I would follow you."

She tipped her head to look at him. "I don't want anyone to follow me."

His brows rose, his look of confused concern.

"I am done." She handed him the pistol as she looked around at the destruction, the smoking ships. She'd never been this close to war and hadn't the stomach for it. She met his gaze. "I threaten more than aid the rebellion. I cannot return to England and in the Colonies . . ." She shook her head. "England still occupies America, Rein. We both could be taken and tried for treason. And we cannot risk starting again there or we endanger our friends." She inclined her head to Nickolas. "Until England recognizes America's independence."

She looked so lost right now, he thought, brushing a strand from her cheek. "We have a home on Sanctuary or Madagascar, Michaela. Whatever you want, we will do."

Her sadness shifted to a look of pure pleasure. "Love me, Rein. For I have the energy to love only you."

"Thank the gods," he groaned, gathering her his arms and brushing his mouth over hers. "I love you."

Over his shoulder and across the water, she recognized Colin standing near Ransom. "However . . . there is one wrong I still must right . . ."

Frowning, Rein twisted, glancing between his brother and his wife's glowering look as she took the pistol and leveled it at Colin.

Colin's eyes widened.

Ransom gaped. "Rein! Control that woman!"

Rein moved alongside her, staring at her profile, how she squinted for aim. "What do you think you are doing?"

Colin folded his arms, daring her.

"Returning the fire you wouldn't because you love him. Well, I don't." She pulled the trigger and the shot hit the deck to the left of Colin's foot. He jerked back, his arms up.

His brother's curses ripped the air blue. Nickolas laughed, and the crews snickered.

Rein smothered his laugh with his hand. "You missed."

She spared him a look, her expression sly. "Did I say I *wanted* to hit him?"

Colin stared at her, his hands slowly lowering to his hips.

Michaela's chin tipped, her gaze full of challenge.

"Want another pistol, my love?" She was so damned righteous sometimes, and he loved her all the more for wanting to defend him.

She kept her gaze on Colin, yet smiled. "One is enough, I think, thank you."

Suddenly, Colin threw his head back and laughed, the rich sound floating across the water. "Damn me, Rein, I like her!"

Michaela scoffed, satisfied the stupid pirate knew he'd crossed the line those weeks past.

"You have that look about you."

She met his gaze, lips twitching. "And what look might that be?"

"That I-have-found-a-new-Montegomery-to-torment look." He nodded to Colin.

She cocked her head, studying her husband. "Nay, you are the only man I wish to vex," she said with a velvety look, the pistol swinging from her fingertip.

Grinning, Rein took the gun. "Good, can we start now?" he asked, passing the spent pistol to Leelan as he wrapped his arm about her waist, steering her toward the ladder, toward their cabin and privacy.

Her laugh was throaty deep as she stopped to kiss him, madly, so thoroughly his knees softened.

"You know, my rebel," he said, his voice far too breathless for a man his age as she left his arms and started down the ladder, "you point weapons at Montegomery men far too often."

She peered up over the edge of the quarterdeck, her smile wreathed in her love for him. "Ahh, but only once, Rein, have I aimed for the heart."

Epilogue

1783

Michaela slipped from the bed, padded across the room on bare feet to the nursery, and pushed open the door. She smiled, leaning against the frame.

Rein sat in a rocker near the window, the warm Carolina air shifting the sheers. He was talking to Jackson, whispering. She moved closer to hear.

"Did you see your mama tonight? She was the most beautiful woman in the room. And the only one, I might add, honored for her bravery, for her part in our country's independence. She was a spy, you know."

Jackson cooed, gazing adoringly with wide blue-green eyes, chubby feet kicking. "Oh, you didn't? I could have sworn I mentioned that."

He rocked the baby, touching his tiny fingers, nibbling on his toes.

"You will know freedom, my son. Because of people like your mother and Uncle Nickolas."

"And you, my love," she whispered.

He twisted, his surprise melting into a tender smile.

"I cannot forget how you joined us even when you did not understand why."

He looked affronted. "I did."

She smiled. "Liar." She came to him, taking Jackson and settling into the window seat. She opened her gown and put the baby to her breast.

Rein propped his bare feet on the seat beside her and sighed with utter contentment.

In the next room two dark-haired boys slept under the blanket of freedom. They were Americans now, yet twice a year they sailed to Madagascar and Mozambique and then to Sanctuary, and Rein knew that Michaela was hinting to return there, to be surrounded by what was most important to her—family. And if she asked, he would go. He would go to the ends of the earth for her, he would die for her. Luckily, since the war was over, he thought with a quirk of his lips, he wouldn't have to make such a noble sacrifice.

She dropped a kiss to their son's head, then swept her hair back off her bare shoulder. God of thunder, she was still an untamed beauty, and continued to stir his blood to unfathomable heights. He loved her more every time he saw her, touched her, and she gave her heart so generously. No longer did he have to control his emotions, for with her, he'd abandoned his old restraints. His lips curved. Hell, she damn well demanded it.

He left the rocker, and she looked up, holding his gaze as he settled to the window seat and bracing his back to the frame. Moonlight spilled over them as she snuggled against him with a soft sigh.

Jackson suckled noisily, and she tipped her head back to look at him. "I love you. Have I mentioned that today?"

His lips curved as he toyed with her curls laying across her breast and he heard her indrawn breath. The breathy sound still drove him mad with desire. "You do not have to speak the words, my rebel." He covered her mouth with his, drinking in her love, cherishing the day she put a bullet in him and pierced his jaded heart. In her, he found more than love, more than a partner in this life and the next. In loving her, he found his own freedom.

And he would spend the next century—listening to it ring.

About the Author

Amy J. Fetzer lives with her family in South Carolina. She is the author of five other historical and time-travel romances published by Zebra Books, including MY TIMESWEPT HEART, THUNDER IN THE HEART, LION HEART, TIMESWEPT ROGUE, and DANGEROUS WATERS. She is currently working on her next historical romance, THE IRISH PRINCESS, which will be published in June, 1999. Amy loves to hear from her readers, and you can write to her at P.O. Box 9241, Beaufort, South Carolina, 29904-9241. Please include a self-addressed stamped envelope if you wish a response. Or you can contact her at http://www.apayne.com/amyfetzer.